Dedicated to My Mother
Late Mrs. Kusum Vijayanand Barfe
— Mrinalini Samson Salve

Dedicated to My Father
Late Mr. Ramesh Janardan Medhekar
— Anagha Ramesh Medhekar

PREFACE

Dear Student - Teachers,

We are very glad to present this textbook of Mathematics (E7) of D. El. Ed. curriculum. You are going to be teachers working in a world of knowledge and technology. The students in your classroom are not just students, who seek knowledge. They are small personalities who are very curious, creative and eager to learn. It is our responsibility to provide proper education to these young ones. This book deals with the nature of mathematics, content matter of mathematics, mathematics syllabus, textbooks, teaching methodology and techniques, evaluation techniques. Continuous and comprehensive evaluation which is an innovation has also been dealt with. This book will make you self-studying and active by providing the right information. Many activities are also included in this book. The ultimate aim is to create an "Ideal Mathematics Teacher".

We are thankful to Shri Dineshbhai Furia and Shri Jignesh Furia of Nirali Prakashan for their co-operation and inspiring us to write and publish this book.

Special thanks to the staff of Nirali Prakashan, especially Mr. Ilyas Shaikh, Ms. Chaitali Takale and Mrs. Yojana Deshpande for error free printing. Also thanks to our family members who have kept the patience and given encouragement in all respects.

Valuable suggestions are always welcome from readers and well wishers for the improvement of this book.

15th September 2016
Anant Chaturdashi

Authors

SYLLABUS AND CONTENTS

✍ ✍ ✍

1

SCOPE OF MATHEMATICS

➲ Chapter Structure ☾

(2) Vygotsky's Theory

(3) Jerome Bruner's Theory

(4) David Ausubel Theory

1.6.1 Piaget's Theory of Cognitive Development

1.6.2 Vygotsky's Cultural-Historical Theory Overview

1.6.3 Jerome Bruner's Cognitive Development

1.6.4 David Ausubel : (Meaningful Verbal Learning)

1.6.5 Influence of Child's Social and Cultural Background on Knowledge of Mathematics

- Exercise

1.1 Objectives

After reading this chapter, you will be able to :

- Explain the place and importance of Mathematics in day-to-day life.
- Explain how Mathematics is the base of day-to-day life.
- Tell how knowledge of Mathematics is useful to carry out daily routine.
- Make use of Mathematics methodically.
- Tell the place and importance of Mathematics at primary level.
- Use Mathematics for intellectual development.
- Explain the meaning of correlation.
- Explain the need of correlation.
- Explain the correlation between Mathematics and other subjects.
- Teach and correlate Mathematics with other subjects, as a teacher.
- Explain the branches, sub-branches and applied branches of mathematics.
- Explain the relation between the branches and the sub branches of mathematics.

- Make use of the principles of applied mathematics.
- Present the structure of each branch in various ways.
- Understand the place of each unit in the structure.
- Understand Theory of Asubel, Piaget, Vygotsky's theorem and theorem of Jerome Bruner and also the use of these theorem's in mathematical study.
- Describe the effect of mathematical concepts on child's mind.
- Understand Concepts in Business Mathematics : Ratio-Proportion, Percentage, Profit-Loss, Simple and Compound interest, Discount, Commission, Postal transactions etc. and Examples based on these concepts.
- Collect information, Classification of information, i.e. frequency distribution.
- Represent the information in graphical form or Read the graph and give the description or write the information from graph.

1.2 Introduction

To facilitate the learning of Mathematics, it has to be taught in an effective and easy manner. To make this task easy, the Mathematics teacher has to be acquainted with the background information relating to the nature of Mathematics, salient features of Mathematics, scope and importance of Mathematics etc. So in this chapter, we are going to study about the place and importance of Mathematics in day-to-day life and also at the primary level. We will also study about the correlation of Mathematics with other subjects.

In this chapter, we are also going to study about the inter-relation between the branches, sub-branches and applied branches of mathematics, structure of mathematics, and concepts and principles in the syllabus of Std. I^{st} to V^{th}. We are also going to study about the presentation of structure, criteria of a good structure, types of subject structure and advantages of structure.

1.3 Concept, Structure, Importance and Characteristics of Mathematics

1.3.1 Concept of Mathematics

The word mathematics comes from the Greek word "Mathema" which is ancient Greek language means "that which is learnt" or "what one gets to know". In other words it can be called "Study" or "Science" or in modern Greek just "lesson".

For more than two thousand years mathematics has been a part of the human research for understanding. In the last century mathematics has been successfully applied to many aspects of life. Learning to think in mathematical terms is an essential part of becoming a liberally educated person.

Mathematics can be defined as a science of numbers and their operations, interrelations, combinations, generalizations and abstractions, measurement, space configurations and transformations.

A mathematical concept is the "why" or "big idea" of mathematics. Knowing a math concept means you know the workings behind the answers.

A mathematical concept is a general idea behind an equation, problems or formula in maths.

In contrast to a math fact, which must be committed to memory, a math concept explains why math works in a certain way.

History of Mathematics

Mathematics has not become important only today but it occupied and kept this important place from the earliest times and is perhaps the only subject which merits its distinction.

In the older times, when man was not civilised and lived in caves and forests, Mathematics played a decisive role in building up our civilisation. In order to conduct his daily routine, man started using an oral language. The base of this oral language was Mathematics. He had to use his fingers for speaking with this sign language. How far is the specific cave ? How much water do you want ? How many fruits will you give me ? Answering such questions led to the discovery of Mathematics. Answering the questions such as How much ? and How many ? led to the discovery of counting. Thus, as they did not know the numbers 1, 2, 3 ......, they would draw lines on the walls of caves or on the bark of trees for counting days or how many people were there in a clan. They started choosing their leader, who had to be a strong man and had to kill more number of animals than the others. This was the beginning of addition. When things became scarce, then they had to be divided among a number of people. This was the beginning of division. Thus, slowly and steadily, Mathematics was discovered.

Initially, Mathematics was very simple. We know that 'Discovery is the outcome of need' and so as the needs of the man increased, it gave rise to more detailed Mathematics. Overall development of mankind led to the discovery of fire, wheels, metals etc. There was also an increase in population and man felt the need of self-protection. All these various changes and needs gave rise to the 'give and take' of daily business. Thus, Mathematics also started getting complicated.

Thus, we can say that "Mathematics is not an invention, but discovery !" as well as "Mathematics is man-made"! Mathematics has not became important only today but it occupied and kept this important place from the earliest times and is perhaps the only subject which merits this distinction.

In earlier days, when education was considered only for the privileged classes, Mathematics was a compulsory subject. Plato advocated the inclusion of Mathematics in the curriculum because Mathematical reasoning disciplines the mind.

Students studied Mathematics for disciplining their mind and at the same time the common man was dependent on Mathematics for its utility in day-to-day life. The number system was developed in countries like India, Egypt and China. Roman numbers were also discovered. The Arabic numericals were changed to 1, 2, 3 ...... 9 by the Europeans.

The Indian numericals are based on the Arabic numericals and hence they are called 'Arabic signs'. The European numericals were accepted as "International Number System".

The Indian Mathematicians made a great discovery by introducing '0' zero for the concept of 'Nothing'. This discovery made great significant changes in Mathematics.

According to Lindsay, "Mathematics is the language of physical sciences and certainly no more marvellous language was created by the mind of man". This definition reveals the unique nature of Mathematics language with its signs, symbols, terms and the operations discovered by man. Thus, we say that "Mathematics is man-made !".

In the earliest civilization on the Indian subcontinent in the Indus Valley Civilization that flourished 2600 BC and 1900 BC in the Indus river basin. Their cities were laid out with geometric regularity, but not known mathematical concepts survive from this civilization.

The Hindu-Arabic numerals were invented by Indian mathematicians in India. Since, they are known as Hindu numerals. They are called Arabic numerals by Europeans. Various symbols sets are used to represent numbers in the Hindu-Arabic numerical system all of which evolved from Brahmi numerals.

1	2	3	4	5	6	7	8	9
−	=	≡	+	h	ꙴ	?	ꙷ	?

Brahmi Numerals

Fig. 1.1

In olden day the mathematical language is developed in symbolic form, at that time numbers can be represented by symbols.

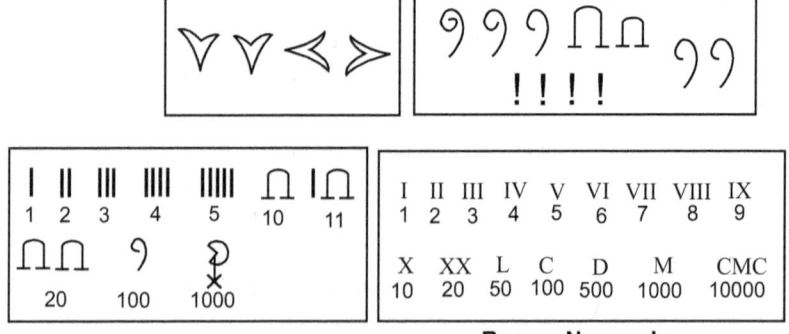

I	II	III	IIII	IIIII	Ⴖ	IႶ
1	2	3	4	5	10	11

ႶႶ	9	ꝑ
20	100	1000

I	II	III	IV	V	VI	VII	VIII	IX
1	2	3	4	5	6	7	8	9

X	XX	L	C	D	M	CMC
10	20	50	100	500	1000	10000

Roman Numerals

Arabic Numerals

Fig. 1.2

> **Activity 1 :** Collect extra information about Mathematics in olden times.

1.3.2 Scope of Mathematics

"Mathematics is the Queen of all Sciences".

The scope of Mathematics can be understood by this statement. The scope of Mathematics is very wide. Mathematics is a basic science and hence it has a wide scope. Mathematics is not limited to the curricula of schools, colleges and universities, but it is also needed for the social and financial development of a country. The base of physical and social sciences is Mathematics. There has been a rapid growth in sciences and all its branches. There is no science, no art and no profession, where Mathematics does not hold a key position. The accuracy and exactness of a science is determined to a major extent by the amount of Mathematics used in it. All sciences like Physics, Chemistry, Biology, Engineering, Economics, Psychology, Marine Sciences etc. have the foundation of Mathematics.

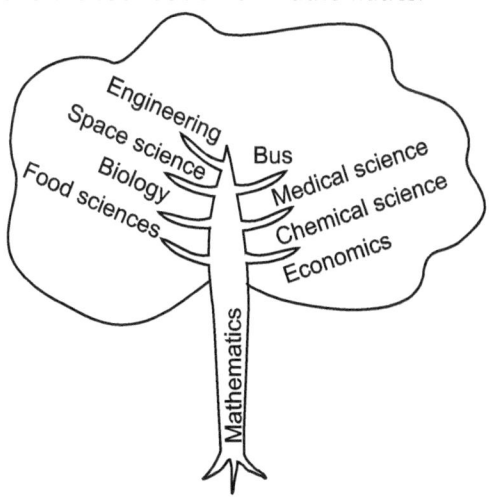

Fig. 1.3

Mathematics holds an important place in man's life also. A small child needs to be taught Mathematics. Addition, subtraction, multiplication and division are the four basic operations which are essential. Mathematics is an important tool of precision in measure involving quantity and time. We use logarithmic tables, calculators and computers in day-to-day life for instant calculations. Recently, computers are widely used to make our life easy. The world is experiencing changes on a large extent. All this development is based on Mathematics. Thus, Mathematics has made itself essential for the existence and progress of the modern world. In this modern world, we have to be more exact and accurate every minute. All this needs a Mathematical understanding.

To conclude we can say, "Mathematics is the soul of all sciences".

Activity 2 :   Make groups in your class. Each group should choose a branch of science and find out how it is based on Mathematics. Discuss it.

1.3.3 Importance and Characteristics of Mathematics

(1) Mathematics for Personality Development

We all know now-a-days more importance is given to personality development of a child. How much knowledge is gained by a child is not important, but a child's all-round development is given more importance. For personality development of a child, more attention is aimed at developing the child's attitudes, abilities and appreciations. As Mathematics is regarded as the mother of all sciences, teaching of Mathematics is aimed at developing the proper abilities, right appreciations and correct attitudes in a child.

If our students are to function effectively in this changing world, they must understand Mathematics and be able to use Mathematics both in their personal and professional lives. For this, they need to have a fully developed personality, which can be acquired through Mathematics.

A person with fully developed personality has certain abilities, attitudes and appreciations. He is able to express his thoughts clearly and accurately and is able to systematically organise and interpret the given data. He is able to analyse a problem and perform original thinking as well as use common-sense. He cultivates proper habits of study and power of concentration. He trains his mind in scientific thinking and logical reasoning towards conclusions. He seeks knowledge with an open mind to build self-confidence which constitutes a strong personality.

All these above abilities and attributes which are imbibed in a person make him a distinguished personality. This is achieved by the study of Mathematics. Thus, Mathematics plays an important role in the development of personality of an individual.

| **Activity 3 :** | While performing Activity 3B try to analyse the individual's (person whom you are interviewing) personality traits from his/her answers). |

(2) Mathematics for Social Development

Mathematics is a subject of great social importance. It is the backbone of our social structure. It helps in the proper organisation and maintenance of our social structure.

Each person is a social being. Society is the result of coming together of such individuals. A society needs laws, rules and traditions. Mathematics helps in formation of laws. In fact whatever balance, equality, harmony, symmetry and competition is seen in the society is due to the impact of Mathematics.

Mathematics plays an important role in the proper organization and maintenance of social institutions such as banks, co-operative societies, railways, post offices, insurance companies, transport companies, navigation industries etc. Effective business transactions in a society cannot take place without Mathematics. Also trade, export - import, trade, commerce and communication are impossible without Mathematics. Napoleon has rightly said, "The progress and the improvement of Mathematics are linked with the prosperity of the state".

The success of an individual in a society depends on how well he is able to become a member of the society and what contributions he can make towards the progress of the society and how well he can be benefitted by the society. An individual can lead a normal social life only when he has elementary Mathematical knowledge to cope up with society demands. As we have seen earlier, an individual acquires certain values, abilities and attributes through learning Mathematics. These acquired traits help him to adjust himself and lead a harmonious life in the society.

| **Activity 4 :** | Study the work of any social reformer and discuss within your group, the qualities of the reformer. |

(3) Mathematics for Development of Nation

The development of a nation is dependent on the scientific and social development of that nation. The rate of development of a country depends on how the society or each individual makes use of science and technology. Higher the use of science and technology, higher is the rate of development in the nation. For example, fully developed countries like Japan and Germany have understood the need of their nation and by making full use of science and technology; they have achieved full development of their country. We also have to think in such terms. Our country is a developing country. Mathematics is needed by all of us whether big or small, rich or poor, younger or older, man or women in every sphere of one's life. In our over-populated country, one must learn to train oneself and make use of modern technology along with Mathematics, to enhance the development of our country.

Mathematics inculcates the habit of self-scrutiny. No other subject demands strict scrutiny of one's own work as in Mathematics. Students are trained to scrutinize each step and make sure that it is right, before they proceed to the next step. The scrutiny improves the student's self-confidence and helps them to assume responsibility for his own work. He also gets prepared to take another responsibility. In fact, through Mathematics we prepare responsible citizens who analyse and scrutinize their work. This finally helps in the development of a nation as responsible citizens are created.

Points to Remember

- Mathematics is involved in all sciences.
- Mathematics is useful in day-to-day life.
- Mathematics helps in development of a person, society and nation.

(4) Mathematics in day-to-day life

Mathematics touches our life at every point. Everyone uses some form of Mathematics directly or indirectly in his daily life. Mathematics plays a predominant role in our life and it has become an important factor for the progress of our present day world.

Our day starts with the use of Mathematics. We get up in the morning at a particular time. The manner in which we brush our teeth is Mathematical. Our breakfast also has a Mathematical angle, for example: Amount of tea, number of bread slices, amount of butter etc. When we go out, for example: college, we start from our house at a particular time, we board a bus or train of certain timing. Our college also has specific timings. The periods are of forty minutes etc.

Everybody has to calculate his income and balance his budget, although all do not undergo university courses. Even an illiterate vendor knows how to make his business. The housewife also needs Mathematics for the smooth running of domestic life, preparing family budget, keeping various accounts, making purchases, controlling expenses etc.

Each and every person, belonging to any class of society uses Mathematics in one form or another. He may be a financier, an industrialist, a doctor or a labourer - he has to make use of Mathematics in his daily life. Various construction works of dams, bridges, buildings, as well as building of ships, aeroplanes, submarines, missiles, rockets and spaceships are possible because of quantitative science. All medical men have to measure doses of medicine, heart beats, blood pressure, body temperature etc.

In many occupations, like banking, accountancy, auditing, book keeping, tailoring, carpentry, postal jobs, taxation, insurance etc. mathematics plays a key role.

Our daily life would be incomplete without acts like painting, drawing, sculpture, music, dancing etc. All these aesthetic acts have a Mathematical touch. Poetry becomes enjoyable with its meter and rhythm. Music becomes sweet due to its mathematically organised sound. Musical instruments are constructed and based on musical scale. Dancing also involves Mathematical steppings. Various martial arts like judo and karate have Mathematical gestures. A beautiful garden, an artistic ornament, a well decorated house, a well designed furniture item etc. all show hidden Mathematical aspects.

Electrical appliances, which are indispensable in our life are also based on Mathematics.

Mathematical knowledge is thus indispensable and no one can progress far if he has no Mathematical knowledge. In this present social set-up, a common man has to face taxes, rates, premia, savings and interests, rents and rises. Only a person with good Mathematical background can be reasonably sure that he is getting his due.

Thus, Mathematics plays an important role in our day-to-day life.

Activity 5 : (A) How is Mathematics useful to you in your daily life ?

(B) Interview any person, for example, engineer, shopkeeper etc. to know how Mathematics is useful for him in his daily life. Make a report.

(a) Place and Importance of Mathematics at Primary Level

(1) Mathematics - Basic Subject in Syllabus

According to Francis Bacon, "Mathematics is the Gateway and key to all sciences". And therefore a subject having such broad scope and utility is given an important place in the curriculum.

Kothari Commission (1964 - 66) also known as National Education Commission has wisely remarked, "Science and Mathematics should be taught on a compulsory basis to all pupils as a part of general education during the first ten years of schooling. In addition, there should be provision of special courses in these subjects at the secondary stage, for students of more than average ability".

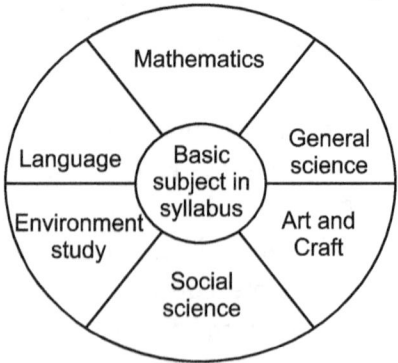

Fig. 1.4

According to the National Education Policy (1986), teaching of Mathematics is compulsory at the primary level i.e. (Std. I to V), higher primary i.e. (Std. VI to VIII), secondary level i.e. (Std. IX to X) and higher secondary level i.e. (Std. XI to XII). Alongwith Mathematics, the other subjects that are included are Language, General Science, Physical Education, Social Science and Arts. As Mathematics is said to be a science of discovery, an intellectual game, the art of drawing conclusions, a system of logical processes and an intuitive method, it is included in the curriculum.

Mathematics at primary level includes teaching of numbers, four fundamental rules, measurement, fractions and geometry. To create skill in the above areas, more emphasis is given on concept formation. For this, 15% of the actual time i.e. 10 periods per week are allotted at primary level and 10% of the actual time i.e. 7 periods per week are allotted at the higher primary level for Mathematics.

Teaching of Mathematics creates values such as practical value, moral value, disciplinary value, cultural value, social value, aesthetic value, intellectual value and international value in students. Therefore, Mathematics is considered as an important subject. The life of man is controlled by Mathematics and hence personality development takes place.

Acharya Vinoba Bhave has quoted, "Other than God, I believe in Mathematics". Thus, Mathematics is included as an important and core subject in school curriculum.

Activity 6 :   Prepare an educational aid to explain how Mathematics is the core subject in school curriculum.

---

(2) Mathematics - Compulsory Subject

As Mathematics has been given the place of core subject in school curriculum, it has been made a compulsory subject. It is made compulsory for the following reasons :

- Mathematics is useful for an individual's day-to-day life.
- Mathematics is the only subject that encourages and develops logical thinking.
- Mathematics as a core subject, lays the foundation for the study of all other subjects.
- Mathematics is the base of higher education.

According to Kothari Commission (1964 - 66), "one of the outstanding characteristics of scientific culture is quantification. Mathematics, therefore, assumes a prominent position in modern education. The advent of automation and cybernetics, in this century, marks the beginning of the scientific industrial revolution and makes it all the more imperative to devote special attention to the study of Mathematics. Proper foundation in the knowledge of the subject should be laid in school".

Accordingly, Mathematics is made a compulsory subject at both the primary and secondary level of school whereas it is an elective subject at the higher secondary level.

Activity 7 : "Mathematics is a compulsory subject". Make a list of points which you will consider, as a teacher, to support the above statement.

---

(3) Key to Various Intellectual Competencies Development

Mathematics! To create a good personality, an individual must possess certain intellectual qualities like power of observation, imagination, memorisation, invention, concentration, originality, creativity, logical thinking and systematized reasoning.

Hubsch has remarked rightly that, "Mathematics is like a wheatstone and by its study one learns to think distinctly, consecutively and carefully".

There is an ocean of knowledge in the world. The important thing is not how much knowledge to acquire but to learn how to acquire knowledge and to use or apply it in solving our problems. To use acquired knowledge properly at the hour of need are only aimed through the teaching of Mathematics.

Actual problem solving in Mathematics is helpful in the proper development of one's mental powers.

Thus, we can say that Mathematics is the key to development of various intellectual competencies.

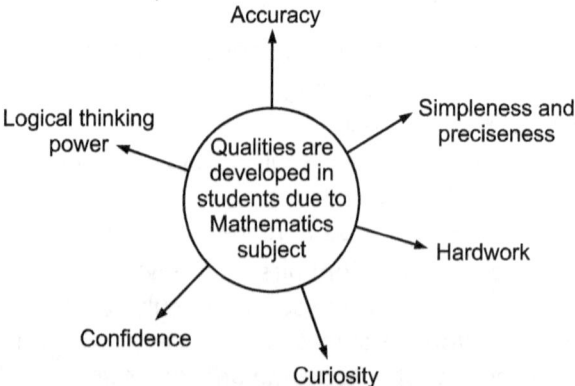

Fig. 1.5

| **Activity 8 :** | "Teaching of Mathematics involves development of various intellectual competencies". Discuss statement with an example. |

Points to Remember

- Mathematics is chosen as a core subject in the school curriculum.
- Mathematics leads to all-round development of a child.
- Mathematics is a compulsory subject in school curriculum.
- Teaching of Mathematics creates good citizens.
- Mathematics is the key to development of various intellectual competencies.
- Mathematics helps in creating moral values in an individual.
- Mathematics subject is not limited to creating Mathematicians only.

(b) Mathematics for Moral Development

Study of Mathematics helps in character formation and moral development. In Mathematics, what is right is always right and what is wrong is always wrong. The answer is always either right or wrong. It cannot be right and wrong at the same time. Thus, Mathematics helps in developing proper moral attitudes as there is no place for biased attitudes, doubts and half-truths. One learns to put check over one's emotions and study the right things and neglect the wrong ones. Greek Philosopher Dutton has rightly said in this connection, "Mathematics does furnish the power for deliberate thought and accurate statement and to speak the truth ...... gossip, flattery, slander, deciet, all speak from a slovenly mind that has not been trained by Mathematics".

Thus, qualities like honesty, self-confidence, truthfulness, patience, self control, punctuality, respect for others opinion, expression of thoughts, observation of rules etc. are inculcated in an individual who studies Mathematics. Therefore, study of Mathematics ultimately leads to moral development.

(c) Characteristics of Mathematics Subject

The characteristics of mathematics that makes it unique among other subjects are :

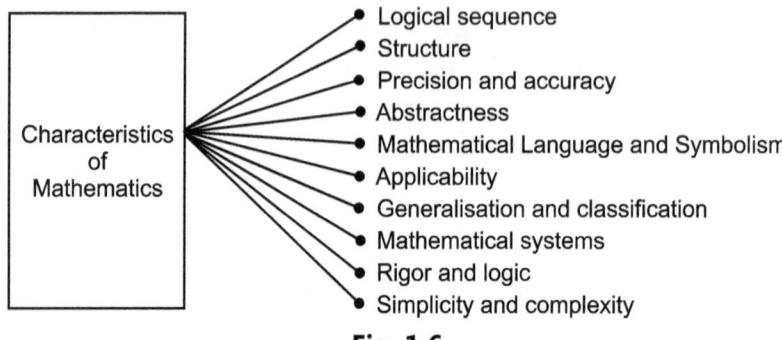

Fig. 1.6

- Mathematics is not just a study of numbers, nor is it simply about calculations. It is not about applying formulas either. It can perhaps be better described as "a field of creation through accurate and logical thinking." Mathematics has a long, rich history and continues to grow rapidly.

- Mathematics is a very diverse field.

- Mathematics is an academic discipline of great depth, with a number of unsolved problems. It has progressed on cumulative contributions from countless mathematicians in the world who have tackled those problems while creating new areas of inquiry.

- Some of the subfields in the appendix, such as fluid mechanics, quantum theory, information and telecommunication, and biology, may seem irrelevant to mathematics at first glance. These fields, however, take mathematical approaches to describing and analyzing phenomena under study.

- They illustrate how a number of subfields of mathematics have benefited from and evolved through interactions with other disciplines. Mathematics, on the other hand, has made considerable contributions to the advancement of other academic fields. In fact, mathematics is often described as the foundation of scientific studies.

- One of the major characteristics of mathematics is its general applicability.

- One equation, for instance, can represent a particular phenomenon in physics as well as certain logic in economics. This general nature of mathematical equations enables unified treatment of diverse phenomena in various academic fields. Furthermore, mathematical theorems have no restrictions of age or seniority: any theorem has to be proven through appropriate mathematical procedures whether you are a novice student researcher or an eminent professor of mathematics. And once proven true, mathematical theorems will never be reversed. This "universality" of mathematics is another important feature that allows the discipline to transcend time and space.

1.4 Structure of Mathematics, Correlation between the Branches and Correlation of Mathematics with Other Subject

1.4.1 Structure of Mathematics

(a) Concept and Need of Structure of Mathematics Subject :

According to Jerome Bruner, all concepts, principles, central ideas and their interrelation play an important role in teaching. Once the student knows and understands this, he himself will be able to collect information and data. Collection of information is the main function of teaching. Information is collected for the fixation of concepts, principles and rules. Thus, interpretation and understanding of concepts and principles is more important.

For the proper transfer of knowledge from one generation to another generation, the subject has to be presented in a methodical manner. This arrangement of knowledge is called as 'structure'.

Structure can be defined as follows :

Definition 1 : The classification of the knowledge of any subject into branches and sub-branches in a methodical manner is called as structure of that subject.

Definition 2 : Structure means the serial and methodical arrangement of units.

Definition 3 : According to Ausubel, the manner in which the subject-matter is collected and grouped is called "subject structure" and the manner in which this knowledge is fixed in a learner's mind is called as "knowledge structure".

The structure of every subject is like a pyramid. If we place the main concept or principle at the top, then below the main concept lies the sub-concepts or sub-topics.

Because of this, the scope of the foundation of the pyramid widens.

Characteristics of Structure :

1. The interrelation among the branches and sub-branches of the subject is understood from the structure.
2. The topics and sub-topics of a sub-branch are understood.
3. The place of each unit and sub-unit in the structure can be decided because of the collective arrangement.
4. The scope of the subject is understood.
5. The structure helps to gain mastery over the teaching-learning subject.

The structure of different subjects can be different. Every teacher has the right to prepare a structure of her own for her subject.

> **Activity 4 :** Explain the meaning of structure of a subject. Explain its need.

(b) Arrangement of the Structure

Following points should be kept in mind while arrangement of structure :

1. While preparing the structure, one must take into account a maximum number of units.
2. Keep the theoretical relation between the units in your mind because :
    (a) One unit may be related to another, or
    (b) Both units may be related to one another, or
    (c) One unit may be related to many other units, or
    (d) Many other units may be included in any one unit.

Thus, keeping the above possibilities in mind, one can prepare the structure.

3. The arrangement of structure should be done diagrammatically.

The most accurate, interesting, eye-catching and understandable structure is the best structure.

(c) Criteria of a Good Structure

1. The structure should be subject-knowledge inclusive in the maximum way.

2. Structure should be meaningful.

3. Structure should be easy, simple and understandable.

4. Structure should be based on theoretical or psychological basis.

5. The structure should explain the concept and laws.

(d) Types of Structures

1. **Classified or categorised structure :** In this type, the subject is divided into branches and sub-branches and are arranged one below the other.

2. **Two-dimensional structure :** Structure is prepared by taking into consideration, the two dimensions of a subject. One dimension is the branch of the subject and the other dimension is the unit. In mathematics, one dimension is the branch and the other dimension is the teaching method.

3. **Three-dimensional structure :** In this type, three dimensions are taken into consideration. The first dimension is the main branch, second dimension is the unit and the third dimension is the analysis of the unit.

   A teacher can decide which three dimensions he can use. This structure has the shape of a cube.

4. **Branched or Tree-like structure :** The trunk of the tree is the main subject, the branches of the tree represent the branches of the subject and the sub-branches of the tree represent the sub-branches of the subject.

5. **Concentric structure :** This structure consists of many circles with one common centre. The circle which is in the centre is representative of the subject. The circles next to the central circle represent the branches of the subject and the outer circles represent the sub-branches of the subject.

(e) Advantages of Structure

1. We come to know the place of any unit in the structure. While comparing any two units, we can find out their places in the structure and relate them.

2. We know the background of an unit from its position in the structure as well as the relation of that unit with other units. This promotes effective teaching.

3. It becomes easy to prepare annual planning and unit planning from the structure.

4. Structure enables a teacher to gain complete knowledge of the subject because one comes to know the branches of the subject.

5. Analysis of the textbook becomes easy.

Activity 5 : Write the criteria of a good structure.

Following are some of the structures of Mathematics.

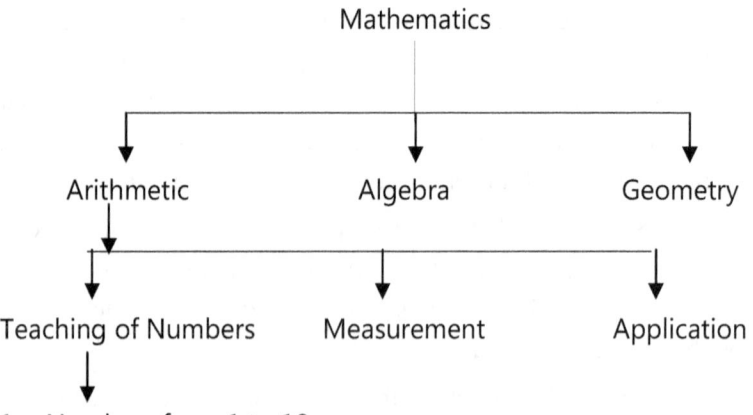

1. Numbers from 1 to 10
2. Comparison of one digit numbers.
3. Concept of zero.
4. Numbers from 11 to 100.
5. Comparison of two-digit numbers.

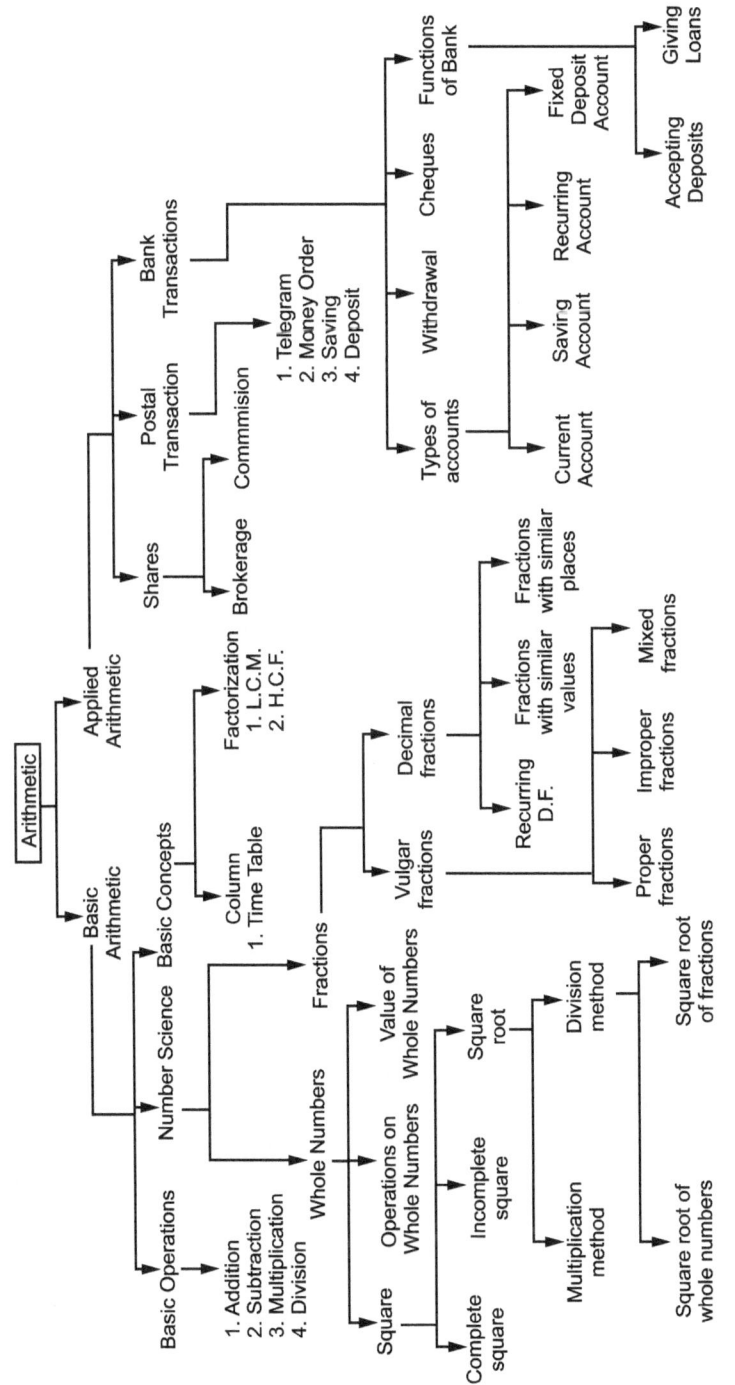

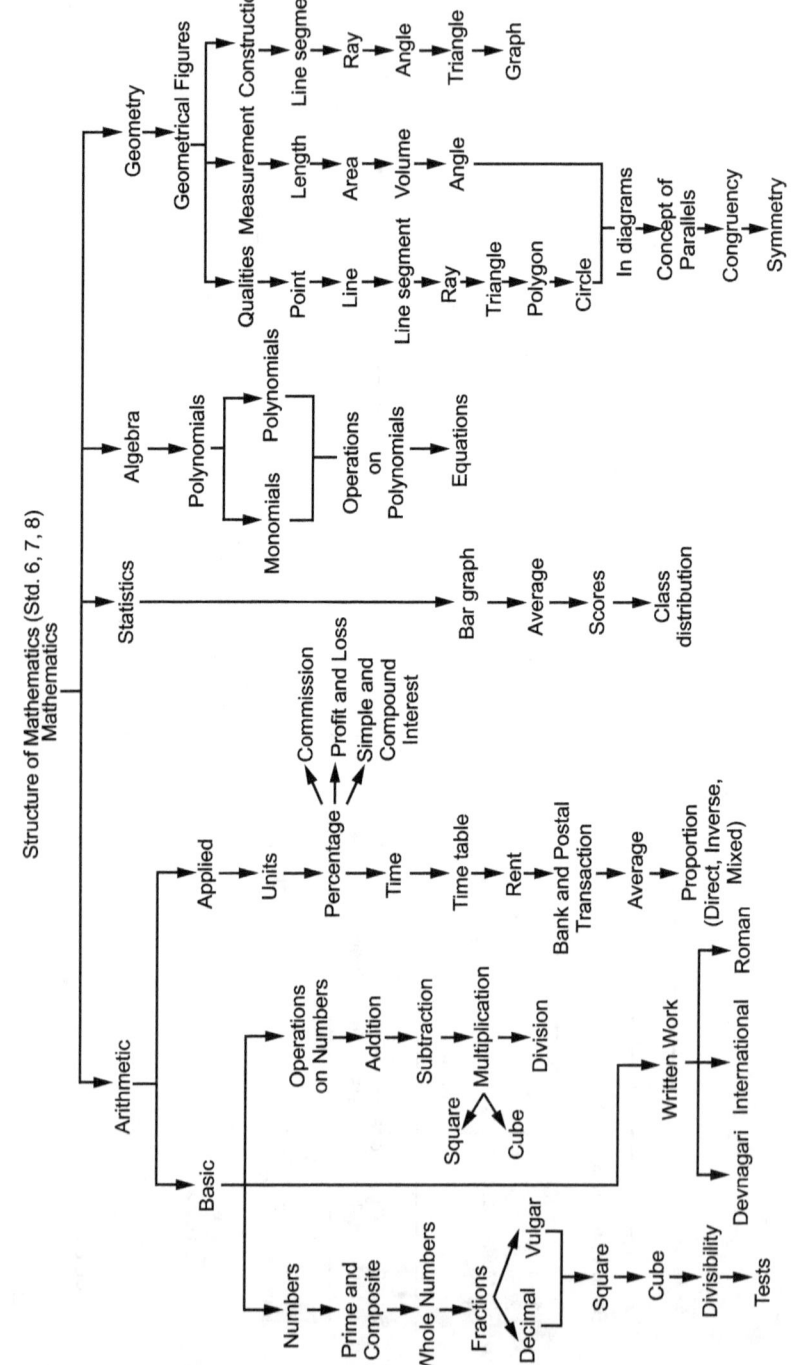

Activity 6 : Which points will you keep in mind while preparing the structure ?

Activity 7 : Prepare a structure of Mathematics subject using your own ideas.

Activity 8 : Prepare structures for each branch of Mathematics.

Points to Remember

- Structure is the methodical arrangement of units.
- A structure has pyramid form. The top consists of the main concept and foundation is made of subtopics.
- Structure of different subjects can be made in different manners.
- While preparing structure, maximum units must be considered alongwith their interrelation.
- Structure must be presented diagrammatically.

Questions

1. What is the meaning of a structure ?
2. Explain the need of a structure ?
3. Write the criteria of a structure.
4. What are the advantages of a structure ?
5. Write about the structure of Mathematics subject in brief.

1.4.2 Correlation between the Branches, Sub-branches and Applied Branches of Mathematics

Arithmetic, Algebra and Geometry are the main branches of mathematics. Arithmetic holds the centre position because we know how mathematics was discovered and it was discovered first as Arithmetic. In order to answer the questions, How much? and How many?, the number system was discovered. This was further developed into Arithmetics. We express ourselves through our language. In the same way, the language used to express the daily measurements and calculations is "Arithmetic language". This language is universally accepted.

There are two sub-branches of Arithmetic :

(i)   Basic Arithmetic

(ii) Applied Arithmetic.

Anything that is basic is always the same everywhere. So also basic arithmetic does not change any of its rules and principles and are always the same anywhere on the earth.

For example, when we say the table of any number, they will remain the same at some other place. i.e. $5 \times 7 = 35$ will remain constant anywhere on the earth. That is why all of us must understand and know all the rules and principles of basic arithmetics. It is also necessary that all should know the four fundamental rules of Arithmetic.

Applied Arithmetic is based on Basic Arithmetic. The rules and principles of applied arithmetic are all derived from basic arithmetic. The nature of arithmetic on the whole is applied. Our daily business becomes easy because of mathematics.

The next branch of mathematics i.e. Geometry has a special meaning in the word. Geometry = Geo + metry.

This suggests that not only can we measure mathematical aspects, but also anything in the universe or on this land. Geometry includes certain rules, principles and theories which do not change anywhere in the world. These principles and theories are the foundations of geometry. We can solve the theorems, questions and problems of geometry with the help of these principles and theories.

Geometry includes angles, geometrical shapes, lines etc. This branch was also discovered like Arithmetic. Man needed to measure land, find out the area and thus geometry was discovered. We come across geometry in our daily life. Geometry helps us to understand the various shapes that we come across in our life. Nature is full of different shapes. Observation will reveal the different shapes of leaves, flowers, fruits, birds etc. Making various rangolis, drawings and decorations is a gift of geometry. The subject of drawing shows relation with geometry by making use of lines, points and circles.

Geometry gives us a chance to derive conclusions and inferences. This is possible when a student studies the various theorems of geometry. Qualities like accuracy, exactness and neatness are inculcated because of geometry. In short, Geometry like arithmetic is an important branch of mathematics.

The third branch of mathematics i.e. Algebra is also called "Alphabetical Mathematics" or "Akshar-Ganit". Famous Indian Mathematician, Bhaskaracharya called algebra as "Unexpressed Mathematics".

We first discussed that Arithmetic has a mathematical language. Similarly, algebra also has a language of its own. The main characteristic is that, this language is symbolic. There are signs, formulae and equations in this branch of mathematics. All of us, as children, have made use of certain symbolic games such as girls play with dolls and small utensils etc. So also algebra makes use of symbolism.

For example, mother gave some amount of rupees to Meena. Meena brought an ice-cream for ₹ 10 and a cadbury for ₹ 12. Now, Meena has 28 rupees with her. So how many rupees did mother give to Meena ?

There is an unknown number in this problem which has to be symbolised or written as 'x', then we solve it as

$$x - (10 + 12) = 28$$

In this way, we can conclude that there is close relation between the branches, sub-branches and applied branches of mathematics. A teacher should not separate them from each other and make them appear as separate subjects. But he/she should be able to interrelate all these branches while teaching, so that the teaching-learning process becomes joyful.

A good teacher interrelates all these three branches while teaching and makes the teaching learning process more joyful.

If we consider the mathematics of Standard II, we come across examples like

$$\Box + 2 = 5$$

$$\Box - 3 = 3$$

Here the blank space is equal to 'x' which is seen in algebra. This above example will show the inter-relation between arithmetic and algebra. Similarly, the formula used to find out the sample interest in arithmetic is related to algebra as letters are used in the formula.

$$I = \frac{PRN}{100}$$

Algebra is also used in preparing the formula to find out the area and volume.

For example,   Area of a square $= l \times l$

Area of a circle $= \pi r^2$

Preparation of a formula and solving problems is infact generalisation of algebra.

We can also solve arithmetical sums in the algebraic manner.

For example, Simplify

$$\frac{324}{729} = \frac{4 \times 9 \times 9}{9 \times 9 \times 9} = \frac{4}{9}$$

Here in this example, instead of doing division directly, we first find out factors and then simplify. Similarly, we can solve algebraic examples using arithmetic operations.

For example, Solve :

$$\frac{x^3 + a^3}{x^2 + 2ax + a^2} = \frac{(x + a)(x^2 - ax + a^2)}{(x + a)(x + a)}$$

$$= \frac{x^2 - ax + a^2}{x + a}$$

The operation of simple division is used in the second step. The four basic operations i.e. addition, subtraction, multiplication and division can be related to one another. For example, we know multiplication is a complex form of addition. The oral and written examples of arithmetic are also interrelated L.C.M. and H.C.F. can be taught after teaching factorisation in algebra. Teaching of algebra also needs knowledge of sets. Various equations and graphs are interrelated. Various topics of geometry like triangle, polygons etc. are dependent on the knowledge of points, lines etc. Thus, we see interrelation between the branches and sub-branches of mathematics.

Activity 9 : Find out more examples to show interrelation between the branches of mathematics.

Activity 10 : Write examples to explain the interrelation between Arithmetic and Algebra.

Activity 11 : Explain with the help of a figure, the practical use of Geometry.

Points to Remember

- Arithmetic is science of numbers.
- Basic Arithmetic and Applied Arithmetic are two sub-branches of Arithmetic.
- Geometry is science of measuring earth surface and universe.
- Any measurement refers to geometry, whereas keeping record of this measurement is arithmetic.
- An alphabet is used instead of a number in algebra.
- Algebra gives importance to signs and symbols.

Questions

1. What is arithmetic ? What are the uses of arithmetic ?
2. How was the use of numbers started ?
3. What are the main branches of Arithmetic ?
4. What do you mean by Basic Arithmetic ?
5. Explain the nature of Applied Arithmetic.
6. Explain the practical use of geometry.
7. "The scope of algebra is very wide." Explain.

1.4.3 Correlation of Mathematics with Other Subjects

1.4.3.1 Concept of Correlation

If we split the word correlation i.e. "co + relation", then the word 'co' means together and thus the word correlation indicates togetherness, intimacy or co-operation. The concept of correlation emphasises on the unity of knowledge rather than its division into small specialised pieces. Correlation in Mathematics may be termed as a technique with the help of which we can bring Mathematics close to our actual life activities and integrate its knowledge with the study of other subjects. A teacher of Mathematics having the knowledge of correlation of Mathematics can increase the effectiveness of her/his teaching by relating it to other areas of study or interest.

1.4.3.2 Need and Importance of Correlation

Some of our great leaders who were also great educationists like Mahatma Gandhiji have emphasised the role of hand, heart and mind in the acquisition of knowledge. Hence, all round development of a child is possible only if he makes use of his personality to gain knowledge. Therefore, correlation is necessary for a child to gain knowledge as a whole by integrating activities related to mind, heart and hand.

Also, the school curriculum is prepared in such a manner that all subjects together aim to develop the intellectual powers of a student. Hence, correlation of one subject with other subjects is necessary.

Similarly, what is taught the previous day has to be linked properly to the knowledge given on next day. Hence, correlation is necessary.

Thus, arises the need and importance of correlating Mathematics with other subjects.

Objectives of Correlation

1. To explain the similar units in Mathematics and other subjects.
2. To explain correlation between the branches of Mathematics.
3. To explain the importance of activities in Mathematics.
4. To create new teaching, learning experiences, as a teacher.
5. To make teaching - learning process joyful.

1.4.3.3 Correlation between Mathematics and Other Subjects

(a) Mathematics and Physics : If we consider the chapter 6 of Standard VIII, i.e. Force and Pressure, we come to know about the formula of pressure which is based on mathematics.

$$\text{Pressure} = \frac{\text{Perpendicular force}}{\text{Area}}$$

The experiment which is given in this chapter also needs mathematical measurements. The experiment is about kneading the clay and placing a brick of 25 × 10 × 5 cm on this dough. The brick has to be kept in such a manner that its broadest side is down. Here the student must also know the broadness of a shape. This is also related to mathematics. To perform the 'Archimedes' principle mathematical numbers and calculation are used.

For example, the water displaced by a slab measuring 4 × 3 × 2 cm will be 24 cc. Also measuring cylinders are used where the level of water which has risen has to be noted. This is also based on mathematics. The following figure will also explain how mathematics is needed in physics in the manner of numbers and symbol of degree.

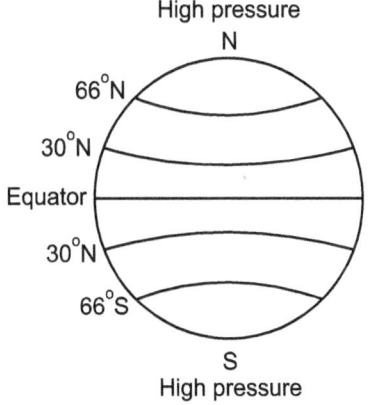

Fig. 1.7

(b) Mathematics and Chemistry : The third chapter of standard VII Heat, includes many tables which have mathematical numbers in it.

Substance	Specific Heat
Water	1 cal/g °C
Mercury	0.033 cal/g °C
Iron	0.125 cal/g °C

The experiment of proving that solid substances expand on heating and contract on cooling involves a scale and a pointer. This is also based on mathematics. The whole concept of the thermometer will be of no use if there was no scale marked on the glass tube. This calibration of thermometer is based on mathematics.

The topic of static electricity of Std. VII includes the use of + and − symbols for changes which are seen in mathematics also.

(c) Mathematics and Biology : Chapter 14 of Standard VI, variety of living things, has a sub-topic of variety in animal life shown by a picture. The variety in shapes is shown where the student comes to know about the shapes of different animals i.e. the shape of an elephant is bigger than a human and he in turn is bigger than the snail. This concept of bigger and smaller is also taught in mathematics.

The following table would be incomplete without the use of numbers :

Animal	Life span
Dog	16 − 18 years
Elephant	70 − 90 years
Housefly	1 − 4 months
Ostrich	50 years

Chapter 9, Internal organs of standard IV includes an activity for the students, where the students have to count their heart beats in one minute. This counting will need the help of mathematics.

(d) Mathematics and Geography : Geography is nothing but scientific and Mathematical description of our earth in its universe. The proper learning of geography is possible only with the sufficient knowledge of Mathematics. Almost all the topics of geography are based on Mathematics. For example, formation of days and nights, solar and lunar eclipses, tides, currents, movements of winds, rainfall, change of reasons.

A geography student has to study maps. Maps are totally based on Mathematics. The drawing, reading and understanding of maps needs thorough knowledge of Mathematics.

Calculation of local, standard and international times is based on Mathematics. Mathematics helps a student to locate the distance between two places.

Mathematics helps in computing the longitude and latitude, in predicting weather conditions and climate changes. It also helps to plan the transportation and communication systems.

(e) Mathematics and History : History is a systematic study of past events which requires Mathematics for its exact description and interpretation. A historical record is meaningful only if it has sufficient concept of time and this is understood only because of Mathematics. The rules and regimes of different kings and emperors are known because of Mathematics. In these olden days, Mathematics dominated every area such as amount of loot taken, amount of king's wealth, number of soldiers in the army, number of horses or elephants in the army, number of queens etc.

Also the dates of birth and death of all kings are known because of Mathematics. Historical maps can be studied with the help of Mathematical knowledge.

(f) Mathematics and Languages : The grammar section of any language is governed by Mathematics. Be it regional, national or international; a language contains grammar, which has rules for every topic. These rules have a Mathematical pattern. For example, we have certain rules of where to put the comma, colon mark, fullstop etc.

Nouns, pronouns, verbs, adjectives and other forms of sentences all follow certain patterns based on Mathematics. The concept of opposite words, similar words and singular and plural have basis of Mathematics.

Also, not only prose, but poetry also follows the rules of Mathematics. The concept of addition is seen when we write two sentences in combined form.

Mathematics and work experience : Work experience is such a subject where there are a lot of activities to be done. The units that are included in this subject are needle work (stitching), knitting, clay - modelling, cane work, woodwork, paper work, metal work, glass painting, gardening, carpentry etc. All these areas need manual work.

If we take any example from the above units and consider the activities carried out in it, we will come to know how it is based on Mathematics. For example, gardening involves all Mathematical operations and activities like survey, measurement, allotment, distribution of land, quantity of seeds or samplings, amount of water to be given, space between two plants, amount of fertilizers and insecticides etc. Thus, work experience is also correlated with Mathematics.

Activity 12 : Make a list of some units of school subjects that show correlation with Mathematics.

1.4.3.4 Correlation of Different Branches of Mathematics

Algebra, Arithmetic and Geometry are the three main branches of Mathematics. All these three branches of Mathematics are correlated. Many times, a teacher treats these branches as different subjects while teaching. And hence students are not able to use the knowledge of one branch to solve problems of another branch. Hence, it is important to study the correlation between these branches.

Arithmetic : According to C.F. Gauss, "Mathematics is the Queen of Sciences and Arithmetic is the Queen of Mathematics".

We come to know the importance of Arithmetic from the above statement. There are two sub-branches of Arithmetic.

(i) Basic Mathematics

(ii) Applied Mathematics.

The first type includes teaching of numbers, four fundamental rules, etc. whereas the second type includes percentage, bank and postal transactions, average, proportion etc. Difficult arithmetic problems can be solved by using algebraic equations.

For example, what number should be added to 53 to get 99 ?

This can be solved by forming an algebraic equation like $53 + x = 99$.

We make use of geometrical figure like circle to explain the concept of time in Arithmetic.

Algebra : Algebra is generalisation of arithmetic. In algebra, alphabets are used in place of numbers. While solving the examples of algebra, one has to make use of arithmetic.

For example, Expansion of $(a + b)^2$.

This can be expanded by multiplying $(a + b) (a + b)$ and collecting the like terms and adding them together i.e.

$$(a + b)^2 = a^2 + 2 ab + b^2$$

We can also make use of geometrical figures to show this expansion.

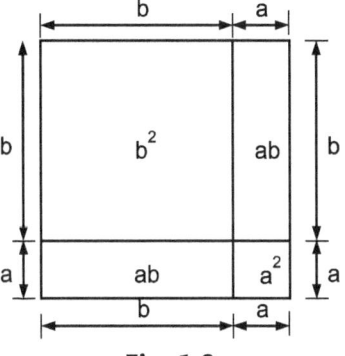

Fig. 1.8

The same formula can be used to solve $(101)^2 = (100 + 1)^2$ in arithmetic.

Geometry : Geometry includes various constructions, area and measuration, geometrical figures and theorems.

As we use letters in algebra, so also we use them in geometry, for example, to name any rectangle, we say ▭ ABCD. We also make use of letters to write formula of finding areas.

For example, Area of a rectangle = Length × Breadth

$$A = l \times b$$

Arithmetic is used in solving the problems of geometry.

Correlation of Mathematics and Co-curricular Activities : Mathematics can be easily included in the co-curricular and extra-curricular activities of the school.

When a school arranges a fete or funfair, the children can learn how to make receipts and also learn how to handle money. They learn to add and subtract while handling rupees and coins.

Similarly, when the school arranges a gathering, students can prepare accounts of all the expenditure. Also they learn more Mathematics if the school sell tickets.

Activity 13 :	Make a list of units that show correlation between different branches of Mathematics.
Activity 14 :	Make a list of co-curricular and extracurricular activities that are correlated with Mathematics.

Points to Remember

- Mathematics teaching should include correlation with other subjects.
- By correlation, the teaching-learning process becomes joyful.
- Mathematics teaching should include correlation between similiar units of school subjects.
- Mathematics is closely related to science, technology and geography.
- The branches of Mathematics are closely related.
- Mathematics is also correlated with the co-curricular and extra-curricular activities.

Questions

1. Discuss the importance of Mathematics in day-to-day life.
2. Explain with examples, how Mathematics is a man-made science.
3. What is the importance of Mathematics in the primary school curriculum ?
4. "Mathematics should be a compulsory subject at school level". Comment with examples.
5. While working as a teacher, which qualities will you inculcate in your students, while teaching Mathematics ? How ?
6. "Mathematics has a wide scope". Explain with examples.
7. Explain the correlation of Mathematics with science and technology.
8. "Mathematics is the foundation of day-to-day life". How will you imbibe this concept in the minds of your students ?
9. Explain with examples how Mathematics can be taught through co-curricular and extra-curricular activities ?
10. Write short notes on :
    (a) Mathematics – A core subject.
    (b) Mathematics and Personality Development.
    (c) Mathematics and Intellectual Development.
11. "Mathematics is a gateway and key to all sciences". Explain with examples.

1.5 Dimensions of Mathematical Knowledge

Creation of nature and mathematics are closely related. The sun, earth, planets stars are of geometrical shape. On the other hand, the natural curiosity of human being might be considered as the source of origin of Mathematics.

Human is the most intelligent creature. In all the spheres of life activities, he make use of his mind. Therefore, at the first stage of his mental development some questions arise like - What, Why, How, How many etc. The search for the solutions of question what and why are originated the spiritual knowledge and the questions like how and how much were concerned with measurement which might have formed the bases for the development of Mathematics. To get answers of these questions human have to make an approach of (i) logical reasoning and (ii) rational thinking.

Mathematics is evolved from its related concepts and assumptions. It provides basis to all the branches of knowledge. Every branch of knowledge whether Art or Science has its involvement. Mathematics is a major source for development of human personality-

- Physical
- Intellectual
- Spiritual

1.5.1 Logical Reasoning

There are different concepts and shapes in mathematics which can be understood with logical reasoning and rational thinking. To clear this, we will see some concepts or branches of mathematics.

Number System : Numbers, Reading, Writing, Big-small number, Concept of zero, Measurement - length, volume, shapes, fractions, equal denominator, unequal denominator, Natural numbers, Whole numbers, Profit-loss, Simple integers, Rational numbers, Graphs.

Algebra : Monomial, Binomial and Polynomials, Equations in one variables, Factorization, Set, Surds, Ratio, Proportion, Statistics.

Geometry : Shapes - square, rectangle, triangles, circle, Angle, Types of angle, Symmetry and Equality of figures.

All above concepts are included in logical thinking.

1.5.2 Symbolic Knowledge

The second part of mathematical knowledge is symbolic knowledge. From symbol we get the knowledge of concept and we do the practical with the help of this knowledge or we use this knowledge in practical life.

The generalization process is done with the help of observation and writing conclusion with the help of observation.

In school curriculum activities, we can see that the logical and symbolic forms are interdependent or depend on each other.

For example : Main four operations in mathematics - Addition, Subtraction, Multiplication, Division. Then Comparison of numbers, Time measurement, Two digit number, Even-odd number, Operations on numbers, Multiplication, Tables, Mathematical symbols and there uses, Factorisation, Commercial mathematics, Simple interest, Compound interest, Area, Volume, Addition-subtraction of fractions, Cube, Cube root, Indices, Percentage, Rational number and operations on rational number, Square, Triangle etc. Area of geometrical shapes, Factorization of equation, Multiplication, Histogram, Simultaneous equations, Polynomial, Bank transactions etc.

1.5.3 Use in Teaching - Learning Process

We have seen logical reasoning and rational thinking. The knowledge of logical and symbolic form is very useful in our day-to-day life. If students can understand these concepts clearly, then there is need to hardwork. They can do the calculations or solve the problems easily.

1.6 Uses of Theories of :
(1) Piaget's Theory
(2) Vygotsky's Theory
(3) Jerome Bruner's Theory
(4) David Ausubel Theory

1.6.1 Piaget's Theory of Cognitive Development

Piaget's theory of cognitive development is a comprehensive theory about the nature and development of human intelligence.

Piaget believed that one's childhood plays a vital and active role in a person's development. Piaget's idea is primarily known as a developmental stage theory. The theory deals with the nature of knowledge itself and how humans gradually come to acquire, construct, and use it. To Piaget, cognitive development was a progressive reorganization of mental processes resulting from biological maturation and environmental experience. He believed that, children construct an understanding of the world around them, experience discrepancies between what they already know and what they discover in their environment, then adjust their ideas accordingly. Moreover, Piaget claimed that cognitive development is at the center of the human organism, and language is contingent on knowledge and understanding acquired through cognitive development. Piaget's earlier work received the greatest attention. Many parents have been encouraged to provide a rich, supportive environment for their child's natural propensity to grow and learn. Child-centered classrooms and "open education" are direct applications of Piaget's views. Despite its huge success, Piaget's theory has some limitations that Piaget recognized himself: for example, the theory supports sharp stages rather than continuous development (decalage).

Assimilation and Accommodation :

Through his study of the field of education, Piaget focused on two processes, which he named assimilation and accommodation. To Piaget, assimilation meant integrating external elements into structures of lives or environments, or those we could have through experience. **Assimilation** is how humans perceive and adapt to new information. It is the process of fitting new information into pre-existing cognitive schemas. In assimilation new experiences are reinterpreted to fit into or assimilate with, old ideas. It occurs when humans are faced with new or unfamiliar information and refer to previously learned information in order to make sense of it. In contrast, **accommodation** is the process of taking new information in one's environment and altering pre-existing schemas in order to fit in the new information. This happens when the existing schema (knowledge) does not work, and needs to be changed to deal with a new object or situation. Accommodation is imperative because it is how people will continue to interpret new concepts, schemas, frameworks and more. Piaget believed that the human brain has been programmed through evolution to bring equilibrium, which is what he believed ultimately influences structures by the internal and external processes through assimilation and accommodation.

Piaget's understanding was that assimilation and accommodation cannot exist without the other. They are two sides of a coin. To assimilate an object into an existing mental schema, one first needs to take into account or accommodate to the particularities of this object to a certain extent. For instance, to recognize (assimilate) an apple as an apple, one must first focus (accommodate) on the contour of this object. To do this, one needs to roughly recognize the size of the object. Development increases the balance, or equilibration, between these two functions. When in balance with each other, assimilation and accommodation generate mental schemas of the operative intelligence. When one function dominates over the other, they generate representations which belong to figurative intelligence.

Sensorimotor Stage:

Cognitive development is Jean Piaget's theory. Through a series of stages, Piaget proposed four stages of cognitive development: the **sensorimotor, preoperational, concrete operational** and **formal operational period**.

Jean Piaget created extensive studies of the intellectual development of children. He believed this to be important because he thought that intellectual development affected all other forms of development in a child's life. Some of his studies were performed on his own children, so he was able to witness cognitive development starting at birth. Piaget designed sets of questions that he would ask the children at different stages in their life. He was not interested in whether they gave him the correct answer or not, instead he was interested in their brain processing and reasoning.

Piaget discovered that the logic of a child is completely different from that of an adult. This meant that knowledge continuously changes throughout life,

Piaget's Four Stages of Cognitive Development

Piaget concluded that there were four different stages in the cognitive development of children. The first was the Sensory Motor Stage, which occurs in children from birth to approximately two years. The Pre-operational Stage is next, and this occurs in children aged around two to seven years old. Children aged around seven to eleven or twelve go through the Concrete Operational stage, and adolescents go through the Formal Operations Stage, from the age of around eleven to sixteen or more.

The following discussion outlines these four stages:

Sensory Motor Stage	Birth or 0 - 2yrs	No thought beyond immediate physical experiences.
Pre-operational Stage	2yrs - 7yrs	Able to think beyond here and now, but egocentric and unable to perform mental transformations.
Concrete Operational Stage	7yrs - 11yrs	Able to perform mental transformations but only on concrete physical objects.
Formal Operations Stage	11yrs - 16yrs	Able to perform hypothetical and abstract reasoning.

Stage 1 : Sensory Motor Stage (Birth or 0 yrs. - 2 yrs.)

Piaget's ideas surrounding the Sensory Motor Stage are centred on the basis of a 'schema'. Schemas are mental representations or ideas about what things are and how we deal with them. Piaget deduced that the first schemas of an infant are to do with movement. Piaget believed that much of a baby's behaviour is triggered by certain stimuli, in that they are reflexive. A few weeks after birth, the baby begins to understand some of the information it is receiving from it's senses, and learns to use some muscles and limbs for movement. These developments are known as 'action schemas'.

Babies are unable to consider anyone else's needs, wants or interests, and are therefore considered to be 'ego centric'.

During the Sensory Motor Stage, knowledge about objects and the ways that they can be manipulated is acquired. Through the acquisition of information about self and the world, and the people in it, the baby begins to understand how one thing can cause or affect another, and begins to develop simple ideas about time and space.

Babies have the ability to build-up mental pictures of objects around them, from the knowledge that they have developed on what can be done with the object. Large amounts of an infant's experience is surrounding objects. What the objects are is irrelevant, more importance is placed on the baby being able to explore the object to see what can be done with it. At around the age of eight or nine months, infants are more interested in an object for the object's own sake.

A discovery by Piaget surrounding this stage of development, was that when an object is taken from their sight, babies act as though the object has ceased to exist. By around eight to twelve months, infants begin to look for objects hidden, this is what is defined as 'Object Permanence'. This view has been challenged however, by Tom Bower, who showed that babies from one to four months have an idea of Object Permanence.

Stage 2 : Pre-Operations Stage (2 yrs. - 7 yrs.)

Piaget's second stage of development, was the Pre-Operations Stage. Children usually go through this stage between the age of two to seven years old.

During this stage, children's thought processes are developing, although they are still considered to be far from 'logical thought', in the adult sense of the word. The vocabulary of a child is also expanded and developed during this stage, as they change from babies and toddlers into 'little people'.

Pre-operational children are usually 'ego centric', meaning that they are only able to consider things from their own point of view, and imagine that everyone shares this view, because it is the only one possible. Gradually during this stage, a certain amount of 'decentering' occurs. This is when someone stops believing that they are the centre of the world, and they are more able to imagine that something or someone else could be the centre of attention.

'Animism' is also a characteristic of the Pre-operational stage. This is when a person has the belief that everything that exists has some kind of consciousness. An example of this is that children often believe that a car won't start because it is tired or sick, or they punish a piece of furniture when they run into it, because it must have been naughty to hurt them. A reason for this characteristic of the stage, is that the Pre-operational child often assumes that everyone and everything is like them. Therefore since the child can feel pain, and has emotions, so must everything else.

Another aspect of the Pre-operational stage in a child, is that of 'symbolism'. This is when something is allowed to stand for or symbolise something else. 'Moral realism' is a fourth aspect of this stage, this is the belief that the child's way of thinking about the difference between right and wrong, is shared by everyone else around them. One aspect of a situation, at one time, is all that they are able to focus on, and it is beyond them to consider that anything else could be possible. Due to this aspect of the stage, children begin to respect and insist on obedience of rules at all times, and they are not able to take anything such as motives into account.

Stage 3 : Concrete Operations Stage (7 yrs. - 11 yrs.)

The Concrete Operations Stage, was Piaget's third stage of cognitive development in children. This stage was believed to have affected children aged between seven and eleven to twelve years old.

During this stage, the thought process becomes more rational, mature and 'adult like', or more 'operational', Although this process most often continues well into the teenage years. The process is divided by Piaget into two stages, the Concrete Operations, and the Formal Operations stage, which is normally undergone by adolescents.

In the Concrete Operational stage, the child has the ability to develop logical thought about an object, if they are able to manipulate it. By comparison, however, in the Formal Operations stage, the thoughts are able to be manipulated and the presence of the object is not necessary for the thought to take place.

Belief in animism and ego centric thought tends to decline during the Concrete Operational stage, although, remnants of this way of thinking are often found in adults.

Piaget claims that before the beginning of this stage, children's ideas about different objects, are formed and dominated by the appearance of the object. For example, these appears to be more blocks when they are spread out, than when they are in a small pile. During the Concrete Operational Stage, children gradually develop the ability to 'conserve', or learn that objects are not always the way that they appear to be. This occurs when children are able to take in many different aspects of an object, simply through looking at it. Children are able to begin to imagine different scenarios, or 'what if' something were to happen. This is because they now have more 'operational' thought. Children are generally first able to conserve ideas about objects with which they are most comfortable.

Once children have learnt to conserve, they learn about 'reversibility'. This means that they learn that if things are changed, they will still be the same as they used to be. For example, they learn that if they spread out the pile of blocks, there are still as many there as before, even though it looks different!

Stage 4 : Formal Operations Stage (11 yrs. - 16 yrs.)

Finally, in the formal operational stage of adolescence, the structures of development become the abstract, logically organized system of adult intelligence. When faced with a complex problem, the adolescent speculates about all possible solutions before trying them out in the real world.

The formal operational stage begins around age 11 and is fully achieved by age 15, bringing with it the capacity for abstraction. This permits adolescents to reason beyound a world of concrete reality to a world of possibilities and to operate logically on symbols and information that do not necessarily refer to objects and events in the real world.

There are 2 major characteristics of formal operational thought.

The first is 'hypothetic-deductive reasoning'. When faced with a problem, adolescents come-up with a general theory of all possible factors that might affect the outcome and deduce from it specific hypothese that might occur. They then systematically treat these hypothese to see which ones do in fact occur in the real world. Thus, adolescent problem solving begins with possibilty and proceeds to reality.

The second important characteristic of this stage is that it is 'propositional' in nature. Adolescents can focus on verbal assertions and evaluate their logical validity without making reference to real-world circumstances. In contrast, concrete operational children can evaluate the logic of statements by considering them against concrete evidence only.

1.6.2 Vygotsky's Cultural-Historical Theory Overview

Lev Vygotsky's, **cultural-historical theory of cognitive development** is focused on the role of culture in the development of higher mental functions, such as speech and reasoning in children. His theory is sometimes referred to as having a sociocultural perspective, which means the theory emphasizes the importance of society and culture for promoting cognitive development.

Vygotsky believed that adults in a society foster children's cognitive development in an intentional and systematic manner by engaging them in challenging and meaningful activities. We will return to our introductory example throughout this lesson to illustrate the principles of Vygotsky's theory. In our intro, the father intentionally engaged with his child to help her understand how to fit the blocks into the designated holes. Without this assistance, she would have continued to be unsuccessful. But with the meaningful directions from her father, she was able to successfully get the blocks into the holes herself.

Assumptions of Vygotsky's Theory :

Six major assumptions guide Vygotsky's theory. We will discuss each one generally. Some assumptions will be covered in greater detail in other lessons in this course.

1. The first assumption of Vygotsky's theory is that, through both informal and formal conversations and education, (*adults convey to children the way their culture interprets and responds to the world.*) Specifically, as adults interact with children, they show the meanings they attach to objects, events and experiences. Returning to our example, the father is now reading to his daughter a book about transportation. The book describes the different modes of transportation we use

in our society (such as cars, trucks and boats). By presenting these concepts, the book shows the little girl how our society classifies modes of transportation.

2. The second assumption of Vygotsky's theory is that *thought and language becomes increasingly independent in the first few years of life*. We will talk specifically about language and speech development later in this lesson.

3. The third assumption explains that *complex mental processes begin as social activities*. As children develop, they gradually internalize processes they use in social contexts and begin to use them independently. This internalization process allows children to transform ideas and processes to make them uniquely their own. Returning to our example, the child and father are simply reading a book, but this social activity is transforming the way the child perceives modes of transportation. She will begin to classify these items herself when she sees cars, trucks and boats in real-life settings.

(a) Vygotsky also introduced the idea that *children can perform more challenging tasks when assisted by more advanced and competent individuals*. Vygotsky identified two levels of development: **actual development**, which is the upper limit of tasks a child can perform individually, and **level of potential development**, which is the upper limit of tasks a child can perform with the assistance of a more competent individual. According to Vygotsky, in order to get a true assessment of a child's actual and potential development, we should assess capabilities both when the child is performing the activity alone and with a more competent individual. For example, our young child exhibited that her actual development was that she knew the blocks belonged in the holes, but she could not quite determine how to actually put them in. Her level of potential development was being able to put the blocks in with the help of her father, an advanced individual. We would not expect the child to then be able to sort the blocks into colours and shapes, or to do anything beyond these skills that she exhibited with the assistance of her father at this point.

(b) Our next assumption is that *challenging tasks promote maximum cognitive growth*. Vygotsky described this as the **zone of proximal development**, or commonly referred to as ZPD. ZPD is the range of tasks that a child can perform with the help and guidance of others but cannot yet perform independently. ZPD will be discussed in more detail in another lesson.

(c) The final assumption is that, *play allows children to stretch themselves cognitively*. Play allows children to take on roles they would normally not be able to perform in real life. Same example of little girl who was playing with the blocks is now five years old. She's playing house with a friend. She is the mother and her friend is the child. Through make-believe play, she is able to exhibit behaviours and be a mommy according to the rules of her society. For example, a mommy takes care of her child, prepares food, etc. That would normally be impossible for a five year old in real-life to do.

1.6.3 Jerome Bruner's Cognetive Development

Jerome Seymour Bruner (Born: October 1, 1915) is an American psychologist who has made significant contributions to human cognitive psychology and cognitive learning theory in educational psychology.

Jerome Bruner and Education:

Cognitive psychologist Jerome Bruner felt the goal of education should be intellectual development, as opposed to rote memorization of facts.

This lesson will discuss Bruner's theory of development and his three modes of representation. We will also explore his beliefs on learning, language and discovery, and differentiate his views from those of Jean Piaget.

Bruner held the following beliefs regarding learning and education:

- He believed curriculum should foster the development of problem-solving skills through the processes of inquiry and discovery.
- He believed that subject matter should be represented in terms of the child's way of viewing the world.

- He believed that curriculum should be designed so that the mastery of skills leads to the mastery of still more powerful ones.

- He also advocated teaching by organizing concepts and learning by discovery.

- Finally, he believed culture should shape notions through which people organize their views of themselves and others and the world in which they live.

Three Stages of Representation:

Jerome Bruner identified three stages of cognitive representation :

1. **Enactive**, which is the representation of knowledge through actions.

2. **Iconic**, which is the visual summarization of images.

3. **Symbolic representation**, which is the use of words and other symbols to describe experiences.

The **enactive** stage appears first. This stage involves the encoding and storage of information. There is a direct manipulation of objects without any internal representation of the objects.

For example, a baby shakes a rattle and hears a noise. The baby has directly manipulated the rattle and the outcome was a pleasurable sound. In the future, the baby may shake his hand, even if there is no rattle, expecting his hand to produce the rattling sounds. The baby does not have an internal representation of the rattle and, therefore, does not understand that it needs the rattle in order to produce the sound.

The **iconic** stage appears from one to six years old. This stage involves an internal representation of external objects visually in the form of a mental image or icon. For example, a child drawing an image of a tree or thinking of an image of a tree would be representative of this stage.

The **symbolic** stage is from seven years and up, when information is stored in the form of a code or symbol such as language. Each symbol has a fixed relation to something it represents. For example, the word 'dog' is a symbolic representation for a single class of animal. Symbols, unlike mental images or memorized actions, can be classified and organized. In this stage, most information is stored as words, mathematical symbols, or in other symbol systems.

Bruner believed that all learning occurs through the stages we just discussed. Bruner also believed that learning should begin with direct manipulation of objects. For example, in math education, Bruner promoted the use of algebra tiles, coins, and other items that could be manipulated.

After a learner has the opportunity to directly manipulate the objects, they should be encouraged to construct visual representations, such as drawing a shape or a diagram.

Finally, a learner understands the symbols associated with what they represent. For example, a student in math understands that the plus sign (+) means to add two numbers together and the minus sign (−) means to subtract.

Discovery Learning

The concept of **discovery learning** implies that, a learner constructs his or her own knowledge for him/herself by discovering as opposed to being told about something.

According to Bruner, the teacher should facilitate the learning process by developing lessons that provide the learner with information they need without organizing it for them.

This idea of discovery learning is often referred to as **constructivism**, which emphasizes the active role of the learner in building understanding and making sense of information.

1.6.4 David Ausubel :
(Meaningful Verbal Learning)

Ausubel whose theories are particularly relevant for educators, considered neo-behaviourist views inadequate. Although he recognized other forms of learning, his work was focused on verbal learning. He dealt with the nature of meaning, and believes that the external world acquires meaning only as it is converted into the content of consciousness by the learner.

Meaningful Verbal Learning:

Meaning is created through some form of representational equivalence between language (symbols) and mental context. Two processes are involved:

1. Reception, which is employed in meaningful verbal learning, and

2. Discovery, which is involved in concept formation and problem solving.

Ausubel's work has frequently been compared with Bruner's. The two held similar views about the hierarchical nature of knowledge, but Bruner was strongly oriented toward discovery processes, where Ausubel gave more emphasis to the verbal learning methods of speech, reading and writing.

Ausubel's focus was on meaningful learning rather than rote learning. To him, new learning was meaningful when it could be related in a non-arbitrary fashion to that which a person already knew. Meaning happens when new information is taken into a person's existing cognitive structure and is related to the previously learned content forming new connections between this new information and the existing information. This is how meaning works according to Auusbel. Rote learning, on the other hand, happens when the new information cannot be related to the previously learned content in any substantive manner. In essence, there is nothing in the person's existing cognitive structure to which she or he can relate the new information to form meaning. Thus, it can only be rotely learned. Meaningful learning sticks and becomes the basis for learning additional information. Rote learning does not stick because it does not have these meaningful connections. Thus, it fades from memory rather quickly.

Ausubel has given instructions about teaching to teachers also. The "Advanced Organizer Model" of teaching is based or Ausubel's "Meaningful Verbal Learning".

An advance organizer is a very useful tool for teachers to help students understand, retain and remember new learning material. When there is an overload of information while studying for examination or while just sitting in a class. Sometimes learning everything that's required can be a overload. Even if one is provided with all the information, it can be hard to remember everything.

This is a challenge teacher's face regularly. Teachers must provide the students with information in such a way that the students understand, retain and remember it.

An advance organizer is a tool used to introduce the lesson topic and illustrate the relationship between what the students are about to learn and the information they have already learned.

The advance organizer model has three phases of activity according to Joyce et al (2000).

Phase - 1 : Presentation of Advance Organiser :

- Clarify the aims of the lesson.
- Present the advance organizer.
- Prompt for awareness of relevant knowledge.

Phase - 2 : Making Links to Form the Organizer :

- Presenting the learning task or material.
- Make organisation and logical order of learning material explicit.

Phase - 3 : Strengthening of the Cognitive Organisation :

- Integrative reconciliation and active reception learning.
- Elicit a critical approach to the subject matter.

The following strategies can be used by the teachers to implement advance organisers :

1. Review basic concepts prior to studying a new concept.
2. Have students identify the characteristics of a known phenomenon and then relate them to new concept.
3. Give a scenario and ask students to infer rules based upon their current knowledge.
4. Use charts, diagrams, oral presentations or concept maps.
5. Ask students to compare and contrast the new content based on what they already know.
6. Identify a problem and ask for a reason why it may occur (before teaching the reason).

Constructivism :

The concept of constructivism has roots in classical antiquity, going back to Socrates's dialogues with his followers, in which he asked directed questions that led his students, to realize for themselves the weaknesses in their thinking.

Jean Piaget and **John Dewey** developed theories of childhood development and education, what we now call Progressive Education, that led to the evolution of constructivisms.

Lev Vygotsky, Jerome Bruner and **David Ausubel** added new perspectives to constructivist learning theory.

Piaget believed that humans learn through the construction of one logical structure after another. Dewey called for education to be grounded in real experience. Inquiry is the key part of constructivist learning. Vygotsky introduced the social aspect of learning into constructivism. He defined the "zone of proximal learning", according to which students solve problems beyond their actual development level under adult guidance. Bruner initiated curriculum change based on the idea that learning is an active, social processes in which students construct new ideas and concepts based on their current knowledge.

Concept of Constructivisms :

Constructivism is basically a theory based on observation and scientific study. It says that people construct their own understanding and knowledge of the world, through experiencing things and reflecting on these experiences.

Definition of Constructivism :

Constructivism is a philosophy of learning founded on the precise that, by reflecting on our experiences, we construct our own understanding of the world in time.

In the classroom, the constructivist view of learning can point towards a number of different teaching practices. In the most general sense, it usually means encouraging students to use active techniques (experiments, real-world problem solving) to create more knowledge and then to reflect on and talk about what they are doing and how their understanding is changing. The teacher makes sure she understands the students pre-existing conceptions, and guides the activity to address them and then build on them.

Constructivist teachers encourage students to constantly assess how the activity is helping them gain understanding. By questioning themselves and their strategies, students in the constructivist classroom ideally become "expert learners". This gives them ever-broadening tools to keep learning. With a well-planned classroom environment, the students learn HOW TO LEARN.

When a student faces an unfamiliar situation or a problem he starts remembering his past experiences. he tries to relate them with the new situations and uses this information to understand the new situation or problem. His understanding process begins at this stage but again some situations occurs which is unfamiliar. Sometimes he does not have any previous knowledge of these new situations. He then starts the process of understanding these new situations by taking the help of processes like imagination, guesswork, reasoning, inference drawing etc. This makes it easy to minimize. The unfamiliarity of the situation or problem. But this may not happen always. Then in this case the student may discuss it with his classmates or the teacher may ask some investigative or searching questions and remove the obstacles in the process of understanding the problem. All this process can be called as creation of knowledge, which is the base of constructivism. Creation of knowledge by students own efforts is the core of constructivism.

According to constructivism following things are necessary for creation of knowledge :

1. Students should be aware of the problem.
2. They should get the inspiration to solve it.
3. They should understand the situation, study the previous knowledge to find the solution or inference.
4. Check the solution properly and then only accept it.

These above four things can be summarized as follows :

1. Determination of unit from curriculum.
2. Motivation.
3. Determination of learning experiences and its implementation.
4. Evaluation.

Guiding Principles of Constructivism :

1. Learning is a search for meaning. Therefore, learning must start with the issues around which students are actively trying to construct meaning.
2. Meaning requires understanding wholes as well as parts. And parts must be understood in the context of wholes. Therefore, the learning process focuses on primary concepts not isolated facts.

3. In order to teach well, we must understand the mental models that students use to perceive the world and the assumptions, they make to support these models.

4. The purpose of learning is for an individual to construct his/her own meaning, not just memorise the 'right' answers and regurgitate someone else's meaning.

Since education is inherently interdisciplinary the only valuable way to measure learning is to make the assessment part of the learning process it provides students with information on the quality of their learning.

Constructivism in Formal Education :

"If one seriously adopts the constructivist approach, one discovers that many more of one's habitual ways for thinking have to be changed".   **– Von Glasersfeld**

Inclusion of constructivism in formal education will need a lot of preparation on the teachers part. A teacher will have to become a "Facilitator". A facilitation means one who facilitates, one who makes it easy and convenient, one who provides conveniences, (for the sake of students). A person who removes the obstacles in a process helps in such a manner that the process becomes easier, is called a facilitator.

A teacher's role in constructivism learning is very important. A teacher should keep following points in mind while making use of constructivism in teaching-learning :

1. A teacher should change his/her outlook about traditional teacher.

2. A teacher should understand his/her new role of assistant/ helper in knowledge, attitude and skill development.

3. A teacher will have to change some of his old habits to new ones i.e. change in attitude.

4. Teacher should keep in mind that students learn a lot from the internet. So many times teacher is not necessary for learning.

5. The teacher should have mastery ever his subject.

6. He should be techno-savvy, so as to give proper experiences to students.
7. Students are going to ask questions, so there should be enough learning material.
8. Teacher should train himself to create constructivist environment in classroom.

1.6.5 Influence of Child's Social and Cultural Background on Knowledge of Mathematics

Social Background :

The nature, extent and quality of mathematics learning among young children cannot be adequately understood without looking at the larger context of education and social background of the children. Society, including schools, characterized by large inequalities impacts mathematics learning.

Mathematics researchers **Vinay Kantha** and **Arindam Bose** have made a study of influence of socio-economic background and cultural practices on mathematics education in India. They observed historical and sociological perspectives and presented an appraisal of need and nature of mathematics learning revealed by field studies in two communities in a deprived rural setting and a low income urban setting, respectively.

While the latter was economically active, the former was such poorer in work and education opportunities, through had richer cultural practices that involved engagement with mathematical riddles, puzzles, folklores and mnemonic tables. In both situations mathematics learning remains disconnected from formal school mathematics. Both the groups presented potentially rich contexts for drawing upon mathematical knowledge everyday that can inform effective mathematics learning.

Information about social background, social support and motivation could lead to an explanation of student attitudes towards maths learning.

Social background of the child refers to the locale of residence, locale of school, type of school, income of parents and literacy of parents.

Child development is also affected by the nature of their family and early educational experiences. The child's learning depends upon the nature of the family whether it is nuclear family or joint family or a single parent family. Parents who are social themselves serve as models for children. The children, who are raised in democratic families, where reasons are given along with rules, are most likely to be socially active and open minder. This helps in mathematics learning.

Several aspects of school's social environment such as teacher support, students-to-student interaction, and the academic and behaviour expectations of teachers plays an important role in shaping the attitude and behaviour of students. When a class environment has supportive beahviour of teachers the students show feelings of control and confidence in their ability to succeed. The way students perceive their teacher's characteristics will affect their attitude towards mathematics.

Students with a higher perception of the learning environment and a more positive perception of their teachers have more positive attitude towards mathematics **Rawnsley** and **Fisher** found out that students had more positive attitude towards mathematic when the teacher was supportive.

The relationship between social aspects of the social environment and student emotional aspects may be mediated by other variables such as control related appraisals and values-related appraisals. Therefore, competence support, expectations and feedback that students receive from others have an impact on their studying attitudes.

Family income and parent literacy have a strong effect on various learning activities including mathematics learning socio-economic disadvantage, lack of maternal education qualifications, were found to have stronger effect childrens learning. They remained powerful in influencing competencies in children of primary school.

Numerous studies have established a link between poverty and children's cognitive abilities and competence. Increases in family income have shown positive impact on children's learning.

Cultural Background :

The cultural tendencies impact the way children participate in education cultured is the characteristics and knowledge of a particular group of people, defined by everything from language, religion, cuisine, social habits, music and arts.

Culture can be defined also as shared patterns of behaviour and interactions, cognitive constructs and understanding that are learned by socialization.

Every student has different cultural background. **Edd Taylor**, an assistant professor at a school of education, has focused his work on how mathematics learning is shaped by one's culture. Culture has a tremendous impact on the way a child learns to count.

All the students in a given class are sharing. The common experiences of their classroom and thus create their own unique classroom environment, each student also brings the cultural sensitivities from their home environment. A teacher should understand how non-verbal cues are seen by their students.

In some cultures, it is considered rude, disrespectful and even confrontational for a student to make eye contact with authority figures. In other cultures, it is actually forbidden to shake hands with a stranger of the opposite gender.

Knowledge of learning styles and of the child's culture helps the teachers examine their own instructional practices.

A growing body of research has indicated that the frequency of religious practice is directly correlated with academic outcomes and educational achievements. Religiously involved students spend more time on homework, work harder in school and achieve more as a result. Frequent religious attendance correlates with lower dropout rates and greater school attachment. Parents also who are religious care more for the welfare of their child. Attendance and achievement in religious schools influence educational performance.

Significant difference in mathematics achievement among students of different countries have been observed in recent international studies. There seems to be an assumption that mathematics is learned roughly the same way through different languages within the field of mathematics education, the central role that language plays in the learning, teaching and doing mathematics is greatly known.

Language plays an important part in mathematics education in the following four areas :

1. Analysis of the development of students' mathematical knowledge.
2. Understanding the shaping of mathematical knowledge.
3. Understanding processes of teaching and learning.
4. Multilingual contexts.

Teachers should keep the following points in mind to handle influence of social and cultural background of students during mathematics learning :

1. Learn about your own culture.
2. Learn about your students culture.
3. Know the social backgrounds of your students.
4. Understand your students linguistic traits.
5. Use this knowledge to inform your teaching.
6. Know about your students home and school relationships.
7. Use multi-cultural books and materials to faster cross cultural understanding.
8. Reducing ignorance that comes from lack of exposure.
9. Providing opportunities for all students to develop cross-cultural competence.
10. Preparing students for the real world.

Points to Remember

- Mathematics is a major source for - Physical, Intellectual, Spiritual development of human personality.
- The knowledge of logical and symbolic form is very useful in our day-to-day life.
- Assimilation means how human perceive and adapt the new information.
- Accommodation is the process of taking new information in one's environment and altering pre-existing schemes in order to fit in the new information.

- Piaget's theory of cognitive development is comprehensive theory about the nature and development of human intelligence.
- Piaget's four stages of cognitive development :
  (i) Sensory Motor Development (0 yrs. - 2 yrs.)
  (ii) Pre-operation Stage (2 yrs. - 7 yrs.)
  (iii) Concrete Operation Stage (7 yrs. - 11 yrs.)
  (iv) Formal Operation Stage (11 yrs. - 16 yrs.)
- Vygotsky's Cultural - Historical Theory of Cognitive Development is focused on the role of culture in the development of higher mental functions, such as speech and reasoning in children.
- **Jerome Bruner and Education :** Cognitive psychologist Jerome Bruner felt the goal of education should be intellectual development as opposed to role memorization facts.
- Ausubel's theories are particularly relevant for educators, considered neo-behaviourist views inadequate.
- Constructivism is basically a theory based on observation and scientific study.

EXERCISE

Q.1. Multiple Choice Questions :

1. Knowledge of _____ styles and of the child's culture helps the teachers examine their own instructional practices.
   (a) knowing   (b) learning
   (c) examining   (d) none of these

2. _____ is basically a theory based on observation and scientific study.
   (a) Knowledge   (b) Teaching
   (c) Constructivism   (d) None of these

3. _____ is involved in all sciences.
   (a) Teaching   (b) Mathematics
   (c) Knowledge   (d) None of these

4. The second part of mathematical knowledge is _____ knowledge.
   (a) symbolic   (b) constructive
   (c) educative   (d) none of these

5. Structure is the methodical arrangement of _____ .
    (a) content   (b) syllabus
    (c) units   (d) none of these

Answers : 1 - (b), 2 - (c), 3 - (b), 4 - (a), 5 - (c).

Q.2. Answer the Following Questions :

1. Explain the Concept of Mathematics.
2. Write Importance and Characteristics of Mathematics.
3. Explain in Brief : Structure of Mathematics.
4. Explain : Importance of Mathematics in day-to-day life.
5. Discuss 'Mathematics for development of nation'.
6. What is mean by Constructivism ?
7. Write the correlation of Mathematics with branches and sub-branches.
8. Explain the correlation of mathematics with other subject.
9. "Influence of child's social and cultural background of knowledge of mathematics". Explain.
10. Explain in brief Jerome Bruner's Cognitive Development Theory.

Q.3. Write Short Notes On :

1. Place and importance of mathematics in primary level.
2. Constructivism.
3. Piaget's Theory of Cognitive Development.
4. Cultural Historical Theory of Vygotsky.
5. Meaningful Verbal Learning.

✍ ✍ ✍

2

CONTENT ANALYSIS OF MATHEMATICS (1ˢᵀ TO 5ᵀᴴ)

➲ Chapter Structure ☾

(2.1)

2.1 Objectives

After reading this chapter, teachers will be able to :

- Explain basic concepts in Geometry.
- Explain two dimensional and three dimensional geometrical figures.
- Explain equality, similarity, and describe the correlation of different types of geometrical figures.
- Explain how to measure the different types of geometrical figures.
- Explain how to calculate area, perimeter and volume of geometrical figures.
- Explain the geometrical patterns and write answers of questions on given patterns.
- Explain the concept of fraction, decimal fraction.
- Explain preparation of algebraic expressions, use of variables and equations with one variable.

2.2 Introduction

In first chapter, we have seen that what is meant by Mathematics? Background information related to the nature of Mathematics, salient features of Mathematics, Scope and Importance of Mathematics.

In this chapter, we have also seen commercial mathematics and use of mathematics in day-to-day life.

Now in this chapter, we will study different types of geometrical figures and basic concepts of geometry and geometrical patterns also.

2.3 Van Hiele Model

In mathematics education, the Van Hiele model is a theory that describes how students learn geometry. This theory originated in 1957 in the doctoral dissertations of Dina van Hiele-Geld and Pierre van Hiele (wife and husband) at Utrecht University, in the Netherlands. The Soviets did research on the theory in the 1960's and integrated their findings into their curricula. American researchers did several large studies on the van Hiele theory in the late 1970's and early 1980's, concluding that (students' law van Hiele levels made it difficult to succeed in proof-oriented geometry courses and advised better preparation at earlier grade levels.) Pierre van Hiele published *Structure and Insight* in 1986. The model has greatly influenced geometry curricula throughout the world through emphasis on analyzing properties and classification of shapes at early grade levels. In the United States, the theory has influenced the geometry strand of the Standards published by the National Council of Teachers of Mathematics and the new Common Core Standards.

2.3.1 Van Hiele Levels

The student learns by role to operate with [mathematical] relations that he does not understand, and of which he has not seen the origin. Therefore the system of relations is an independent construction having no rapport with other experiences of the child. This means that, the student knows only what has been taught to him and what has been deduced from it. He has not learned to establish connections between the system and the sensory world. He will not know how to apply what he has learned in a new situation. (by *Pierre van Hiele, 1959*.)

The best known part of the van Hiele model is the five levels which the van Hiele postulated to describe how student learn to reason in geometry. Students cannot be expected to prove geometric theorems until they have built-up an extensive understanding of the systems of relationships between geometric ideas. These systems cannot be learned by role, but must be developed through familiarity by experiencing numerous examples and counter examples, the various properties of geometric figures, the relationships between the properties, and how these properties are ordered. The five levels postulated by the van Hiele describe how students advance through this understanding.

The five van Hiele levels are sometimes misunderstood to be descriptions of how students understand shape classification, but the levels actually describe the way that students reason about shapes and other geometric ideas. Pierre van Hiele noticed that his students tended to "plateau" at certain points in their understanding of geometry and he identified these plateau points as *levels*. In general, these levels are a product of experience and instructions rather than age. This is in contrast to Piaget's theory of cognitive development, which is age-dependent. A child must have enough experiences (classroom or otherwise) with these geometric ideas to move to a higher level of sophistication. Through rich experiences, children can reach Level 2 in elementary school. Without such experiences, many adults (including teachers) remain in Level 1 all their lives, even if they take a formal geometry course in secondary school. The levels are as follows:

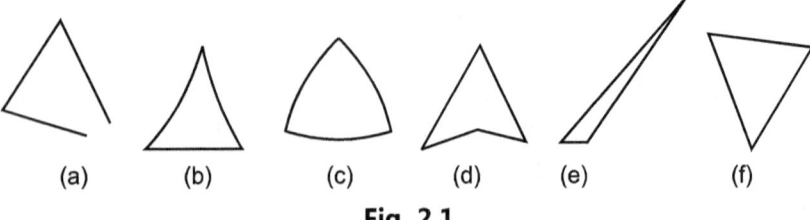

| (a) | (b) | (c) | (d) | (e) | (f) |

Fig. 2.1

Children at Level 0 will often say all of these shapes are triangles, except E, which is too "skinny". They may say F is "upside down". Students at Level 1 will recognize that only E and F are valid triangles.

Level 0: Visualization: At this level, the focus of a student's thinking is on individual shapes, which the student is learning to classify by judging their holistic appearance. Student simply says, "That is a circle," usually without further description. Students identify prototypes of basic geometrical figures i.e. triangle, circle, square.

These visual prototypes are then used to identify other shapes. A shape is a circle because it looks like a sun; a shape is a rectangle because it looks like a door or a box; and so on. A square seems to be a different sort of shape than a rectangle, and a rhombus does not look like other parallelograms, so these shapes are classified completely separately in the student's mind. Student view figures holistically without analyzing their properties. If a shape does not sufficiently resemble its prototype, the child may reject the classification. Thus, student at this stage might balk at calling a thin, wedge-shaped triangle (with sides 1, 20, 20 or sides 20, 20, 39) a "triangle", because it is so different in shape from an equilateral triangle, which is the usual prototype for "triangle". If the horizontal base of the triangle is on top and the opposing vertex below, the child may recognize it as a triangle, but claim it is "upside down". Shapes with rounded or incomplete sides may be accepted as "triangles" if they bear a holistic resemblance to an equilateral triangle. Squares are called "diamonds" and not recognized as squares if their sides are oriented at 45° to the horizontal. Children at this level often believe something is true based on a single example.

Level 1: Analysis: At this level, the shapes become bearers of their properties. The objects of thought are classes of shapes, which the student has learned to analyze as having properties. A student at this level might say, "A square has 4 equal sides and 4 equal angles. Its diagonals are congruent and perpendicular, and they bisect each other." The properties are more important than the appearance of the shape. If a figure is sketched on the blackboard and the teacher claims it is intended to have congruent sides and angles, the students accept that it is a square, even if it is poorly drawn. Properties are not yet ordered at this level. Students can discuss the properties of the basic figures and recognize them by these properties, but generally do not allow categories to overlap because they understand each property in isolation from the others.

For example, they will still insist that "a square is not a rectangle". (They may introduce extraneous properties to support such beliefs, such as defining a rectangle as a shape with one pair of sides longer than the other pair of sides.) Students begin to notice many properties of shapes, but do not see the relationships between the properties; therefore they cannot reduce the list of properties to a concise definition with necessary and sufficient conditions. They usually reason inductively from several examples, but cannot yet reason deductively because they do not understand how the properties of shapes are related.

Level 2: Abstraction: At this level, properties are ordered. The objects of thought are geometric properties, which the student has learned to connect deductively. The student understands that properties are related and one set of properties may imply another property. Students can reason with simple arguments about geometric figures. A student at this level might say, "Isosceles triangles are symmetric, so their base angles must be equal". Learners recognize the relationships between types of shapes. They recognize that all squares are rectangles, but not all rectangles are squares, and they understand why squares are a type of rectangle based on an understanding of the properties of each. They can tell whether it is possible or not to have a rectangle; that is, for example, also a rhombus. They understand necessary and sufficient conditions and can write concise definitions. However, they do not yet understand the intrinsic meaning of deduction. They cannot follow a complex argument, understand the place of definitions, or grasp the need for axioms, so they cannot yet understand the role of formal geometric proofs.

Level 3: Deduction: Students at this level understand the meaning of deduction. The object of thought is deductive reasoning i.e. simple proofs, which the student learns to combine to form a system of formal proofs (Euclidean geometry). Students can construct geometric proofs at a secondary school level and understand their meaning. They understand the role of undefined terms, definitions, axioms and theorems in Euclidean geometry. However, students at this level believe that axioms and definitions are fixed, rather than arbitrary, so they cannot yet conceive of non-Euclidean geometry. Geometric ideas are still understood as objects in the Euclidean plane.

Level 4: Rigor: At this level, geometry is understood at the level of a mathematician. Students understand that definitions are arbitrary and need not actually refer to any concrete realization. The object of thought is deductive geometric systems, for which the learner compares axiomatic systems. Learners can study non-Euclidean geometries with understanding. People can understand the discipline of geometry and how it differs philosophically from non-mathematical studies.

American researchers renumbered the levels as 1 to 5 so that they could add a "Level 0" which described young children who could not identify shapes at all. Both numbering systems are still in use. Some researchers also give different names to the levels.

2.3.2 Properties of the Levels

The van Hiele levels have five properties:

1.   Fixed sequence: The levels are hierarchical. Students cannot "skip" a level. The van Hieles claim that much of the difficulty experienced by geometry students is due to being taught at the deduction level when they have not yet achieved the Abstraction level.

2.   Adjacency: Properties which are intrinsic at one level become extrinsic at the next. The properties are there at the Visualization level, but the student is not yet consciously aware of them until the Analysis level. Properties are in fact related at the Analysis level, but students are not yet explicitly aware of the relationships.

3.   Distinction: Each level has its own linguistic symbols and network of relationships. The meaning of a linguistic symbol is more than its explicit definition; it includes the experiences the speaker associates with the given symbol. What may be "correct" at one level is not necessarily correct at another level. At Level 0 a square is something that looks like a box. At Level 2 a square is a special type of rectangle. Neither of these is a correct description of the meaning of "square" for someone reasoning at Level 1. If the student is simply handed the definition and its associated properties, without being allowed to develop meaningful experiences with the concept, the student will not be able to apply this knowledge beyond the situations used in the lesson.

4. Separation: A teacher who is reasoning at one level speaks a different "language" from a student at a lower level, preventing understanding. When a teacher speaks of a "square" she or he means a special type of rectangle. A student at Level 0 or 1 will not have the same understanding of this term. The student does not understand the teacher, and the teacher does not understand how the student is reasoning, frequently concluding that the student's answers are simply "wrong". The van Hieles believed that this property was one of the main reasons for failure in geometry. Teachers believe they are expressing themselves clearly and logically, but their Level 3 or 4 reasoning is not understandable to students at lower levels, nor do the teachers understand their students' thought processes. Ideally, the teacher and students need shared experiences behind their language.

5. Attainment: The Van Hieles recommended five phases for guiding students from one level to another on a given topic:

- **Information or inquiry:** Students get acquainted with the material and begin to discover its structure. Teachers present a new idea and allow the students to work with the new concept. By having students experience about the structure of the new concept in a similar way, they can have meaningful conversations about it. (A teacher might say, "This is a rhombus. Construct some more rhombi on your paper.")

- **Guided or directed orientation:** Students do tasks that enable them to explore implicit relationships. Teachers propose activities of a fairly guided nature that allow students to become familiar with the properties of the new concept which the teacher desires them to learn. (A teacher might ask, "What happens when you cut out and fold the rhombus along a diagonal? the other diagonal?" and so on, followed by discussion.)

- **Explicitation:** Students express what they have discovered and vocabulary is introduced. The students' experiences are linked to shared linguistic symbols. The van Hieles believe, it is more profitable to learn vocabulary *after* students have had an opportunity to become familiar with the concept. The discoveries are made as explicit as possible. (A teacher might say, "Here are the properties we have noticed and some associated vocabulary for the things you discovered. Let us discuss what these mean.")

- **Free orientation:** Students do more complex tasks enabling them to master the network of relationships in the material. They know the properties being studied, but need to develop fluency in navigating the network of relationships in various situations. This type of activity is much more open-ended than the guided orientation. These tasks will not have set procedures for solving them. Problems may be more complex and require more free exploration to find solutions. (A teacher might say, "How could you construct a rhombus given only two of its sides?" and other problems for which students have not learned a fixed procedure.)

- **Integration:** Students summarize what they have learned and commit it to memory. The teacher may give the students an overview of everything they have learned. It is important that the teacher is not present any new material during this phase, but only a summary of what has already been learned. The teacher might also give an assignment to remember the principles and vocabulary learned for future work, possibly through further exercises. (A teacher might say, "Here is a summary of what we have learned. Write this in your notebook and do these exercises for homework.") Supporters of the Van Hiele model point out that traditional instructions often involves only this last phase, which explains why students do not master the material.

Points to Remember

- Van Hiele model is a theory that describes how students learn geometry.
- Description of figures made by the students is not wrong.
- Guide to students to do the practical in a simple way.

2.4 Two and Three Dimensional Shapes

2.4.1 Two Dimensional Shapes/Figures

(A) Point : Point is just a position on a plane. It is denoted by a dot (•). A point has no length, no breadth and no thickness. A point is always named by any capital alphabet.

For example : Point A, M etc. See Fig. 2.2.

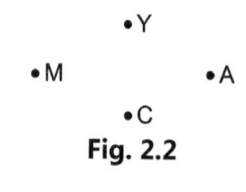

Fig. 2.2

(B) Collinear points : The points which are contained in one single straight line are called collinear points.

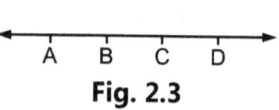

Fig. 2.3

(C) Non-collinear points : When three or more points are such that they cannot be contained in a single straight line, then these points are called non-collinear points. A, B, C, D cannot be contained in a single straight line. So, they are called non-collinear points.

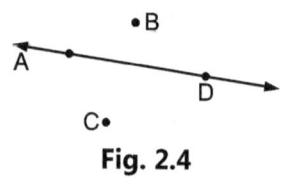

Fig. 2.4

(D) Line : The union of two opposite rays is called as line. A line extends infinitely on both the sides. Infinite number of lines can be drawn through *one* point.

Two distinct points determine one and only one line.

When two lines intersect, they can intersect in one and only one point.

The lines are called intersecting lines and the point at which they intersect is called point of intersection.

(E) Line segment : A set of two points, and all the collinear points in between these two points is called a segment. There are limited number of end points in a line segment. We can measure the length of a line segment. Two segments are said to be congruent when their lengths are same.

For example,

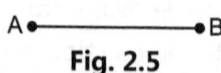

Fig. 2.5

(F) Ray : If a line segment is extended on one side, then the figure so formed is called a ray. In a ray, one side of the segment contains infinite points, having one end point on the other side. That end point is called the origin of the ray or the vertex of the ray.

For example,

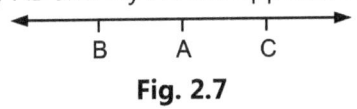

(a)   (b)

Fig. 2.6

While naming a ray, we should write the name of the vertex first and then any other point on the ray. For example, ray in Fig. 2.6 (a) is ray AB and not ray BA, ray in Fig. 2.6 (b) is ray YX and not ray XY.

(G) Opposite rays : Two collinear rays having the same vertex one extending on one side and the other extending on the other side in opposite direction are called opposite rays. The vertex of the ray is common to both the rays.

For example, ray AB and ray AC are opposite rays.

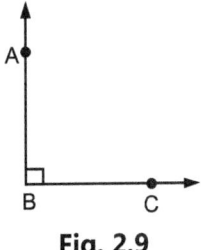

Fig. 2.7

Angles and Types of Angles

(A) Angle : An angle is the union of two non-collinear rays with a common origin.

The common origin is called the vertex and two rays are the sides of the angle.

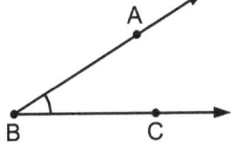

Fig. 2.8

(A) Right angle : An angle whose measure is 90° is called a right angle.

Fig. 2.9

(B) Acute angle : An angle whose measure is less than 90° is called an acute angle.

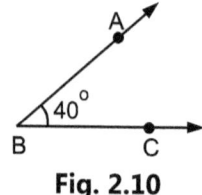

Fig. 2.10

(C) Obtuse angle : An angle whose measure is greater than 90° is called an obtuse angle.

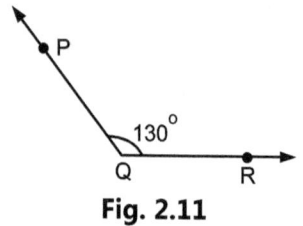

Fig. 2.11

(D) Parallel lines : The lines which never intersect to each other are called as parallel lines.

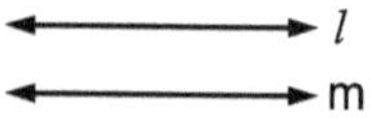

Fig. 2.12

Points to Remember

- Distance between parallel lines is same everywhere.
- There are three types of angles right angle, acute angle and obtuse angle.

Triangles and Types of Triangle

The three segments joining three non-collinear points form a triangle. A triangle is a closed figure having three sides and three vertices and has three angles.

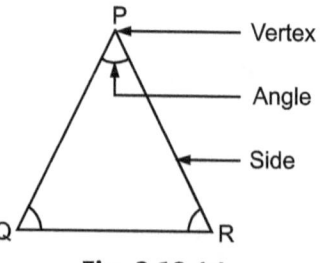

Fig. 2.13 (a)

In Δ PQR, seg PQ, seg PR and seg QR are its sides.

Point P, point Q and point R are its vertices.

∠ PQR, ∠ PRQ and ∠ QPR are its three angles.

TYPES OF TRIANGLES

Triangles are classified on the basis of angles and sides :

(I) Based on Angles, triangles can be classified as:

    (a) Acute angled triangle : A triangle which has all its angles acute, is called an acute angled triangle.

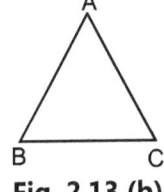

Fig. 2.13 (b)

    (b) Right angled triangle : A triangle that has one of its angles as right angle, is called a right angled triangle.

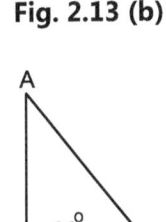

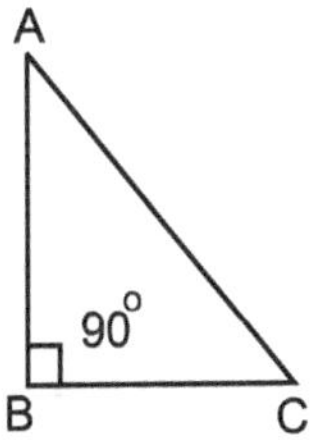

Fig. 2.14

    (c) Obtuse-angled triangle : A triangle that has one of its angles obtuse, is called an obtuse-angled triangle.

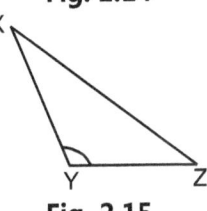

Fig. 2.15

(II) Based on its sides, triangles can be classified as :

    (a) Equilateral triangle : A triangle that has all its sides equal is called an equilateral triangle. All the angles of an equilateral triangle are congruent, each measuring 60°.

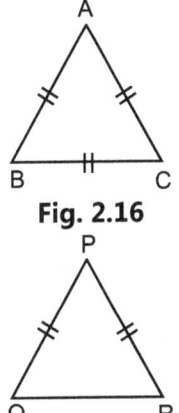

Fig. 2.16

    (b) Isosceles triangle : A triangle that has any two of its sides congruent, is called an isosceles triangle. In case of an isosceles triangle, the angles opposite to the congruent sides are also congruent.

    side PQ ≅ side PR and ∠ PQR ≅ ∠ PRQ

Fig. 2.17

(c) Scalene triangle : A triangle that has no two sides congruent is called a scalene triangle.

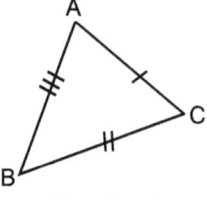

Fig. 2.18

Points to Remember

* Addition of measure of three angles of triangle is equal to 180°.
* There are three types of triangle based on angle - Acute angled triangle, Right angled triangle, Obtuse angled triangle.
* Types of triangle based on sides - Equilateral triangle, Isosceles triangle, Scalene triangle.

Square : Types and Properties

(a) Square : A rhombus having all its angles right angles is called a square.

Properties of a Square :

1. All the sides of square are congruent.
2. Both diagonals of a square are congruent.
3. All the angles of a square are congruent.
4. Diagonals of a square bisect each other at right angles.

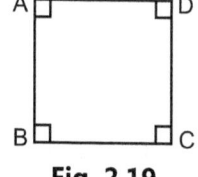

Fig. 2.19

(b) Rectangle : A parallelogram having each of its angles a right angle, is called rectangle.

Properties of a Rectangle :

1. Diagonals are congruent.
2. Diagonals bisect each other.
3. Opposite sides are congruent.

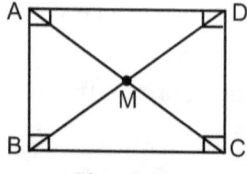

Fig. 2.20

(c) Rhombus : A parallelogram with all its sides congruent is called a rhombus.

Properties of Rhombus :

1. The diagonals of a rhombus bisect each other at right angles.
2. The opposite angles of a rhombus are congruent.

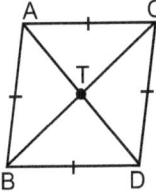

Fig. 2.21

(d) Parallelograms : If the opposite sides of a quadrilateral are parallel, the quadrilateral is called parallelogram.

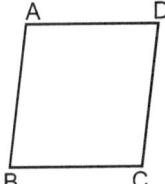

Fig. 2.22

Properties of Parallelogram :

1. Diagonals of a parallelogram bisect each other.
2. Opposite sides of a parallelogram are congruent.
3. Opposite angles of a parallelogram are congruent.

(e) Trapezium : If only one pair of its opposite sides is parallel, the quadrilateral is called trapezium. [Fig. 2.23 (a)]

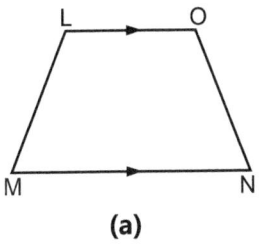

(a)

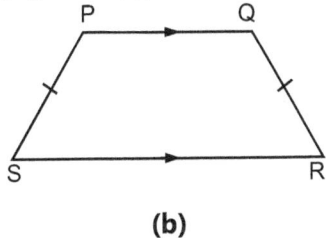

(b)

Fig. 2.23

Isosceles Trapezium : When the lengths of the non-parallel sides are equal it is an isosceles trapezium. [Fig. 2.23 (b)]

Points to Remember

- All sides of squares are equal.
- Opposite sides of rectangle are equal.
- Diagonals of rectangle are congruent.
- Diagonals of a parallelogram bisect each other.

Circle : Terms and Definition

(1) Radius : All the points on the circle lie at equal distance from its centre. This distance is known as the radius. All the radii of a circle are congruent.

(2) Chord : A segment obtained by joining any two points on the circle is called its chord. The circle has many chords.

(3) Diameter : A chord passing through the centre of the circle is called its diameter. The circle has many diameters. The diameter of a circle is the largest chord of the circle. The diameters of the circle are congruent. A diameter = $2 \times$ radius.

(4) Secant : A line which intersects a circle in two distinct points is called its secant.

(5) Tangent : A line which lies in the plane of a circle and touches the circle in one and only one point is said to be a tangent to the circle. The point in which the tangent touches the circle is called the point of contact. The tangent to a circle is perpendicular to its radius at the point of contact.

Points to Remember

- Centre, radius, chord, diameter, secant, tangent are parts of circle.
- Diameter is the largest chord of the circle.
- The line which intersects a circle in two distinct points is called secant.
- The line which touches to the circle into one and only one point is called tangent.

Characteristics of Two Dimensional Figures

Activity : Count the sides and corners of the following figures.

Fig. 2.24

Perimeter

Activity 1 : I have a handkerchief want to trim it with lace.
How much lace do I need ?

Activity 2 : A fence of a single wire has to be put around a rectangular field.
How much wire is required to fence the field ?

In both the cases, we have to find the length of lace and wire.

The sum of the length of all four sides of the handkerchief and rectangular field will tell us the length of lace and wire need respectively.

This is called as *perimeter*.

Questions

Complete the following sentences :

1. Perimeter of rectangle is ......

Fig. 2.25

2. Addition of measure of three sides of triangle means ......

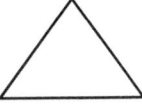

Fig. 2.26

3. To find the perimeter of a circle, we count ......

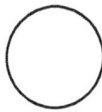

Fig. 2.27

Points to Remember

- Addition of measure of three sides of triangle is called as perimeter of triangle.
- If we know the measure of side of a square then we can calculate perimeter of square.
- If perimeter and measure of three sides of rectangle is given then we can find out measure of fourth or remaining side of rectangle.

Formula for Perimeter of Rectangle :

Activity :

Draw ☐ ABCD. Now take measure of each side of rectangle.

Take thread and rotate with four sides of rectangle after that measure the length of rectangle.

Observation :

l(AB) = 6 cm l(CD) = 6 cm   ($\because$ l = length

b(BC) = 2 cm   b(AD) = 2 cm   b = breadth)

Length of thread (Perimeter) = 16 cm

Perimeter of rectangle ABCD = 6 + 2 + 6 + 2

$$16 = 6 + 6 + 2 + 2$$
$$16 = (2 \times 6) + (2 \times 2)$$
$$16 = 2(6 + 2)$$

$\therefore$ | Perimeter of rectangle = 2 (length + breadth)
= 2 (l + b)

Points to Remember

- Perimeter of rectangle = 2(l + b)
- Perimeter of square = 4 (side)
- Perimeter of equilateral triangle = 3 (side)
- Perimeter of circle = 2 × π × r
- Perimeter of triangle = Side + Side + Side

Questions

Complete the following sentences :

1. Perimeter of rectangle PQRS is ...... cm.

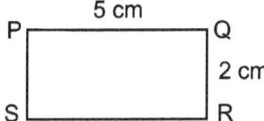

Fig. 2.28

2. Perimeter of ∆ABC is ...... cm.

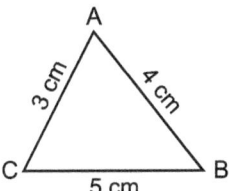

Fig. 2.29

3. Perimeter of ☐ LMNO is ...... cm.

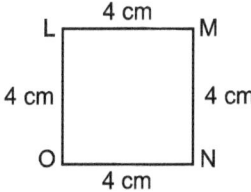

Fig. 2.30

4. Write the difference between area and perimeter ?

Area

1. Draw triangle, square and circle. Colour it.

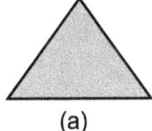 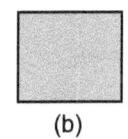 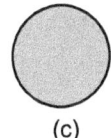

    (a)   (b)   (c)

Fig. 2.31

The colour part of each figure shows the area of that figure.

Questions

1. Coloured part of each figure shows ......

2. Make list of areas of different shapes. For example, area of black board, area of table, area of wall, area of farm, area of garden.

3. Take a square shape paper. Pest small size squares on it.

   Check whether the whole paper is covered or not with small parts of paper ?

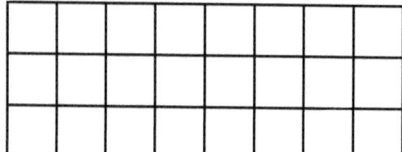

Fig. 2.32

How many parts/squares required to cover the complete paper ?

The part of paper covered with small square is called as ......

Points to Remember

- Any figure can occupy a space is called as area of figure.
- Area can be measured in square unit.

To find the formula of area of rectangle.

Practical 1 :

Take one rectangular shape paper. Make 8 folds of that paper horizontally (in length) and make four folds vertically (in width). Now, remove the folds and observe the shapes of folds on paper. How many squares on that paper ? How many square unit place is occupied by the rectangle ?

By counting these squares, we get area of rectangle.

What is the correlation of this area and multiplication of length and width of rectangle.

Observation :

1. By making fold on paper, we get number of small squares on paper.

2. Small squares occupy the space on rectangular shape paper. It is called as area of rectangle.

3. If we count the length of rectangle there are 8 squares.

4. If we count the width of rectangle there are 4 squares.

5. In all there are 32 squares in rectangle.

6. $32 = 8 \times 4$.

$$\therefore \quad \text{Area of rectangle} = \text{length} \times \text{breadth}$$
$$= l \times b$$

Activity :

Take a rectangle shape paper. Do the same procedure as discussed above. Count the number of squares. Find the length and breadth of rectangle with the help of scale. Find the multiplication of length and breadth. Check whether the multiplication is equal to number of squares.

Question : Prove the following formulae's with the help of practical method. OR Practically verify the following formulaes.

1. Area of square $= (\text{side})^2$.

2. Area of triangle $= \dfrac{1}{2} \times \text{Base} \times \text{Height}$.

3. Area of circle $= \pi r^2$.

4. Area of parallelogram $= \text{Base} \times \text{Height}$.

Preparation of Two Dimensional and Three Dimensional Figures:

(1) Draw different types of rectangles and colour it.

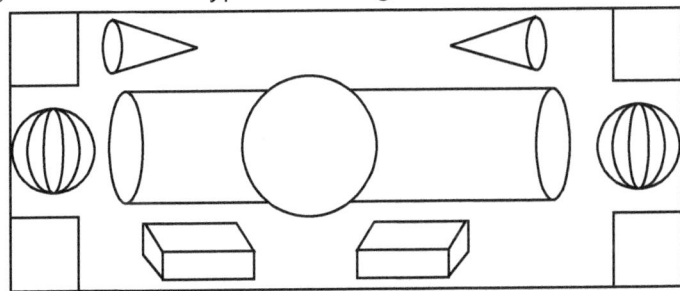

Fig. 2.33

(2) Make different types of geometrical shapes by using tangram.

Steps to prepare tangram :

Step 1: Take a cardboard, cut a square shape from it.

Step 2: As shown in Fig. 2.34 below, cut the different shapes from the square.

Step 3: Join all these shape in different manner and make new shapes.

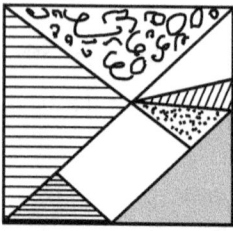

Fig. 2.34

(3) **Nets :** A two dimensional figure mean **nets**.

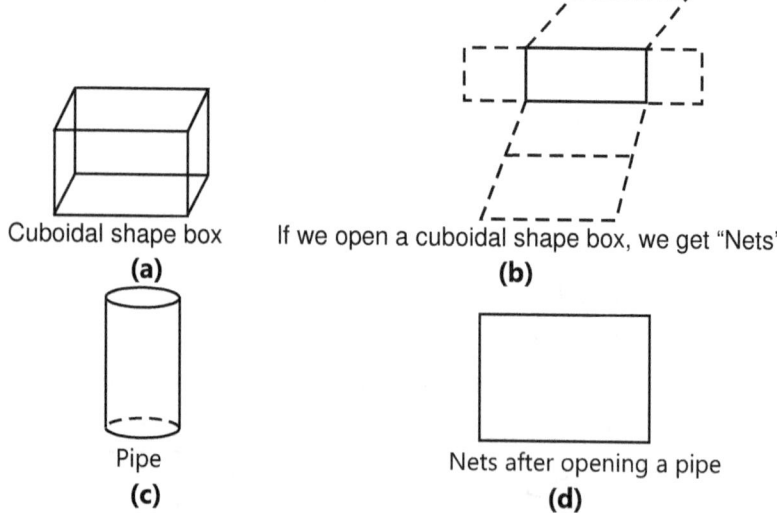

Cuboidal shape box   If we open a cuboidal shape box, we get "Nets"

(a)   **(b)**

Pipe   Nets after opening a pipe

(c)   **(d)**

Fig. 2.35

2.4.2 Three Dimensional Shapes/Figures

Three Dimensional Objects

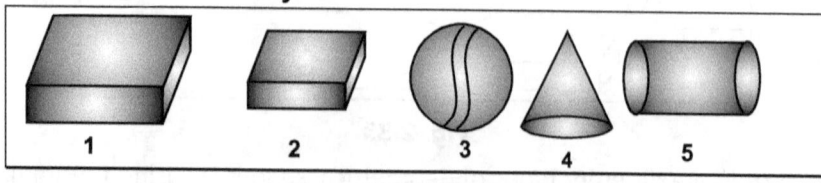

Fig. 2.36

Activity 1: Make a list of objects in your surrounding which are similar to the above given figures.

Activity 2: Classify the following things into two dimensional three dimensional, cylindrical, cone shape figures.

Apple, Medicine bottle, Ice-cream cone, medicine box, pumpkin, locky, water melon, gas cylinder, onion, paper, boll, pipe etc.

Three Dimensional Shapes

(1) Cube

- Six faces of equal length.
- Each two faces are perpendicular to each other.
- Eight vertices.
- Twelve edges.

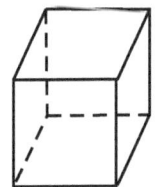

Fig. 2.37

(2) Cuboids

- Total six faces.
- Two faces are of equal length.
- Faces of equal length are parallel to each other.
- Eight vertices.
- Twelve edges.

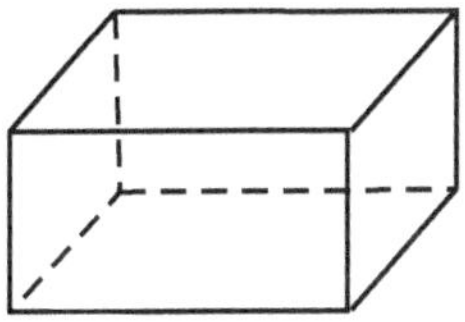

Fig. 2.38

(3) Cylinder

The figure alongside is called as cylinder.

1. What is the shape of base and top of the figure ?

2. What is the shape of one rupee coin ?

Fig. 2.39

Open a cylindrical shape box and observe the shape carefully :

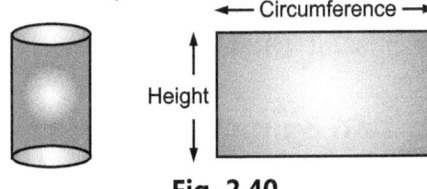

Fig. 2.40

Surface area of cylinder = Area of base × Height = $\pi r^2 \times$ Height

Volume of round = Circumference × Height = $2 \pi r^2 \times$ Height

(4) Cone :

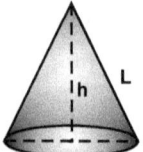

Fig. 2.41

Surface area of cone = Area of base + Area of slanting height

$$= \pi r^2 + \pi r L$$

Volume of cone $= 1/3 \, \pi r^2 \, h$ (h = height)

(5) Round :

Fig. 2.42

Surface area of round $= \dfrac{1}{3} \pi r^3$

Volume of round $= \dfrac{4}{3} \pi r^3$ (r = radius)

Points to Remember

- In two dimensional geometrical shapes, square have four equal sides, angles and vertices.
- Rectangle has four sides, angles and vertices.
- Triangle has three sides, three angles and three vertices.
- How to make/draw square, rectangle, triangle ?

Activity 1 : Make different types of geometrical shapes by using nets.

Activity 2: Make different types of geometrical shapes by using tangram.

Similar Figure and Symmetric Figures

Similarity - Definition : (Equal figures)

The figures which are same in shape but different in size are called as similar figure.

For example :

(a)   (b)

Fig. 2.43

From Fig. 2.43 (a) and (b) it is clear that both figures are same in shape, but they are different in size. We say that Fig. 2.43 (a) is similar with Fig. 2.43 (b).

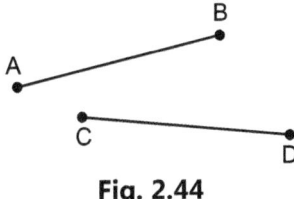

Fig. 2.44

In Fig. 2.44 above, segment AB is similar with segment CD.

Symmetrical Figures : If a figure can be divided by at least one line into two parts which fit on each other exactly, the figure is called as symmetrical figure.

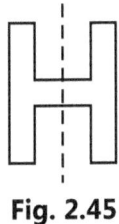

Fig. 2.45

Activity 1 : As shown in Fig. 2.46 below, cut a paper in triangle shape. Draw a dotted line from center. Make a fold on dotted line of a paper and observe it.

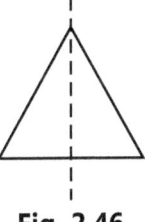

Fig. 2.46

Observation : The dotted line divide the paper in two parts which fits on each other exactly. The Fig. is symmetric.

Activity 2 : As shown in Fig. 2.47, the dotted line cannot divide the figure in two equal parts.

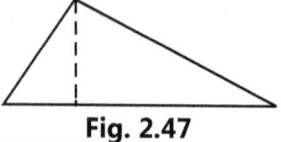

Fig. 2.47

Observation : The dotted line cannot divide the figure in two equal parts. The figure is not symmetrical figure i.e. asymmetric figure.

Activity 3 : Observe the following figure and check whether the given letters in figure are symmetrical or asymmetrical.

A B Y X Z

Fig. 2.48

Points to Remember

• If two parts are fit to each other exactly then they are called as symmetric.

Questions

1. If two figures are fit on each other exactly then they are called ......
2. If two figures are not fit on each other exactly then they are called ......
3. Match the following :

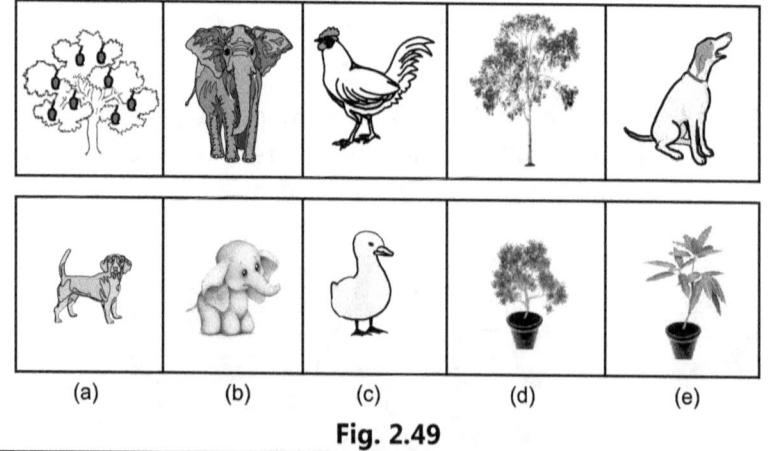

| | | | | |
| (a) | (b) | (c) | (d) | (e) |

Fig. 2.49

4. Draw the similar figures.

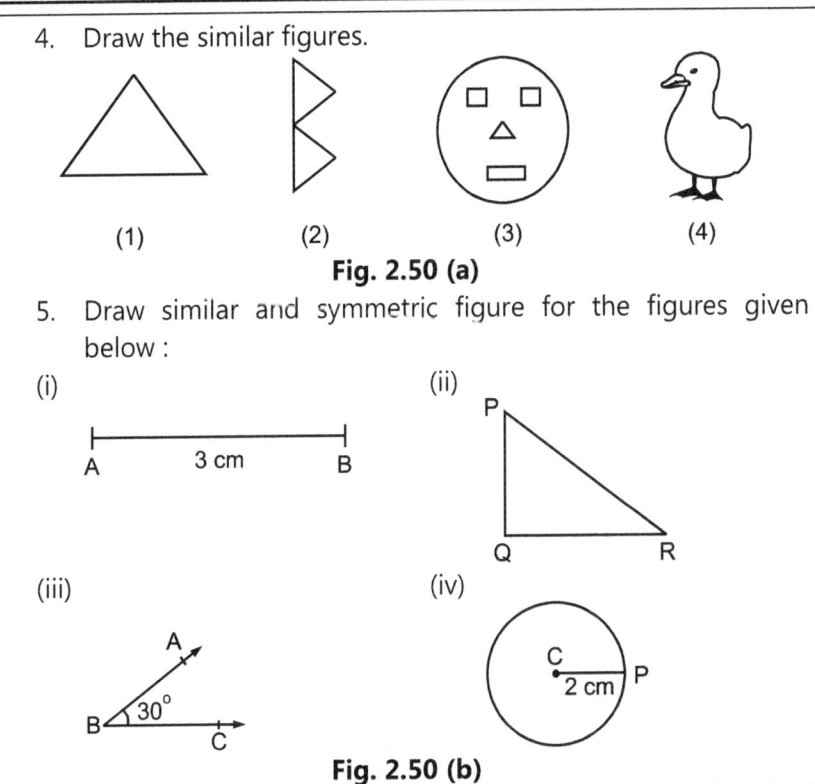

(1)   (2)   (3)   (4)

Fig. 2.50 (a)

5. Draw similar and symmetric figure for the figures given below :

(i)

A   3 cm   B

(ii)

P

Q   R

(iii)

A

B   30°   C

(iv)

C   2 cm   P

Fig. 2.50 (b)

2.5 Geometrical Shapes and Measurement

Sr. No.	Name	Figure	Formula of Area
1.	Triangle (Any)	a units, c units, b units	Area of triangle = Multiplication of three sides = $a \times b \times c$
2.	Triangle (Any)	a units, b units	Area of triangle = $\frac{1}{2} \times$ base $\times$ height = $\frac{1}{2} \times a \times b$

... (Contd.)

Sr. No.	Name	Figure	Formula of Area
3.	Right Angle Triangle	a units, b units	Area of right angle triangle $= \dfrac{1}{2}$ [product of sides of the right angle] $= \dfrac{1}{2} \times a \times b$
4.	Equilateral Triangle	a units	Area of an equilateral triangle $= \dfrac{\sqrt{3}}{4} \times (\text{side})^2$ $= \dfrac{\sqrt{3}}{4} \times a^2$ {a = side}
5.	Square	a units	Area of a square $= (\text{side})^2$ $= (a)^2$
6.	Rectangle	a units, b units	Area of rectangle $= \text{length} \times \text{breadth}$ $= a \times b$
7.	Parallelogram	D, C, h, A, M, B, a	Area of parallelogram $= \text{base} \times \text{height}$ $= a \times h$ {a = l (AB) · h = l (DM)}
8.	Rhombus	D, A, C, B	Area of rhombus $= \dfrac{1}{2} \times$ product of diagonals $= \dfrac{1}{2} \times d_1 \times d_2$ {d_1 = (BD), d_2 = (AC)}

... (Contd.)

Sr. No.	Name	Figure	Formula of Area
9.	Trapezium		Area of trapezium = $\frac{1}{2}$ [sum of parallel sides] $\times$ height $= \frac{1}{2}$ [a + b] h {a = l (DC), b = l (AB), h = l (DM)}
10.	Quadrilateral		Area of quadrilateral $= \frac{1}{2} \times$ Diagonal $\times$ Sum of the offset $= \frac{1}{2} \times$ AC $\times$ [(DE) + (BF)]
11.	Regular Hexagon		Area of regular hexagon $= \frac{3\sqrt{3}}{2} \times$ (side)^2 $= \frac{3\sqrt{3}}{2} \times a^2$

Note : Offset means perpendicular dropped on the diagonal.

Formulae :

1. Area of a square = $\frac{1}{2}$ (diagonal)^2 sq. units

2. Side of a square = $\sqrt{area}$ linear units.

3. Perimeter of a rectangle = 2 (length + breadth) linear units.

4. Perimeter of a square = (4 $\times$ side) linear units.

5. (i) Diagonal of a square = side $\sqrt{2}$ linear units.

   (ii) Diagonal of a square = $\sqrt{2 \times area}$ linear units.

6. (i) Area of four walls of a room =

   [2 (length + breadth) $\times$ height] sq. units.

   (ii) Area of the four walls of a room = (perimeter of floor $\times$ height) sq. units.

7. Area of an isosceles triangle $= \frac{a}{4}(4b^2 - a^2)$ sq. units, where a, b are in same units.

8. (i) Circumference of a circle $= 2\pi r$ sq. units.

   (ii) Area of a circle $= \pi r^2$ square units, where r is the radius of circle.

   (iii) Area of a circle $= \pi \left(\frac{d}{2}\right)^2$ sq. units, where 'd' is the diameter

   $= \frac{1}{2}$ circumference × radius sq. units

9. Area of a quadrilateral $= \frac{1}{2}$ (diagonal) × (sum of the offsets) sq. units.

10. Side of a rhombus $= \frac{1}{2}\sqrt{d_1^2 + d_2^2}$ sq. units, where d_1 and d_2 are lengths of the diagonals.

11. Height of trapezium $= \left[\dfrac{2 \times \text{Area}}{\text{Sum of parallel sides}}\right]$ units.

Note: Linear unit means measuring unit.

Surface Area and Volume

Definition : Anything which occupies space is called a solid. It has three dimensions – length, breadth, and height or thickness.

Important Formulae :

1. If 'l' be the length, 'b' be the breadth and 'h' be the height of a cuboid, then

   (i) Total surface area of a cuboid $= 2(lb + bh + lh)$ sq. units.

   (ii) Volume of a cuboid $= (l \times b \times h)$ cubic units.

2. (i) Total surface area of a cube $= 6\,(\text{side})^2$ sq. units.

   (ii) Volume of a cube $= (\text{side})^3$ cubic units.

   (iii) Diagonal of a cube $= \sqrt{3}\,(\text{side})$ units.

3. (i) Lateral surface area of a prism = (perimeter of the base) × (height) sq. units.

   (ii) Volume of a prism = (area of the base) × (height) cubic units.

4. (i) Area of slant surface of a pyramid $= \frac{1}{2}$ (perimeter of the base) × slant height sq. units.

    (ii) Volume of a pyramid $= \frac{1}{3}$ (area of the base) × height cu. units.

5. If 'r' is the radius of the base of a right circular cylinder and 'h' its height, then
    (i) Curved surface area of a cylinder $= 2\pi rh$ sq. units.
    (ii) Total surface area of a cylinder $= 2\pi rh \, (r + h)$ sq. units.
    (iii) Volume of a cylinder $= \pi r^2 h$ cu. units.

6. If 'h' is the height of cone, 'r' radius of base, and 'l' is slant height then
    (i) Lateral surface area of a cone $= \pi r \, l$ sq. units, where $l = \sqrt{h^2 + r^2}$ units.
    (ii) Total surface area of a cone $= (\pi rl + \pi r^2) = \pi r \, (r + l)$ sq. units.
    (iii) Volume of a cone $= \frac{1}{3} \pi r^2 h$ cubic units.

7. If 'r' is the radius of a sphere, then
    (i) Total surface area of a sphere $= 4\pi r^2$ sq. units.
    (ii) Volume of a sphere $= \frac{4}{3} \pi r^3$ cu. units.

8. (i) Total surface area of a hemisphere $= 3\pi r^2$ sq. units.
    (ii) Volume of a hemisphere $= \frac{2}{3} \pi r^3$ cu. units.

2.6 Measurement

2.6.1 Length

1. Length : We write the measurement of length in millimetres, centremetres, metre, kilometre.

1 centimetre (cm)	= 10 millimetres (mm)
1 metre (m)	= 100 centimetres (cm)
1 kilometre (km)	= 1000 metres (m)

Solved Examples

1. The timetable below lists the places between Pune and Ahmednagar and their distances in kilometres. Study it and answer the following questions.

Pune	Sanaswadi	Shikrapur	Ranjangaon	Shirur	Supa	Ahmednagar
0	30	35	40	65	97	122

(i) How far is Ranjangaon from Pune ?

Solution : Ranjangaon is 40 km from Pune.

(ii) What is the distance between Shirur and Supa ?

Solution : The distance between Shirur and Supa is

97 km – 65 km = 32 km.

(iii) What is the distance between Shikrapur and Supa ?

Solution : The distance between Shikrapur and Supa is

97 km – 35 km = 62 km

4. Solve the following examples :

(i) How many kilometres are equal to 6874 metres ?

Solution : $\dfrac{6874}{1000}$ = 6.874 km

(ii) How many pieces each of 2 cm can be cut out from a ribbon 1.80 metres long ?

Solution : Convert 1.80 metres into cm i.e.

1.80 × 100 = 180 cm = $\dfrac{180 \text{ cm}}{2}$ = 90 pieces.

(iii) How many kilometres are equal to 5 km and 40 metres ?

Solution : 5 km and 40 mts. = 5 × 1000 + 40 mt = 5040 mts. = 5.04 km.

Questions

1. If a tailor cuts 2 m and 25 cm from a piece of cloth 5 m long. How much cloth is left over ?

2. Mr. Kumar travelled 475 km by train, 56 km 975 m by car and 20 km 720 m by scooter. What is the total distance that he covered ?

3. Total length of a road is 2 km, out of which 1400 metres have been completed. How much road is left incomplete ?

2.6.2 Weight

Mass or weight is measured in grams, kilograms, tons etc. Grains, metals, vegetables are measured in grams and kilograms.

We are going to learn about the below mentioned units to measure weight.

1 centigram = 10 milligrams

1 gram = 100 centigrams

1 kilogram = 1000 grams.

For Example

1. What is a quarter kilogram ?

    1 kilogram is 1000 gram.

    $\frac{1}{2}$ a kilogram will be 500 gm and $\frac{1}{4}$ a kilogram will be $\frac{1}{2}$ of

    $\frac{1}{2}$ kilogram is 250 gm.

    So the answer, is 250 gms.

2. How many grams are 5 kilograms ?

    1 kilogram = 1000 grams

    ∴ 5 kilograms = 1000 × 5 = 5000 gms

3. Convert 6500 gms into kilograms and grams ?

    6500 gm = 6 kg 500 gm

4. Convert 9 kg 400 gms into grams ?

    9 kg 400 gm = 9400 gms

5. How many gram is one and a quarter kilogram ?

    One and a quarter kilograms means 1000 grams + 250 gram = 1250 grams.

    Therefore one and a quarter kilogram means 1250 gms.

Units to Measure Weight :

10 milligram = 1 centigram.

10 centigram = 1 decigram.

10 decigram = 1 gram.

10 grams = 1 decagram.

10 decagram = 1 hectogram.

10 hectograms = 1 kilogram.

But we are going to study only the below mentioned topics.

1 kilogram : 1000 grams.

1 gram : 100 centigrams.

1 centigrams : 10 milligrams.

Solved Examples

Solve the following examples :

1. From 3 kg sugar, 2.200 kg sugar has been used. How much sugar is left ?

Solution : 3 kg = 3000 gm and 2.200 kg = 2200 gm.

Now 3000 gm – 2200 gm = 800 gm sugar is left.

2. Ramesh weighs 38 kg. The weight of Mahesh is 20 kg 500 gm less than that of Ramesh. What is the weight of Mahesh ?

Solution :

$$38 \text{ kg} = 38000 \text{ gm}$$
$$12 \text{ kg } 500 \text{ gm} = 12000 + 500 = 12500 \text{ gm}$$
∴ Weight of Mahesh = 38000 – 12500 = 25,500 gm
∴ Weight of Mahesh = 25 kg 500 gm.

3. Two different bags hold 15 kg 750 gm and 12 kg 500 gm of pulses respectively. Then how much is the total weight of pulses in kilograms ?

Solution :

Pulses in bag 1 = 15 kg 750 gm = 15750 gm
Pulses in bag 2 = 12 kg 500 gm = 12500 gm
∴ Total weight of pulses = 28250 gm
∴ Total weight of pulses = 28 kg 250 gm.

Questions

Q. Solve the following examples.

1. A pocket contains 250 gms of salt. How many packets can be filled with 11 and 3 quarters kilogram of salt ?

2. There are 7 sacks each containing 80 kg grain. This grain was put into cans. If each can is of 16 kg, how many such cans will be needed ?

3. Weight of ☐ pouches of 100 gms is 2000 gms.

4. 7800 gm + 400 gms = ... kg ...... gm.

2.6.3 Volume and Capacity

Kilolitre, Hectolitre, Decalitre, Litre, Decilitre, Centilitre, Millilitre are the units of capacity. As we go from the smaller unit to the larger unit, every unit is 10 times larger than the preceding unit.

10 millilitres = 1 centilitre

10 centilitre = 1 decilitre

10 decilitres = 1 litre

10 litres = 1 decalitre

10 decalitres = 1 hectolitre

10 hectolitres = 1 kilolitre

The units of capacity given below are to be learnt.

1 kilolitre = 1,000 litres

1 litre = 100 centilitre

1 centilitre = 10 millilitres

1 litre = 1000 ml

We use litre and millilitres to measure liquids like milk, oil, diesel and petrol. Litre is written as '*l*' and milliliter is written as 'ml'.

1 litre *(l)* = 1000 millilitre (ml)

For example :

1. 4 litres = ... millilitre

Solution :   1 litre = 1000 millilitre

∴   4 litre = 4 × 1000 = 4000 millilitre

2. How many ml is 1.25 *l* ?

Solution : 1.25 *l* = 1 *l* 25 ml = 1000 ml + 25 ml = 1025 ml

3. Liquid ink is sold in bottles each of capacity 125 ml. How many bottles will be required to fill 3 litres of ink ?

    (a) 16   (b) 8   (c) 32   (d) 24

Solution : 3 litre = 3000 ml

∴ Number of bottles required = $\dfrac{3000}{125}$ = 24

4. A bottle contains 1 litre and 750 ml of water. Out of which 0.25 litre water is spoiled. How much water remained ?

Solution : 1 litre and 750 ml = 1,000 ml + 750 ml = 1750 ml.

0.25 litre water is spoiled, it means that 0.25 × 1,000 = 250 ml. water is spoiled.

∴ Water remained = 1750 − 250 = 1,500 ml = $\dfrac{1,500}{1,000}$ = 1.5 litre.

∴ 1.5 litre water remained in a bottle.

Questions

1. Each student is given 125 ml of milk. What is the quantity of milk in litres required for 30 boys ?

2. In school, 250 students are given milk. Each child is given 140 ml milk. How much litre milk will be required ?

3. If there is 600 litre 400 ml. of water in one barrel, 300 litre 460 ml. of water in the second barrel and 400 litre 340 ml. in the third barrel. What is the total quantity of water ?

4. One container holds 18 litre of milk and the other, 11 *l* 300 ml milk. How much more milk does the first container hold ?

Coins and Currency

Coins

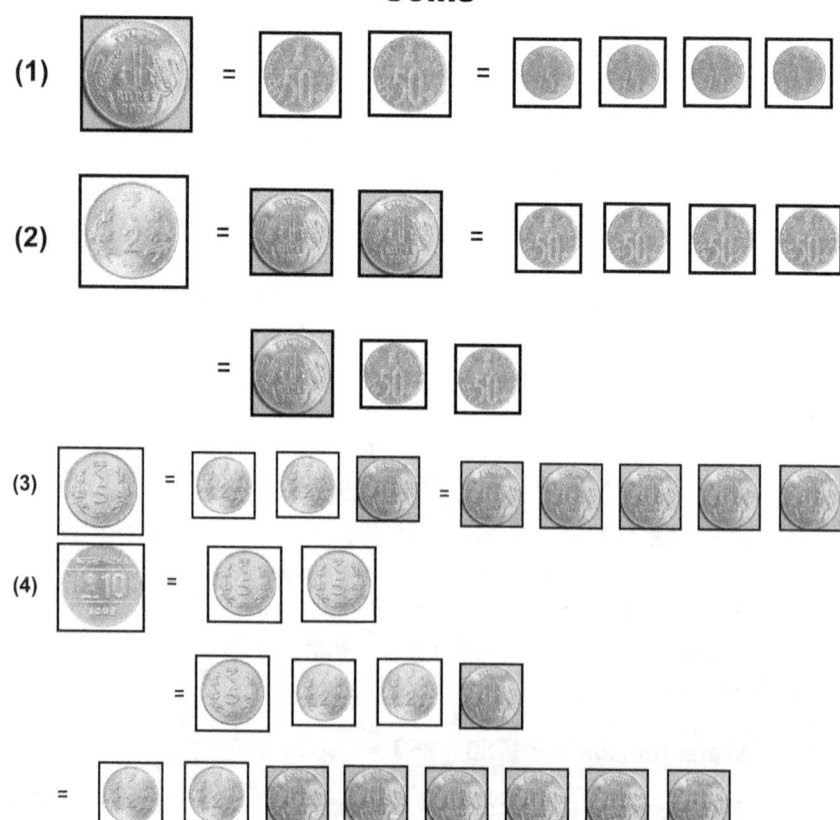

Notes

(1)

(2)  =

(3)  =

=

(4)  =

=

(5)

=

=

(6)  =

=

(7)

=

(8)

=

Time Measurement, Calendar

Time: Time can be measured with units - seconds, minutes and hours.

$$1 \text{ minute} = 60 \text{ seconds}$$
$$1 \text{ hour} = 60 \text{ minutes}$$
$$1 \text{ day} = 24 \text{ hours}$$
$$30 \text{ days or } 31 \text{ days} = 1 \text{ month}$$

(Except February have 28 or 29 days).

$$1 \text{ year} = 12 \text{ months}$$

The Calendar :

7 days : 1 week

4 weeks : 1 month : 30 days or 31 days.

52 weeks : 12 months : 1 year.

365/366 days make a year : In a year 7 months i.e. January, March, May, July, August, October and December have 31 days. 4 months i.e. April, June, September, November have 30 days. February has 28 days in normal year and 29 days in a leap year.

July and August are the two successive months having 31 days. If Monday fall on 5th day of the month, then the next Monday will fall on 12th day of that month. Thus, the difference between the two consecutive Mondays is of 7 days. Similar thing happens in case of Tuesday, Wednesday, Thursday, Friday, Saturday and Sunday.

In the year, there are 12 months and 365 days. In leap year there are 366 days and February is of 29 days.

What is a leap year ? If the number of a year is completely divisible by four, it is a leap year. How to find out a leap year ?

For example : Find out whether 1996 is a leap year or not ?

Answer : 1996 is a leap year because it is completely divisible by 4.

$$
\begin{array}{r|l|l}
4 & 1996 & 499 \\
\hline
  & -\ 16 & \\
\hline
  & 39 & \\
  & -\ 36 & \\
\hline
  & 36 & \\
  & -\ 36 & \\
\hline
  & 00 &
\end{array}
$$

A centenary year whose number is not divisible by 4 is not a leap year.

For example : 1900 year was not a leap year but 2000 is a leap year.

Points to Remember

- We measure the length in metres.
- We measure the weight in kilogram.
- Volume can be measured in litre units.
- 1 kilogram = 1000 gram
- 1 kilometre = 1000 metre
- 1 Litre = 1000 millilitres
- We measure time in units such as seconds, minutes, hours.

2.7 Number System and Operations on Numbers

2.7.1 Number System / Knowledge of Numbers

To explain the number system or concept of numbers from 1 to 9, we can do the following activity.

Activity : Take beads 1 to 9 and also prepare cards of numbers from 1 to 9. Read the card and match the pair. OR

Fill the beads to prepare a lace.

1 Ten's = 10 beads	
10 Beads or 10 units	

$$1 \text{ Ten's} = 10 = \text{Ten}$$
$$2 \text{ Ten's} = 20 = \text{Twenty}$$
$$3 \text{ Ten's} = 30 = \text{Thirty}$$
$$9 \text{ Ten's} = 90 = \text{Ninety}$$

Now to explain the concepts of numbers 11 to 20, use flannel board or beads strip.

○○○○○○○○○○	⊡	One tens and One units	Eleven	11
○○○○○○○○○○	⊡ ⊡	One tens and two units	Twelve	12
○○○○○○○○○○	⊡ ⊡ ⊡	One tens and three units	Thirteen	13
○○○○○○○○○○	⊡ ⊡ / ⊡ ⊡	One tens and four units	Fourteen	14
○○○○○○○○○○	⊡ ⊡ ⊡ / ⊡ ⊡	One tens and five units	Fifteen	15
○○○○○○○○○○	⊡ ⊡ ⊡ / ⊡ ⊡ ⊡	One tens and six units	Sixteen	16
○○○○○○○○○○	⊡ ⊡ ⊡ ⊡ / ⊡ ⊡ ⊡	One tens and seven units	Seventeen	17
○○○○○○○○○○	⊡ ⊡ ⊡ ⊡ / ⊡ ⊡ ⊡ ⊡	One tens and eight units	Eighteen	18
○○○○○○○○○○	⊡ ⊡ ⊡ ⊡ ⊡ / ⊡ ⊡ ⊡ ⊡	One tens and nine units	Nineteen	19
○○○○○○○○○○ / ○○○○○○○○○○		Two tens	Twenty	20

Place Value and Expanded form of Numbers :

Activity : Show number 67 with the help of practical method.

Material : Strips of Beads, flannel board

$$67 =$$

$$= 6 \text{ Tens and 7 Units}$$
$$= 60 + 7$$

In number 67, the place value of 6 is 60 and place value of 7 is 7. The expanded form of 67 is as follows :

$$67 = 60 + 7$$

To find the place value of a digit in a number :

The place value of digit at unit's place = Digit at units place × 1.

The place value of digit at Ten's place = Digit at tens place × 10.

The place value of digit at hundredth place = Digit at hundredth place × 100.

The place value of digit at thousandth place = Digit at thousandth place × 1000.

Knowledge of Numbers :

Even Numbers : The numbers which are completely divisible by 2 are called as even numbers. For example, 2, 4, 6, 8, 10, 12, 14, ...

Odd Numbers : The numbers which are not completely divisible by 2 are called as odd numbers.

For example 1, 3, 5, 7, 9, 11, ...

Natural Numbers (N) : We naturally start counting from 1 and go on as 1, 2, 3, ... whenever we are asked to count anything.

So, these numbers are called natural numbers.

- The set of natural numbers is defined as

  N = (All positive numbers excluding zero)

- It can be written in set notation as

  $N = \{x \mid x \in N, x > 0\}$

- The smallest number in series is 1 and has not biggest or largest number. Therefore it is also called as an infinite or never ending set.

  N = {1, 2, 3, ...}

  Here, the dots after the ',' comma shows infinity.

Whole Numbers (W) : Whole numbers are all positive numbers including zero.

- Set of whole numbers :

  W = {0, 1, 2, 3, 4, ...}

  Or $W = \{x \mid x \in W, x \geq 0\}$

- The smallest number in this set is '0'. and there is no biggest or largest number.

- Therefore, this is also an infinite set.

Roman Numerals

Roman Numbers	International Numbers	Roman Numbers	International Numbers
I	1	XI	11
II	2	XII	12
III	3	XIII	13
IV	4	XIV	14
V	5	XV	15
VI	6	XVI	16
VII	7	XVII	17
VIII	8	XVIII	18
IX	9	XIX	19
X	10	XX	20

Points to Remember

- '0' is neither positive nor negative.
- The sum of first n even numbers = $n(n + 1)$.
- The sum of first n odd numbers = n^2.

2.7.2 Operations On Numbers

(1) Addition :

Sum, in all, altogether are the words which describe the concept of addition. This can be explained with the help of practical work.

Madhu have 3 birds and Sonu have 2 birds with her. In all how many birds they have.

For example :

Madhu and Sonu have in all 5 birds with them.

First give practical knowledge how to do the addition of single/ one digit numbers.

$$\begin{array}{r} 5 \\ + 4 \\ \hline 9 \end{array}$$

Activity : Write different examples of addition having answer is equal to 8.

Observation : 7 + 1 = 8   1 + 7 = 8   2 + 6 = 8   5 + 3 = 8

3 + 5 = 8   4 + 4 = 8   6 + 2 = 8   etc.

In this way, we can explain the concept of addition.

(2) Subtraction :

As like addition, we can explain the concept of subtraction.

For example : (1) Shweta purchased a uniform worth ₹ 372 and a school bag worth ₹ 250. How much more does she spend on the uniform than a bag ?

Cost of uniform = ₹ 372

Cost of bag = ₹ 250

$$\therefore \quad \begin{array}{r} 372 \\ - 250 \\ \hline 122 \end{array}$$

Shweta spend ₹ 122 more on the uniform than a bag.

The words how much, more/less, how many left etc. are the words which explain the concept of subtraction.

(3) Multiplication : Multiplication concept with the help of addition :

(i) 2 × 3 = 6,   (ii) 3 × 2 = 6

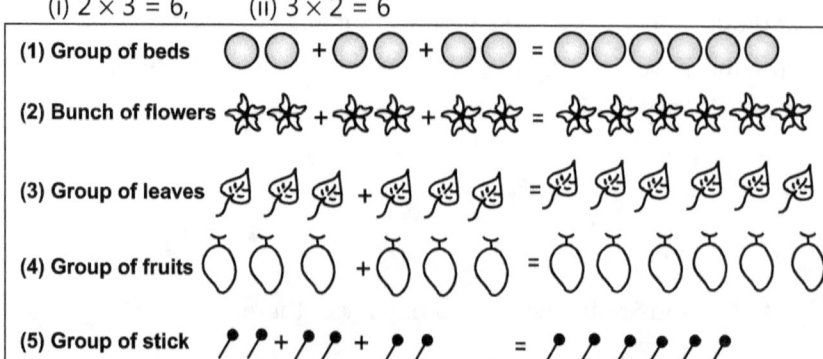

(1) Group of beds	
(2) Bunch of flowers	
(3) Group of leaves	
(4) Group of fruits	
(5) Group of stick	

DIVISIBILITY TESTS

A number (x) is said to be completely divisible by (y), when on carrying the actual division (x ÷ y) we get remainder as zero.

Tests of Divisibility :

Number	Test of Divisibility
2	The number is divisible by 2 when its units place digit is even or zero.
3	The number is divisible by 3 when the sum of the digits is divisible by 3.
4	The number is divisible by 4 when the number formed by its last two digits to the right is divisible by 4 or if the last two digits are zero.
5	The number is divisible by 5 when unit place digit is 5 or zero.
6	The number is divisible by 6 when it is divisible by both 2 and 3.
7	A number is said to be divisible by 7 if, difference between double the digit in units place and the remaining number is divisible by 7.
8	The number is divisible by 8 when the number formed by its last three digits to the right is divisible by 8 or if the last three digits are zero.
9	The number is divisible by 9 when the sum of the digits is divisible by 9.
10	The number is divisible by 10 when its units place digit is zero.
11	The number is divisible by 11 when the difference between sum of the even place digits and the sum of the odd place digits is a multiple of 11 or is zero.
12	The number is divisible by 12 when it is divisible by 3 and 4.
15	The number is divisible by 15 when it is divisible by 3 and 5.
25	The number is divisible by 25 when the number formed by the last two digits to the right is divisible by 25 or last two digits are zero.

A method to find out whether the given number is divisible by any another number.

Points to Remember

- In all, altogether, sum are the words which explain the concept of addition.
- More or less, left etc. are the words which explain the concept of subtraction.
- The number x is said to be completely divisible by (y), when on carrying the actual division (x ÷ y), we get remainder as zero.

2.7.3 Examples in Day-to-day Life

Addition/Subtraction/Multiplication/Division in day-to-day life

Solved Examples

1. The cost of one note book is 5 rupees. Find the cost of 9 note books.

Ans. : We have to add 5, 9 times.

∴ 5 + 5 + 5 + 5 + 5 + 5 + 5 + 5 + 5 = ₹ 45

∴ 5 × 9 = ₹ 45

∴ Cost of 9 note books is ₹ 45.

2. In a row there are 30 students, then how many students in 6 rows ?

Ans. : ∴ 30 × 6

	3	0	Students in one row
	×	6	Number of rows
1	8	0	Total number of students

3. Add the fowllowing :

7856 + 8437

Ans. :

	Th	H	T	U
	1		1	
+	7	8	5	6
	8	4	3	7
1	6	2	9	3

7856 + 8437 = 16293

(1) Addition of numbers at units place is 6 + 7 = 13

∴ 3 units and 1 will be carry to tens

(2) Addition of numbers at tens place is 1 + 5 + 3 = 9

(3)   Addition of numbers at hundredth place is $8 + 4 = 12$

∴   2 hundred and 1 will carry to thousand place.

(4)   Addition of numbers at thousand place $= 1 + 7 + 8 = 15$

4. With the help of number prepare example of multiplication. Use ₹ 235 and number 37 to form example of multiplication. The cost of one chair is ₹ 235. Find the cost of 37 chairs.

235×37

```
     235
×     37
    1645
+   7050
    ————
    8695
```

First multiply by the number at units place.
Now, multiply by the number at tens place and write 0 at unit's place

2.8 Classification of Data

2.8.1 Collection of Data

For example : (1) Oral Discussion :

- Make list of objects in your house.
- Tell name of animals in your surrounding.
- To whom you invite on your birthday.
- What is the menu of lunch on your birthday ?

(2) Ask questions about fun fair.

(3) Collection of information.

Collect the information of plants in your garden.

- How many big trees are in the garden?
- How many flowering plants are in the garden?
- How many bushes in the garden?

(4) Ask students to draw a table of collected information and ask questions to each other.

Plants in garden	Number of plants

Activity : Guide students wherever they required.

Table 1

Information	Numbers

Table 2

Information	Numbers
Farmers	150
Grocery shops	5
Cloth shops	2
Medicine shops	1
Stationary shops	2

Table 3

Information	Numbers
Old people	60
Young people	500
School going children	125
Children's not going to school	150

Activity: Ask students to make a list of different types of flowers and represent the information in tabular form.

Classification of data with the help of tally marks :

- Collect different types of flowers and put them in a basket.
- Ask student to pick one flower one-by-one and tell the name of flower.

Information in table, for example :

Read the information; like there are 13 Jasmine flowers in a basket.

- How many flowers of Champa?
- How many flowers of Aboli?
- How many flowers of Mogra?
- How many flowers of Hibiscus?

Types of Flowers	Tally Marks
Jasmine	卌 卌 |||
Champa	卌 |||
Aboli	卌 卌 卌
Mogra	卌 卌 卌 卌 ||
Hibiscus	卌 卌 卌 |||

Activity : Read the information in the following table and answer the questions.

Table 4 : Classification of school going children

School going children	Tally Marks
Boys by walking	卌 卌 卌 卌 卌 卌 卌 卌 卌 卌 卌 |||
Boys by cycling	卌 卌 卌 卌 卌 卌 卌 ||||
Girls by walking	卌 卌 卌 卌 卌 卌 卌 卌 卌 卌 卌
Girls by cycling	卌 卌 卌 ||
By Bus	卌 卌 卌 卌 卌 |||
By Rickshaw	卌 卌 卌 卌 卌 ||||

1. By which mode of transport more number of children go to school.

2. How children do not have mode of transport to go to school?

3. How many more number of children go to school by walking than by cycle ?

4. How many number of children come to school by Rickshaw?

Table 5 : Marks of Students in Mathematics Subject

Marks in Mathematics Subject (out of 100)	Number of Students
90 - 100	07
80 - 89	22
70 - 79	35
60 - 69	33
50 - 59	40
40 - 49	15
less than 40	05

1. Which group gets more number of marks in mathematics subject?

2. How many number of students got more than 50% marks?

3. How many number of students need guidance to improve in mathematics subject ?

2.8.2 Pictographs : Construction, Reading and Draw Conclusion

Sometimes the information is collected and information is presented in picture format is called as pictograph.

For example : (1) Sunil brought different types of flowers for a function. He make bunch of 10 - 10 flowers.

Rose - 100 flowers - 10 bunches.

Lily - 150 flowers - 15 bunches.

Astor - 50 flowers - 5 bunches.

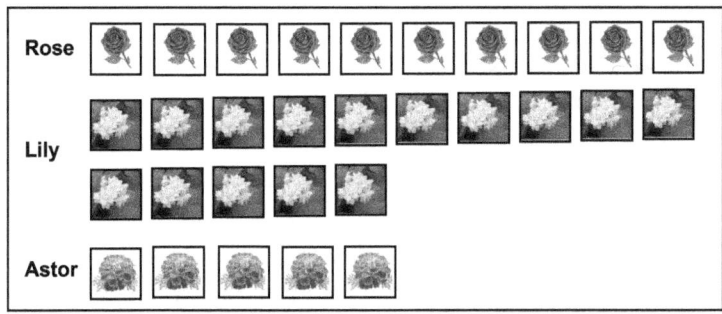

Points to Remember

- To draw pictograph, we have to take a scale to represent the given information.

   For example : 1 picture = 10 flowers etc.

Read the pictograph and answer the following questions :

The following pictograph show the information of trees in school premises.

   1 picture = 3 number of trees.

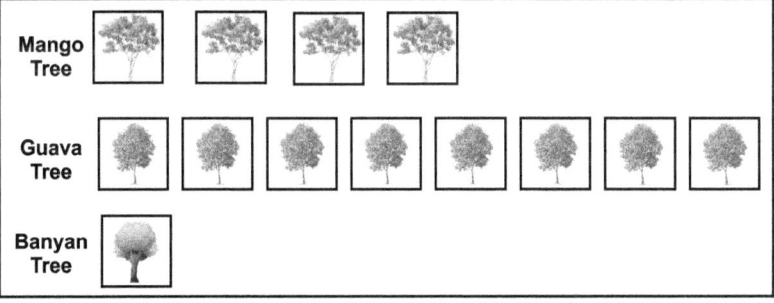

Questions

1. Which type of trees are more in number?
2. Which type trees are less in number?

   From pictograph the given information is 1 picture represents 3 number of trees.

   Number of Mango trees = 4 × 3 = 12 trees.

   Number of Guava trees = 8 × 3 = 24 trees.

   Number of Banyan trees = 3 × 3 = 9 trees.

Ans. 1: Guava trees are more in numbers.

Ans. 2: Banyan trees are less in numbers.

2.9 Patterns

2.9.1 Geometrical Patterns

We generally observe various patterns in our daily life. We use them and many times place them according to our requirement. Here students are supposed to observe the geometrical patterns and answer the question.

1. Observe the pattern and answer the questions given below.

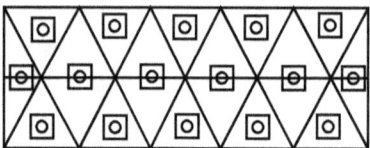

Fig. 2.51

1. How many geometrical shapes are there in the above figure.

   (1) 4   (2) 5

   (3) 6   (4) 7

2. What is the pattern followed in a time table ?

   (1) Numbers in the units place is in decreasing value.

   (2) Numbers in the tens place are in decreasing value.

   (3) Numbers in the units place is in increasing value.

   (4) Numbers in the tens place are in increasing value.

Questions

1. Complete the following patterns :

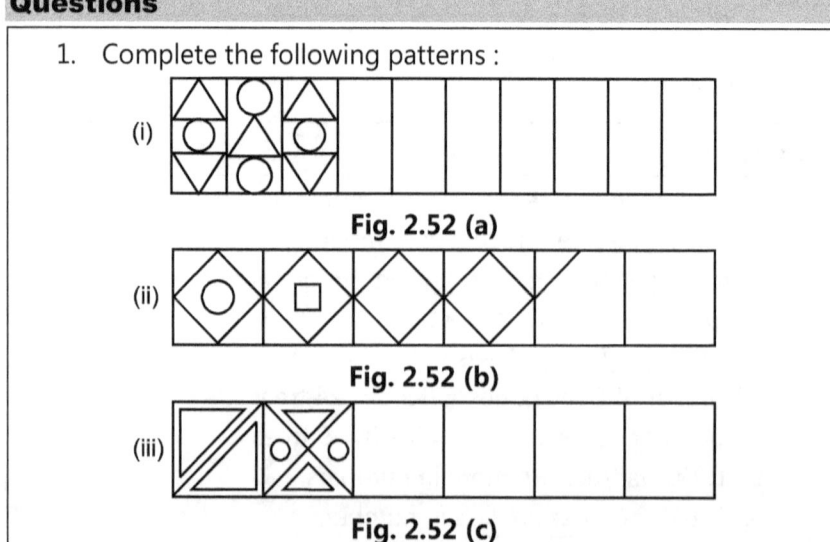

(i)

Fig. 2.52 (a)

(ii)

Fig. 2.52 (b)

(iii)

Fig. 2.52 (c)

Formation of Patterns with the help of Geometrical Shapes :

Activity 1: Observe the pattern given below carefully.

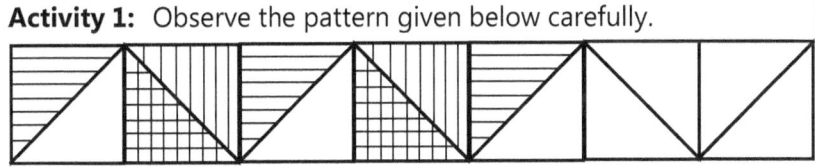

Complete the pattern.

Activity 2: As shown in Fig. (1) take rectangle shape paper.

(1)

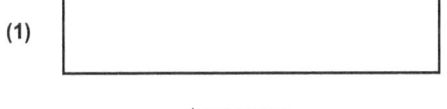

(2)

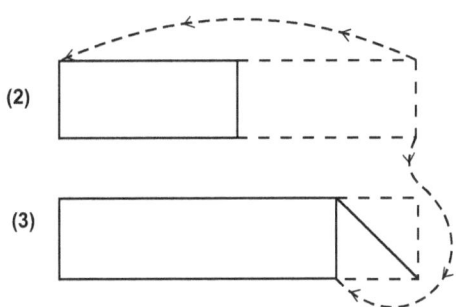

(3)

As shown in Fig. (2) and (3) fold the paper. After the completion of folding, open the folds. Observe the folds carefully and fill it with colours.

In the same way make different types of patterns.

Activity 3: 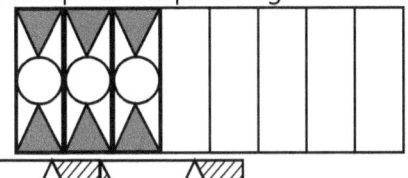 as shown the Fig. along side cut the paper and complete the pattern given below.

Activity 4:

Complete the pattern.

Activity 5: By using symmetric figures, flowers and objects prepare different types of patterns.

> **Activity 6:** By using different geometrical shapes prepare different types of patterns.

Points to Remember

- If we arrange geometrical figures in systematic manner the pattern of geometrical figure will form.
- Examples of pattern : Decoration of house, black board, wall etc.
- Attractive design on cloth.

2.9.2 Patterns in Numbers

By using different numbers, we can make different patterns. As discussed above, if we use different types of shapes. For example, $\triangle$, $\bigcirc$ and $\square$, with the help of these shapes, we can form different types of patterns.

By using $\triangle$, $\bigcirc$ and $\square$, we have forms a picture, it is called as pattern. In the same way, we can form pattern of numbers.

For example : Writing number :

(i)   1, 2, 3, 4, 5, 6, 7, 8, 9, ...

(ii)   Even numbers : 2, 4, 6, 8, ...

(iii) Odd numbers : 1, 3, 5, 7, 9, ...

In the above pattern;

(i)   There is increment in each number such as $1 + 1 = 2$, $2 + 1 = 3$, $3 + 1 = 4$ this is called as series. There is an increment in each number by 1.

(ii)   In 2nd pattern there is an increment by 2 in each number. But the series start from 2 and so it is even number series.

(iii) In the same way, in 3rd pattern there is an increment by 2 in each number. But the series start from 1 and so it is odd number series.

By using different objects, we can make different patterns of numbers. For example, balls, fruits etc.

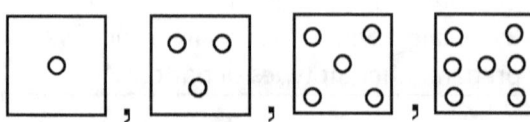

Number Pattern

1. For Example : Observe table of 9.

09	• The numbers at units place are in decreasing order from 9 to 0.
18	
27	• The numbers at tens place are in increasing order form 0 to 9.
36	
45	• Addition of digits in each number in the table is equal to 9.
54	
63	
72	
81	
90	

2. Find the pattern in given table. For example table of 16.

16	• The digit at unit's place of each number is the number at unit place in table of 6.
32	
48	• The digit at ten's place in table is obtained as the number at ten's place of 16 is 1 the number next to 1 is 2, 1 + 2 = 3 etc.
64	
80	
96	
112	
128	
144	
160	

3. Find the pattern in table of 9.

Pattern in table of 9 is.

19	• The digits at unit's place of number in table are in decreasing order from 9 to 0.
38	
57	• The digit at ten's place of number is odd number. For example : 1, 3, 5, 7, 9, ...
76	
95	
114	
133	
152	
171	
190	

2.10 Fractions

2.10.1 Meaning

A quantity that expresses a part of the whole quantity is called a fraction. The part above the horizontal line is called a numerator. The part below the horizontal line is called a denominator.

The diagram is divided into two equal parts. One part is shaded. The shaded part of the diagram is $\frac{1}{2}$. It is read as one half.

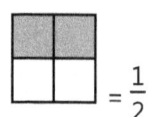

$= \frac{1}{2}$

Fig. 2.53 (a)

The figure is divided into four equal parts and one part is shaded. The shaded part of the diagram is $\frac{1}{4}$ and it is read as one over four. It is one fourth or a quarter.

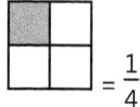

$= \frac{1}{4}$

Fig. 2.53 (b)

The figure is divided into four equal parts and three parts are shaded. It is called (3/4) three fourth or three quarter. It is read as three over four.

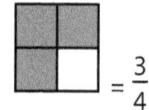

$= \frac{3}{4}$

Fig. 2.53 (c)

Mixed Fraction :

A fraction like $2\frac{1}{4}$ or $3\frac{1}{2}$ is called mixed fraction.

For example, when we divide 4 apples equally among 3 people we can do this in two ways.

Method 1	Method 2
Divide each apple equally into 3 parts Each person gets $\frac{1}{3}$ of each apple or one part of each apple. In this	First give each person 1 whole apple. Then divide the remaining apple into three equal parts. Give each person one part of the fourth apple that

way, each person gets 4 parts of $\frac{1}{3}$ of each apple. Therefore each person gets $\frac{1}{3} \times 4 = \frac{4}{3}$ apples $= 1\frac{1}{3}$	is $\frac{1}{3}$ apple. Each person gets 1 whole apple and $\frac{1}{3}$ apple $= 1 + \frac{1}{3} = 1\frac{1}{3}$

A fraction like $1\frac{1}{3}$ is called a mixed fraction.

Reading of Fraction :

   Example 1 : $2\frac{3}{4}$ is read as

Solution : Two and three quarters.

   Example 2 : The fraction Ten and a half is

Solution : $10\frac{1}{2}$.

Solved Examples

Q. Solve the following examples.

   1. $\frac{5}{7}$ is read as five over seven.

   2. $\frac{6}{7}$ is read as six over seven.

Questions

Q. Solve the following examples.

   1. Write shaded portion in fraction.

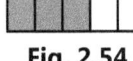

Fig. 2.54

   2. Read the fraction : $\frac{14}{18}$

   3. $\frac{4}{8}$ Read as =

Q. Solve the following examples :

   1. Three quarter is written as :

(1) $\frac{3}{4}$ (2) $\frac{1}{4}$ (3) $\frac{3}{6}$ (4) $\frac{2}{6}$

2. $\dfrac{4}{8}$

(1) numerator 8 denominator 4

(2) 4 by 8

(3) 8 divided four

(4) numerator 4 denominator 8

3. Three over five is written as ....

(1) $\dfrac{5}{3}$ (2) $\dfrac{3}{5}$ (3) 3 = 5 (4) 5 = 3

4. Seven over nine is written as ....

(1) $\dfrac{9}{7}$ (2) 9 = 7 (3) $\dfrac{7}{4}$ (4) $\dfrac{7}{9}$

Solved Examples

Q. Solve the following examples :

1. Write fraction in words : $\dfrac{1}{2}$

Solution : One half.

2. Write in numerical form : Numerator 8 denominator sixteen.

Solution : $\dfrac{8}{16}$.

3. Numerator 4 denominator 6

Solution : $\dfrac{4}{6}$.

Questions

1. Look at the given figures and find the fraction from the figures.

(i)

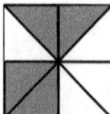

Fig. 2.55

(ii)

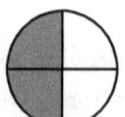

Fig. 2.56

2.10.2 Decimal Fractions

Decimal Numbers

The numbers written in decimal form are called decimal numbers or simply decimals.

Concept of Decimal Fraction

A decimal fraction is a fraction whose denominator is 10 or 100 or 1000 etc. Thus, $\dfrac{1}{10}, \dfrac{3}{10}, \dfrac{17}{100}, \dfrac{1}{100}, \dfrac{57}{100}$ etc. are all decimal fractions. There is a special way of writing names of such fractions. The fraction $\dfrac{1}{10}$ names the number as one-tenth. It can also be written as 0.1.

Conversions

(A) Convert the decimal fraction into decimal number.

For example, We can convert a decimal fraction with denominator 10, 100, 1000 etc. easily into a decimal number.

For example, $\dfrac{3}{10} = 0.3, \dfrac{4}{10} = 0.4, \dfrac{25}{100} = 0.25, \dfrac{75}{100} = 0.75, \dfrac{36}{10} = 3.6$

While putting a decimal point, we have to consider the following steps :

(1) See that the denominator is 10, 100, 1000 etc.

(2) Write the numerator and start counting digits from right to left. Put the decimal point just before as many digits, as the number of zeros in the denominator.

For example, (1) $\dfrac{3}{10}$ 10 has 1 zero.

∴   Write 3, then put decimal point just before digit. It will look $\overset{\leftarrow}{0.3}$. We put a zero to make the readability of the decimal point clear.

For example, (2) $\dfrac{23}{10} = 2.3$

For example, (3) $\dfrac{23}{100} = 0.23$

For example, (4) $\dfrac{23}{1000} = 0.023$

(B) Converting the non-decimal fraction into decimal fraction. The fraction in which the denominator is not 10, 100, 1000 we should be able to convert it into decimal fraction by finding an equivalent fraction for it such that the denominator becomes 10, 100, 1000 etc.

(1) Convert the given fraction into a decimal fraction.

For example, $\dfrac{2}{5} = \dfrac{2 \times 2}{5 \times 2} = \dfrac{4}{10} = 0.4$

or $\dfrac{3}{25} = \dfrac{3 \times 4}{25 \times 4} = \dfrac{12}{100} = 0.12$

For example, $\dfrac{1}{2} = 0.5$, $\dfrac{1}{4} = 0.25$, $\dfrac{3}{4} = 0.75$ etc.

(2) But if even that is not possible, we can find the decimal number by actually dividing the numerator by the denominator.

For example, $\dfrac{2}{3} = 0.666$, $\dfrac{7}{8} = 0.875$, $\dfrac{25}{11} = 2.272$

Place Value of Decimal Numbers

For example, Find the place value of the underlined digit in the following number :

(1) 687.4368

Since 3 is second after the decimal point, the place value of 3 is $3 \times \dfrac{1}{100} = \dfrac{3}{100} = 0.03$

(2) 348.24569

6 is fourth after the decimal point.

Therefore place value of 6 is $6 \times \dfrac{1}{10,000}$ or $\dfrac{6}{10,000}$, 6 ten thousandth = 0.0006

Equivalent Decimals

As we have equivalent fractions, in the same way, we have equivalent decimals. The value of decimal does not change, if at the end of any decimal place, we add on any number of zeros.

Now, $\dfrac{2}{10} = \dfrac{20}{100} = \dfrac{200}{1000}$

∴ 0.2 = 0.20 = 0.200 ....

Operations Involving Decimal Numbers

(I) Addition/Subtraction of Decimal Numbers :

For example, (1) Addition : 36.2408 + 423.048

```
      3  6 .  2  4  0  8
  +   4  2  3 .  0  4  8
      4  5  9 .  2  8  8  8
```

In the answer also, place the decimal point just below the above two decimal points.

(2) Subtract : 369.4298 – 32.43

```
    369.4298
  –  32.43
    336.9998
```

(II) Multiplication of Decimal Numbers :

In multiplication, if a decimal number is multiplied by any other decimal number, then the following steps are to be taken :

(1) Ignoring decimal points, multiply the given numbers.

(2) Then count the total number of decimal places in the multiplicand and the multiplier taken together.

(3) Put the decimal point after leaving that many decimal places to the right as the total of decimals found in step 2.

For example, (1) $43.28 \times 3.6 = 155.808$

(2) $48.96 \times 12.5 = 612.000 = 612$

(3) $47.3796 \times 100 = 4737.9600 = 4737.96$

Note : In case any decimal number, if multiplied by 10, 100, 1000, 10000 etc. the number as such does not change, but only the decimal place gets shifted to the right, as many places as the number of zeros in the multiplier.

For example, (1) $364.2498 \times 1000 = 364249.8$

(2) $32.497 \times 10 = 324.97$

(3) $846.4596 \times 10000 = 8464596$

(III) Division of Decimal Numbers :

For dividing a decimal number by a whole number, carry out the division in the normal manner and put decimal point in the quotient while taking the tenth digit down.

For example, 125 ÷ 2.5 should be changed to 1250 ÷ 25 and hence, we get the answer 50.

$$\text{Or} \quad 125 \div 2.5 = 125 \div \frac{25}{10}$$

$$= \frac{125 \times 10}{25}$$

$$= 5 \times 10 = 50$$

Recurring Decimal Numbers

While expressing rational numbers into decimal numbers, sometimes, it so happens that a certain set of numbers go on repeating itself after the decimal point. These types of digits keep on repeating infinitely and we do not get a finite decimal number. These numbers are called recurring decimal numbers.

For example, $\dfrac{5}{3}$ = 1.6666 .... = $1.\bar{6}$

```
        1.6666 ...
    3 |  5.0
      -  3
         ___
         20
      - 18
         ___
         20
      - 18
         ___
         20
          :
```

The recurring digits in a decimal number are denoted by putting a bar over the numbers which recurred as shown in $\dfrac{5}{3}$ = $1.\bar{6}$.

Conversion of Recurring Decimals into Fractions

If there is a recurring decimal, then it can be easily converted into a fraction. For doing this, the following steps are required.

(1) The number formed by the recurring digits should be put as the numerator.

(2) Put as many 9's in the denominator, as the number of recurring digits.

For example, $3.\overline{3} = 3\dfrac{3}{9} = 3\dfrac{1}{3}$

$$7.\overline{45} = 7\dfrac{45}{99}$$

$$= 7\dfrac{5}{11} \quad \text{... reducing to its lowest forms}$$

For example : In the following Fig. 2.57 there are 10 rows and 10 columns of square. In all there are 100 squares. In first column 2 squares are coloured i.e. $\dfrac{2}{10}$ is fraction, it can be written as 0.2.

In the same Fig. 2.57 in last column 2 squares out of 100 squares are coloured   i.e. $\dfrac{2}{100}$ it can be written as 0.02.

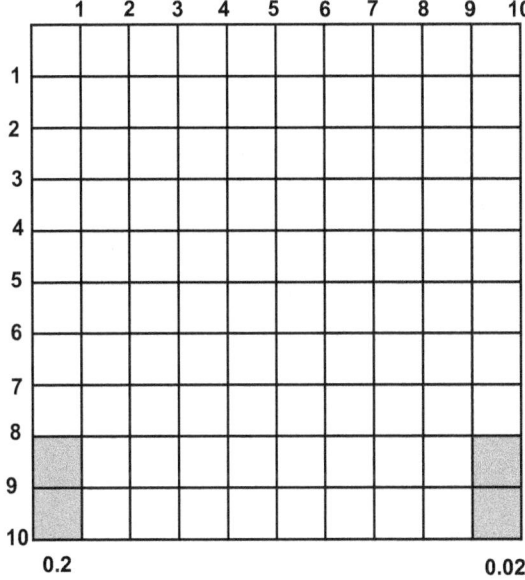

Fig. 2.57

2.11 Algebra : Introduction

2.11.1 Polymers

Many times we use letters to denote numbers. At such times, we can use small-letters and not capital letters to denote these numbers.

For example : When we say twice a number, it can be expressed arithmetically as $2 \times x$. If only multiplication is involved, we can write $2 \times x$ as $2x$.

Any letter from a, b, c, d, ... x, y, z can be taken. In this type of number, the numeral is called the constant or co-efficient and the alphabet part is called the variable. A variable can be in the form of one or more alphabets. As we perform all the operations of addition, subtraction, multiplication, division etc. in case of numbers, the same can be done in these letters also. These numbers/expressions using letters are called algebraic expressions. In algebra, they are also called terms. A term has one constant, and one variable.

2.11.2 Concept of Variable

A letter used in an algebraic expression which takes different values is called a variable.

2.11.3 Concept of Equation

An algebraic expression, having some constants and some variables, related with an equality sign is called as equation.

In an equation, the expression is divided into two sides with the help of an equal sign. The terms to the left of the equal sign are called the left hand side and the terms to the right side of the equal sign are called the right hand side or simply L.H.S. and R.H.S.

In an equation, there is a value of the variable, which satisfies the given equality. Finding this value of the variable means solving the equations. And the values thus received, is called the solution set. The method of finding the solution set is called the "solving of the equation".

Rules

Some rules have to be considered while solving the equations.

1. The equation does not change if the same number is added on both the sides or subtracted from both the sides.

2. The equation does not change if both the sides of the equation are divided by or multiplied by the same non-zero number.

For example :

(1) x + 5 = 7

This is an example of an equation. In this equation, x + 5 is the left hand side, and 7 is the right hand side.

We can solve it by subtracting 5 from both the sides.

$$x + 5 - 5 = 7 - 5$$

∴ $$x = 2$$

Hence, the solution is 2.

This means the above equation stands true if the value of the variable x is 2.

(2) 3y – 5 = 10

Here, we first have to separate the variable from the constant,   i.e. take the constant to the right hand side. This can be done by adding 5 to both the sides. So, we get,

$$3y - 5 + 5 = 10 + 5$$

∴ $$3y = 15$$

Now, if we divide both the sides by 3, we can easily get the solution.

∴ $$\frac{3y}{3} = \frac{15}{3}$$

∴ $$y = 5$$

Solved Examples

1. If $16 \times x + 2 = 162$ then find value of x.

Ans.:

$$16 \times x + 2 = 162$$
$$\therefore \quad 16 \times x = 162 - 2$$
$$16 \times x = 160$$
$$x = \frac{160}{16}$$
$$x = 10$$

2. Find the value of $\sqrt{(x-y)^2}$ if x = 15 and y = 10.

Ans.: x = 15   and   y = 10   ... (Given)

$$\sqrt{(15 - 10)^2} = \sqrt{5^2}$$
$$= \sqrt{25} = 5$$

3. Find the value of x if $6(x - 1) = 5(x + 1)$.

Ans.: The given equation is

$$6(x - 1) = 5(x + 1)$$
$$\therefore \quad 6x - 6 = 5x + 5$$
$$6x - 5x = 5 + 6$$
$$x = 11$$

4. From the equation for 'The difference between two natural numbers is 76'.

Ans.: The two natural numbers are x and x + 1.

The difference between the two numbers is given as 76.

$$(x + 1) - x = 76$$

EXERCISE

Multiple Choice Questions :

1. In mathematics education, the Van Hiele model is a theory that describes how students learn _____ .

   (a) Mathematics   (b) Algebra

   (c) Geometry   (d) None of these

2. The points which are contained in one single _____ line are called collinear points.

   (a) straight   (b) perpendicular

   (c) parallel   (d) none of these

3. An angle is the union of two non-collinear rays with a _____ origin.

   (a) one   (b) two

   (c) common   (d) none of these

4. An angle whose measure is less than _____ is called an acute angle.

   (a) 180°   (b) 360°

   (c) 90°   (d) 270°

5. The lines which never intersect to each other are called _____ lines.

   (a) parallel   (b) perpendicular

   (c) intersecting   (d) none of these

6. A parallelogram with all its sides congruent is called a _____ .

   (a) rectangle   (b) rhombus

   (c) square   (d) none of these

7. Addition of measure of three sides of a triangle is called as _____ of triangle.

   (a) perimeter   (b) area

   (c) base   (d) none of these

8. Any figure can occupy a space is called as _____ of figure.

   (a) perimeter   (b) area

   (c) both (a) and (b)   (d) none of these

9. Surface area of cylinder = _____ .

   (a) πr^2 (b) $2\pi d$

   (c) $\pi r^2 h$ (d) none of these

10. The figures which are same in shape but different in size are called _____ figures.

   (a) similar   (b) symmetric

   (c) both (a) and (b)   (d) none of these

11. 1 centimetres = _____ millimetres.

   (a) 10   (b) 100

   (c) 1000   (d) none of these

12. 1 kilogram = _____ grams.

   (a) 100   (b) 500

   (c) 1000   (d) none of these

13. A quantity that expresses a part of the whole quantity is called a _____ .

   (a) numerator   (b) denominator

   (c) fraction   (d) none of these

14. A letter used in algebraic expression which takes different values is called a _____ .

   (a) constant   (b) variable

   (c) both (a) and (b)   (d) none of these

15. An algebraic expression, having some constant and some variables, related with an equality sign is called as _____ .

   (a) expression   (b) variable

   (c) equation   (d) none of these

Answers : 1 - (c), 2 - (a), 3 - (c), 4 - (c), 5 - (a), 6 - (b), 7 - (a), 8 - (b), 9 - (b), 10 - (a), 11 - (a), 12 - (c), 13 - (c), 14 - (b), 15 - (c)

Q.2. Answer the Following Questions :

1. State the properties of Van Hiele levels.

2. Explain how you can use Van Hiele levels to learn geometry.

3. Explain with example two dimensional figures.

4. Explain the concept of similar figure and symmetric figures on the basis of pre-primary level.

5. Using the given information, find the perimeter of the figure. (∠ X and ∠ W are right angles)

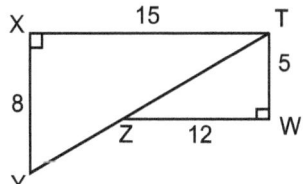

Fig. 2.58

6. From the information given in the figure below, find the area of trapezium ABCD.

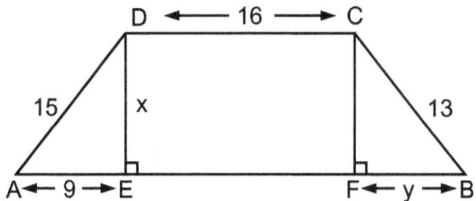

Fig. 2.59

7. ABCD is parallelogram. $l(BC) = 6$, m ∠ A = 30° find DP.

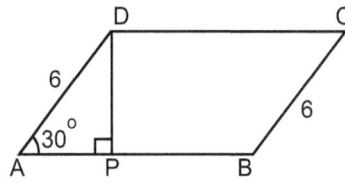

Fig. 2.60

8. Complete the pattern given below :

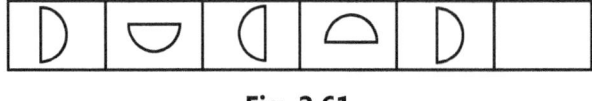

Fig. 2.61

Fig. 2.62

Q.3. Write Short Notes On :

1. Two Dimensional Figures.

2. Three Dimensional Figures.

3. Pictograph.

4. Patterns.

5. Equation in One Variable.

✍ ✍ ✍

3

SYLLABUS OF MATHEMATICS AND MATHEMATICS TEXTBOOK, TEACHING METHODS AND TECHNIQUES

➲ Chapter Structure ☯

3.1   Objectives

3.2   Introduction

3.3   Syllabus of Mathematics

    3.3.1   Concept

    3.3.2   Principles of Syllabus Preparation

    3.3.3   Structure of Syllabus

    3.3.4   Linear Approach

    3.3.5   Logical and Psychological Approach

    3.3.6   Integrated Approach

    3.3.7   Spiral or Concentric Approach

    3.3.8   Analysis of Syllabus Standard 1st to 5th

3.4   Mathematics Textbook

    3.4.1   Textbook Meaning

    3.4.2   Relation between Syllabus and Textbook

    3.4.3   Critical Analysis of Textbook (1st to 5th)

    3.4.4   Content Analysis of Textbook

    3.4.5   Importance and Usefulness of a Mathematics Textbook

        3.4.5.1   Usefulness for a Teacher

        3.4.5.2   Usefulness for a Student

        3.4.5.3   Usefulness for the Parents

3.5 Teaching and Learning of Mathematics : Methods and Techniques
    3.5.1 Rules of Maths Technology (Aims and Objectives)
    3.5.2 Teaching Methods in Mathematics
3.6 Planning in Teaching
    3.6.1 Importance of Planning
    3.6.2 Annual Planning
        3.6.2.1 Objectives of Annual Planning
        3.6.2.2 Points to be Considered for Annual Planning
        3.6.2.3 Advantages of Annual Planning
    3.6.3 Unit Planning
        3.6.3.1 What is a Unit ?
        3.6.3.2 Need for Unit Planning
        3.6.3.3 Steps in Unit Planning
        3.6.3.4 Advantages of Unit Planning
    3.6.4 Lesson Planning of Content-Cum-Methodology
    3.6.5 Maxims of Teaching
3.7 Teaching Techniques in Mathematics
    3.7.1 Question-Answer/Questioning Technique
    3.7.2 Revision Technique (Assignments)
    3.7.3 Supervise of Study Technique
    3.7.4 Diagnostic Test
    3.7.5 Remedial Teaching, Feedback
    3.7.6 Computer Assisted Teaching
3.8 Retention of Technological Process of Mathematics
    3.8.1 Mathematics Laboratory
    3.8.2 Mathematics Club
    3.8.3 Mathematical Fair
    3.8.4 Arranging Maths Fair
    3.8.5 Compact Disc
    3.8.6 Teleconference
    3.8.7 Teaching-learning Process of Mathematics with Fun
        3.8.7.1 Mathematical Puzzles
        3.8.7.2 Mathematical Games
        3.8.7.3 Magic in Mathematics
    3.8.8 Vedic Mathematics : Introduction
    3.8.9 Abacus
• Exercise

3.1 Objectives

After reading this chapter, you will be able to :

- Understand the concept and types of syllabus organisation.
- Understand the information about the analysis of syllabus of Standard 1st to 5th by concentric method.
- Understand the concept of new information about the content with the help of the computer.
- Do the arrangement of any syllabus from Standard 1 to 8 by concentric method.
- Understand the importance and usefulness of a textbook.
- Understand the criteria of a model textbook.
- Understand the relation between the content of mathematics textbooks and its objectives at lower primary level.
- Understand the review of content of one unit of mathematics.
- Explain the basic objectives of mathematics.
- Explain the objectives of teaching mathematics at lower primary level.
- Explain the various teaching methods of mathematics.
- Explain the utility of various teaching methods of mathematics.
- Make use of various teaching methods, to teach various units of mathematics.
- Explain various techniques of mathematics.
- Understand the concept of Planning in Teaching.
- Understand the concept of mathematical teaching aids.
- Get knowledge about mathematics games and other co-curricular activities.

3.2 Introduction

In this chapter, we are going to study about the types of syllabus arrangement, the analysis of Syllabus of standard 1st to 5th by concentric approach and new information about the content with the help of a computer.

In this chapter, let us study about the importance and usefulness of a textbook of mathematics with reference to teachers, students and parents. Also we will study the criteria of a good textbook and relation between the objectives and content of the textbook. You will also understand how to review the content of any unit.

We have seen the place and importance of mathematics as well as the uses and characteristics of structure of mathematics. Let us now study the basic aims of mathematics, objectives of mathematics at the lower primary, level. We shall also study the fixation and application of concepts at lower primary level which are useful at the secondary level.

In the chapter, we also studied about the planning of mathematics teaching, its necessity and importance. We also studied about unit plan, annual plan and lesson plan of content-cum-methodology. In this unit we are going to study about the various teaching methods Inductive and deductive method, Analysis and synthesis method, Self-search, Problem solving, Demonstration super method and mathematics games and co-curricular activities.

3.3 Syllabus of Mathematics

3.3.1 Concept

A syllabus is an outline and summary of topics to be covered in an education or a training courses.

Definition of Syllabus :

- An outline or other brief statement of the main points of a discourse, the subjects of a course of lectures, the contents of a curriculum.
- A compendium containing the heads of a discourse, and the like; an abstract.
- An integrated course of academic studies.
- A description of the contents of a course of instruction and the order in which they are to be taught.

A syllabus lets the students know what the course is about, why the course is taught, where it is going and what will be required for there to be successful in the course.

Characteristics of a Syllabus :

- Syllabus has explicit objectives.
- It is a public document.
- It has a time schedule.
- It consists of a comprehensive list of content items.
- It specifies learning tasks and activities. Describes appropriate procedures and course policies.
- Contains information useful for evaluation.
- Helps students by being a learning tool. So that students become more effective learner in the course.
- Focuses or students and what they need to be effective learners.

Purpose of Syllabus :

A syllabus is a contract between the teacher and students. By reading the syllabus, the student should gain a clear understanding of the goals of the course, what activities they need to engage in to achieve the course objectives and how they will be graded.

Advantages of Good Syllabus :

A well designed syllabus benefits the teacher and the students :

1. It requires you to think about the course and to organize early.
2. It helps students understand how the course fits into their educational plans.
3. It communicates your expectations. When students know what to expect, they can plan their own work for the semester.
4. It establishes class policies, assignments and deadlines.
5. It gives relevant information.
6. It helps to establish the classroom climate.

3.3.2 Principles of Syllabus Preparation

The strongest syllabi are built on a solid foundation of course design. In course design the instructor first chooses learning goals that are appropriate for the level of the class. These are goals that can be achieved in one semester and that are rooted in discipline. After selecting learning goals, the instructor/teacher decides how to measure whether students have achieved those goals. Then he decides what learning experiences in and outside the classroom will help his students learn.

While constructing a syllabus following basic things must also be included in it along with the content :

1. **Basic information :** Title of the course, contact location, office hours, name.

2. **Course description :** Prerequisites, overview of the course, student learning objectives.

3. Materials needed for the courses.

4. **Requirements :** Exams, quizzes, assignments, problem sets, reports etc.

5. **Policies :** Grading procedure, attendance, class participation, exams or assignments, late policies etc.

6. **Schedule :** Tentative calendar of topics, dates of exams and assignments.

7. **Resources :** Tips for success, model student assignments glossaries of terms, links to support materials on web, space for students to prepare study circle.

8. Evaluation of course and assessment of student learning.

3.3.3 Structure of Syllabus

There are various approaches or methods of structure of syllabus. They are :

1. Topical approach or Topic method.

2. Linear approach.

3. Logical and Psychological approach.

4. Integrated approach.

5. Spiral or Concentric approach.

(1) Topical Approach

After selecting the topics, the curriculum has to be organized maintaining the mathematical sequence and continuity. In topic methods, those topics which have similar characteristics or properties are brought together and arranged systematically. While teaching, a teacher concentrates only on one topic and hence that topic is grasped quickly by the learner.

In topical approach, a topic once presented should be completely finished in the same class. This method demands that the entire topic, as well as its subtopics, whether easy or difficult, should be covered in the same stage.

For example: In standard 5, the topic of Numbers and Numeration includes subtopics like Addition, Subtraction, Multiplication, Division, examples of daily life, Divisibility, Prime factors, L.C.M., H.C.F, Unitary Method and Average. All these subtopics have to be covered once the topic is started in a class.

3.3.4 Linear Approach

In this method, one topic is taken or taught in different standards. But the information of one topic in a particular standard is different from the topic of another standard. Sometimes it so happens that a learner may not understand the topic at one standard as well as another standard. So in the end he may not understand that topic at all.

For example: The topic of fractions is taught in standard 3, 4, and 5 as well. But though the topic is similar, the information is different.

3.3.5 Logical and Psychological Approach

Teaching of mathematics from the view of a mathematician will have logical approach whereas a teacher of mathematics will have a psychological approach. But these two approaches do not differ and hence the organisation of a syllabus should have logical as well as psychological approach.

Psychology should decide what kind of logic is appropriate for the pupils of certain age and which type of topics will be most suitable for the development of such logical thinking. Logic will help in maintaining the link and sequence of topics which are useful and meaningful for the child.

For example, the idea of a fraction should be known before its notation. So both logic and psychology require it to be taught after vulgar fractions.

3.3.6 Integrated Approach

The main aim of education is acquisition of knowledge and the transfer of knowledge to study other subjects and to solve successfully the problems that arise in everyday life. However, the subjects are taught in water-tight compartments without relating them to life. Instead the study of every subject should stress the importance of "Unity of Knowledge ". While teaching any subject, the teacher has to explain that "knowledge is an integrated whole", and knowledge gained through various subjects, together constitutes the " whole ". This is the integrated approach of syllabus.

3.3.7 Spiral or Concentric Approach

Contrary to the other approaches, spiral or concentric approach demands the division of the topic into a number of smaller independent units in order of difficulty. Arrangement of syllabus according to its order of difficulty is one of the principles of curriculum organisation. The organisation of the content should be in increasing order of difficulty.

The mental level and power of comprehension of the pupils is taken into account while arranging the syllabus. Thus, the learning proceeds from "simple to complex". The difficulty level of a topical is to be judged from the view of the pupil, based on mental development and capabilities of the pupils.

This approach is based on the principle that a topic cannot be exhaustive treatment at one stage like the topic method.

Thus, we can define concentric arrangement of syllabus as :

Organisation of or arrangements of contents of a curriculum or syllabus, by spreading it to different grades or standards, by covering the easier portion in the lower standards and the difficult portion in the higher and higher standards gradually, is called as concentric arrangement of syllabus.

Advantages of Spiral or Concentric Method :

1. As the subject-matter is introduced in the order of difficulty, it helps in better understanding of the content.

2. It provides sufficient motivation for students to learn.

3. It provides opportunities for revision.

4. It provides opportunities to relate the topics with other topics, other branches and other subjects.

5. As it also has a psychological approach it satisfies the psychological needs of students.

For example, observe how the topic "Addition" is included from Std. 1 to 4 in increasing order of difficulty.

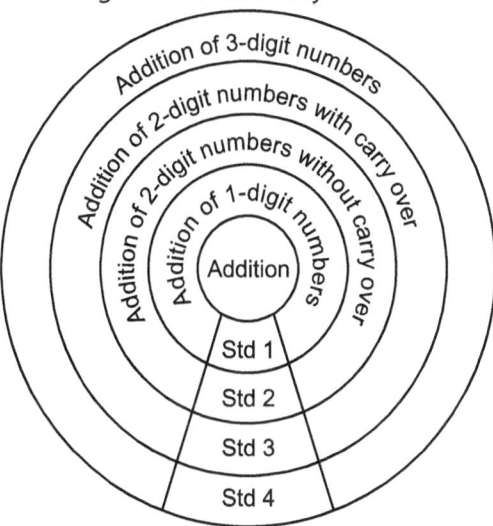

Fig. 3.1

Relation and Difference between Curriculum and Syllabus :

Many times the words curriculum and syllabus are used synonymously. But it is wrong. They are not the same. Curriculum has wider scope than syllabus. Syllabus is a part of curriculum.

Difference between Curriculum and Syllabus :

Curriculum	Syllabus
1. This concept has a broader scope. More comprehensive in nature.	1. Syllabus is a limited part of curriculum.
2. Curriculum is prepared for	2. Syllabus is prepared

different levels like pre-primary level, primary level, secondary level.	specifically for a standard.
3. Long term objectives are considered.	3. Short term objectives to be achieved in one standard are considered.
4. General objectives, teaching methods, evaluation approaches are considered in broader aspect.	4. Specific objectives, teaching methods, evaluation approaches for that specific standard are considered.

3.3.8 Analysis of Syllabus Standard 1st to 5th

Analysis of syllabus includes study of :

1. Type of syllabus arrangement.
2. Objectives of syllabus.
3. Scope and nature of content.
4. Core units included in the content.
5. Values developed through the content.
6. Evaluation scheme.

Importance of Analysis of Syllabus :

1. All the minute details of the content are understood.
2. Objectives of content teaching are made clear.
3. The core units and values in the content are understood.
4. New words, concepts, rules, characteristics, principles are understood.
5. Place of concept in the structure is known.
6. Learning experiences become clear.
7. Selection of suitable teaching method can be done.
8. Selection of suitable teaching aids can be done.
9. Proper selection of suitable evaluation scheme can be done.

Content Analysis :

Content means meaningful information and analysis means breakdown of units to study and correlate them. Thus, the main theme of teaching methods is to analyse the content units, give them a logic sequence, decide the objectives followed by selection of suitable teaching method and planning of teaching.

Following points should be taken into consideration while doing content analysis.

1. Name of Unit :

A unit consists of comprehensive series of related and meaningful activities so developed as to achieve pupils purpose, provide significant educational experiences and results in appropriate behavioural changes.

For example, in standard four the 10th chapter is "Fractions", it consists of : Meaning of fractions, Reading and writing fractions, Some more fractions, Different meanings of fractions, Mixed fractions, Comparing fractions and fractions related to sets. All these together make one unit "Fractions".

2. Place of Unit in the Structure :

The actual place of a unit in the structure of the subject must be known. For example while teaching "Mixed Fractions" in standard 5.

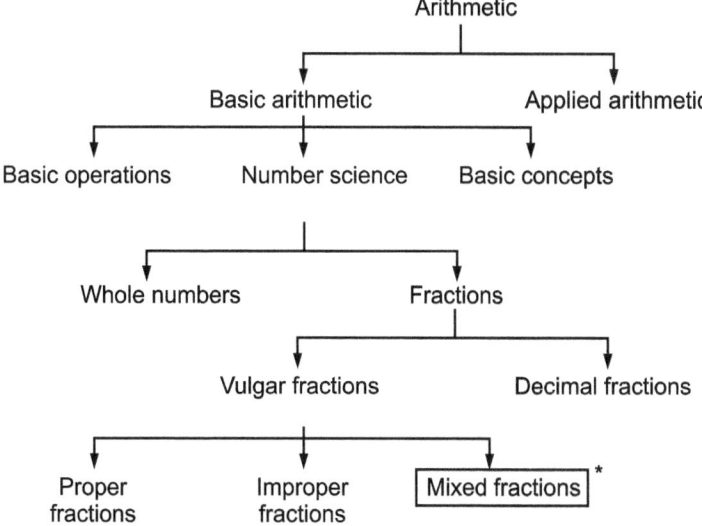

3. Core Units included in the Content :

National policy of education has included these following ten core units :

(i)　History of Indian Movement of Freedom.

    (ii)   Indian Constitutional Responsibilities.

    (iii) Content necessary for National Integration.

    (iv) Inheritance of Indian Heritage

    (v)   Equality, Secularism and Democracy.

    (vi) Equality among Men and Women.

    (vii) Conservation of Environment.

    (viii) Removal of Social Evils.

    (ix) Model of 'Small Family'.

    (x)   Enhancement of Scientific Outlook.

4. Values Developed through the Content :

    (i)   Patriotism.

    (ii)   National Integration.

    (iii) Secularism.

    (iv) Equality of Men and Women.

    (v)   Dignity of Labour.

    (vi) Scientific Outlook.

    (vii) Sensitivity.

    (viii) Punctuality.

    (ix) Courtesy and Respect.

    (x)   Neatness.

5. Concept :

Concept is a set or group of abstract ideas with similar characteristics. Concepts have a specific name, characteristics and examples. Mathematics is full of concepts, for example, sets, congruency, interest etc.

6. Rule/Law :

A rule or law is a statement prepared by bringing together of several facts. Rules and laws are prepared for completion of any activity.

For example : Sum of lengths of all sides of a closed figure is called perimeter. The rules here are :

    1. The figure should be closed one.

    2. Addition should be done of lengths of all sides.

7. Principle :

It is a general law that is used as a basis for a theory.

For example : Diameter of a circle is twice that of the radius.

8. Formula :

It is a mathematical relationship expressed in symbols.

For example : Area of a circle = πr^2.

9. Characteristics :

It is a statement used to describe the specialities or qualities of a concept, figure, or situation.

For example : Characteristics of a protractor Std. V :

- Semicircular in shape.
- Semicircular edge divided in 180 equal parts.
- Each part is called degree.
- Degrees are marked clockwise and anticlockwise.

10. Facts :

Fact is a statement that reveals actual reality or it is an information known to be true.

For example : A triangle has three sides.

11. Terms :

It is a word or phrase used to describe a thing or express an idea. For example : Area, Volume.

12. Assumptions :

Assumptions means facts which are assumed or accepted. In mathematics, we have to assume many things.

For example : The unknown number - x.

13. Theory :

Facts that are result of experimentations and those can be proved are together called as theory.

14. Theorem :

Theorem is a general proportion or since that can be proved by reasoning.

For example : Pythogoras theorem.

15. Figure :

It is symbolic, graphic or pictorial presentation.

According to the new education policy a new improved syllabus was decided for Standard 1 to 5. Later on changes were made and the curriculum was based on level of competencies and least competency level.

Let us now study the concentric arrangement of each area in the syllabus.

Activity 1 :	Prepare concentric arrangement of syllabus using the figure form for at least five areas.

Points to Remember

- There are five types of arrangements of syllabus. Out of those, the most widely used arrangement for mathematics syllabus is the concentric or spiral type of arrangement.
- Concentric arrangement also has a psychological angle to it.
- We can get new information about the content with the help of the computer.

Questions

1. What are the various types of arrangement of syllabus ? Explain.
2. Explain the concentric form of syllabus organisation. Analyse how it will be suitable for any topic of lower primary level.

3.4 Mathematics Textbook

3.4.1 Textbook Meaning

The mathematics textbook is one of the most important resources for teaching and learning mathematics. Whereas a number of studies have examined the use of mathematics textbooks by teachers there is a dearth of research into the use of mathematics textbooks by students. In this paper results of an empirical investigation of the use of mathematics textbooks by students as an instrument for learning mathematics are presented. Firstly, a method to collect data on student's use of mathematics textbooks is introduced. It is explicated, that this method is capable to explore the actual use of the mathematics textbook by students, and a way of recording the use of the mathematics textbook whenever and wherever students use it. Secondly, results from the study are presented. The results outlined in this paper focus on typical self-directed uses of the mathematics textbook by students.

3.4.2 Relation between Syllabus and Textbook

(a) Focus on understanding avoiding information load.
(b) Provide space to subject-specific pedagogy in-built in the content.
(c) Integrate assessment within the content and learning.
(d) Must be interactive.
(e) Provides space for learning beyond the textbook.
(f) Soften the boundaries between different subject areas.
(g) Provide adequate space for hands-on experience, arts and crafts. Incorporates social concerns related to gender, marginalised groups, health and work.

3.4.3 Critical Analysis of Textbook (1st to 5th)

Concept of Analysis :

The textbook plays an important role in teaching and learning. Textbook provide organized units of work. The material to be covered and the design of each lesson are carefully spelled out in detail. Textbooks are detailed sequence of teaching procedures that tell you what to do and when to do it. Good textbooks are excellent teaching aids. They are a resource for both teachers and students.

Some textbooks may fail to arouse student interest and they may reject such textbooks. So the textbooks have to be as good as teachers. So whether a textbook is really good for the students has to be decided by doing critical analysis.

Analysis means a systematic examination or evaluation of data or information, by breaking it into its component parts to uncover their interrelationships.

Analysis is a careful study of something to learn about its parts, what they do and how they are related to each other.

Wikipedia defines analysis as the process of breaking a complex topic or substance into smaller parts in order to gain a better understanding of it.

A critical analysis is subjective writing because it expresses the writer's opinion or evaluation of text.

Analysis of Textbooks from Std. 1 to 4 :

Standard 1 :

The mathematics textbook of standard one is divided into two parts.

Part - I :

This part includes words of comparison, counting, numerals, writing numbers, numbers in words, before, after and middle number, smaller and bigger numbers, addition, introducing zero, introducing ten and coins and currency, notes.

'Words of Comparison' is explained very properly by many pictures. Some of these pictures are based on stories, for example, to explain the concept of small-big, in-out and far-near, pictures of three stories i.e. The mouse and the lion, The sparrow and the crow and The hare and the tortoise are given. Family background picture is given for up-down and nearest-farthest. Students like sweets and chocolates, so the pictures of sweets and chocolates are used in explaining 'less-more'. The picture of class students is used to explain the concept of "equal".

There are two poems in this Part - I, to teach the unit of "Counting" and "The Song of Zero".

The units of 'counting' and 'numerals' too have many beautiful pictures and charts. Introduction of every numeral is done by giving many examples though pictures and specific facts of nature has also been told in this introduction such as - one tail, two horns, three wheels of rickshaw, four legs of cow, five fingers, six legs of butterfly, seven colours of rainbow, eight legs of spider etc. Lot of practice activities are given in order to practice for numerals from 1 to 9.

This is followed by the concept of 'Bigger-Smaller' which is again explained by pictures. The concept of "addition" is properly introduced without the plus sign (+) initially. Then afterwards (+) sign as been introduced.

Word problems, introducing zero and introducing ten also are explained with the help of many pictures "coins and currency notes" unit has actual pictures of the money.

Part - II :

This part contains comparison, subtraction, introducing 'tens', introduction of 11 to 19 numerals, smaller and bigger numbers, addition, patterns in series, 1 to 9 tens, reading and writing members from 20 to 29, 30 to 39 and so on till 90 to 99, introduction of 100, counting big number on string of beads, measurement of time, days of the week, classifying things, handling data and fun with numbers.

All these above units of Part II are very well explained with the help of pictures, figures, drawings and charts. Students will know how to study from these colourful pictures as they like colourful pictures at their age. A story has been given in the second part to explain sharing and dividing between friends. Measurement of time has examples based on actual life such as travelling by train, aeroplane and cycle. Travelling by boat and swimming, and filling of water in small bucket and big bucket. Day of the week are taught through a beautiful poem. Fun with numbers contains a story with dialogues which can be enacted in the class.

Table 3.1 : The mathematics textbook of standard 1 fulfils the following core units, values and objectives

Page No.	Core Unit	Value	Objective
1.	Protection of environment	Sensitivity	Concept of small-big
2.	Protection of nature	Sensitivity	Concept of in-out
3.	Principle of small family	Sensitivity	Concept of up-down
4.	–	Punctuality	Concept of near-far

... *(Contd.)*

Page No.	Core Unit	Value	Objective
5.	Equality among men and women	Dignity of labour	Concept of nearest-farthest
6.	–	Equality	Concept of less-more
7.	Equality among men and women	Sensitivity	Concept of equal
12.	Protection of environment	Sensitivity	Concept of introducing 1 & 2
14.	Protection of environment	Sensitivity Neatness	Concept of 3 & 4
16.	Protection of environment	Dignity of labour	Concept of 5 & 6
19.	Protection of environment	Sensitivity	Concept of 8
20.	National Integration	National integration	Concept of 9
24, 25	Protection of environment	Dignity of labour	Concept of nos. 1 to 9
26.	–	Dignity of labour	Concept of nos. 1 to 9
28.	–	–	Concept of before-after
29	–	–	Concept of smaller and bigger numbers
31.	Protection of environment	Dignity of labour	Concept of addition
34.	National Integration Secularism	Dignity of labour	Concept of addition word problems

... (Contd.)

Page No.	Core Unit	Value	Objective
37.	Protection of environment	–	Concept of zero
38.	Protection of environment	–	Concept of zero
41.	National integration	Dignity of labour	Concept of coins and currency notes
44.	Protection of environment	–	Concept of breadth
45.	Protection of environment	–	Concept of height
46.	Indian Constitutional Responsibilities	–	Concept of tallest-shortest
47.	–	Dignity of labour	Concept of weight
48., 49.	Protection of environment	–	Concept of subtraction
51.	Protection of environment equality	Dignity of labour Sensitivity	Concept of division
55.	Protection of environment	Dignity of labour Sensitivity	Concept of 11 - 19
75.	National integration	–	Concept of time
76.	–	Dignity of labour	Concept of before and after
77.	Protection of environment	–	Concept of week
79.	National integration	–	Concept of data
80. 81.	Protection of environment	–	Concept of fun while learning numbers

Standard 2 :

The textbook of mathematics of standard 2 is divided into two parts.

Part - I : This part includes :

Left-Right, Behind - In front of

Introducing Geometrical Shapes

Edges and Corners

Surfaces of Objects

Introducing the Line

Drawing Lines and Shapes

Using Objects

Use of Curved and Straight Lines

Recognizing Geometrical Shapes

Measurement : Length

Weight (Mass)

Weight

Ordinal and Cardinal Numbers

A Feast in the Forest

Read the Numbers

Numbers - Counting Forward

Clap Your Hands

Snap Your Fingers : A Game

Counting

A Counting Game

Numbers in Tens and Units Form

Two-digit Numbers on a String of Hundred

Numbers in Tens and Units Form

Writing Numbers in Words

Revision : Addition and Subtraction

Addition : By Counting Forward

Addition : Using Tens-Units

Adding Zero and Subtracting Zero

Another Meaning of Subtraction

The Relationship between Addition and Subtraction

Subtraction by Counting Forward

Subtraction

Word Problems

Days of the Week

Yesterday, Today and Tomorrow

Measurement of Time

Smaller and Bigger Numbers

Part - II : This part includes :

The Ascending and Descending Order of Numbers

Introducing : Numbers in Steps

Numbers in Steps : By Counting Forward

Addition by Carrying Over Preparation

Addition by Carrying Over, Word Problems : Addition

Introducing Coins and Currency Notes

Coins and Currency Notes

Subtraction : By Counting Backward

Addition by Increasing in 10's and Subtraction by Taking away 10's

Addition and Subtraction (in Steps)

Subtraction : Preparation

Addition and Subtraction

Necklaces and Bracelets of Beads

Subtraction (By Untying a Ten) :

Preparation

Subtraction : By Untying a Ten

Subtraction

Multiplication and Division - Preparation

Multiplication : Preparation

Multiplication Tables : Preparation

The 2 Times Table

The 3 Times Table

The 4 Times Table

Tables of 5 and 10

Pictorial Information (Classification)

Patterns in Our Surroundings

Patterns

Handling Data

Word Problems

The Number Ladder : A Game

All the concepts and units, sub-units are described and explained with the help of colourful pictures, charts and figures. Various pictures of day-to-day family life, classroom environment, situations from the garden, scenes from the playground, various scenes from stories, and various pictures of currency notes and coins are given appropriately.

A beautiful poem describing the various geometrical shapes is given to explain the unit number 2. The poem also gives the information about the growth of vegetables i.e. where they grow. For example, carrots growing under the ground and tamarind on trees.

To explain the concept of ordinal numbers. The units like 'counting forward, smaller and bigger numbers, addition and subtraction have been explained through a conversation. The concept of addition and subtraction is also explained by a short story of 'cap seller and the monkeys'.

The concept of 'weight' and 'subtraction by untying a ten' is done through a dialogue writing. The book has many charts, pictorial as well as numerical charts.

Activity : Prepare a table as shown in Table 3.1 to enlist the core units, values and the objectives included in the textbook of mathematics for Std. 2.

Standard 3 :

The textbook of standard 3rd mathematics is divided into two parts.

Part - I : This part includes

Introduction to Geometrical Figures
Number Work
Addition without Carrying Over
Subtraction without Borrowing
Multiplication
Coins and Currency Notes
Measurement
Patterns
Symmetry

Part - II : This part includes

Addition of Carrying Over
Subtraction by Borrowing
Multiplication
Division
Measurement of Time
The Calendar
Fractions
Handling Data

The mathematics textbook of Std. 3 is based on following seven areas of study :

1. Geometry
2. Numbers
3. Operations on numbers
4. Measurement
5. Fractions
6. Handling data
7. Patterns

The mathematics textbook of standard 3 has various colourful pictures, figures, drawings, numerical charts, pictorial charts.

Various figures are given to explain the concept of geometrical figures and fractions. The book also contains the explanation through activities as given on page numbers 2, 4, 47, 42, 35. Many concepts like smaller-bigger, multiplication, measurement, subtraction by borrowing, multiplication, division, time concept and handling data are explained with the help of dialogues between students and teacher.

Activity : Prepare a table to enlist core units, values and objectives included in the textbook of mathematics of standard 3 (as shown for standard 1).

Standard 4 :

The textbook of mathematics of standard 4 is divided into two parts :

Part - I : This part includes

Geometrical Figures
Number Work
Addition
Subtraction
Multiplication : Part I
Division : Part I
Coins and Notes
Measuring Time

Part - II : This part includes

Word Problems : Addition and Subtraction
Fractions
Measurement
Perimeter and Area
Multiplication : Part II
Division : Part II
Pictographs
Patterns

The mathematics textbook of standard 4 is based on the following seven areas of study :

1. Geometry
2. Numbers
3. Operations on numbers
4. Measurement
5. Fractions
6. Graphs
7. Patterns

Units like geometrical figures, patterns, area, volume, weight, kilometer, fractions, coins and notes and division have been explained through nice colourful pictures. Almost all the units have various mathematical activities that are to be done by the students. Different numerical and pictorial charts have been given to explain units like number work, geometrical figures, calendar, leap year, fractions and measurement. Different units like break-up of numbers, international numbers, inter-relationship between division and multiplication, dividing zero by non-zero number, coins and notes, leap year, measurements, perimeter and area of pictographs have been explained through dialogues between the students and the teacher or dialogue in their family.

Core units, values and objectives from mathematics textbook of Std. 4.

Sr. No.	Unit	Core Unit	Value	Objectives
1.	Geometrical figures	Protection of environment	Dignity of labour	Concept of angles, Concept of types of angles.
2.	Number work	National integration	Neatness	Concept of four digit numbers, Concept of five digit numbers. Concept of expanded form

3.	Addition	–	Neatness	Concept of addition
4.	Subtraction	Protection of environment	Neatness	Concept of subtraction
5.	Multiplication	National integration	Sensitivity	Concept of multiplication
6.	Division	Equality of men and women	Sensitivity	Concept of division
7.	Coins and notes	–	Dignity of labour	Concept of coins and notes
8.	Measuring time	National integration Secularism	Dignity of labour Punctuality	Concept of measuring time
9.	Addition and subtraction word problems	1. Protection of environment. 2. National integration 3. Constitutional responsibilities 4. Principle of small family	Sensitivity neatness	Concept of word problems on addition and subtraction
10.	Fractions	Principle of small family	Sensitivity (sharing)	Concept of fractions, mixed fractions comparing fractions and fractions related to sets.
11.	Measurement	National integration	Neatness punctuality Dignity of labour	Concept of length and weight
12.	Perimeter and Area	–	Sensitivity	Concept of area and perimeter

13.	Multiplication	National integration Protection of environment	–	Concept of multiplication
14.	Division	Protection of environment	Sensitivity Neatness	Concept of division
15.	Pictographs	Protection of environment	Sensitivity Neatness	Concept of pictographs
16.	Patterns	–	Neatness	Concept of patterns

3.4.4 Content Analysis of Textbook

Analysis of Mathematics Syllabus at Primary Level :

Analysis of mathematics syllabus means analysis of units and sub-units of syllabus, in short it means content analysis of syllabus. Let now study the content analysis of standard 4th mathematics syllabus.

Standard 4th syllabus is divided into 7 study areas of fields : They are :

Sr. No.	Study Area	Units	Sub-units
1.	Geometry	1	2
2.	Numbers	1	6
3.	Operations or Numbers	7	16
4.	Measurement	4	9
5.	Fractions	1	3
6.	Graphs	1	1
7.	Patterns	1	1
	Total	**16 units**	**38 sub-units**

(1) Area : Geometry :

    Objectives :

1. Draws different types of angles.
2. Draws circle using a compass.
3. Free hand drawing of rectangle, square and triangle.

Content points :

1. Angles, types of angles.
2. Circle, drawing a circle.
3. Geometrical figures : Vertex and side.

Core units of the content :

1. Equality of men and women.
2. Model of small family.
3. Mathematical outlook.
4. Dignity of labour.
5. Neatness.

New words, concepts in the content :

1. **Angle :** Two lines meet to form an angle.
2. **Right angle :** 3 O'clock, 9 O'clock are right angles.
3. **Acute angle :** Angle smaller than right angle.
4. **Obtuse angle :** Angle bigger than right angle.
5. **Chord :** Line joining two points on edge of circle.
6. **Diameter :** Line dividing circle in two equal halves.
7. **Radius :** Half of diameter.
8. **Vertex :** Point where two lines meet.

Characteristics in content :

1. **Angle :** Point where two lines meet.
2. **Right angle :** Angle between minute hand and hour hand at 3 O'clock.
3. **Acute angle :** Angle smaller than right angle.
4. **Obtuse angle :** Angle bigger than right angle.
5. **Chord :** Line joining two points on a circle.
6. **Diameter :** Biggest - longest chord.
7. **Centre :** Mid-point of circle.
8. **Radius :** Half of diameter.
9. **Vertex :** Point where two lines meet.

Activity : Write content analysis of 'Geometry' of Std. 5.

(2) Area Numbers :

Objectives :

Recognizes four digit numbers, reads them and writes in words. Reads and writes five digit numbers, writes the expanded form of a number, understands the different breakups of a numbers, writes before and after members, writes ascending and descending numbers, recognizes odd and even numbers, understands international numbers.

Content points :

1. Four digit numbers.
2. Introducing five digit numbers.
3. Expanded form of numbers.
4. Different breakups of a number.
5. Before and after.
6. Ascending and descending order.
7. International numbers.

Core units of the content :

1. Removal of social evils.
2. Model of small family.
3. Inheritance of Indian heritage.
4. Equality among men and women.
5. National integrity.
6. Secularism.
7. Neatness.

New words and concept :

1. **Expanded form :** Arrangement of number in expanded form such as, T Th + Th + H + T + U.
2. **Place value :** Place of a digit in the number and its value.
3. **Breakup of number :** For example : 125 = One hundred and twenty five units.

   125 = Twelve tens and five units.

   125 = One hundred, two tens and five units.

4. **Before and after :**

   Number before a number → Subtract by one.

   Number after a number → Add one.

5. **Ascending and Descending order :**

   Ascending order : Arrangement of numbers from lowest to highest value.

   Descending order : Arrangement of numbers from highest to lowest value.

6. **International numerals :** English numerals.

Activity : Write the characteristics of the above field.

(3) Area Operations on Numbers :

Objectives :

1. Adds with carrying over.
2. Adds four digit numbers.
3. Subtracts four digit numbers without borrowing.
4. Subtracts by borrowing.
5. Subtraction of five digit number with and without borrowing.
6. Solves oral sums of addition and subtraction.
7. Multiplies a three digit number by two digit number.
8. Understands the inter-relationship between division and multiplication.
9. Divides a two digit number by one digit number.
10. Solves mixed problems of addition and subtraction.
11. Multiplies three digit number by one digit number.
12. Solves word problems on division.

Content points :

1. Addition with carrying ones.
2. Addition of four digit numbers.
3. Subtraction of four digit number with and without borrowing.
4. Subtraction of five digit number with and without borrowing.
5. Oral sums of addition and subtraction.

6. Multiplication of three digit number by two digit number.
7. Inter-relationship between division and addition.
8. Division of two digit number by one digit number.
9. Mixed problem on addition and subtraction.
10. Multiplication of three digit number by one digit number.
11. Word problems on division.

Core units in the content :

1. Inheritance of Indian heritage.
2. Equality, democracy and secularism.
3. Protection of environment.
4. Indian constitutional responsibilities.
5. Model of small family.

Place in structure :

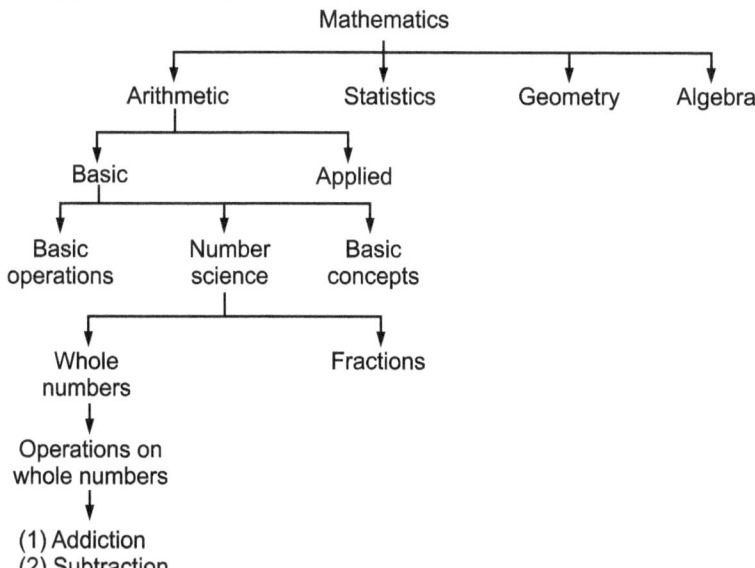

Values seen in the content :

1. National integration.
2. Secularism.
3. Equality of men and women.

4. Dignity of labour.

5. Neatness.

6. Courtesy and respect.

Concepts in the content :

1. Addition with carrying over.

$$\begin{array}{r} 5462 \\ +\ 4179 \\ \hline 9641 \end{array}$$

2. Addition of four digit numbers.

6785 + 7453

3. Subtraction of four digit number without borrowing.

$$\begin{array}{r} 5795 \\ -\ 2183 \\ \hline 3612 \end{array}$$

Subtraction with borrowing :

$$\begin{array}{r} 4215 \\ -\ 2649 \\ \hline 1566 \end{array}$$

4. Subtraction of five digit numbers without borrowing and with borrowing.

Same method should be used like subtraction of four digit numbers with and without borrowing.

5. Oral sums of addition and subtraction.

6. Multiplication of three digit numbers by two digit numbers.

$$709 \times 76 = ?$$

709 = 700 + 0 + 9

76 = 70 + 6

X	700	0	9
70	49000	0	630
6	4200	0	54

$$\begin{array}{r} 49000 \\ +\ 4200 \\ +\ 630 \\ +\ 54 \\ \hline 53884 \end{array}$$

7. Interrelationship between division and subtraction.

$$6 \times 7 = 42$$

$$42 \div 7 = \square \qquad 42 \div 6 = \square$$

8. Division of two digit numbers by one digit.

$$84 \div 4 = \square \qquad 4\overline{)84}$$

9. Mixed problems on addition and subtraction.

For example : There are 42,306 trees in a forest. Of these 23,479 are teak trees and 16,675 are other trees. How many other trees are there in the forest ?

10. Multiplication of three digit number by one digit number.

For example 300×7

X	300	10	5
70	2100	70	35

+	2100
+	70
	55
	2205

11. Word problems on division.

For example : If 40 children stand in 5 equal rows for a drill, how many children will be there in each row ?

Activity : Study the content of the area, "Operations on Numbers" of Std. 3.

---

(4) Area - Measurement :

Objectives :

1. Exchanges big coins and notes for smaller ones.
2. Uses the terms : A quarter past, half past and a quarter to.
3. Understands the calendar.
4. Understands the concept of length.
5. Understands the concept of kilometer.
6. Understands the concept of mass (weight).
7. Understands the concept of perimeter.
8. Understands the concept of area.

Content points :

1. Exchanging big coins and notes for smaller ones.

2. Use of terms like - A quarter to half past and a quarter past.
3. Calendar.
4. Length.
5. Kilometer.
6. Mass (weight).
7. Perimeter.
8. Area.

Core units of the content :

1. Constitutional responsibilities.
2. Removal of social evils.
3. Courtesy.
4. Dignity of labour.
5. Environment protection.
6. Secularism.
7. Model of small family.
8. Equality of men and women.
9. Sensitivity.
10. Neatness.

New words, concepts in the content :

1. Big coins and notes can be exchanged for smaller ones.
2. Small notes and coins can also be exchanged for bigger note or coins.
3. Quarter of an hour = 15 minutes.
   Half an hour = 30 minutes.
   Three quarters of an hour = 45 minutes.
4. Calendar :
   Leap year : When there are 29 days in February then it is a leap year. Leap year comes once in four years.
5. Length : Concept of measurement.
6. Kilometer : 1000 m = 1 km.
7. Mass (weight)
   Gram : Unit for measuring weights.

8. Perimeter : Sum of length of sides of a closed figure.

9. Area : On any surface, the measure of the place occupied by a figure is the area of that figure.

Activity : Study the content of "Measurement" of Std. 4.

(5) Area - Fractions :

Objectives :

1. Understands the meaning of fractions.
2. can read and write fractions.
3. Understands the concept of "Quarter".
4. Understands the concept of "three quarters".
5. Understands the concept of mixed fractions.
6. Understands comparing of fractions.
7. Understands fractions related to sets.

Content points :

1. Meaning of fractions.
2. Reading of fractions.
3. Writing of fractions.
4. Concept of "Quarter".
5. Concept of "Mixed Fractions".
6. Concept of "Three Quarters".
7. Mixed Fractions.
8. Comparing fractions.
9. Fractions related to sets.

Core units of the content :

1. Equality of men and women.
2. Neatness.
3. Secularism.
4. Environment preservation.
5. Model of small family.

New words, concepts in the content :

1. **Fraction :** When an object is divided into parts, each part is a fraction.

2. **Reading of fraction :** $\frac{1}{2}$ = One half.

3. **Quarter :** One part out of four of an item divided equally into four parts.

4. **Mixed fraction :** Fraction like $1\frac{1}{2}$ is a mixed fraction.

5. **Comparison of fractions :**

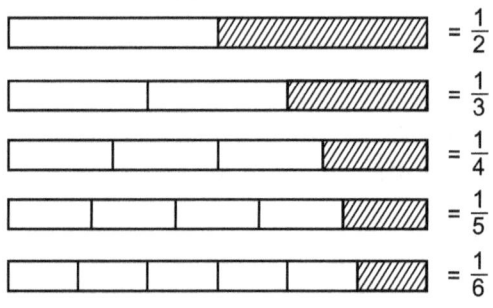

Fig. 3.2

Which is bigger ?

Which is smaller ?

6. **Fractions related to sets :**

<table>
<tr><td>●</td><td>●</td><td>●</td><td>○</td></tr>
<tr><td>●</td><td>●</td><td>●</td><td>○</td></tr>
<tr><td>●</td><td>●</td><td>●</td><td>○</td></tr>
</table>

Fig. 3.3

4 sets of 3 balls.

3 sets are coloured.

It means $\frac{3}{4}$ part is coloured $\frac{3}{4}$ of 12 is 9.

Activity : Study and write the content of "Fractions" of Std. 4.

(6) Area - Graph :

Objectives :

1. Understands the concept of pictographs.

2. Understands the information presented in the form of pictorial charts.

Content points :

1. Reading pictograph.

2. Answering questions given below pictographs.

Core units :

1. Protection of nature.
2. Equality among men and women.
3. Sensitivity.
4. Neatness.
5. Indian constitutional responsibilities.

New words and concept :

1. Pictorial chart : Chart having information in form of pictures.

(7) Area - Patterns :

Objectives :

1. Understands the geometric patterns.
2. Studies geometric patterns made from free hand shapes.
3. Understand the patterns in multiplication tables.

Content points :

1. Geometric patterns.
2. Geometric patterns from free hand shapes.
3. Patterns in multiplication tables.

Activity : Write the core units and content matter of this area.

Points to Remember

- Review means finding whether a textbook content is able to achieve the objectives.
- Review includes points like language, rules, definitions, concepts, figures, model examples and assignment.

Questions

1. Explain the importance of analysis of content.
2. What is the need of figures and diagrams in the content ?
3. "The language of the content should be exact and accurate"? Explain.

Assignments

1. What are the objectives-based criteria of a model textbook ?
2. What are the criteria of the external qualities of a model textbook ?

3. "The internal qualities of a textbook are the core of the book". Explain.

4. Write short notes on :

   (a) Importance of textbook.

   (b) Analysis of content.

   (c) Use of textbooks for parents.

   (d) Content of unit.

3.4.5 Importance and Usefulness of a Mathematics Textbook

Textbook plays an important role in the present-day teaching and learning of mathematics. What is to be taught and learnt in a particular class is entirely based on the prescribed textbooks of mathematics for that class. The textbook decides for the teacher his teaching, for the student his learning and for the examiner his examining task. Thus, care should be taken in the selection of proper textbooks and they should be used in a proper way. Then and then only, will the textbooks become useful to teachers, students and parents.

3.4.5.1 Usefulness for a Teacher

1. The textbook helps the teacher in planning his lessons, deciding his method of teaching and preparing suitable aids.

2. A textbook is written according to the syllabus. Therefore, it helps the teacher to decide about the limits and depth of the content to be presented to the students.

3. Content presented in the textbook is in a well organised and systematic form. Hence, the logical and psychological sequence followed in the textbook proves to be useful for the teachers.

4. A textbook is written by an experienced teacher of mathematics. A beginner teacher can avail the experience and expertise of authors.

5. Textbook of mathematics presents worked out or solved examples on each topic. It makes the task of a teacher easy as he becomes acquainted with different types of problems and

the method to solve them. This gives him more self-confidence while teaching.

6. The textbooks of mathematics, provides well-graded exercises after every topic. This helps the teacher in giving suitable assignments for practice and drill.

7. A textbook saves a lot of time for the teacher as he need not spend time to prepare problems and the solutions are available in the textbook.

8. Because of the textbook, a teacher remains on the track and thus teaches for the achievement of the objectives that are set up.

9. The task of paying individual attention to the students becomes quite simple to the teachers by making use of the textbooks.

3.4.5.2 Usefulness for a Student

1. The textbook helps the students, what they are learning to life.

2. The students come to know what is to be studied in a particular class. Clarity of objectives helps in maintaining interest in the study.

3. Textbook provides for important source of materials for the review and recapitulation of lessons taught in the class.

4. Textbooks help in pre-preparation. At their home, students may prepare themselves by studying for the next-day lessons.

5. Textbooks save the time and energy of the students. They need not copy the illustrative examples or problems written on the blackboard.

6. A textbook provides sufficient material for drill and practice and thus helps in fixing the mathematical principles and formulae in the minds of the students.

7. It encourages self-study and independent work among the students.

8. Sometimes students commit mistakes in copying the formulae, symbols, definitions and principles from the blackboard. Sometimes there are gaps due to their slow

writing or inability of quick understanding. In such times, a textbook helps a lot in supplementing as well as correcting the class notes.

9. New learning activities such as individual projects, laboratory experiments and demonstrations suggested in the textbook can be carried out by the students. It permits each student to read and carry out the activity at his own rate of comprehension.

10. Textbook provides opportunities for understanding, practicing and using the learned facts and inculcation of desired interests, habits and aptitudes in students.

3.4.5.3 Usefulness for the Parents

1. Textbooks also play an important role in guiding the parents. They come to know what content is being taught in the classroom.

2. Parents also come to know the progress of their child. They can find out by comparing their child's knowledge with that of given in the textbook. Thus, they come to know, how much their child knows.

3. They also come to know the portion given for examination and guide their child's study.

4. A parent has completed studies many years before that of his child. Hence in order to take study of his child, he must have recent knowledge. The textbook helps the parents in renovating their knowledge. Thus, the parents come to know about the recent and new teaching methods and new methods of solving examples.

5. Students have to appear for ability tests, skill tests, competitive exams. etc. Textbooks become foundation books and act as guide for parents.

Questions

1. Why is the textbook needed by students ?
2. What do mean by content analysis ?

3.5 Teaching and Learning of Mathematics : Methods and Techniques

Every subject included in the curriculum has distinct and unique aims. These aims give a direction for the education process. The aims of mathematics are related to the broad aims or goals of education.

(1) Utilitarian or Practical Aim :

Teaching of mathematics enables a student to have clear ideas about the number concept. An individual gets an understanding of the ideas and operations in numbers and quantity needed in daily life. He also gets a clear idea about how the number is applied to all measures particularly to those frequently used concepts such as length, volume, area, weight, temperature, speed etc.

Teaching of mathematics makes an individual proficient in the four fundamental operations of addition, subtraction, multiplication and division. This provides a basis of mathematical skills and processes which will be needed for vocational purposes. The learner acquires and develops mathematical skills and attitudes to meet the demands of daily life. He is also able to do work in related fields. All this helps the individual ultimately to apply his mathematics to a wide range of problems that occur in daily life.

(2) Disciplinary Aim :

Teaching and learning of mathematics inculcates the following disciplinary qualities in an individual :

(i) Independence and confidence.

(ii) Originality and creativity in thinking.

(iii) Exactness of thought and language.

(iv) Disciplining of mental faculties.

(v) Concentration.

(vi) Constructive imagination.

(vii) Use of reasoning power.

(viii) Systematic and orderly habits.

(3) Cultural Aim :

Mathematics helps an individual to appreciate the part played by mathematics in the culture of the past and that it continues to play a part in the present world. The individual also appreciates the role played by mathematics in preservation and transmission of our cultural traditions. Through mathematical ideas, an individual is provided, aesthetic and intellectual enjoyment and satisfaction. The mathematical ideas also give an opportunity for creative expression.

A student of mathematics appreciates various cultural arts like drawing, design-making, painting, poetry, music, sculpture and architecture. Thus, a learner can explore creative fields like art and architecture. Mathematics also develops an aesthetic awareness of mathematical shapes and patterns in nature as well as the products of our civilization.

Thus, mathematics creates an understanding, in the individual, about the contribution of mathematics in the development of culture and civilization.

(4) Social and Moral Aim :

Mathematics provides the individuals with a knowledge of science and technology which is necessary for adjusting the rapidly changing society and social life. It helps him in the formation of social laws and social order needed for social harmony. It enables a learner of mathematics to understand how the methods of mathematics, such as scientific, intuitive, deductive and inventive methods are used to investigate, interpret and to make decisions in human affairs.

Mathematics helps an individual to acquire an awareness of the mathematical principles and operations which will enable the individual to understand and participate in the general social and economic life of his community. Thus, mathematics helps an individual to acquire social and moral values to lead a fruitful life in the society.

3.5.1 Rules of Maths Technology
(Aims and Objectives)

All these aims are very broad and general in nature. It is practically impossible for a teacher to achieve these aims within a short span of school time. Also these aims do not fit in the framework of curriculum, for they involve a total programme of education including even out-of-classroom experiences. Thus, it becomes necessary to form objectives which are directed towards the aims. Objectives are more specific, precise and observable in nature. They are short-term goals and are attainable within the educational system. They are specific for each course and vary from course-to-course.

The term 'objective' may be defined as : *'An objective is an end point of the possible achievement in terms of what a student is able to do when the whole educational system is directed towards educational aims'.*

Thus, an objective is a statement of expected results. It is a description of the learning outcome that the teacher hopes to achieve from instruction. It is a statement of what the students must be able to do at the end of learning period which they could not do before hand. Thus, an objective is a part of an aim which the school can hope to achieve.

Objectives of Mathematics

(According to curriculum of primary education 1988)

(I) Objectives of Mathematics at Lower Primary Level i.e. (Std. 1 to 5) :

Following are the objectives of mathematics at lower primary level.

To enable the student :

1. To understand the concept of grouping, sub-grouping and concept of size and shape.

2. To understand number concept and symbols, their sequence and comparison.

3. To understand and correlate the four fundamental operations i.e. addition, subtraction, multiplication and division.

4. To acquire skill to solve oral and word problems based on whole numbers, vulgar fractions and decimal fractions.

5. To understand the concept of distance, time, weight, coins, area, volume, and capacity in daily life measurement.

6. To recognise the characteristics of geometrical shapes.

7. To understand basic idea of space and infinity.

Points to Remember

- The main aims of teaching of mathematics are utilitarian or practical aim, disciplinary aim, cultural aim and social and moral aim.
- Mathematics teaching inculcates certain important disciplinary values in a person.
- There are seven objectives of mathematics at lower primary level.

Activity 1 : Make a list of various competencies of mathematics at standard I level.

Activity 2 : Find out the relation between objectives and competencies.

Questions

1. What are the aims of teaching mathematics ?
2. Which disciplinary values are inculcated by the teaching of mathematics ?
3. What are aims and objectives ?
4. Explain the difference between aims and objectives.
5. What are the objectives of mathematics at the lower primary level ?
6. What are the objectives of mathematics at the higher primary level ?
7. What do you mean by objectives of mathematics ?
8. Which qualities are inculcated in an individual by learning of mathematics ?

3.5.2 Teaching Methods in Mathematics

There are various methods in teaching mathematics. They are not mutually exclusive and shade into each other. In the olden times, the individuality of the student was scarcely considered. But now-a-days, educationists have given importance to child centered approach of teaching. Freedom in the field of learning is the order of the day. Opportunity is provided for practical work and greater responsibility is thrown on the pupil. Thus, a student derives formulae, rules and principles and no stress is laid on memory work.

(I) Inductive and Deductive Methods :

(i) Inductive Method :

Inductive method takes into account induction. Induction is the process of proving a universal truth or theorem by showing that if it is true for any particular case, it is true for the next case in the same serial order and hence true for any such cases. Thus, it is a process which involves observations of enough cases so as to arrive a particular formula. A rule or a formula is generally accepted when it applies to a particular case and is applicable to other similar cases.

Therefore in this method, we proceed from particular to general, from concrete situations to abstract situations and from simple examples to complex formula.

While using this method, a student is required not to accept the already discovered formula without knowing how it has been discovered. They have to find it by adopting inductive reasoning.

Example : The sum of the angles in a triangle is 180°. A student measures the angles of different types of triangles. He finds that in each case, the sum is equal to 180°. Thus, he has sufficient background to realise that the sum of angles of a triangle is 180°.

Steps in Inductive Method :

1. Selection of a number of cases.
2. Observation of the case under given conditions.
3. Investigation and analysis.
4. Finding common relations.
5. Arriving at generation.
6. Verification or Application.

Merits of Inductive Method :

1. It helps understanding.
2. It is a logical method and develops critical thinking.
3. It encourages active participation of the students in learning.
4. It provides ample opportunities for observation.
5. It sustains the students' interest as they proceed from known to unknown.

6. It curbs the tendency of rate learning as it clears the doubts of students.
7. It facilitates meaningful learning.
8. It enhances self-confidence.
9. Students learn to find out the accurate conclusions.
10. If a student forgets a discovered rule, he can find it again.

Demerits of Inductive Method :

1. Its application is limited to very few topics in mathematics.
2. It is lengthy and time-consuming method.
3. This method is not suitable for higher classes as higher order mathematical principles cannot be generalised through observations of concrete cases.
4. It is not useful for practice.
5. Sometimes insufficient observations may lead to wrong generalisations.
6. This method only facilitates the formation of a rule or formula. Supplementary exercises are needed for fixation.
7. It makes mathematics lengthy and dull for gifted students.

(ii) Deductive Method :

It is the opposite of inductive method. It is based on deductive reasoning. It proceeds from general to particular, abstract to concrete and formula to problems. Deductive reasoning is the process of drawing logical inferences from established facts. In this method, the teacher presents the known facts or generalisation and draws inferences regarding the unknown. This approach is not suitable for exploration, but appropriate for a final statement of mathematical results. In this method, we began with a rule, formula or generalisation and apply it to a particular case. A pre-established formula is given to the students and they are asked to solve the relevant problems using that formula. It involves application of the formula problems.

The teacher announces the topics of the day and immediately gives a relevant formula. Then he explains the application of the formula by solving one/two problems on the board. The students understand how to solve the problems by using the formula. They are then given some more problems to solve by using the formula in the same way. The formula and the application are memorised for further use.

Example : We have to teach the topic, "Perimeter of Rectangle". The teacher starts by first telling the formula.

Perimeter of Rectangle = Sum of the length of all four sides
of the rectangle

$$= 2l + 2b$$

The teacher proceeds to explain what 'l' and 'b' stand for. The teacher then solves two examples. This is followed by students solving some more examples.

Steps in Deductive Method :

1. Clear recognition of the problem.
2. Search for tentative hypothesis.
3. Formulation of tentative hypothesis.
4. Verification.

Merits of Deductive Method :

1. It saves times and labour of both students and teachers. The solving of problems by pre-established formula takes little-time and effort.
2. It helps in increasing the memory power of students as students are required to memorize a large number of rules, formulae, laws etc.
3. It is adequate especially at the revision and application stage. It thus helps in fixation of the formula.
4. It is the complement of inductive method.
5. It increases speed, skill and efficiency in solving problems.
6. Rules and formulae can be applied by this method.
7. Discovering a formula is difficult for a student, the formula can be applied by just memorising it for use.

Demerits of Deductive Method :

1. It is not suitable for the beginners as it is difficult for a beginner to understand an abstract formula, if it is not preceded by a number of cases.

2. It demands blind cramming of formulae.

3. It does not cater to thinking, reasoning and discovery.

4. As it puts more emphasis on memory, the child's mind is burdened.

5. It does not clarify the doubts of the students regarding generalisation and hence learning is incomplete.

6. Once the formula or rule is forgotten, it is not possible for the students to rediscover.

Questions

1. What do you mean by inductive method ?

2. What do you mean by deductive method ?

(II) Analytic and Synthesis Method

(i) Analytic Method :

The word 'analytic' is derived from the word 'analysis' which means 'breaking-up'. Analysis means breaking-up of the problem in hand so that it gets connected with something already known. It is the process of opening-up or unfolding of the problem to know its hidden interior. We start with what is to be found out. Then we think of further steps to connect the unknown with the known. Hence, in this method can proceed from unknown to known, abstract to concrete and from complex to simple.

Algebraic identities and geometrical concepts can be explained by this method. In these cases, the problem is made-up of two parts i.e. known and unknown. The known part is called 'given' and unknown part is to be 'proved'. We start with unknown part as our starting point, analyse the statement of our problem, work out step-by-step requirements, connect the unknown with the known and conclude that the unknown stands proved.

Merits of Analytic Method :

1. It is a psychological method.

2. It leaves no doubts in the minds of the students as every step is justified.

3. It suits the learner as it facilitates understanding.

4. It involves active participation of students.

5. The student handles the problem intelligently and confidently as he is faced with a lot of questions.

6. It helps in developing the spirit of enquiry and discovery.

7. No cramming is needed.

8. As students participate actively, there is longer retention of knowledge and easy recall.

Demerits of Analytic Method :

1. It is lengthy, time-consuming and therefore not economical.

2. It is difficult to acquire speed and efficiency.

3. It is not suitable for all topics.

4. It is not beneficial for below average students.

5. Information is not permitted in well-organised manner.

(ii) Synthetic Method :

'Synthetic' is derived from the word 'Synthesis'. It means to combine. It is the opposite of analytic method. In this method, we start with something known and connect it with the unknown part. Thus, in this method we proceed from known to unknown. The usual forms of statements of proofs found in textbooks are examples of synthetic method.

Merits of Synthetic Method :

1. This method is logical as it proceeds from known to unknown.

2. It is a short and elegant method.

3. It facilitates speed and efficiency.

4. It is more effective for slow learners.

5. It glorifies memory as it involves cramming.

Demerits of Synthetic Method :

1. It leaves many doubts in the minds of the learner and offers no explanation for them.

2. It does not provide clarity and understanding.

3. There is no scope for discovery and enquiry.

4. Memorisation of homework is likely to be heavy.

5. As it does not justify all steps, recall of all the steps may not be possible.

6. If the student forgets the sequence of steps it would be difficult to write the proof.

Questions

1. What do you mean by Analytic method ?
2. What do you mean by Synthetic method ?

(III) Experimental Method :

It is also called as laboratory method. This is a method in which we try to make the students learn mathematics by doing experiments and laboratory work in the mathematics room or laboratory on the same lines as they learn sciences by performing experiments in the science rooms or laboratories.

Experimental method is a procedure to stimulate activities of students and encourage them to do discoveries. In this method, one proceeds from concrete to abstract. It provides a practical base to our inductive reasoning. It is based on principles such as "Learning by doing" and "Learning by observation". This process makes learning more interesting, lively and meaningful.

Experimental method can be used to teach geometry and arithmetic.

Example :

To calculate the area of a square :

1. Ask the students to take a square cardboard of 10 cms.

2. Let them divide the length and breadth into 10 equal parts vertically and horizontally. The square piece will be divided into 100 similar square pieces. $10 \times 10 = 100$.

3. Ask them to measure area of 1 square. It will be 1 sq. cm. In this way the area of 40 pieces will be 40 sq. cm.

4. The above experiment should be repeated with the help of other squares of different dimensions and the students derive the formula of area of a square whose sides are equal.

Merits of Experimental Method :

1. It is based on the principle of learning by doing.
2. It stimulates the interest of the students to work with concrete material.
3. It provides an opportunity for the students to verify the validity of mathematical rules through their application.
4. Knowledge and skills acquired through experiments help in better understanding and retention.
5. It develops self confidence and self-reliance in a student.
6. This method involves social interaction and co-operation among students.
7. Develops scientific outlook in students.

Demerits of Experimental Method :

1. It needs experience and requires lot of time and energy.
2. If teacher is not competent, there may be total chaos during teaching by this method.
3. Maintenance of laboratory needs more manpower and hence more staff.
4. Sometimes there is much expectation from the students which the students may not be able to fulfill.
5. Laboratory methods do not contribute towards mental development.
6. All topics cannot be taught by this method.
7. It is suitable for lower classes only.

Question

1. Write a detailed note on "Experimental Method".

(IV) Self Search Method :

It is also called a heuristic method. The term 'heuristic' is derived from Greek word 'Heurisco' which means 'I have found out' or 'I discover'. This method was originated by Professor H. E. Armstrong. He writes, "Heuristic method is the method of teaching which places the students as far as possible in the attitude of a discoverer".

Thus, heuristic or self search method aims to develop a heuristic attitude in the students. The student is not just a passive listener, but he changes into an active investigator. It is a method in which student discovers facts and information by himself. The method is based on the principle of learning by doing.

When a teacher uses this method, he puts a problem before the students. Each one is asked to solve the problem. The students have to perform the thinking. Teachers acts as a guide. The teacher only asks thought provoking questions that may lead the students to the solution of the problem. The tact lies in the manner of framing questions for example, a question such as, Is ABC a triangle ? is incorrect. One has to ask "What type of figure is this ?" The questions must be thought provoking.

Merits and Self Search Method :
1. The student becomes an active participant in the process of learning.
2. It develops a mathematical sense.
3. The teacher comes in close contact with the students. This helps in strengthening the teacher student relationship.
4. It is a psychologically sound method as it aims at utilising the constructive and active tendencies of the learner.
5. The student develops real understanding of the subject.
6. Student becomes self-reliant.
7. It emphasizes practical work and careful observation making the child independent thinker.
8. It develops scientific attitude.
9. Home study and cramming is reduced.

Demerits of Self-Search Method :
1. It demands extra time, labour and preparation on part of the overburdened teacher.
2. A child left on his own may not be able to discover certain things and he gets discouraged.
3. The self-search is slow in the beginning.
4. All topics cannot be covered by this method.

5. If students copy from the books, this method fails.

6. Teacher must be competent to frame good questions.

7. There is too much expectation from students and teachers.

8. As it is time consuming, the syllabus cannot be covered.

Questions

1. What do you mean by self search method ?

(V) Problem Solving Method :

Mathematics is a subject of problems. Problem solving is the main activity in the learning of this subject.

According to James Ross, "Problem solving is an educational device whereby the teacher and the pupils attempt in a conscious, planned and purposeful manner to arrive at an explanation or solution to some educationally significant difficulty".

The process of problem solving is a systematic and orderly process. The student is faced with a problem or a difficulty. The student has to think over the problem from all possible angles. Sometimes, at this stage, the student may not be able to find out the solution. But then he makes use of his previous knowledge and experiences and tries to find out the solution of problem.

Steps in Problem Solving :

1. Recognising the problem.

2. Defining the problem.

3. Collection of information.

4. Organising and evaluating data.

5. Formulating tentative solutions.

6. Arriving at correct solution.

7. Verification of results.

Merits of Problem Solving Method :

1. It allows the students to learn by self effort.

2. It prepares the student to solve, problems of future life.

3. It inculcates the habit of thinking and reasoning.

4. It develops and strengthens the student-teacher relationship.

5. It is a psychological method as it is child-centered.

6. The student becomes self-reliant and confident.

7. It takes into account individual differences as there are no limits on student achievement.

Demerits of Problem Solving Method :

1. It is not suitable for all students as all are not problem solvers.

2. It is time-consuming method.

3. Not all teachers can use this method effectively.

4. It becomes impossible to use this method in overcrowded classes.

5. It is not suitable for lower classes.

6. It demands a lot of preparation and study from the teachers.

Question

1. What do you mean by problem solving method ?

(VI) Demonstration Method :

Demonstration method involves the process of explaining "how to do or perform" certain activities. For example, while teaching geometrical constructions the teacher explains how to construct geometrical figure and at the same time she demonstrates how to carry out the construction following certain steps.

The demonstration method is used when the students have to learn the process from the teacher and also when it is not possible to allow students to perform some activity.

Following things should be kept in mind while using this method :

1. Explanation done during demonstration should be to the point.

2. Material should not be distributed to the students during demonstration.

3. Teacher should give adequate instructions to the students.

4. There should be correlation between explanation and action.

5. Teacher's activity must be visible for all students.

6. Teacher must make adequate preparations for arrangement of equipments.

7. Teacher should instruct the students on how to do observation.

8. Students must be instructed and pre-taught, how to write conclusions.

9. Teacher should keep all things in proper place after use.

10. Student activities should be supervised and given personal guidance.

Merits of Demonstration Method :

1. It is suitable for all students of varying abilities.

2. It is an economical method.

3. It encourages students', participation in learning.

4. It trains mental attributes of students.

5. It is a psychological method.

Demerits of Demonstration Method :

1. If method involves only demonstration by the teacher, then students do not get first-hand experience.

2. It caters only to the need of average students as clever students get bored by observing.

3. It cannot be applied for higher mathematics.

4. If students are not attentive, they fail to observe minute details of demonstration.

Question

1. What is the meaning of demonstration method ?

Points to Remember

- Teaching method is a planned scheme to achieve the teaching objectives.
- There are various types of teaching methods. They are all student centered.
- Inductive method is based on the principle of particular to general and concrete to abstract.
- Deductive method proceeds from general to particular and abstract to concrete.
- Analysis means 'breaking-up'. This method proceeds from unknown to known, abstract to concrete and complex to simple.

- Synthesis means 'to combine'. It proceeds from known to unknown and concrete to abstract.
- Experimental method provides practical base to inductive reasoning.
- Self search or Heuristic method changes a passive listener (student) to active investigator.
- Problem solving method is the main part of mathematics subject.
- Demonstration method involves the process of explaining "how to do".

For example, Standard I :

Addition of two digit number with one digit number.

Following type of criterion – test can be prepared for the unit – Addition of two digit numbers with one digit numbers (Nos. 1 to 20).

Question : Fill in the blank squares with correct answers by doing addition as shown in the solved example :

1. $15 + 2 = \boxed{17}$ 6. $16 + 3 = \square$

2. $11 + 8 = \square$ 7. $13 + 6 = \square$

3. $12 + 3 = \square$ 8. $15 + 3 = \square$

4. $14 + 5 = \square$ 9. $17 + 4 = \square$

5. $19 + 1 = \square$ 10. $12 + 2 = \square$

Mastery level/criterion : Students should solve at least seven problems. If student solves only 5 or less than 5, then remedial teaching is needed.

Question

1.	Explain the importance of criterion tests.

3.6 Planning in Teaching

Planning is a must for the successful completion of a task or project. It not only caters to the proper realisation of the aims of the task but also helps in proper utilisation of the time and energy on the part of human and material resources. The same is equally true for teaching-learning process.

The teachers who plan their work properly prove quite effective in their teaching job. That is why a mathematics teacher should concentrate on wise planning of his teaching.

The planning in teaching includes consideration of the following points :

1. Difficulty level of topics.
2. Age group of students.
3. Time available for teaching.
4. Periods which may be cancelled without notice.
5. Objectives.
6. Evaluation.
7. Available teaching aids.
8. Ability of students and individual differences.
9. Surrounding and environment.
10. Rural or Urban area.

3.6.1 Importance of Planning

1. It is necessary for the achievement of objectives.
2. For teaching of various concepts as most concepts of mathematics are abstract.
3. For the effectiveness of teaching methods.
4. For proper utilisation of time and energy.
5. For proper execution of a teaching task.

Need for Planning :

As there are various educational schemes for the educational development of a nation, so also every subject needs meticulous and proper planning. Thus, planning is needed for :

1. Completion of syllabus in specific time.
2. Deciding the difficulty level of a unit for effective teaching.
3. Achievement of specified units.
4. Decision of direction of teaching - learning process.
5. Measurement of student's progress.

6.   Teaching according to individual differences.

7.   Creating expected behavioural changes in students.

8.   Selection of suitable teaching methods and aids.

There are three types of planning :

1.   Annual Planning (Year Plan)

2.   Unit Planning.

3.   Lesson Planning.

3.6.2 Annual Planning

Annual Planning is done by the teacher at the beginning of the year for the entire course. In such type of planning, a teacher of mathematics tries to take a complete view of what he has to do in the whole session regarding the instructional work of a particular mathematics class.

For example, a teacher who teaches a course in mathematics for a particular class plans the curricular and co-curricular activities as per the syllabus for the entire academic year. Thus, we can define Annual Planning as follows :

Definition 1 : *"An annual plan is the planning of mathematics syllabus of the whole year for a particular standard"*.

Definition 2 : *"Annual plan is a sessional programme, that has to be chalked out by the teacher in his subject of teaching, with reference to teaching-learning activities to be carried out with his students"*.

3.6.2.1 Objectives of Annual Planning

To enable a teacher :

1.   Divide the number of periods according to the scope and difficulty level of units, in order to achieve the objectives of mathematics.

2.   To complete the syllabus in specific planned time for effective teaching.

3.   Select suitable teaching aids.

4.   Select suitable problems to inculcate specific values.

3.6.2.2 Points to be Considered for Annual Planning

A teacher has to prepare annual plan by keeping in mind the following points :

1. Confirming the number of periods : The total number of working days and weeks available for the teaching-learning subject have to be counted. Alongwith this, total number of periods available also has to be counted. All the long vacations, government holidays, examinations, unit tests, gathering trips, sport's competitions etc. also have to be considered because they have to be deducted from the total number of days.

For example, Std. V has single period for three days and a double period for two days. Thus, there are seven periods in a week.

Months	Weeks	Periods	Periods that may be cancelled	Available periods for teaching
June	3	3 × 7 = 21	–	21
July	4	4 × 7 = 28	–	28
August	4	4 × 7 = 28	3	25
September	4	4 × 7 = 28	2	26
October	3	3 × 7 = 21	2	19
November	1	1 × 7 = 07	07 (Half-yearly exam)	–
December	3	3 × 7 = 21	3	18
January	3	3 × 7 = 21	3	18
February	4	4 × 7 = 28	1	27
March	4	4 × 7 = 28	–	28
April	Final Examination			
Total	**33**	**231**	**21**	**210**

2. Unitwise division of periods : After the total number of periods are counted for the year, the units have to be allotted number of periods for completion of syllabus. The unitwise allotment of periods is based on the scope, difficulty level and total marks of that unit.

For example, standard V : No. of periods.

Numbers and Numeration	40 periods
Geometry	78 periods
Applied Mathematics	22 periods
Measurement and Mensuration	16 periods
Algebra	42 periods
Statistics	12 periods
Total	**210 periods**

3. Objectivewise allotting of periods : All the units should be divided according to the various objectives i.e. knowledge, comprehension, skill and application and periods allotted accordingly. While doing this, some periods must be kept for evaluation. The evaluation technique should be selected at the same time.

4. Selection of Educational activities : Various educational activities and projects should be selected in order to achieve the objectives and make teaching-learning joyful.

Thus, above four points should be kept in mind by a teacher while doing the Annual Planning.

ANNUAL PLANNING

Standard - Vth   **Subject – Mathematics**

Periods of a Week   **Total Periods**

Month	Week	Unit/ Subunit	Objectivewise periods			Educational activities	Evaluation technique	Total periods
Total								

3.6.2.3 Advantages of Annual Planning

1. It helps the teacher in planning of the entire course for the whole of the academic year.
2. It keeps the teacher on the right track.

3. It enables the teacher to cover the syllabus within the allotted time, as planning saves time and energy.

4. It helps the teacher in orderly and systematic teaching.

5. A teacher can arrange the units according to the changes in the surrounding.

6. Difficulties which may arise later on can be perceived and solved.

7. As the teacher comes to know the scope and difficulty level of an unit earlier, he learns to allot appropriate time for it.

8. Appropriate educational projects can be decided beforehand.

9. Previously done annual planning helps a teacher to eliminate his drawbacks in the new annual planning.

10. It gives a lot of self-confidence to the teacher as he is sure of what is expected of her during each period/week/month/term.

Activity 1 : Make a list of those units from the syllabus which are related with daily life.

Activity 2 : Which values can be inculcated from each unit ?

Activity 3 : Prepare an annual plan of the responsibility of some work given to you.

3.6.3 Unit Planning

3.6.3.1 **What is a Unit ?**

Preston defines unit as, "a large block of related subject matter as can be overviewed by a learner".

According to H.C. Morrison, "A unit consists of comprehensive series of related and meaningful activities so developed as to achieve pupil's purposes, provide significant educational experiences and results in appropriate behavioural changes".

Characteristics of a Good Unit :

1. A unit should be meaningful segments of well organised subject matter.

2. A unit can be broken into inter-related sub-units.

3. The segments in units should be linked together by a unifying idea or principle.

4. A unit should not be too lengthy or short.

5. A unit, after being taught, should bring about behavioural changes.

Unit planning is a part of annual plan.

Definition : Unit planning may be defined as 'a plan chalked out for the   teaching - learning of a particular unit, mentioning   the method of teaching with proper realisation of its objectives'.

3.6.3.2 **Need for Unit Planning**

1. To analyse the contents of the unit.

2. To explain the objectives of the content.

3. To explain and give information about the concept, rule, principle, formulae etc.

4. To understand the core-matter and values.

5. To select the educational activities, teaching aids and learning experiences.

6. To decide the direction of evaluation of content-cum-methodology.

3.6.3.3 **Steps in Unit Planning**

Unit planning involves the following steps or stages :

1. **Content Analysis [What to teach ?] :** After choosing the unit, the teacher has to do a detailed analysis of the contents of the unit to get detail knowledge of the terms, concepts, principles consisting the unit. This helps the teacher to break-up the units into meaningful sub-units and lessons retaining the continuity throughout the unit.

2. **Stating the general and specific objectives [Why to teach ?] :** The teacher should identify the general and specific objectives or learning outcomes to be achieved as a result of learning the unit.

3. **Selection of teaching methods [How to teach ?] :** Proper decision should be taken about the method and technique used for teaching the unit. Planning of the learning activities must be done suitably.

4. **Use of Teaching aids :** The fourth step is to carefully choose what type of teaching aids will be used while teaching. In order to give suitable learning experiences, suitable aids have to be selected.

5. **Evaluation Procedure :** The last stage of unit planning is to select appropriate evaluation tools and techniques to assess the content coverage, the realisation of the stated objectives and the effectiveness of teaching methods.

Proper decision should be taken for the evaluation of the unit covered. For this purpose, it is always better to prepare an unit test before hand. The time and resources needed for the administration of unit test should also be well decided.

3.6.3.4 Advantages of Unit Planning

1. Unit plan breaks-up a lengthy unit into smaller subunits so that pupils can easily grasp the scope of these during a brief overview.

2. It helps the teacher to present the various principles and concepts constituting the unit in an orderly and systematic manner, without losing the continuity.

3. It enables the pupils to see clearly the relationship between various facts, processes, and principles that make-up the unit.

4. It helps the teacher to plan a variety of learning experiences, keeping in mind the individual differences, the nature of the content and objectives to be achieved.

5. It provides various opportunities for the students to review and reorganize their learning.

6. It helps the teacher to plan definite outcomes of learning so that they are clear, not only to the teacher, but also to the students.

Activity 4 :	Discuss which examples of our daily routine are included in certain units of mathematics. Name the units and examples.
Activity 5 :	Select a unit from the syllabus of mathematics of any standard. Make a list of all the new concepts, formula, rules, definitions and terms from it.
Activity 6 :	Make a planning table of your daily routine work.

3.6.4 Lesson Planning of Content-Cum-Methodology

(1) Concept and Meaning

According to Good, "*A lesson plan is an outline of the important points of a lesson arranged in the order in which they are to be presented to students by the teacher*".

According to Bossing, "A lesson plan is the title given to a statement of the achievement to be realised and the specific means by which these are to be realised as a result of the activities engaged in during the period. It is the teacher's mental and emotional visualisation of the classroom experience as he plans it to occur".

Lesson planning of content-cum-methodology is the planning which involves consideration of the content, the core-matter, values, the objectives, teaching method, learning experiences and various teaching aids to teach a unit in one period.

(2) Need for Lesson Planning of Content-Cum-Methodology

This type of lesson planning is a new concept in this educational programme. Previously the way of presenting the content was given more importance, no matter what content it was. But the content and methodology are the two sides of a same coin. Both of them should not be separated. A need has arisen to keep the content at centre place and making use of an effective teaching technique to teach the unit effectively. Hence, lesson planning of content-cum-methodology has arisen.

According to Dr. H. N. Jagtap,

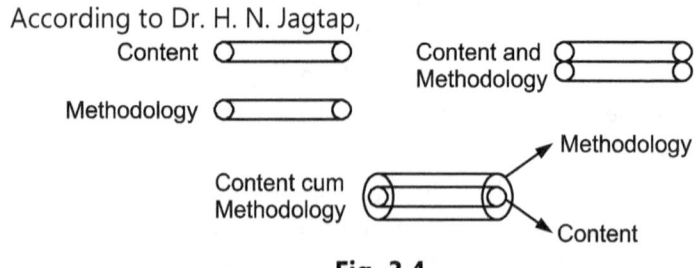

Fig. 3.4

(3) Importance of Lesson Planning of Content-Cum-Methodology

1. It makes the work of the teacher more regular, organised and systematic.

2. It delimits the teacher's field of work and thus enables him to define his aims and objectives more clearly.

3. It helps in consideration of objectives, selection of subject matter, selection of procedure, planning of activities and planning of evaluation devices.

4. It prevents waste of time as every step has been planned with forethought. Unnecessary repetition is avoided.

5. It creates self-confidence in a teacher as it paves way for the teacher to enter the class without anxiety.

6. It facilitates appropriate use of teaching aids at appropriate places.

7. It helps to pick and choose particular aspects that need emphasis.

8. It helps in providing drill and practice in mathematics.

9. It keeps the teacher on the right track as he is conscious of every step he has to take.

10. It helps the teacher to visualise student's difficulty and plan for remedial programmes.

(4) Points to be Considered for Lesson Planning of Content-Cum-Methodology

John Fredrick Herbart, a German Philosopher and educationist (1776-1841) advocated pedagogy - based lesson planning. Pedagogy means science of teaching. His approach is called as "Herbart's 5-point Approach." This approach to lesson planning involves the following steps :

1. Introduction
2. Statement of Aim
3. Presentation
4. Recapitulation
5. Assignment.

While writing the lesson plan, a student must know the objectives and its explanations. They are as follows :

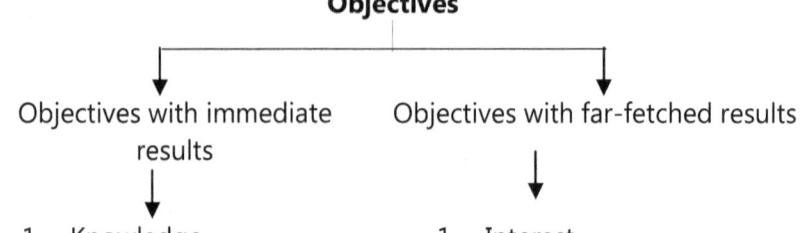

Objectives

Objectives with immediate results

1. Knowledge
2. Comprehension
3. Application
4. Skill

Objectives with far-fetched results

1. Interest
2. Mathematical Outlook
3. Appreciation

Care should be taken to write one objective per sentence.

(5) Objectives and Explanations of Mathematics Teaching

Objectives	Explanation of Objectives or Specific Learning Outcome
1. Knowledge : The pupil acquires knowledge of terms, symbols, concepts, definitions, principles, processes and formulae in mathematics.	The pupil, • recognises • recalls or reproduces concept/ term/etc. • defines • states theorems • lists properties
2. Comprehension : The pupil develops an understanding of terms, symbols, concepts, definitions, principles, processes and formulae.	The pupil : • gives examples • explains • describes • illustrates • gives reason for • establishes relation • detects errors • substitutes the values • identifies • compares • discriminates/distinguishes

	• classifies as per criteria
	• proves the result/theorem
	• estimates the result
	• translates verbal statements into symbolic form and vice versa.
	• interprets
	• infers
3. Application : The pupil applies knowledge and understanding of mathematics to unfamiliar or new situations.	The pupil : • analyses what is given and what is to be found out. • selects suitable method/ appropriate formula. • predicts. • judges the sufficiency of the given data. • formulates hypothesis. • suggests alternative method. • verifies the result.
4. Skill : (i) The pupil develops skill in drawing figures.	The pupil : • draws fairly accurate free-hand figures. • selects appropriate geometrical instruments. • handles geometrical instruments with ease. • measures with speed and accuracy. • constructs according to the given specification. • draws neatly and correctly.

(ii) The pupil develops skill in drawing graphs.	• tabulates correctly. • selects appropriate scale. • plots the points neatly and correctly. • draws the graph neatly and correctly. • interprets the graph correctly.
(iii) The pupil develops skill in reading table.	• reads the table correctly. • reads the table with speed and accuracy.
(iv) The pupil develops skill in computation.	• does oral calculation with speed and accuracy. • does written calculations with speed and accuracy. • does written calculations neatly.
5. Interest : The pupil develops an interest in mathematics.	The pupil : • reads literature on mathematics. • solves mathematical puzzles. • writes popular articles on mathematical topics for school magazines. • gives short cuts for solving problems. • does additional study in mathematics. • does problems which are not related to the syllabus. • participates in mathematics debates, quiz contest etc.

6. Positive Attitude : The pupil acquires a positive attitude towards mathematics.	The pupil : • likes his teacher of mathematics. • exhibits enthusiasm in learning mathematics. • promotes the activities of the mathematics club in the school.
	• enquires about TV programmes on mathematics. • listens with enthusiasm any talk on mathematics. • help students who are weak in mathematics. • engages in doing recreational activities such as doing puzzles, reading mathematical literature etc.
7. Mathematical Attitude : The pupil develops mathematical attitude through the study of mathematics.	The pupil : • accepts a proposition only when logically proved. • examines all aspects of a problem. • points out error boldly if convinced. • accepts errors without hesitation. • respects the opinions of others. • keeps on open mind and does not record any argument as final.

(6) Lesson Plan of Content-Cum-Methodology

(A) Initial Preparation :

Before writing a lesson plan initially, one has to do some of the following preparations :

(i) Analysis of syllabi of different standards.

(ii) Study and analysis of the scope of various concepts.

(iii) Classification and planning of various learning experiences according to the age of students.

(iv) Selection of teaching methods for explanation of various concepts.

(v) Preparation of various diagnostic tests according to standards.

(vi) Preparation of various remedial teaching schemes.

(B) Objectives of Lesson Planning :

(i) Planning of objectives for a single lesson according to the unit.

(ii) Laying more emphasis on skills because of student – centered methodology.

(C) Content :

(i) Content analysis has to be done.

(ii) Objectives according to the standards.

(iii) Teaching methods.

(iv) Techniques of teaching.

(v) Teaching aids.

(vi) Evaluation technique.

Above points can be arranged in columns.

(D) Learning Experiences and Teaching Methods :

(i) Learning experiences have to be selected according to the objectives.

(ii) Teaching method has to be selected according to the student's capacity, learning experiences and the content.

(E) Evaluation :

(i)   Evaluation should be objective based.

(ii) Evaluation should be continuous and comprehensive.

(iii) Evaluation should be based on learning experiences and teaching aids.

(iv) Evaluation should be activity based as well as knowledge based.

(v)   Evaluation should be followed by remedial teaching.

The lesson planning cum-methodology expects the teaching of one unit by three different methods or teaching of one unit to three different standards according to the depth and scope of the unit.

When a teacher teaches a unit by three different methods, she can choose a correct method from those methods. When a teacher teaches a same unit to three different standards, she has to think about the age, maturity, mental capacity of the students.

Sometimes this lesson planning-cum-methodology has some limitations. Sometimes the teaching in different standards is done not considering the capacities of the students. By using three methods, the teacher has to use one method out of it just for the sake of it. If these limitations are overcome, then the teaching according to content-cum-methodology will be lively.

Following is an example of Lesson Plan.

Name of the student teacher :

Roll No. :

Subject : Mathematics

Unit : Angle

Subunit : Drawing an angle of the given measure

Standard : V

Division : A

Number of Students : 40

Age Group of Students : 10 - 11 years

Time limit : 35 Minutes

Previous knowledge :

(i) Student knows properties of a parallelogram.

(ii) Student knows how to handle geometrical instruments.

Teaching method　:　Experimental method

Teaching aids　　:　Blackboard, cut-out of angle, Compass box.

Introduction　　:　Teacher shows cut-out of a angle and asks the students to identify it.

Teacher also asks students to measure of given angle.

Questions

1. Explain the meaning of annual planning and also state its importance.

2. Explain the meaning of unit planning and the various points to be kept in mind while doing unit planning.

3. "Annual planning does not become successful unless we do unit planning also". Discuss the statement.

4. Explain the meaning of unit planning and proceed to write an unit plan for any unit.

5. Explain the advantages of :

    (i) Annual Planning

    (ii) Unit Planning

    (iii) Lesson Planning

6. Which points should a teacher keep in mind while doing lesson planning ?

7. Prepare a lesson plan for unit of Standard IV.

8. Write short notes on :

    (i) Lesson planning of content-cum-methodology.

    (ii) Need for Annual planning.

3.6.5 Maxims of Teaching

Maxims of Teaching are the universally facts found out by the teacher on the basis of experience. The knowledge of different maxims helps the teacher to proceed systematically. It also help to find out his way of teaching, especially at the early stages of teaching.

The different maxims of teaching are as follows :

(a) From known to unknown: When a child enters into school, he possess some knowledge and it is the duty of teacher to enlarge his previous knowledge. Whatever he possesses should be linked with the new knowledge. If we link new knowledge with the old knowledge our teaching becomes clearer and more definite. This maxim facilitates the learning process and economises the efforts of the teacher and the taught. This way the teaching becomes definite, clearer and more fruitful.

(b) From simple to complex: The main objective of teaching is to teacher and the learner's objective is to learn something. In this process of teaching and learning, simple or easy things should be first presented to the students and gradually he should proceed towards complex or difficult things. The presentations of simple material make the learners interested, confident and feel encouraged. As they will show interest towards the simple material, they become receptive to the complex matter. On the other hand, if complex matter is presented first, the learners becomes upset, feel bored and finds himself in a challenging situation. For example, in mathematics we first explain the concept of addition, subtraction, multiplication and then division. When the student as he proceeds further he becomes familiar with the complex material like matrices, integration, differentiation etc. In this way a learner shows interest by proceeding from simple mathematics to complex one. Simplicity or complexity of the subject matter should be determined according to the view point of the students. It makes learning convenient and interesting for the students.

(c) From concrete to abstract: Concrete things are solid things and they can be visualized but abstract things are only imaginative things. The student understands more easily when taught through their senses and never forget that material. On the other hand if abstract things or ideas are presented, they forget it soon. Through this process, the students understand the materials more easily. Some power of imagination also develops in them. But if we reverse the situation, it will become difficult for learners to understand anything.

(d) From analysis to synthesis: When we divide a thing into easy parts or separate elements in order to understand it easily is called analysis. It is the process which helps in understanding the hidden elements of a thing or the cause of some incident or behaviour. For instance, in order to tell about the structure or functions of heart, the parts of the heart are shown separately and knowledge of every part is given. After it the students are made to understand the structure or system of working of the heart. In this way, even a very difficult thing can be easily understood. Synthesis is just opposite of analysis. All parts are shown as a whole. The process of analysis is easier than synthesis for understanding a thing. This process develops the analytical power of the students. It is the best method of starting the teaching process.

(e) From particular to general: A teacher should always proceed from particular to general statements. General facts, principles and ideas are difficult to understand and hence the teacher should always first present particular things and then lead to general things.

(f) From empirical to rational: Empirical knowledge is that which is based on observation and first and experience about which no reasoning is needed at all. It is concrete, particular and simple. We can feel and experience it. On the other hand rational knowledge is based upon arguments and explanations. This maxim is an extension of some of the previous maxims, namely proceed from simple to complex proceed from concrete to abstract and from particular to general.

(g) From induction to deduction: The process of deriving general laws, rules or formulae from particular examples is called induction. In it if a statement is true in a special situation, it will also be true in other similar situations. It means drawing a conclusion from set of examples. While using this process in teaching, a teacher has to present particular examples or experiences and tell about similarity of their attributes. Deduction is just opposite of induction. In it, we derive a certain particular conclusion from general laws, rules or principles.

(h) From psychological to logical: Modern education gives more emphases on psychology of the child. The child`s psychological development is of utmost important than any other thing. A teacher while teaching should follow this maxim viz from psychological to logical. Psychological approach takes into consideration the pupil his interests, abilities, aptitudes, development level, needs and reactions. The teacher should keep in mind the psychological selection of the subject matter to be presented before the pupils. Logical approach considers the arrangement of the choosen content into logical order and steps. It is student centered maximum.

(i) From Actual to Representative: First hand experiences makes learning more vivid and efficient than to give them representative ones. A teacher while selecting the content for presentation should make all efforts possible to present it through actual, natural or real objects than from their improvised representative one's like pictures, models etc. Representative forms should be used at the higher classes than in lower classes.

(j) From Whole to Parts: This maxim is the offshoot of gestalt theory of learning whose main emphasis was to perceive things or objects as whole and not in the form of parts. Whole is more understandable, motivating and effective than the parts. In teaching, the teacher should first give a synoptic view of lesson and then analyze it into different parts.

(k) From definite to indefinite: A teacher should always start from definite because definiteness has its limited boundaries and jurisdiction than indefinite things. We always have confidence on definite and tested things. We learn easily indefinite things on the basis of definite things. Hence a teacher while teaching any content should first present definite things, concepts and then he can learn indefinite things easily. Definite things, definite rules of grammar help the learner to have good knowledge. Gradually he can be taught about indefinite things.

3.7 Teaching Techniques in Mathematics

3.7.1 Question-Answer/Questioning Technique

Good questioning techniques have long being regarded as a fundamental tool of effective teachers. Unfortunately, research shows that 93% of teacher questions are "lower order" knowledge based questions focusing on recall of facts (Daines, 1986). Clearly this is not the right type of questioning to stimulate the mathematical thinking that can arise from engagement in open problems and investigations. Many Primary teachers have already developed considerable skill in good questioning in curriculum areas such as Literacy and History and social studies, but do not transfer these skills to Mathematics. Teachers' instincts often tell them that they should use investigational mathematics more often in their teaching, but are sometimes disappointed with the outcomes when they try it. There are two common reasons for this. One is that the students are inexperienced in this approach and find it difficult to accept responsibility for the decision-making required and need a lot of practise to develop organised or systematic approaches. The other reason is that the teachers have yet to develop a questioning style that guides, supports and stimulates the children without removing the responsibility for problem-solving process from the children.

Types of Questions

Within the context of open-ended mathematical tasks, it is useful to group questions into four main categories. These questions can be used be the teacher to guide the children through investigations while stimulating their mathematical thinking and gathering information about their knowledge and strategies.

1. Starter Questions or Beginning Question:

These take the form of open-ended questions which focus the student's thinking in a general direction and give them a starting point. For example, The questions ask at starting of following type :

1. What can be made from....?
2. How many different .... can be found?

3. How many ways can you find to .... ?

4. What happens when we .... ?

5. How could you sort these.......?

2. Questions to Stimulate Mathematical Thinking :

These questions assist student to focus on particular strategies and help them to see patterns and relationships. This aids the formation of a strong conceptual network. The questions can serve as a prompt when children become 'stuck'.

For example :

1. What is different?

2. What do think comes next? Why?

3. What would happen if....?

4. Is there a way to record what you've found that might help us see more patterns?

5. How can this pattern help you find an answer?

6. What is the same?

7. Can you group these items in some way?

8. Can you see a pattern?

3. Assessment Questions :

Questions such as these ask student to explain what they are doing or how they arrived at a solution. They allow the teacher to see how the children are thinking, what they understand and what level they are operating at. Obviously they are best asked after the children have had time to make progress with the problem, to record some findings and perhaps achieved at least one solution.

Examples:

1. Why do you think that?

2. How did you find that out?

3. What have you discovered?

4. What made you decide to do it that way?

4. Final Discussion Questions:

These questions draw together the efforts of the whole class and prompt sharing and comparison of solutions and strategies. This is a vital phase in the mathematical thinking processes. It provides further opportunity for reflection and realisation of mathematical ideas and relationships. It encourages children to evaluate their work.

Examples:

1. Why/why not?
2. Are everybody's results the same?
3. Have we found all the possibilities?
4. How do we know?
5. Have you thought of another way this could be done?
6. Do you think we have found the best solution?
7. Who has the same answer/ pattern/ grouping as this?
8. Who has a different solution?

Levels of Mathematical Thinking

Another way to categorise questions is according to the level of thinking they are likely to stimulate, using a hierarchy such as Bloom's taxonomy (Bloom, 1956). Bloom classified thinking into six levels:

1. Memory,
2. Comprehension,
3. Application,
4. Analysis,
5. Synthesis, and
6. Evaluation.

Sanders separated the Comprehension level into two categories, Translation and Interpretation, to create a seven level taxonomy which is quite useful in mathematics. As you will see as you read through the summary below, this hierarchy is compatible with the four categories of questions already discussed.

1. **Memory:** The student recalls or memorises information.
2. **Translation:** The student changes information into a different symbolic form or language.

3. **Interpretation:** The student discovers relationships among facts, generalisations, definitions, values and skills.

4. **Application:** The student solves a life-like problem that requires identification of the issue and selection and use of appropriate generalisations and skills.

5. **Analysis:** The student solves a problem in the light of conscious knowledge of the parts of the form of thinking.

6. **Synthesis:** The student solves a problem that requires original, creative thinking.

7. **Evaluation:** The student makes a judgement of good or bad, right or wrong, according to the standards he values.

Combining the Categories

The two ways of categorising types of questions overlap and support each other.

For example, the questions as follows :

1. Do you think we have found the best solution? encourage Evaluation.
2. Have you thought of another way this could be done?
3. How do we know?
4. How did you find that out?
5. How can this pattern help you find an answer? relate to Interpretation, and; the questions
6. Can you see a pattern?
7. What have you discovered?
8. Why do you think that? require Analysis, and; the questions:
9. Have we found all the possibilities?

In process of working with teachers on this topic, a table was developed which provides examples of generic questions that can be used to guide student through a mathematical investigation, and at the same time prompt higher levels of thinking.

Eight Tips for Asking Effective Questions:

1. Anticipate student thinking.
2. Link to learning goals.

3. Pose open Questions.

4. Pose questions that actually need to be answered.

5. Incorporate verbs that Elicit higher levels at bloom's taxanomy.

6. Pose questions that open-up the conversation to include others.

7. Keep Questions Neutral.

8. Provide wait time.

3.7.2 Revision Technique (Assignments)

Assignment is an important part of teaching. It is a good way of encouraging students to do independent work. Certain amount of teaching time should be allotted for assignments.

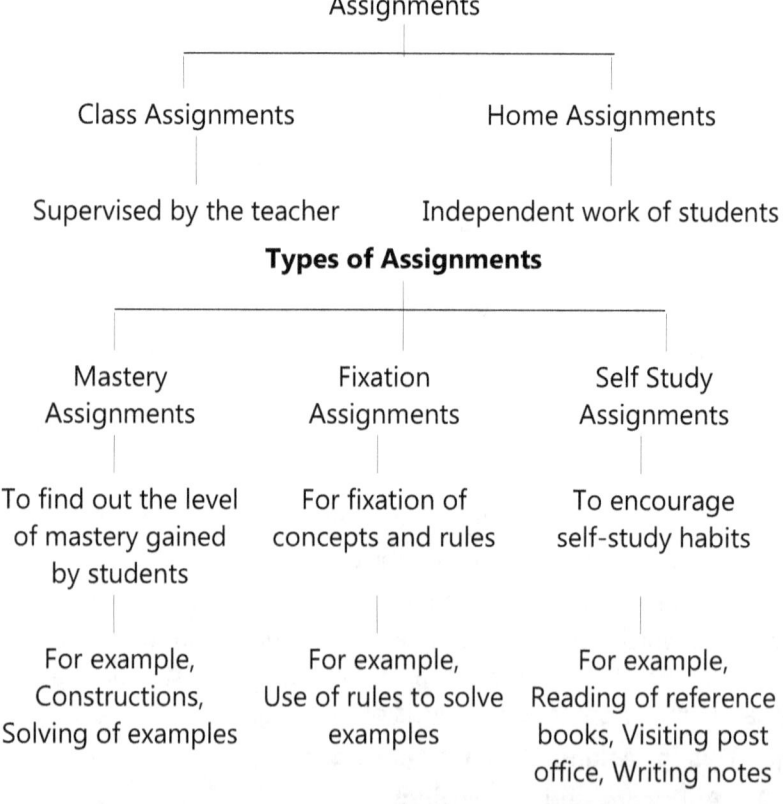

Sometimes assignments can also be given as group assignments. A group of students work collectively to work out the assignment.

Criteria of a Good Assignment :
1. Assignment should be related to topic under study.
2. It should have clear cut objectives.
3. Assignment should stimulate self-study and reflective thinking.
4. Assignment should be brief and to the point.
5. Language should be understood by students.

Steps in Giving Assignments :
1. Planning of assignment.
2. Presentation.
3. Accessing students understanding.
4. Supervising assignment.
5. Evaluation.

Advantages/Uses of Assignment :
1. It helps the teaching-learning, process.
2. It helps in measuring student's progress and achievements.
3. Differentiated assignments help in judging the pupil's understanding.
4. Assignments motivate further learning.
5. Students can learn at their own pace.

3.7.3 Supervise of Study Technique

Supervised study means study under supervision. When the learning activities are properly organised under the supervision of the teachers, it is called supervised study.

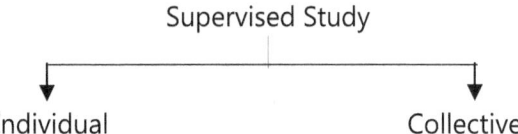

This means self study or group study may take form of supervised study. The students have to consult their teachers for planning and performing certain learning activities. The teacher acts as a guide. All the students in the group of supervised study are of different mental abilities. Because of this, their way and capability of learning also differs. The difficulties faced by each of student may also be different and of various levels. Whatever is taught in the class may leave some unanswered questions in the minds of the students. These problems can be solved during supervised study. Instead of doing the homework or assignment at home, the student does it under the guidance of teachers in supervised study.

Objectives of Supervised Study :

1. To inculcate good study habits in students. To inculcate self-study habits in students.
2. To give personal attention and solve the difficulties of students.
3. To reduce the load of some assignments.
4. To find out the difficulties and arrange for remedial teaching.

Merits of Supervised Study :

1. Provides organised supervision on work of students.
2. Students get proper guidance at proper time.
3. Develops good relationship among teachers and students.
4. Inculcates habit of systematic work.
5. Reduces chances of wastage and stagnation.
6. Encourages self learning in students.
7. Builds self confidence in students.
8. Irresponsible students, who do not do their homework regularly, can be properly looked after.

Demerits of Supervised Study :

1. Demands too much work from the teacher.
2. Crowded classes may not show successful results.
3. Too much guidance may spoil the habits of students or non-availability of guidance may discourage them.
4. Supervision done only for finding faults is incorrect. Teachers should have correct attitude of supervised study.

3.7.4 Diagnostic Test

Diagnostic tests measure students' understanding of a subject area or skills base. Teachers typically administer diagnostics for reading and math skills, using the results to provide remedial instruction or place students within appropriately leveled classes. Many content teachers, though, give formative assessments to gauge what knowledge students bring to class. Some schools also diagnose concepts as a whole, aiming to reveal commonly held misconceptions in specific subjects.

Diagnostic testing in mathematics typically provides a level for the child's mathematical skills in this case not just related to grade level but also math topic. Schools often use such diagnostic testing to place students in appropriate math classes, for instance, by determining if they have the prerequisite skills necessary for a higher-level class such as calculus or trigonometry. However, educators use math diagnostics to boost student achievement by encouraging high achievers and offering remedial instruction, including summer school programs, to those who are struggling.

3.7.5 Remedial Teaching, Feedback

The Process of Remedial Teaching can be describe with the help of flow chart as given below which is very useful/helpful for teachers in the individual teaching.

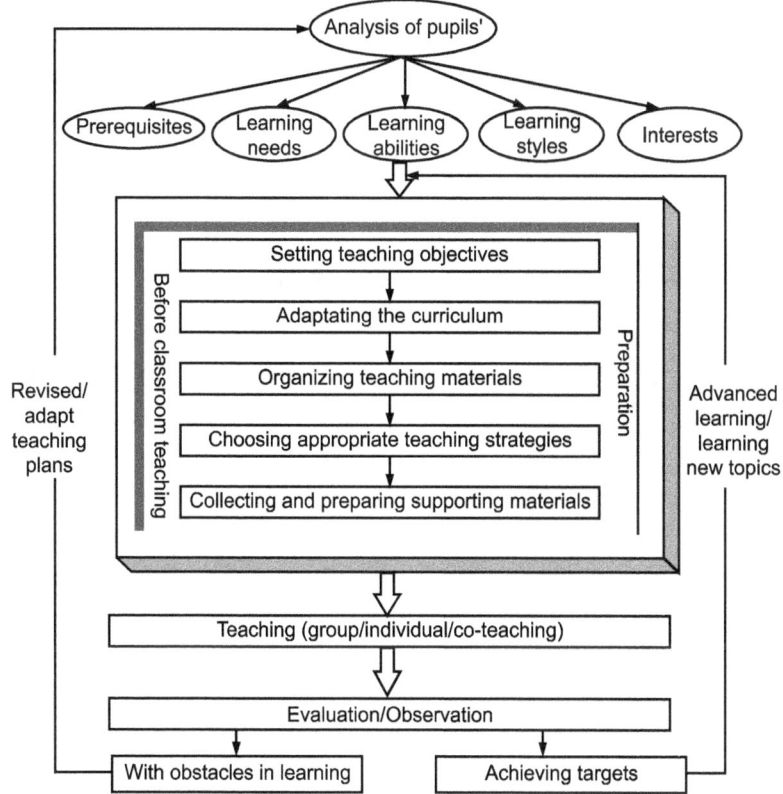

Objectives of Remedial Teaching :

1 Each pupil is different in terms of learning ability, academic standards, classroom learning and academic performance, and each has his own in learning. The aim of IRTP is to provide learning support to pupils who lag far behind their counterparts in school performance. By adapting school curricula and teaching strategies, teachers can provide learning activities and practical experiences to students according to their abilities and needs. They can also design individualized educational programmes with intensive remedial support to help pupils consolidate their basic knowledge in different subjects, master the learning methods, strengthen their confidence and enhance the effectiveness of learning.

2. Throughout the teaching process, teachers should provide systematic training to develop pupils' generic skills, including interpersonal relationship, communication, problem-solving, self-management, self-learning, independent thinking, creativity and the use of information technology. Such training can lay the foundation for pupils' life-long learning, help them develop positive attitudes and values, as well as prepare them for future studies and career.

3.7.6 Computer Assisted Teaching

The impact of computers on *teaching* and *learning* activities at all levels of education is considerable, and the extent of use increases as computers become more convenient to use and less expensive to purchase and maintain. Every area of post-secondary education is affected. A medical student practices diagnosis and prescription on a wide variety of hypothetical patients simulated by computer programs. A group of engineering student's uses computer assistance to solve problems in analysis and design that otherwise would not be approachable. A student aide develops a program to help a professor of mathematics evaluate the effectiveness of questions on a multiple-choice quiz.

Points to Remember

- Teaching method is a planned scheme to achieve the teaching objectives.
- There are various types of teaching methods. They are all student centered.
- Inductive method is based on the principle of particular to general and concrete to abstract.
- Deductive method proceeds from general to particular and abstract to concrete.
- Analysis means 'breaking-up'. This method proceeds from unknown to known, abstract to concrete and complex to simple.
- Synthesis means 'to combine'. It proceeds from known to unknown and concrete to abstract.
- Experimental method provides practical base to inductive reasoning.
- Self search or Heuristic method changes a passive listener (student) to active investigator.
- Problem solving method is the main part of mathematics subject.
- Demonstration method involves the process of explaining "how to do".

3.8 Retention of Technological Process of Mathematics

3.8.1 Mathematics Laboratory

In our schools, laboratories are generally meant for science subjects. But we should not forget that mathematics subjects are also a science and every science should have a laboratory. Thus, a mathematics laboratory should be there in all schools. A mathematical laboratory should have the following equipments and materials :

1. Different types of pictures and charts.
2. Models.
3. Measuring equipments.

4.   Drawing instruments.

5.   Bulletin Board.

6.   Blackboard.

7.   Concrete materials such as beads, balls etc.

8.   Computing devices like calculator and computers.

Advantages of Mathematics Laboratory :

1.   It makes mathematics more interesting.

2.   It enables students to develop proper skills of handling equipments.

3.   It provides safe and proper place for placing all equipments.

4.   It gives proper opportunity for students to satisfy their urge of mathematics experiments.

5.   Gifted children are more happy in a mathematical laboratory.

6.   Students develop the power of observation.

3.8.2 Mathematics Club

Mathematics club plays an important role in the students life as it provides a good opportunity for the students to express themselves and work differently. In this club more importance is given to the students. All the activities are chosen by the student. It is run by the students under the guidance and observation of the teacher.

Organisation of Mathematics Club :

President	:	A senior most mathematics teacher or the principal
Vice President	:	Mathematics teacher
Treasurer	:	Senior student
Programme Secretary	:	Student
Members	:	8 to 10 students

Objectives of mathematics club :

1.   To help the student in proper utilisation of leisure time.

2.   To help in arousal of interest in mathematics.

3.   To provide a healthy social atmosphere.

4. To help student to inculcate qualities like co-operation and adjustment.

5. To provide for exchange of mathematical ideas.

6. To provide good platform for students.

7. To supplement classroom teaching.

8. To engage students of field work.

Activities of Mathematics Club

1. Conducting individual or group projects.

2. Writing articles related to mathematics.

3. Organising lectures and seminars of experienced and learned teachers.

4. Arranging for watching of T.V. programmes.

5. Organising workshops in mathematics.

6. Organising recreational activities like mathematical puzzles, riddles, games etc.

7. Organising mathematical fairs and exhibitions.

8. Helping in maintenance of mathematics library.

9. Preparing charts, models etc. for the mathematics laboratory.

10. Publication of newsletter and bulletin of the club.

11. Organising inter-school and inter-class competitions of mathematics.

12. Celebration of historical mathematical days.

3.8.3 Mathematical Fair

A mathematical fair is sort of exhibition which can be held at the centre of the city or any other main area or school and where many schools come together, to exhibit their mathematical aids and devices. There are various games based on mathematics, various mathematical competitions and lectures. Thus, a student can enjoy all these in a mathematical fair.

Objectives of Mathematical Fair :

1. To provide rich and meaningful experiences to the students.

2. To elicit meaningful responses from the students as they actually participate in various activities.

3. To develop mathematical attitude.

4. To provide suitable chances for the students to prove their ability.

5. To improve the interrelation between the schools, teachers, students and parents.

6. To make use of leisure time.

7. To inculcate creativity in students.

8. To enable, all to know the various devices of mathematics.

9. To create feeling of responsibility in students.

10. To provide a better link between school and community.

3.8.4 Arranging Maths Fair

Many school programs are broadcast on the radio. These programs are preplanned and the planning is sent to different schools in advance. These programs are based on all subjects for all standards. As the leaflet of planning is sent beforehand, a teacher comes to know which program will be broadcast on a particular day, for which standard, of which subject and what time. These lessons are taken by experienced teachers who have a good voice for explanation or lecture. Thus, it becomes a model lesson. These programs are broadcast two times, once before the school begins and second, during the school time. The main aim is that, the teacher should listen first, prepare for that lesson, prepare students also for that lesson, test their previous knowledge etc. Then the students can listen during the school time. Thus, lessons taken on the radio are a joyful experience both for the teachers and the students.

3.8.5 Compact Disc

Compact disc CD is a type of format of optical disk. Optical disc is a type of storage media. The CD format is most widely used today. CD drives are standard on many computer systems. CDs can store from 650 MB (mega bytes) to 1 GB (giga byte) of data on one side. In other words, it can store about 60 - 65 crore words.

One important characteristic of CDs is their rotational speed. This speed is important because it determines how fast data can be transferred from the CD.

3.8.6 Teleconference

The planning of teleconference is done similar to the planning of radio programmes. Teleconference is organised and telecast through satellites. Many people are benefitted at a time.

A teleconference is such a technique in which the student under training can discuss any point or ask any difficulty to the guide or lecturer, while the programme is being telecast online. Through this medium, the person under training can observe and hear the lecturer on T.V. through the satellite.

The first educational satellite ATS - F was sent by America. This satellite was first used for India on 1st August, 1975. The first satellite programme was called SITE i.e. satellite instruction television experiment. This SITE programme was for the year 1975 - 76.

Activity 4 :	Arrange a workshop in your school for any topic.
Activity 5 :	Arrange group discussion on any topic of your own choice.
Activity 6 :	Arrange for viewing of any educational C.D.

3.8.7 Teaching-learning Process of Mathematics with Fun

A critical challenge in improving the quality of mathematics education is in motivating students to take interest in studies in the presence of easy availability of alternate recreational activities that are perceived as enjoyable. Recreational mathematics identifies math activities including puzzles that can be enjoyed by adults and children. The Sudoku puzzle is a very good example of this. At present, such puzzles have a very limited role in classrooms because there are only a small number of math lessons that can be taught with these puzzles. Puzzle problems are particularly suitable for teaching creative problem solving. Puzzle problems are often hard enough and require application of a variety of problem solving strategies. Reflecting on the process permit further learning about mathematics.

Mathematics subject can be taught with different ways, like :

(i)   Mathematical puzzles.

(ii) Mathematical games.

(iii) Magic in mathematics OR Mathematical magic.

3.8.7.1 Mathematical Puzzles

Mathematical puzzles' make an integral part of recreational mathematics. They have specific rules as do multiplayer games, but they do not usually involve competition between two or more players. Instead, to solve such a puzzle, the solver must find a solution that satisfies the given conditions. Mathematical puzzles require mathematics to solve them. Logic puzzles are a common type of mathematical puzzle.

Many of the puzzles are well known because they were discussed by Martin Gardner in his "Mathematical Games". Mathematical puzzles are sometimes used to motivate students in teaching elementary school math problem solving techniques.

List of some types of mathematical puzzles :

1.   Numbers, arithmetic and algebra.

    (i)   Cross-figures or cross number puzzle.

    (ii) Four fours.

    (iii) Verbal arithmetics.

    (iv) Dyson numbers

2.   Combinatorial

    (i)   Cryptograms - N-puzzle/Fifteen puzzle.

    (ii) Sudoku

    (iii) Tower of Hanoi

3.   Analytical or differential - Ant on a rubber rope.

4.   Probability - Monty Hall problem.

Completed puzzles are always a type of Latin square with an additional constraint on the contents of individual regions. For example, the same single integer may not appear twice in the same 9×9 playing board row or column or in any of the nine 3 × 3 sub-regions of the 9×9 playing board.

The puzzle was popularized in 1986 by the Japanese puzzle company Nikoli, under the name Sudoku, meaning *single number*.

Example 1 : Solve the following puzzle.

5	3			7				
6			1	9	5			
	9	8					6	
8				6				3
4			8		3			1
7				2				6
	6					2	8	
			4	1	9			5
				8			7	9

Solution :

5	3	4	6	7	8	9	1	2
6	7	2	1	9	5	3	4	8
1	9	8	3	4	2	5	6	7
8	5	9	7	6	1	4	2	3
4	2	6	8	5	3	7	9	1
7	1	3	9	2	4	8	5	6
9	6	1	5	3	7	2	8	4
2	8	7	4	1	9	6	3	5
3	4	5	2	8	6	1	7	9

Example 2 : What patterns do you observe in the table below ?

Numbers	Product
4, 3, 25	300
4, 4, 25	400
4, 21, 25	2100
4, 28, 25	2800
4, 18, 25	1800

Solution : (i) To look for patterns, look for similarities between entries in each row and for similarities between different columns. We observe that the product is the same as the middle number followed by 0. In general, if we have a product of a series of numbers that includes 2 and 5, then do the following: (a) replace 2 and 5 by 10, (b) multiply the rest of the numbers (c) multiply the product by 10.

Because multiplying by 10 can be done easily by adding a zero at the end of the number, this re-ordering allows us to do the multiplication faster.

(ii) 120

(iii) 720

(iv) 180

(v) 300

(vi) To look for patterns, look for similarities between entries in each row and for similarities between different columns. We observe that the product is the same as the middle number followed by 00. In general, if we have a product of a series of numbers that include 4 and 25, then do the following: (a) Replace 4 and 25 by 100. (b) Multiply the rest of the numbers (c) Multiply the product by 100. Because multiplying by 100 can be done easily by adding two zeros at the end of the number, this re-ordering allows us to do the multiplication faster.

Questions

1. What patterns do you observe in the table below ?

Numbers	Product
2, 3, 5	30
2, 4, 5	40
2, 21, 5	210
2, 28, 5	280
2, 18, 5	180

Now, try the following products using the pattern you observed.

2. $2 \times 3 \times 4 \times 5$

3. $2 \times 3 \times 4 \times 5 \times 6$

4. $2 \times 3 \times 5 \times 6$

5. $2 \times 2 \times 3 \times 5 \times 5$

3.8.7.2 Mathematical Games

A **mathematical game** is a game whose rules, strategies, and outcomes are defined by clear mathematical parameters. Often, such games have simple rules and match procedures, such as Tic-tac-toe and Dots and Boxes. Generally, mathematical games need not be conceptually intricate to involve deeper computational under-pinnings.

For example, even though the rules of Mancala are relatively basic, the game can be rigorously analyzed through the lens of combinatorial game theory.

Mathematical games differ sharply from mathematical puzzles in that mathematical puzzles require specific mathematical expertise to complete, whereas mathematical games do not require a deep knowledge of mathematics to play. Often, the arithmetic core of mathematical games is not readily apparent to players untrained to note the statistical or mathematical aspects.

Some mathematical games are of deep interest in the field of recreational mathematics.

When studying a game's core mathematics, arithmetic theory is generally of higher utility than actively playing or observing the game itself. To analyze a game numerically, it is particularly useful to study the rules of the game insofar as they can yield equations or relevant formulas. This is frequently done to determine winning strategies or to distinguish if the game has a solution.

3.8.7.3 Magic in Mathematics

Look at the following examples :

Example 1 : Favourite number = 5

$5 \times 2 = 100$

$10 \times 5 = 50$

50 ... drop the zero = 5!

Example 2 : Favourite number = 32

$32 \times 2 = 64$

$64 \times 5 = 320$

320 ... drop the zero = 32!

Mathematical magic is also a process of learning with magic. This types of magical examples are also given in mathematics text book. For example, see the following magical box.

2	9	4
7	5	3
6	1	8

There are nine parts in a square with number 1 to 9. If you observe this box carefully then we get the addition of number's horizontally, vertically or diagonally both are equal i.e. 15.

All additions are equal is a magic.

In this way we can prepare a magical box or table with different numbers with different operations such as - multiplication, division. In this way you can teach mathematics to students with the help of magic of geometric shapes also.

| **Activity 15** : Arrange a workshop in your school for any topic. |
| **Activity 16** : Arrange group discussion on any topic of your own choice. |
| **Activity 17** : Arrange for viewing of any educational C.D. |

3.8.8 Vedic Mathematics : Introduction

Other than counting, addition is perhaps the most basic mathematical operation. As such there are relatively few techniques to improve its efficiency, those techniques that exist are basically ways to organise the calculation to make it simpler to compute mentally. Subtraction is similar, but in this case there are also some techniques to help with the carry/borrow process which unlike addition can run across multiple digits. You will no doubt already use most of the addition and subtraction techniques described here intuitively without thinking about them, many of the techniques may seem to be so basic that they don't deserve explanation, but it is worth re-iterating them even if just to make you aware that you are probably already using techniques that can be expanded upon to improve your arithmetic ability.

Memory versus Calculation :

It is a basic fact of arithmetic that the more you memorise the less you have to calculate. The first thing you learn about numbers is how to count. You can think of this as the ability to add one to any number.

For example : $0 + 1 = 1$, $4 + 1 = 5$, $7 + 1 = 8$, $9 + 1 = 10$, $10 + 1 = 11$, $19 + 1 = 20$, $56 + 1 = 57$. You instinctively know the answer to these sums, they have been memorised from an early age by repeatedly counting from 1 to 100.

Once you have learnt to count, you learn to add by counting, that is, repeatedly adding one (at first often using your fingers). Indeed addition is implicitly defined as the repeated addition of one.

For example, Add 6 + 3

$$6 + 3 = 6 + 1 + 1 + 1$$
$$= 7 + 1 + 1$$
$$= 8 + 1$$
$$= 9$$

It is not long before you have memorised the results of adding smaller numbers so you no longer have to count, (on your fingers or otherwise!), to find the answer to simple additions.

This pattern repeats itself again and again. When learning a new arithmetic operation, you initially learn how to perform it, then after practising you tend to memorise the results of the operation on the most common (often smaller) numbers so you don't actually have to perform the operation to get to the answer. This is perhaps the first and most basic arithmetic technique, i.e. **memorise and you don't have to calculate.**

- All sums up to 10.

$$2 + 6$$
$$5 + 4 \text{ etc.}$$

- All compositions of 10

$$1 + ? = 10$$
$$4 + ? = 10 \text{ etc.}$$

Just memorising the above lets you calculate any sum of two single digit numbers by partitioning and reorganising, but it saves a lot of time to also memorise the sum of all pairs of single digit numbers and not just those sums up to 10.

For example, All single digit sums

$$2 + 8 = ?$$
$$9 + 5 = ? \text{ etc.}$$

Note that it is perhaps surprising how few people have memorised the above sums. You may think you have them memorised, but consider carefully; are you actually recovering the results from memory or are you working them out by partitioning and reorganisation.

Addition is Associative :

The most basic law of addition is that addition is associative. That is, if you have a number of additions to perform it doesn't matter which order you do them in.

For example, $(3 + 5) + 4 = 3 + (5 + 4) = 12$

Generally it can be written as,

$$(a + b) + c = a + (b + c) \qquad \text{(law of associative)}$$

Subtracting 9

Subtracting 9 is a very easy way. For example : 10 – 1 = 9, 100 – 1 = 99.

Here, we observe that while subtracting 1 from 0's we net the answer is only as 9's

Subtraction from a power of 10 :

You will see in the multiplication section the Vedic Mathematics Sutra Vertically and Crosswise is used to multiply numbers near a power of 10,

For example, 10, 100, 1000, etc.

The first step in this technique is to subtract the numbers you are working with from the nearest power of 10.

Luckily another sutra can help with this initial subtraction.

All from 9 and the last from 10 tells us how to subtract a number from the next highest power of 10.

We simply subtract each digit of the number in question from 9 apart from the last one which we subtract from 10. It is very simple method.

For example : Subtract 8675 from 10000

$$
\begin{array}{cccc}
9 & 9 & 9 & 10 \\
8 & 6 & 7 & 5 \; - \\
\downarrow & \downarrow & \downarrow & \downarrow \\
1 & 3 & 2 & 5
\end{array}
$$

$$10000 - 8675 = 1325$$

Vedic Mathematics : Multiplication

There are a wide range of multiplication techniques, the one perhaps most familiar to the majority of people is the classic long multiplication algorithm.

For example, 23958233×5830

$$
\begin{array}{r}
23958233 \\
\times \; 5830 \\
\hline
00000000 \\
71874699 \\
191665864 \\
119791165 \\
\hline
139676498390
\end{array}
\begin{array}{l}
\\
\\
(= 23{,}958{,}233 \times 0) \\
(= 23{,}958{,}233 \times 30) \\
(= 23{,}958{,}233 \times 800) \\
(= 23{,}958{,}233 \times 5{,}000) \\
(= 139{,}676{,}498{,}390)
\end{array}
$$

While this algorithm works for any pair of numbers, it is long winded, requires many intermediate stages, and requires you to record the results of each of the intermediate stages so you can sum them at the end to produce the final answer. However, when the numbers to be multiplied fall into certain categories, short-cuts can be used to avoid much of the work involved in long multiplication. There are many of these 'special cases' some of them allow seemingly difficult multiplications to be completed mentally, literally allowing you to just write down the answer.

Special Cases of Multiplication :

There are a number of simple techniques that can be used when multiplying by certain numbers. They are very useful in their own right but can be even more useful when combined with other techniques where they can facilitate the solution of more difficult problems.

Multiplying by 11 :

To multiply any number by 11 do the following steps :

Working from **right** to **left**.

Step 1: Write the rightmost digit of the starting number down.

Step 2: Add each pair of digits and write the results down, (carrying digits where necessary right to left).

Step 3: Finally write down the left most digit (adding any final carry if necessary).

Step 4: It is as simple as that.

For example, Multiply 712 × 11

$$
\begin{array}{cccc}
7 & 1 & 2 \\
7 & 8 & 3 & 2
\end{array}
$$

712 × 11 = 7832

The reason for working from right to left instead of the more usual left to right is so any carries can be added in.

For example, Multiply 8738 × 11

$$
\begin{array}{cccccccc}
8 & & 7 & & 3 & & 8 \\
9 & \leftarrow 1 & 6 & \leftarrow 1 & 1 & \leftarrow 1 & 1 & & 8
\end{array}
$$

8738 × 11 = 96118

Multiplying two single digit numbers :

Although most students have memorised multiplication tables from 1×1 to 10×10, one of the Vedic Sutras, (Vertically and Crosswise), allows you to multiply any pair of single digit numbers without using anything higher than the 5x multiplication table. While this may not be particularly useful, the algorithm is a good introduction to some of the ideas behind the Vedic techniques and so is worth taking the time to learn and understand as the basic idea is expanded upon later. Because of this I will go through the procedure in more detail than it probably deserves. The technique is as follows:

If either of the numbers are below 6 then just recall the answer from memory. If instead both numbers are above 5 then continue.

Write, (or imagine), the two single digit numbers one above the other with an answer line below.

Subtract each number from 10 and place the result to the right of the original number.

Vertically: Multiply the two numbers on the right and place the answer underneath them on the answer line. Since the original numbers were above 5, these numbers will always be below 5 (because the original numbers were subtracted from 10) so you won't need anything above the 4x multiplication table. If the answer to the multiplication is 10 or more, just place the right-most digit on the answer line and remember to carry the other digit to the next step.

Crosswise: Select one of the original numbers, and subtract the number diagonally opposite it. If there was no carry from the previous step just place the result on the answer line below the original numbers, if there was a carry add this to the result before you place it on the answer line.

That's it, the number on the answer line is the final answer. The technique is very simple but looks more complicated than it actually is when written down step-by-step. The following examples should clarify the procedure.

Multiply 7×8

$$
\begin{array}{cc}
7 \longrightarrow 3 \\
8 \longrightarrow 2 \\
\hline
\end{array}
\;\Rightarrow\;
\begin{array}{cc}
7 & 3 \\
 & \downarrow \\
8 & 2 \\
\hline
 & 6 \\
\end{array}
\;\Rightarrow\;
\begin{array}{cc}
7 & 3 \\
 & \nearrow \\
8 & 2 \\
\hline
5 & 6 \\
\end{array}
$$

Giving an answer of 56 as expected. The next example involves a carry between the last two stages.

Multiply 7 × 6

$$
\begin{array}{cc} 7 \to 3 \\ 6 \to 4 \\ \hline \end{array} \Rightarrow
\begin{array}{cc} 7 & 3 \\ 6 \;\; 1 & 4 \\ \hline & 2 \end{array} \Rightarrow
\begin{array}{cc} 7 & 3 \\ 6 \;\; 1 & 4 \\ \hline 3 & 2 \end{array} \Rightarrow
\begin{array}{cc} 7 & 3 \\ 6 & 4 \\ \hline 4 & 2 \end{array}
$$

As you can see the multiplication in the second (Vertically) stage (3 × 4) results in 12, the 2 is written down and the 1 is carried. The subtraction in the Crosswise stage (6 − 3) results in 3, but you have to add the carried 1 from the previous step resulting in 4. The final answer is 42.

This may all seem like a lot of work for doing simple multiplications that you can just recall from memory, but the important thing here is to learn the technique as it is expanded upon later. If you are interested in improving your mental arithmetic skills, learn to do this procedure in your head by visualising the numbers laid out as above. Before going on to the next technique, try it now; close your eyes and multiply 6 × 6 using the procedure above. You should have imagined the following:

Multiply 6 × 6

$$
\begin{array}{cc} 6 \to 4 \\ 6 \to 4 \\ \hline \end{array} \Rightarrow
\begin{array}{cc} 6 & 4 \\ 6 \;\; 1 & 4 \\ \hline & 6 \end{array} \Rightarrow
\begin{array}{cc} 6 & 4 \\ 6 \;\; 1 & 4 \\ \hline 2 & 6 \end{array} \Rightarrow
\begin{array}{cc} 6 & 4 \\ 6 & 4 \\ \hline 3 & 6 \end{array}
$$

Combining techniques :

One of the key ideas of the Vedic system is that you can combine techniques to solve problems. You should look at problems in a flexible way and use the combination of techniques that best suits a particular problem. It is perhaps a little early to be discussing this since we have only covered one major technique so far, but even at this stage it is possible to combine the Vertically and Crosswise multiplication technique with the special case multiplication techniques already described to handle the situation when both numbers are further away from 100, 1000, etc.

For example, using the 'by 10 and half again' rule to multiply by 15 lets you easily deal with numbers further away from 10, 100, 1000, etc., if one of the numbers is 15 away from your 'base' number.

For example, Multiply 66 × 85.

$$
\begin{array}{l}
66 \longrightarrow 34 \\
85 \longrightarrow 15 \\
\hline
\end{array}
\Rightarrow
\begin{array}{cc}
66 & 34 \\
85 \; _5 & 15 \\
\hline
& 10
\end{array}
\Rightarrow
\begin{array}{cc}
66 & 34 \\
85 \; _5 & 15 \\
\hline
51 & 10
\end{array}
\Rightarrow
\begin{array}{cc}
66 & 34 \\
85 & 15 \\
\hline
56 & 10
\end{array}
$$

$$66 \times 85 = 5610$$

You can see here that the vertically multiplication results in 510 (34 × 15 = 340 'and half again' = 340 + 170 = 510). 510 have 3 digits so we write down the last two digits (10) and carry the leading 5. We then do the Crosswise subtraction along the easiest diagonal (66 – 15 = 51) and add the carry (5) before writing down the final answer (56).

Extending the Multiplication Technique :

The same vertically wise technique described above works for any numbers but it is particularly useful for numbers near a power of 10, i.e. 10, 100, 1000, 10000, 100000, etc. As long as the initial subtraction results in numbers that are 'easier' to multiply it is a useful technique.

For example, Multiply 1232 × 1003

$$
\begin{array}{l}
1232 \longrightarrow 232 \\
1003 \longrightarrow 3 \\
\hline
\end{array}
\Rightarrow
\begin{array}{cc}
1232 & 232 \\
1003 & 3 \\
\hline
& 696
\end{array}
\Rightarrow
\begin{array}{cc}
1232 & 232 \\
1003 & 3 \\
\hline
1235 & 696
\end{array}
$$

$$1232 \times 1003 = 1235696$$

Since we are dealing with numbers near 1000 here we find the initial differences from 1000 instead of 100 and we only carry if the vertically multiplication is 1000 or greater.

Multiply 9960 × 9850

$$
\begin{array}{l}
9960 \longrightarrow 40 \\
9850 \longrightarrow 150 \\
\hline
\end{array}
\Rightarrow
\begin{array}{cc}
9960 & 40 \\
9850 & 150 \\
\hline
& 6000
\end{array}
\Rightarrow
\begin{array}{cc}
9960 & 40 \\
9850 & 150 \\
\hline
9810 & 6000
\end{array}
$$

$$9960 \times 9850 = 98106000$$

In this case, the numbers are slightly below 10000 so we initially subtract from 10000, we also subtract in the Crosswise stage, and we only carry if the vertically multiplication is 10000 or more.

Multiply 89684 × 99989

89684 → 10316		89684	10316		89684	10316		89684	10316
99989 → 11	⇒	99989	11	⇒	99989	11	⇒	99989	11
			13476		89673	13476		89674	13476

89684 × 99989 = 8967413476

Note the combination of techniques in the above example, i.e. the difference between 89684 and 100000 is easily derived using the special case technique for subtracting from a power of 10, (i.e. using the sutra all from 9 and the last from 10). The special case technique for multiplication by 11 is also used.

Multiply 98688 × 99997

$$
\begin{array}{r}
98688 \\
99997 \times \\
\hline
690816 \ (= 98688 \times 7) \\
8881920 \ (= 98688 \times 90) \\
88819200 \ (= 98688 \times 900) \\
888192000 \ (= 98688 \times 9000) \\
8881920000 \ (= 98688 \times 90000) \\
\hline
9868503936
\end{array}
$$

98688 × 99997 = 9868503936

In this example the numbers are slightly less than 100000 so the initial subtraction is from 100000. The thing to watch out for here is that the result of the vertically multiplication must be padded out to 5 digits by adding an extra zero on the left (03936 instead of 3936). This is also true generally, i.e. the number of digits in the result of the vertically multiplication must always be the same as the number of zeroes in the 'base' number (i.e. 100, 1000, 100000, etc.).

It is worth remembering how far we have come even at this early stage. Even if you are writing the calculations down, it is still much more efficient to do the multiplication above the Vedic way than using traditional long multiplication.

For example, Multiply 98688×99997 using long multiplication

$$
\begin{array}{r}
98688 \\
\times\ 88887 \\
\hline
690816\ (= 98688 \times 7) \\
7895040\ (= 98688 \times 80) \\
78950400\ (= 98688 \times 800) \\
789504000\ (= 98688 \times 8000) \\
7895040000\ (= 98688 \times 80000) \\
\hline
1666544256
\end{array}
$$

This multiplication technique can be extended further to cover cases where one number is slightly above a power of 10 and one slightly below the same power of 10. In this case it is advantageous to note whether the original numbers are greater or smaller than the 'base' power of 10 using + or − symbols accordingly.

Multiplying Two Numbers that are 'Closely Related' :

We are now ready to extend the multiplication technique described above to the most general case, i.e. the multiplication of any two numbers that are 'closely related'. The precise definition of 'closely related' is:

"Numbers that are a small distance away from a 'proportional power of 10' such that the differences between the original numbers and this proportional power of 10 are simple to multiply".

This may sound very complicated, but it is actually quite simple. The extended technique is simply the addition of the sub sutra Anurupyena or Proportionately to the technique already described above. The complete description of the extended Vertically and Crosswise technique is:

(i)   Place the two numbers you wish to multiply one on top of the other, leave an answer line below.

(ii) Choose a 'working base' that is close to both numbers, this must be a 'proportional power of 10'. The 'theoretical base' is the actual power of 10 before you have multiplied or divided it to get your 'working base'.

For example, If the 'working base' is 25 then the 'theoretical base' would be 100. Remember the 'proportionality' of what you have done, you will use this 'proportionality' correct the left hand side of the answer.

(iii) Subtract the 'working base' from each of the original numbers and place the results to the right of each. We will call these results the 'residuals'.

(iv) Vertically multiply the 'residuals' obtained above noting the sign of the result, i.e. if the signs of the 'residuals' are different then the sign of the multiplication result will be negative, if the signs of the 'residuals' are the same then the result will be positive. We will call this the 'Vertically Result'.

(v) Add or Subtract Crosswise following the sign present on the particular diagonal chosen.

(vi) 'Correct' the 'Crosswise Result' by repeating the 'proportionality' used to create the 'working base'. Note that if the proportionality was a division, and if this resulted in a result with a fractional part, then this fractional part must be transferred to the right hand side of the answer by adding the same fractional proportion of the theoretical base to the previously calculated 'Vertically result'.

(vii) If there are now too many digits in 'Vertically Result' i.e. more than the number of zeroes in the 'theoretical base', then you have to carry the leading digit(s) to the next stage remembering to preserve the signs. We will call the result of the Vertically multiplication after any carry has been removed the 'remainder'.

(viii) If the 'remainder' is positive you can just place it on the answer line, if it is negative, it must be replaced with it's compliment before placing it on the answer line. If you have to compliment the 'remainder' to make it positive then you must also reduce the carry by 1, if there is no carry yet then the carry becomes −1.

(ix) Add or Subtract any carry according to it's sign to the corrected Crosswise result above, place this result in the answer line to the left of the 'remainder' part of the answer.

(x) That is it, the digits on the answer line are the results of the original multiplication.

Now, that all sounds terribly complicated, but it really is much harder to write the steps than to actually follow them. In fact you have already followed all the steps in the many previous examples, the only additional steps are the 'proportionately calculations.

3.8.9 Abacus

The abacus (plural abaci or abacuses), also called a counting frame, is a calculating tool that was in use in Europe, China and Russia, centuries before the adoption of the written Hindu–Arabic numeral system and is still used by merchants, traders and clerks in some parts of Eastern Europe, Russia, China and Africa. Today, abaci are often constructed as a bamboo frame with beads sliding on wires, but originally they were beans or stones moved in grooves in sand or on tablets of wood, stone, or metal.

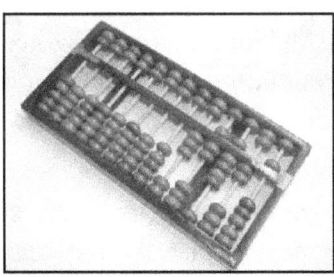

Fig. 3.5

What is Abacus ?

Abacus is an instrument that was invented some 2500 years ago primarily in China, which later on spread through countries like Korea, Japan, Taiwan, Malaysia etc. It was used in the ancient times for calculating numbers through basic arithmetic system. It has now been proven as a complete brain development tool over last two decades.

Abacus became popular over the world after being transformed from a calculating instrument into a system having immense power to benefit children of small ages by expanding the brain usage, in addition to making maths learning easy and effective.

Getting Friendly with Abacus:

The image displayed is that of a structure of an abacus.

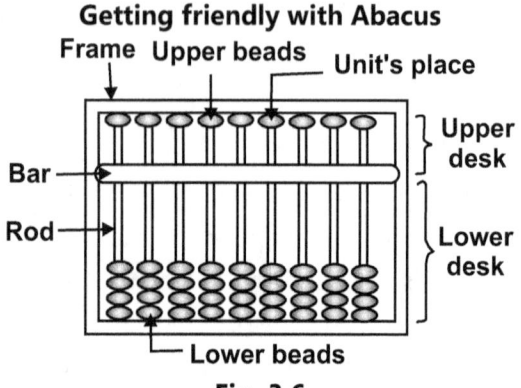

Getting friendly with Abacus

Frame Upper beads   Unit's place

Bar

Rod

Upper desk

Lower desk

Lower beads

Fig. 3.6

Functions of Abacus:

An abacus instrument allows performing basic operations like Addition, Subtraction, Multiplication and Division. It can also carry out operations such as counting-up to decimal places, calculates sums having negative numbers etc.

Advantages of Abacus:

(i) When a child works on abacus it uses both its hand to move the beads. The finger movement of both hands activates the sensors of brain, the right hand co-ordinates with left brain and the left hand coordinates with right brain.

This facilitates the functioning of "The whole brain" and helps in added intellect, thereby creating 'child maths prodigy'.

(ii) Visualization: Ms. Kimiko Kawano, Researcher, Nippon Medical School, Center for Informatics and Sciences, is of the opinion that abacus users simply visualize an image of abacus in their head. They do not replace the image into words. This difference can be seen clearly in the EEGs. What is important is that the ability to visualize can be put to use for other subjects.

(iii) Concentration: The study indicated that increased concentration of the abacus students was one of the pre-dominating effects of the training program.

(iv) Logical reasoning: In addition, a positive effect was seen, not only in mathematical problems with integers and decimals, but also in those with fractions, especially when higher level of logical thinking is required to solve them.

(v) Photographic memory: Abacus learners were found to score higher than non-abacus learners... It can be speculated that the training to obtain the abacus image visually had the effect of making students sensitive towards spatial arrangement or enhanced photographic memory.

(vi) Recall: "Some abacus experts use their ability for memorizing whole page of textbook or years in history. The ability developed by abacas can be used effectively in different ways" such as the capability to recall.

(a) Orient the abacus correctly: A basic abacus consists of two rows of beads arranged in a variable number of columns. Each column in the top row should have one or two beads per row, while each column in the bottom row should have four. When you start, all of the beads should be up in the top row, and down in the bottom row. The beads in the top row represent the number value 5 and each bead in the bottom row represents the number value 1.

Once you become more familiar with the function of the abacus, you can assign different values to the beads in the bottom row to perform more complex operations. The beads in the top row, however, need to be 5 times the value of each bead in the bottom row for the abacus method to work.

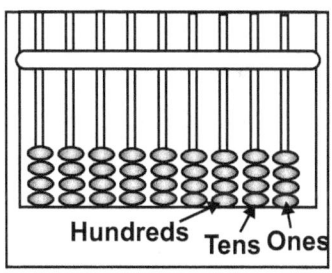

Fig. 3.7

2. Place Value: As on a modern calculator, each column of beads represents a "place" value from which you build a numeral. So, the farthest column on the right would be the "ones" place (1-9), the second farthest the "tens" place (10-99), the third farthest the hundreds (100-999), and so on.

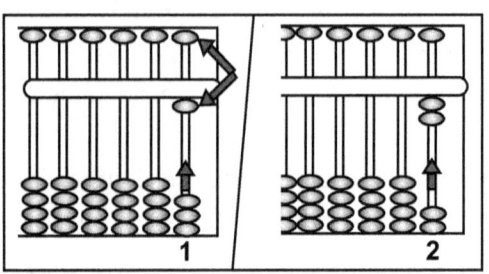

Fig. 3.8

3. Start counting: To count a digit, push one bead to the "up" position. "One" would be represented by pushing a single bead from the bottom row in the farthest column on the right to the "up" position, "two" by pushing two etc.

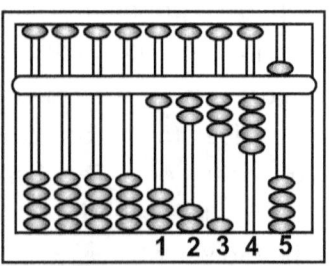

Fig. 3.9

4. Complete the "4/5 exchange": Since there are only four beads on the bottom row, to go from "four" to "five," you push the bead on the top row to the "down" position and push all four beads from the bottom row down. The abacus at this position is correctly read "five." To count "six," push one bead from the bottom row up, so the bead in the top row is down and one bead from the bottom row is up.

The process is essentially the same across the abacus. Go from "nine," in which all the beads in the ones place are pushed up and the bead in the top row is pushed down, to "ten," in which a single bead from the bottom row of the tens place is pushed up.

For example : 12345 would be represented with the top bead down in the ones place, four beads from the bottom row of the tens place pushed up, three beads up in the bottom row of the hundreds place, two beads up in the bottom row of the thousands, and a single bead from the bottom row of the ten-thousand place.

It is easy to forget to push the beads in the bottom row down when exchanging a place, making the board will show the wrong value. It's easy enough to keep track of when you are counting, but when you get into complicated arithmetic it becomes more difficult.

Part - I : Adding and Subtracting

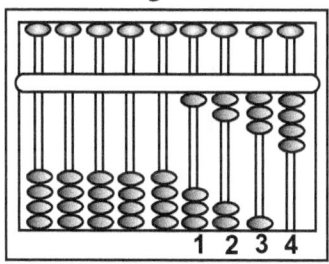

Fig. 3.10

1.   Input your first number: You have to add 1234 and 5678. Enter 1234 on the abacus by pushing up four beads in the ones place, three in the tens place, two in the hundreds place, and one in the thousands place.

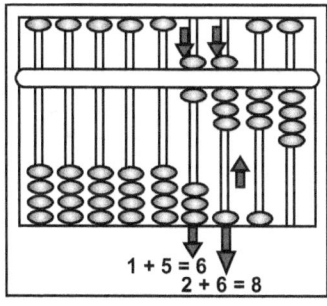

Fig. 3.11

2. Start adding from the left: Unlike traditional arithmetic, in which you start from the ones column and move left, the abacus works from left to right. So, the first numbers you will add are the 1 and the 5 from the thousands place, in this case moving the single bead from the top row of that column down to add the 5, and leaving the lower bead up for a total of 6. Likewise, you'll move the top bead in the hundreds place down and three more beads from the bottom up to get an 8 in the hundreds place.

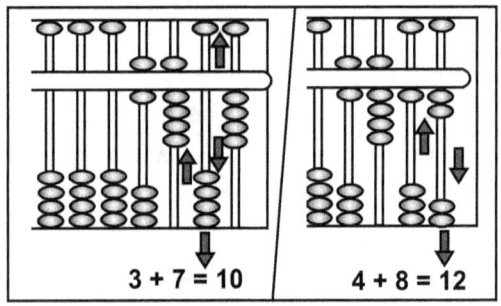

3 + 7 = 10   4 + 8 = 12

Fig. 3.12

3. Complete an exchange: Here's where things get creative. Since adding the two numbers in the tens place will result in 10, you will carry over a 1 to the hundred place, making it a 9 in that column. Next, put all the beads down in the tens place, leaving it zero.

In the ones column, you will do essentially the same thing. 8 + 4 = 12, so you'll carry the one over to the tens place, making it 1, leaving you with 2 in the ones place.

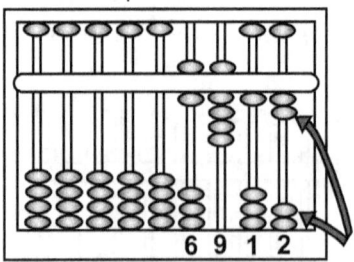

6 9 1 2

Fig. 3.13

4. Count up your beads. You are left with a 6 in the thousands column, a 9 in the hundreds, a 1 in the tens, and a 2 in the ones: 1234 + 5678 = 6912.

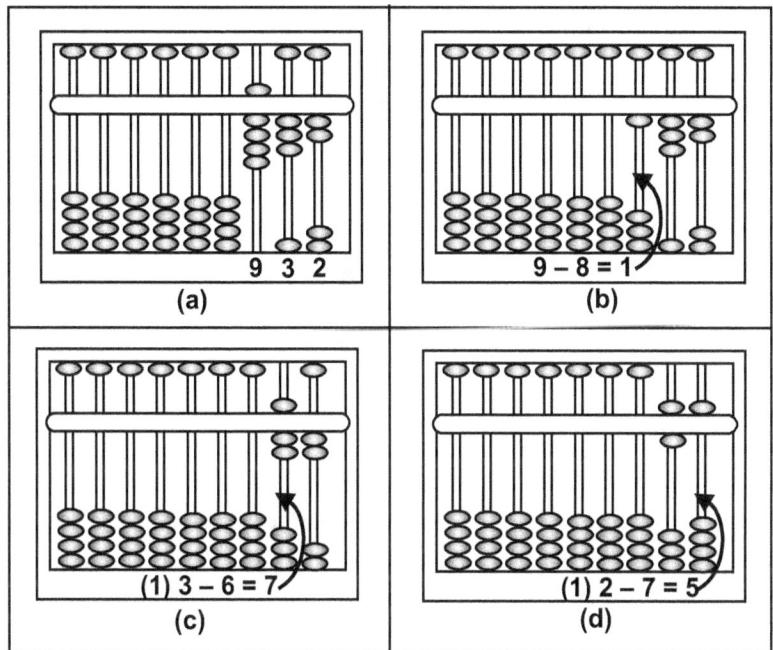

(a) 9 3 2

(b) 9 – 8 = 1

(c) (1) 3 – 6 = 7

(d) (1) 2 – 7 = 5

Fig. 3.14

5. To subtract, do essentially the exact same process in reverse: Borrow digits from the previous column instead of carrying them over. i.e. Subtracting 867 from 932. After entering 932 into the abacus i.e. the upper bead in the up position and all four lower beads up in the hundreds column, three lower beads up in the tens column, and two lower beads up in the ones column, start subtracting column-by-column starting on your left.

8 from 9 is one, so you will leave a single bead up in the hundreds place. In the tens place, you can't subtract 6 from 3, so you'll borrow the 1 in the hundreds place leaving it zero; and subtract 6 from 13, making it 7 in the tens place i.e. the upper bead up and two lower beads. Do the same thing in the ones place, "borrowing" a bead from the tens place making it 6 to subtract 7 from 12 instead of 2. There should be a 5 in the ones column: 932 – 867 = 65.

PART II : Multiplying

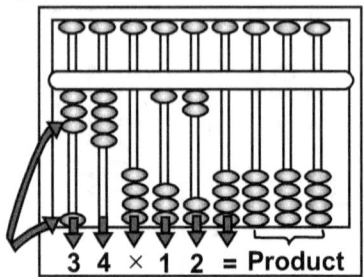

$3\ 4 \times 1\ 2$ = Product

Fig. 3.15

1. Transpose the problem onto the abacus: Unlike adding, it helps to start at the farthest left column of the abacus when multiplying. Say you're multiplying 34 and 12. You need to assign columns to "3" "4" "X" "1" "2" "=" and leave the rest of the columns to the right of them blank for your product. For this problem, you will need at least three.

The "X" and the "=" should just be spaces that you leave blank, to keep your numbers separate, so it will take a total of six columns to enter "34 × 12 =" into the abacus.

The abacus should have 3 beads up in the farthest column left, four up in the next farthest, a blank column, one bead up, two beads up, another blank column, and at least three columns open to record the product.

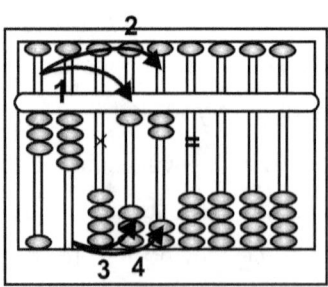

Fig. 3.16

2. Multiply by alternating columns: The order here is critical. You need to multiply the first column by the first column after the break, then the first column by the second column after the break. Next, you will multiply the second column before the break by the first column after the break, then the second column before the break by the second column after the break. It should always be done in this order.

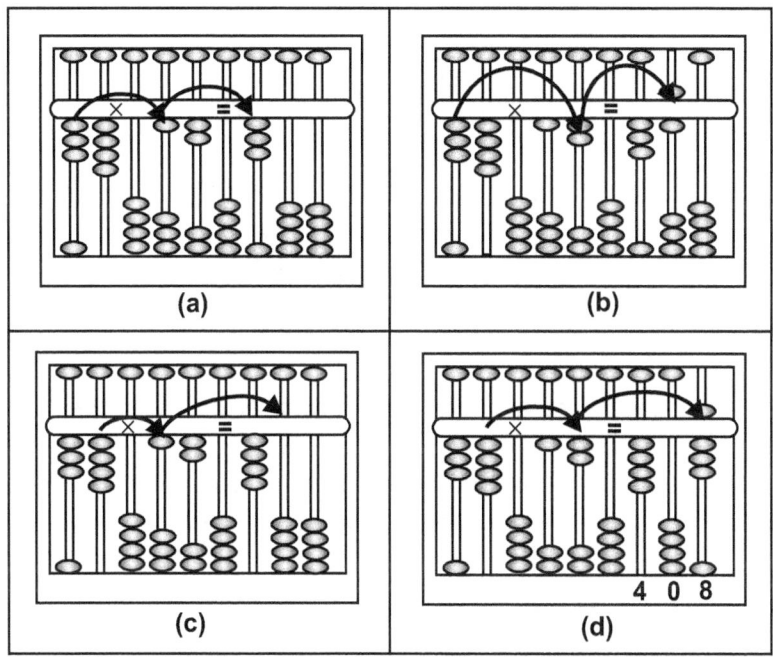

(a)

(b)

(c)

(d)

Fig. 3.17

3. Record the products in the correct order: First, you will multiply 3 and 1, recording their product in the first answer column, which in this case will be the seventh column from the left, accounting for each digit and each necessary blank column. Push three beads up in that seventh column. Next, multiply the 3 and the 2, recording their product in the eighth column. Push up the upper bead and one lower bead in that column.

When you multiply the 4 and the 1, you will need to add that product to the eighth column, the second of the answer columns. The product of 4 and 1 is 4, and since you are adding a 4 to a 6 in that column, you will need to carry one bead over to the first answer column, making it a 4 in the seventh column and a zero in the eighth.

Multiply the last two digits in the problem, 4 and 2, and record that product in the ninth column, putting an 8 in the last of the answer columns, which should now read 4, blank, and 8, making your answer 408.

PART III : Dividing

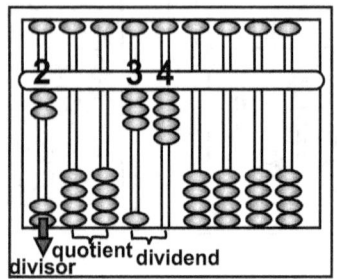

Fig. 3.18

1. To divide, leave space for the answer between the divisor and the dividend: Division is a more fluid process than multiplication, and it works best when you don't leave blank spaces between the numbers involved. The left-most column on the abacus will be the divisor, the number being divided by. The next spaces to the right should be left for the answer.

Say you are dividing 34 by 2. You know the answer will be at least two columns, so leave two columns between 2 on the right and the 3 and the 4.

To summarize, to enter 34 divided by 2 on the abacus, you should have 2 in the left most column, two columns to record the answer, the 3 in the fourth column, and the 4 in the fifth.

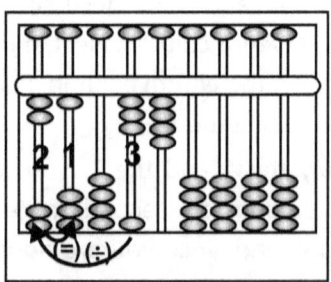

Fig. 3.19

2. Record the quotient: Take the first number in the dividend (3) and the divisor (2) in the first answer column. 2 goes into 3 once, so record a 1 in column 2.

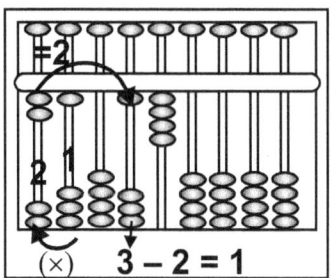

Fig. 3.20

3. Determine the remainder: Next, you need to multiply the quotient in column two (1) by the dividend in column one (2) to determine the remainder. This product (2) needs to be subtracted from column four. The divisor should now read 14.

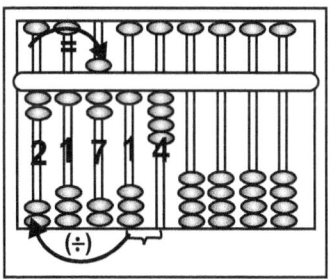

Fig. 3.21

4. Repeat the process: Record the next digit of the quotient in the third column, subtracting the product from the divisor (here, eliminating it). Your board should now read 2, 1, 7, leaving your dividend and the quotient, 17.

EXERCISES

Q.1. Multiple Choice Questions :

1. A syllabus is an _____ and summary of topics to be covered in education or a training courses.

    (a) outline   (b) explanation

    (c) both (a) and (b)   (d) none of these

2. Content means _____ information and analysis means _____ of units to study and correlate them.
   - (a) meaningful
   - (b) breakdown
   - (c) meaningful, breakdown
   - (d) none of these

3. Concept is a set or group of abstract ideas with similar _____ .
   - (a) idea
   - (b) concepts
   - (c) characteristic
   - (d) none of these

4. A _____ is a statement prepared by bringing together of several fact.
   - (a) rule
   - (b) law
   - (c) both (a) and (b)
   - (d) none of these

5. The _____ plays an important role in teaching and learning process.
   - (a) textbook
   - (b) syllabus
   - (c) both (a) and (b)
   - (d) none of these

6. There are _____ objectives of mathematics at lower primary level.
   - (a) eight
   - (b) seven
   - (c) nine
   - (d) none of these

7. Mathematics teaching indicates certain important _____ values in a person.
   - (a) disciplinary
   - (b) constructive
   - (b) both (a) and (b)
   - (d) none of these

8. Deductive method is the _____ of inductive method.
   - (a) similar
   - (b) opposite
   - (c) equal
   - (d) none of these

9. Experimental method is also called as _____ method.
   - (a) laboratory
   - (b) explanatory
   - (c) both (a) and (b)
   - (d) none of these

10. Self search method is also called as _____ method.
    - (a) problem solving
    - (b) practical
    - (c) heuristic
    - (d) experimental

11. _____ is the main activity in the learning of this subject.
    (a) Problem solving   (b) Practical
    (c) Heuristics   (d) Experiment

12. An _____ is the planning of mathematics syllabus of the whole year for a particular standard.
    (a) lesson plan   (b) annual plan
    (c) unit plan   (d) none of these

13. A _____ plan is an outline of the important points of a lesson arranged in the order in which they are to be presented to student by the teacher.
    (a) lesson   (b) annual
    (c) unit   (d) none of these

14. When a teacher teaches a unit by three different methods, she can choose a _____ method from those methods.
    (a) first   (b) second
    (c) third   (d) correct

15. Supervised study means study under _____ .
    (a) supervision   (b) instruction
    (c) both (a) and (b)   (d) none of these

Answers : 1 - (a), 2 - (c), 3 - (c), 4 - (c), 5 - (a), 6 - (b), 7 - (a), 8 - (b), 9 - (a), 10 - (c), 11 - (a), 12 - (b), 13 - (c), 14 - (d), 15 - (a)

Q.2. Answer the Following Questions :

1. Explain the difference between inductive and deductive method.

2. How are Analysis and Synthesis method supplementary to each other ?

3. Explain the importance of experimental method at the lower primary level.

4. Choose a topic of standard 6 and explain how you will teach it by self-study method.

5. Prepare a list of all the units of standard 7 mathematics which can be taught by inductive - deductive method.

6. Explain the memory model of teaching with an example.

7. Prepare a lesson plan using concept attainment model.

8. Make a list of all co-curriculum and extra-curricular mathematical activities and write their importance.

9. What are the objective of the concept of mathematic with fun ?

10. Explain the concept of vedic maths in brief.

Q.3. Write Short Notes On :

1. Mathematical Game

2. Vedic Maths.

3. Abacus.

4. Unit Plan.

5. Annual Plan.

6. Lesson Plan.

✍ ✍ ✍

4

GENERALISATION AND CONTENTION OF MATHEMATICS

⊃ Chapter Structure ⊂

4.1   Objectives

After reading this chapter, teacher/students will be able to understand :

– Meaning of generalization.
– Rationalization by inductive method.
– Rules, Definition, Formula and Theorems in Mathematics.

(4.1)

- Mathematics laboratory and characteristics of mathematics teacher.
- The concept of action research, report writing and innovation.

4.2 Introduction

Education is imparted for achieving certain ends and goals. Various subjects of the school curriculum are different means to achieve these goals. The term aim of teaching mathematics stands for the goals, targets or broader purposes that may be fulfilled by the teaching of mathematics in the general scheme of education. Aims are like ideals. Their attainment needs a long-term planning. Their rationalization is not an easy task. While studying mathematics education, we discuss the theory of Piaget, Vygotaski, Bruner and Asubel and use of these theorem's in the teaching - learning process.

In this chapter, we will study the teaching methodology and planning in teaching. While studying these concepts, we will also see the rules, definitions, formulae, and theorems in mathematics with the help of rationalization. Even as we study the concept of action research, reports writing and innovation, we shall also study about the organisations of mathematics teacher.

4.3 Generalisation Method

4.3.1 What is Generalisation ?

To understand the meaning of generalization, we will do the following activity.

Activity : Study the measure of angles of a triangle.

Step - 1: Draw a triangle.

Step - 2: Measure the angles of triangle.

m∠A = 35°, m∠B = 120°, m∠C = 25°

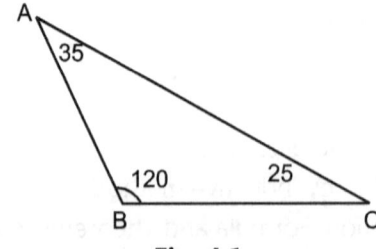

Fig. 4.1

Step - 3: Add the measures of three angles.

Teacher will write the observations on black board as follows :

Observation Table

Sr. No.	Measure of Angle			Total
	Angle (1)	Angle (2)	Angle (3)	
1.	35°	120°	25°	180°
2.	40°	70°	70°	180°
3.	45°	65°	70°	180°
4.	75°	43°	62°	180°
5.	65°	45°	70°	180°
6.	20°	85°	74°	179°
7.	67°	38°	76°	181°

From observation table we can ask :

1. What is the difference between the triangles ?
2. What is the similarity in triangles ?
3. Measure of angles of triangle are different.

From observation table, we can conclude that measures of angle of triangle are different, but addition of angles of each triangle is equal to 180°.

Generalization :

Definition : A generalization is a concept in the inductive sense of that word, or an extension of the concept to less-specific criteria.

Generalization posit the existence of a domain or set of elements, as well as one or more common characteristics shared by element (which forms conceptual mode).

In this method, a student himself prepares a rule or a concept by experimenting in different ways and thus as he himself has done it, he gets mental satisfaction and happiness. So a teacher should provide ample opportunities for the students to search and find out for themselves.

The rules and concepts obtained should be ascertained by teacher by giving another example. This will enhance the confidence of the students.

As the student participation is maximum, they will create more interest in the subject.

Even if the student forgets any formula, he is confident enough to prepare it again. But it is the teacher's responsibility to mould him in such a manner.

Many things happen around us in this world. We observe them minutely and then arrive at some conclusions. Then we try to act according to these experiences. This is generalization. We do not come to any conclusion immediately. We have to go through many experiences and then we decide our behaviour. This process of thinking is most needed in the generalization process.

Inductive Method :

Inductive method is a method of logical thinking, drawing inferences and making conclusions. This method is based on the psychological processes like sensation, perception and conception. Also this method is based on the teaching maxim of specific to general.

Generalisation process is the main base of inductive method. This method includes the following steps :

1. Observation.
2. Comparative observation.
3. Meditative or contemplative thinking.
4. Drawing conclusion.

These steps lead to formation of a general rule. This is generalization.

4.3.2 Use of Generalization Method in Day-to-Day Life

Activity : Read the following example.

Sunil earn ₹ 5000 per month. Expenditure of Sunil's family is

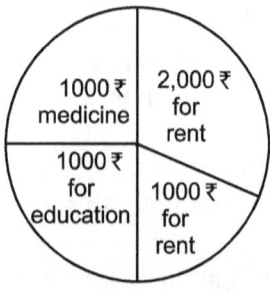

Fig. 4.2

From the above information answer the following questions :

1. What is monthly expenditure of Sunil's family ?
2. Family members of Sunil's family are always happy. Give reason.
3. What is Sunil's monthly income ?

In the same way, do the survey of family in your area and discuss it.

From this, we can conclude that in real life situation we can do our daily life simple, easy and happy by using the mathematical terms like Profit-Loss, Commission, Discount, Percentage.

With the help of generalization method, we can do Bank/Postal transaction easily.

Activity 1 : Observe the daily transactions in your life, make list and compare it and write conclusion.

4.3.3 Use of Internet for Reference in Mathematics Education

Now-a-days, new technologies are developed very fast. Teacher and students need to be familiar with a variety of technologies and understanding of how technology relates to the teaching-learning process of mathematics. New technologies like internet offers opportunities not only to address old purposes, goals and means in new ways but also to define new purposes, new goals and new means that have not been considered before.

Advantages of Internet :

1. **Source of information :** Students have access to articles, reports, web-based instructional material etc.
2. **Source of classroom material :** It provides ideas and resources for teachers and students to prepare lessons or classroom reports or talks.
3. **Learning system :** It supports students during their home work and allows them to ask individual questions via internet.
4. There are possibilities of getting dynamic visualization of theorems and proofs.
5. Interactive opportunity.

6. Reading interesting material.

7. Reference material.

8. Communication and

9. Problem solving etc.

Internet for Future Teachers (present student-teachers) :

One of the most important issues that teacher education programs/courses are facing is the use of technology by the student teachers. In response to the growing need for technological literacy in student-teachers certain goals have to be attained as follows :

1. Providing students with the opportunity to learn specific technological resources in mathematical contexts.

2. Focusing student attention on how and when to use technology appropriately in mathematics classroom.

3. Giving opportunities for students to apply their knowledge of technology and its uses the teaching and learning of mathematics.

Uses of Internet :

Since the internet has become popular, its being used for many purposes :

1. E-mail : By using internet now we can communicate in a fraction of a second with a person who is in the other part of the world. There are plenty messenger services and e-mail services offering this service for free. Student-teachers can establish global friendship global friendship for sharing thoughts and exploring other cultures.

2. Information : The internet and the world wide web makes it easy for all to access information of all types. Student-teachers can get any type of information on any topic.

3. Communication : This area frequently uses internet because of its low cost, less efforts and speed. Communication takes place in forms of e-mails, chats, video and conferences.

4. Another growing use of internet is to build and take part in discussion forums as per interest and express one's ideas. Almost every site provides a blog page to make the consumers and internet users provide their views easily.

5. e-marketing : This is the most recent but now a very common use of internet. This involves buying and selling over the internet.

6. Access of internet : Common methods of internet access by users include Dial-up with a computer modern via telephone circuit, broadband over coaxial cable, fiber optics or copper wires, wi-fi, satellites and cellular telephone technology (3G, 4G).

The internet can be accessed almost anywhere by numerous means including mobile internet devices, mobile phones, data cards, hand held game consoles and cellular routers that allow users to connect to internet wirelessly.

Points to Remember

- Generalization is a concept in the inductive sense of that word, or an extension of the concept to less specific criteria.
- Inductive method, is a method of logical thinking, drawing inferences and making conclusions.
- Internet is the most important thing in the teachers education program.

Activity 2 : Collect information from different web sites about the mathematical concepts, and discuss them with your teacher and other students.

Questions

1. Write the definition of Generalization ?
2. State the advantages of internet.

4.4 Mathematical Concepts

4.4.1 Mathematical Concepts and Definitions

(1) Mathematical Signs and Symbols :

Mathematical signs and symbols have a decisive role for coding, constructing and communicating mathematical knowledge.

For example : To do the operation with numbers such as addition, subtraction, multiplication, division, equality, unequal number, greater than, less than we use 0, 1, 2, ..., 9, + −, ×, ÷, =, ≠, >, < etc.

(2) Mathematical Language :

The language of mathematics is the system used by mathematicians to communicate mathematical ideas among themselves. This language consists of a substrate of some natural language i.e. English using technical terms and grammatical compositions that are peculiar to mathematical discourse supplemented by a highly specialized symbolic notation for mathematical formula.

For example, if $\triangle ABC$ is equal to $\triangle PQR$ then in mathematical language, we can write this statement as follows :

$$\triangle ABC = \triangle PQR$$

(3) Concept :

Concept is a set or group of abstract ideas with similar characteristics. Concepts have a specific name, specific characteristics and specific examples. Mathematics is full of concepts.

For example, concept of sets, concept of profit and loss etc.

(4) Principle :

Principle is a general law that is used as a basis for a theory or system

For example, "Diameter of a circle is twice of the radius".

(5) Rule :

Rule is a statement prepared by bringing together of several facts.

In mathematics rule can be defined, as 'a standard method or procedure for solving a class of problems'.

For example, Law of Indices

$$a^x \times a^y = a^{(x+y)}$$

(6) Mathematical Formulae :

In mathematics, a formula is an entity constructed using the symbols and formation of rules of a given logical language. It is a mathematical relationship expressed in symbols.

For example, (i) To determine the volume of a sphere the particular formula is

$$V = \frac{4}{3}\pi r^3$$

(ii) Area of circle, $A = \pi r^2$

(iii) $(a+b)^2 = a^2 + 2ab + b^2$

(iv) $a^2 - b^2 = (a-b)(a+b)$

(7) Definition :

Definition is the formal statement of the meaning or significance of a word or object from which we get exact idea or meaning of the object or shape. In mathematics, definitions are generally not used to describe existing terms, but to give meaning to a new form. The meaning of mathematical statement changes if definition change.

For example : **Equilateral triangle : Definition :** A triangle in which all sides are of equal length is called as equilateral triangle.

(8) Theorem :

In mathematics, a theorem is a statement that has been proven on the basis of previously established statements, such as other theorems and generally accepted statements, i.e. axioms.

For example : **Pythagoras theorem -** Pythagoras theorem is a fundamental theorem of a fundamental relation in Euclidean Geometry among the three sides of a right angle triangle. Theorem is addition of square of two sides of a triangle is equal to square of hypotenuse i.e.

$$(\text{Hypotenuse})^2 = (\text{One side})^2 + (\text{Second side})^2$$

(9) Figure :

A drawing that shows size and shape is called as figure.

For example : (i) Figure of circle.

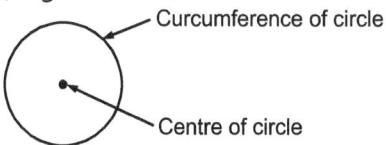

Fig. 4.3

4.4.2 Correlation between Signs, Symbols Language, Formula, Definition, Theorem and Figures

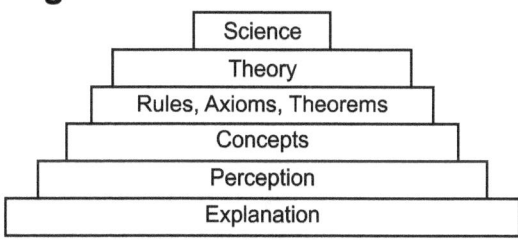

Cognition Process
Fig. 4.4

To understand the concept and structure of mathematics, we require the following things in effective manner.

1. Learning with understanding.

2. Proper arrangement of mathematical operations for solving the problem.

3. Explanation of concepts or equations with the help of mathematical language.

4. Use of mathematical knowledge in day-to-day life.

Primary Education Curriculum 2012 :

Curriculum of mathematics subject can be divided in two parts : 1st to 5th std. (Pre-primary level/low level) and for 6th std. to 8th std. (Primary level/ high level).

Pre-primary Level or Lower Level (Area/Units)

1. Geometry
2. Measurement
3. Number system
4. Operations on number
5. Classification of data
6. Pictorial representation

Higher Level (Units) :

1. Geometry
2. Mensuration
3. Number system
4. Operations on numbers
5. Fractions
6. Algebra
7. Commercial mathematics
8. Presentation or classification of data

The co-ordination between the units of primary level can be seen clearly shown in Fig. 4.4.

Correlation of one unit to other unit.

Area/Unit - Operation on numbers

Square : Square means the multiplication of a number with the same number - Rule, definition.

Area/Unit - Geometry

Area of square is equal to square of side - Theorem.

Area/Unit - Algebra

$(a + b)^2 = a^2 + 2ab + b^2$ - Formula, Signs, Rules.

In short, the co-ordination between mathematical concepts depend on each other. Therefore, the mathematical terms have an important place in mathematical sciences.

Activity 1 : Explain the co-ordination between operations on number while studying the properties of triangle.

4.4.3 Gradation of Mathematical Signs, Languages, Rules, Theorems, Definitions, Formulaes and Figures

[Primary Education Curriculum 2012]

Now-a-days use of mathematical terms/concepts is going on increasing in every field. As per grade, the increasing order of these terms is as shown below. For example :

(1) Geometry

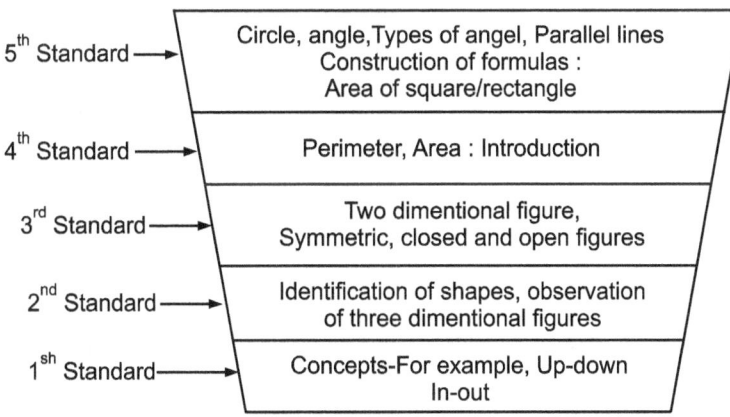

Fig. 4.5

(2) Number system :

1st Std. : Introduction of '0', Introduction of 1 to 9 numbers, Concept of tens.

2nd Std. : Concept of two digit numbers, Expanded form of number, Place value of number.

3rd Std. : Introduction of three digit numbers. Expanded form of three digit numbers place value of three digit numbers etc.

4th Std. and 5th Std. : Arrangement of numbers in increasing order.

Advantages of Activity :

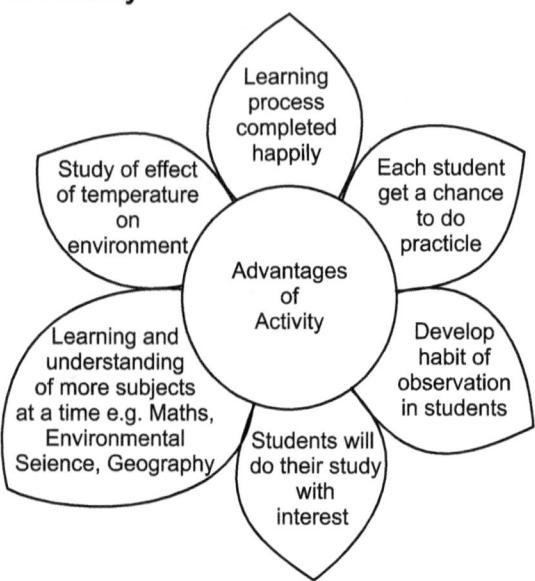

Fig. 4.6

Activity 3 : Draw a figure as per gradation of Geometry, Algebra, Classification of data.

Assignment

1. Make list of mathematical concepts as per the syllabus/curriculum of 1st Std. to 5th Std.

2. Explain the characteristics of mathematical concepts from 1st Std. to 5th Std. in your day-to-day life.

Points to Remember

- Definition is a formal statement and meaningful significance of a word or object.
- Theorem is a statement that has been proven on the basis of previously established statements.
- Formulae is very important thing in mathematics.

Questions

1. Write the definition or meaning of following terms :

(a) Definition, (b) Formulae, (c) Theorem, (d) Concept, (e) Mathematical symbols, (f) Figure

4.5 Creative Thoughts in Mathematics

4.5.1 Development of Creative Thoughts in Mathematics

A creative thought is very important part in Mathematics Education. Creativity in mathematics is not just about what students do but also what we do as a teacher. If teachers are thinking creatively about the mathematical experiences teacher can offer their students, they can open up opportunities for them to be creative.

Problem solving is a creative process. Students do not generally expect to be challenged by an unknown/unfamiliar situation. When students are placed in problem-solving situations it is nearly always within a context that is very familiar.

For example, a problem involving the application of a mathematical concept the students have just been taught. In such a situations students are aware of boundaries, and have been given some clear ideas about knowledge to apply. Such problems often seen closed with very little room to explore and be creative.

Problem solving should be about valuing independence and individual ideas, and being given some mathematical space to develop a "habit of mind" that gives opportunities to experience.

A teacher can think creatively and give a chance to students to do the mathematical things in different way with creative thinking.

For example : 1. Use geometrical figures and make different designs with the help of it.

Fig. 4.7

2. Read the table alongside :

* In the table at unit place of 19 the number is 9.

* Each number in the table is at unit place is in decreasing order from 9 to 0.

* If we look after the tens place of 19 number is 1, if we add 1 and 2, we get the number at tens place of next number such as $1 + 2 = 3$; $3 + 2 = 5$; $5 + 2 = 7$ ... etc.

18
38
57
76
95
114
133
152
171
190

Fig. 4.8

4.6 Critical Thinking in Mathematics

(A) Concept of Critical Thinking :

Educational psychologists frame critical thinking as a set of generic thinking and reasoning skills, including a deposition for using them, as well as a commitment to using the outcomes of critical thinking as a basis for decision-making and problem solving. Critical thinking is esta - as a general standard for making judgements and decisions. Critical thinking can be as much a part of mathematics class as learning concepts, computations, formulae and theorems. Activities that stimulate critical thinking will also encourage the students to think and speak in mathematical terms.

Critical thinking is a key factor in separating those students who can "do" maths from those who truly "understand" what they are doing. When students do maths, they can perform computations and explain concepts because they have learned formulae and definitions through practice and rote memorization. Likewise, they may not know how some ancient mathematician defined the concept, but they know the definition.

On the other hand, students who have been taught to think critically in maths can explain why a formula works and they can trace the steps used to define a concept. Not only can, they solve a problem, they can explain the logic behind the process they used to reach a solution.

Let us take the example of Pythagorean theorem and its related formula. Most of the students learn the formula of the theorem and use it to find the length of the hypotenuse. They can solve problems involving right triangles using the formula, provided they are given enough information, whereas the students who are taught to think critically can explain why the theorem works.

(B) Asking Questions in Critical Thinking :

To think critically is to follow a clear line of logical steps and reasoning. To solve critical thinking problems, mathematics teacher should model the way they think when solving a problem. Students can internalize a set of questions to ask that will help them think their way to solution. These questions could be as follows :

- What is the problem ?
  What am I trying to figure out ?
- What do I know ?
  What is the given information ?
- What do I need to know to solve the problem ?
- Have I solved any problems of this type before ?
  Which problems have I solved ?
- What solutions could work ? What strategies will work best in this situation ?

After student attempts a problem and gets a solution, they can further ask.

- Why did my solution work ? or they might try to understand why their solution didn't work ?

(C) Bell Ringers :

Bell ringers stimulate critical thinking bell ringers are short activities that students are asked to do at the beginning of a class or as a warm-up exercise. Normally, these activities require the students to practice or apply skills they have already learned.

For example : A critical thinking math bell ringer might ask the students to evaluate a pattern and determine a missing piece such as

What number would come next ?

3, 6, 9, 12, 15, 18, ..., ?

Steps of critical thinking :

1. Identify an objective (Problem).
2. Conduct research (Ask questions).
3. Generate ideas.
4. Develop solutions.
5. Check opportunities of solution.

(D) Definition of Critical Thinking :

Critical thinking is defined as meaningful, unbiased decisions or judgements based on the use of interpretation, analysis, evaluation, inferences and explanations of information as it relates to the evidence applied to specific discipline.

Critical thinking differs from student to student as they have different levels of interpretations. A mathematics teacher should keep this in mind.

The question, "Why" is a great sign of critical thinking. Most of the students just follow what they have learnt from their teachers, books or any digital source. But few student try to learn about what it is and ask why it is being followed.

This enthusiastic nature makes them special from the rest of the world.

"Learning stops at an answer. Thinking happens during questioning!"

(E) Critical Thinking in Daily Life :

When an individual can determine whether a problem is under control or beyond his control and can recognize his limitations regarding money, time and power, then he is using critical thinking in his day-to-day life.

Ask any mother in a family how the uses critical thinking if she trying a new recipe. Working in a kitchen requires a wide range of mathematical knowledge followed by critical thinking. More maths is found the kitchen than anywhere else in the house. Cooking and baking are sciences and can be some of the most rewarding (delicious) ways of introducing mathematics to children in kitchen. After all, recipes are really just mathematical algorithms or self-contained step-by-step sets of operations to be performed.

One of the most obvious places to find people using mathematics with critical thinking everyday is the grocery store. Grocery shop requires a broad range of mathematical thinking from multiplication, addition, subtraction to estimation and percentages.

Ask any contractor or construction worker, they will tell you how they do the figuring of total amount of bags of concrete needed for a slab, accurately measuring lengths, widths and angles and estimating project costs.

Critical thinking comes in handy while travelling and shows-up in various ways from estimating the amount of fuel you'll need to plan out a trip based on kms per hour; paying the tolls, checking tyre pressure, etc. Teaching students how to read maps using their maths skills wil make them safer travelers.

Many experts agree that without critical mathematical thinking skills, it would be difficult for people to invest, save or spend money. A student who thoroughly grasps the concepts of exponential growth and compound interest will be more inclined to manage debt.

Points to Remember

- Critical thinking is very important and useful in daily life.
- Critical thinking develop thinking power of student for problem solving.
- Creativity develop habits in students to find new thoughts or short-cuts in mathematics.

EXERCISE

Q.1. Multiple Choice Questions :

1. _____ differs from student-to-student as they have different levels of interpretations.
   (a) Creative thoughts
   (b) Critical thinking
   (c) Bell ringers
   (d) None of these

2. _____ are short activities that students are asked to do at the beginning of a class as a warm-up exercise.
   (a) Creative thoughts
   (b) Critical thinking
   (c) Bell ringers
   (d) None of these

3. _____ in the mathematics classroom is not just about what students do but is what we do as teachers.
   (a) Creativity
   (b) Activity
   (c) Both (a) and (b)
   (d) None of these

4. A _____ is a concept in the inductive sense of that word, or an extension of the concept to less-specific criteria.
   (a) Generalization
   (b) Creation
   (c) Both (a) and (b)
   (d) None of these

5. _____ is a statement prepared by bringing together of several facts.

(a) Formula   (b) Theorem
(c) Principle   (d) Rule

Answers : 1 - (b), 2 - (c), 3 - (a), 4 - (a), 5 - (d).

Q.2. Answer the Following Questions :

1. State meaning of Generalization Method.
2. Explain the Inductive Method.
3. State the use of generalization method in day-to-day life.
4. State and explain the uses of internet in mathematics education.
5. State the uses of internet.
6. State and explain the different mathematical concepts.
7. What are the advantages of activity ?
8. Explain in brief : "Creative thoughts in Mathematics".
9. Explain the concept of critical thinking.
10. Write the definition of critical thinking.

Q.3. Write Short Notes On :

1. Inductive Method.
2. Role of Internet in Mathematics Education.
3. Gradation of Mathematical Sign and Formulae.
4. Correlation between Signs and Symbols.
5. Creative thoughts in Mathematics.
6. Critical thinking in Mathematics.

✍ ✍ ✍

5

EVALUATION

➲ Chapter Structure ☾

5.1 Objectives

After reading this chapter, teachers will be able to :

- Tell more information about evaluation in mathematics.
- Explain the importance of evaluation.
- Know the method of evaluation.
- Understand the importance of formative and summative evaluation.
- Understand the concept of unit test.
- Preparation of question paper.
- Formation of different types of questions.

5.2 Introduction and Meaning of Evaluation

Evaluation in general is a process which allows one to make judgement. Evaluation is a systematic process which is continuous and comprehensive. Evaluation determines the effectiveness of learning experiences provided in the classrooms. Evaluation determines how well the goals of education have been achieved. Evaluation is integrated with the educational task and its purpose is to improve instruction not merely measure achievements. That is, it has qualitative and quantitative aspect.

For example: If a student gets 70 marks in an educational test, then it is a measure performance. This measure can also be made meaningful in perspective of any established standard or norm or situation such as average, above the average, below the average or fail. This process is called as evaluation.

In mathematical language, evaluation is

$$\text{Evaluation} \rightleftharpoons \text{Measurement + Judgement}$$

By this process, any mental ability is measured through a test.

Definition by Bred Field:

"Evaluation is the assignment of symbols to phenomena in order to characterize, the worth of value of a phenomena usually with reference to some socio-cultural or scientific standards.

5.3 Importance of Evaluation in Mathematics

Importance of Evaluation :

Fig. 5.1

Advantages of Evaluation :

1. Helps to assess the student's progress.
2. Helps to bring improvement in the students.
3. Gives regular feedback to teachers and parents.
4. Students can acknowledge their shortcomings and work on them.
5. Promotes competition in students.
6. Helps in evaluation of teaching methods.
7. Helps in identifying problems in teaching.
8. Helps in determining whether objectives have been achieved or not.
9. Evaluation serves as a useful tool of guidance and counselling.

Concept :

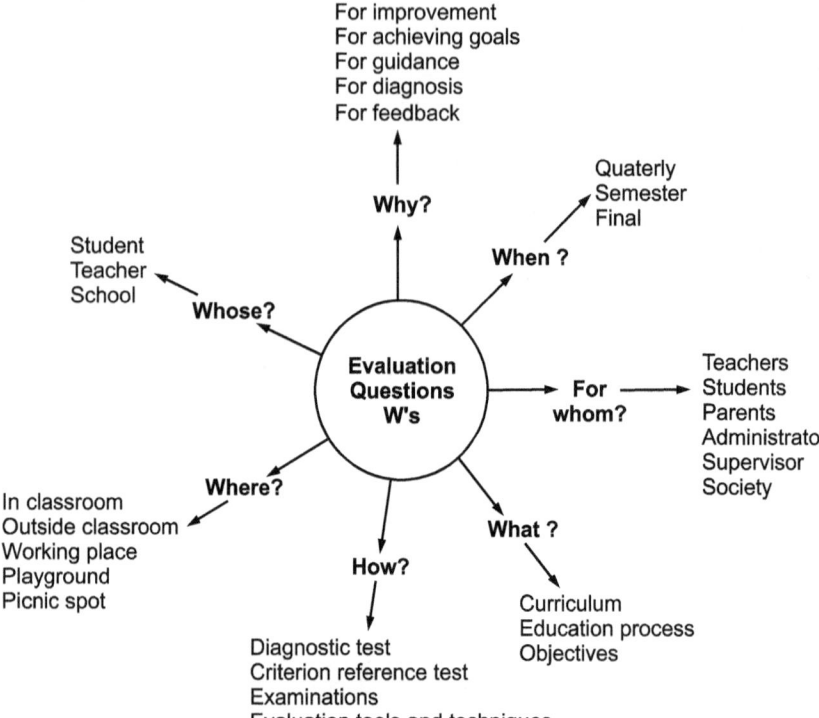

Fig. 5.2

Types of Evaluation :

1. Preparative evaluation.
2. Formative evaluation.
3. Diagnostic evaluation.
4. Summative evaluation.

Types of Evaluation Approaches :

1. Self evaluation approach.
2. Teacher evaluation approach.
3. Parent evaluation approach.
4. Institutional evaluation approach.

Evaluation has an important place in educational process. In current situation teaching-learning process, role of evaluation is very important.

Evaluation has various functions in teaching-learning of any subject. The functions of evaluation in mathematics subject are :

(i)   Norm reference functions.

(ii) Criterion referenced functions.

(iii) Dual purpose functions.

Activity 1 : For example :

(i)   There are 30 students in std. VIIIth. Out of 30 students Vishal gets 95 marks out of 100. From this, we can say that Vishal is intelligent in Mathematics.

(ii) In a class of 15 students. Tushar get 99 marks and 5 students get out off marks in mathematics.

Questions

1.   Read the above examples and give your remark.
2.   Whether Tushar is intelligent in mathematics?

Activity 2 :   Prabha is in 5th Std. While doing addition of fraction she works as

$$\frac{3}{5} + \frac{4}{7} = \frac{3+4}{5+7} = \frac{7}{12}$$

From this it is clear that Prabha can not understand the concept of fraction. To do the addition of fraction there is a need to make both the denominators equal.

From Prabha's behaviour it is clear that she is not understood the concept and there is a need to give her more explanation to clear the concept of addition of fraction with unequal denominator.

The objective of evaluation is, to make expected changes in behaviour in the form of learning products of content gained through instruction.

From the analysis of score or the marks obtained by the students and its inferences, the judgement about the effectiveness of teaching devices, instructional materials and strategies relevancy of objectives, weakness of learners etc. can easily obtained and for all these things evaluation is very important.

5.3.1 Steps in Evaluation OR Evaluation Programme

Evaluation is a comprehensive and continuous process. It starts with the beginning of education process. The teachers can evaluate the students during whole year with the help of oral questions, test assignment and also with co-curricular activities etc.

In evaluation, there are three main steps :

1. Fixed educational objectives.
2. Arrangement of learning activities.
3. The evaluation is executed by comparing the actual change in behaviour of the student.

Steps in Evaluation :

In the step of evaluation, the behavioural changes occurred in the student are compared with the expected changes. If the behavioural changes occurred are very near to the expected behavioural changes, then teaching work is considered as satisfactory.

The last step of evaluation process is, the application of results as a feedback. From evaluation, it is known whether specific objectives of teaching have been achieved or not. If these objectives are achieved, it works as feedback for further teaching - learning process. If the objectives are not achieved then the teacher modifies his teaching method on the basis of the result.

Thus, the result of evaluation can provide feedback to make the teaching-learning process effective and it also helps in the attainment of the specified objectives.

5.3.2 Place of Evaluation in the Process of Education

Many a times we have certain purpose in our mind. We make different efforts to fulfill the purpose. Ultimately we review the extent to which our purpose is realised. Similar is the process of 'education'. Take an example of teaching Marathi to Class IV. Initially, we will have to chalk out yearly plan, which will have to be followed by unit-planning. When we plan teaching strategy for certain unit, we have to set objectives for teaching the unit. Then in the second phase, we make efforts to satisfy the objectives. We have to decide during this process, the 'learning experiences' to be given to the students. In the third and the last phase we will have to take the review of the extent to which the objectives have been satisfied. This review-phase is the phase of evaluation. This is in short, the description of 'educational process'. This description can be represented diagramatically as under.

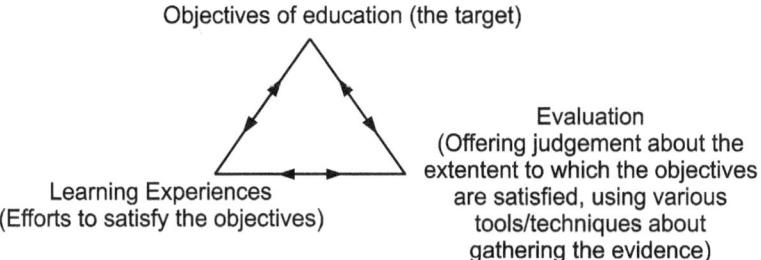

Objectives of education (the target)

Evaluation
(Offering judgement about the extentent to which the objectives are satisfied, using various tools/techniques about gathering the evidence)

Learning Experiences
(Efforts to satisfy the objectives)

Fig. 5.3: The triangle of the process of education

Interpretation of various aspects of the diagram are discussed in the following paragraphs.

5.3.2.1 The Objectives of Education

'Educational objectives' are indicated at the vertex of the triangle. The process of education has to begin with identification of the 'objectives'. The objective helps us to list the changes needed in the behaviour of students. The objectives enable us to make focussed teaching i.e. teaching becomes streamlined. More specific the objectives, more specific becomes the teaching and evaluation.

Let us take an example. If our objective is to teach the students to do good loud-reading, then first question will be what we mean by 'good quality reading'. The objective needs to be spelt out clearly. If we need to visualise the changes in the reading behaviour of students who have satisfied this objectives.

For example :

1. Student reads smoothly.
2. Student duly acknowledges the punctuation marks while reading.
3. Student does meaningful reading.

The list can be continued further. The clarity about the objectives will help the teachers to develop better and more specific plan for teaching. Thus, we proceed to second vertex of the triangle viz. 'learning experiences'.

5.3.2.2 Learning Experiences

We consciously and carefully select educational experiences which help in achieving educational objectives in stipulated time. These experiences may be called as 'learning experiences'.

Achievement of objectives means change in the behaviour of students in desired direction. The teacher has to help the students to achieve these changes in stipulated time. Teacher organises 'learning situations' to facilitate the changes which gives 'learning experiences' to the students. Let us consider the objective of inculcation of good reading habits among students. One of the strategies to achieve this is demonstration of 'Model reading' by the teachers. Another one may be listening to the audio cassettes demonstrating model reading. Teacher, also, may be required to diagnose difficulties in good reading and organise remedial program to remove them. These learning situations are organised as per objective. Pupils gain learning experiences when involved in these situations. Consequently they will gradually develop good reading habits.

After spelling out objectives and making efforts to achieve them through organising learning experiences we come to the third stage i.e. evaluating indicated at the third vertex of the triangle.

5.3.2.3 Evaluation

At the stage of evaluation, teachers try to find out the extent to which behavioural changes envisaged have occurred. For gathering the evidence for changes various tools and techniques are employed. If we want to get evidence of good reading in previous example, what are we required to do ? We need to select/develop appropriate reading matter while doing so. We will have to take into consideration the factors which will help to test 'good reading' like length of a sentences, punctuation marks, conjuct letters, difficulty of the content etc. Then we will have to let the students the paragraphs so designed. We will have to observe the process of reading of students and record observations about the change in the behaviour with respect to good reading. Ultimately, we will be able to offer our judgement about the behavioural changes based on this objective records.

In this example, the paragraph designed specifically is the 'tool' of testing while asking the students to read them loudly is the 'technique' of the testing. Various tools/techniques need to be employed for gathering objective evidence about behavioural changes. Written, oral or practical examinations are some such techniques used extensively. The selection of tools depends upon the objective to be examined. For example, oral techniques will not be useful to test good hand writing or orthography. Here, the proper option will be written examination.

The information we receive by employing these tools or techniques is partly quantitative (in the form of numbers) and partly qualitative (of descriptive nature). We are able to offer our judgement about the achievement of objectives on the basis of this information. This in short is the process of evaluation.

The arrow-signs indicate the direction of the process. We observe two arrow signs on each of the sides at the triangle indicating opposite direction. Let us see how to interpret these signs.

(a) If we read the signs in anticlockwise direction starting from upper vertex, we understand the sequence of educational process i.e. objectives → learning experiences → evaluation.

(b) If we read clockwise starting from the vertex of 'evaluation', we understand that process of education does not end at evaluation. The clockwise arrows suggest reverse process of thinking i.e. evaluation → learning experiences → objectives. This means that when we observe failure in achievement of objectives at the stage of evaluation we need to examine the suitability of learning experiences given. If we find no shortcoming in the learning experiences we need to look back to the objectives and examine their suitability to the age group of students etc. We need to make necessary corrections when we find shortcomings at any of the stages.

Both of these anticlockwise and clockwise cycles in the educational process are equally important. The cycles continue till the educational objectives are achieved at the desired level.

(c) Every side of the triangle has two arrow signs.

This means, the two processes indicated at the end points of the side are mutually related.

(d) Evaluation has important role in the process of education. Evaluation triggers the review of entire process of education when objectives are not achieved. Thus, evaluation helps us to maintain the expected output/quality of the educational process.

Read and think over ...

We advocate that 'the purpose of testing should not be competing with others, but competing with the self.' Do you find the view to be practical ?

5.4 Evaluation Tools of Mathematics Subject

Evaluation is a process of determining to what extent the objectives are being realized. But to check whether these objectives have been achieved or not, a teacher or an evaluator needs some tools to carry out the process of evaluation. Following classification will give a class picture of the evaluation tools of mathematics subject.

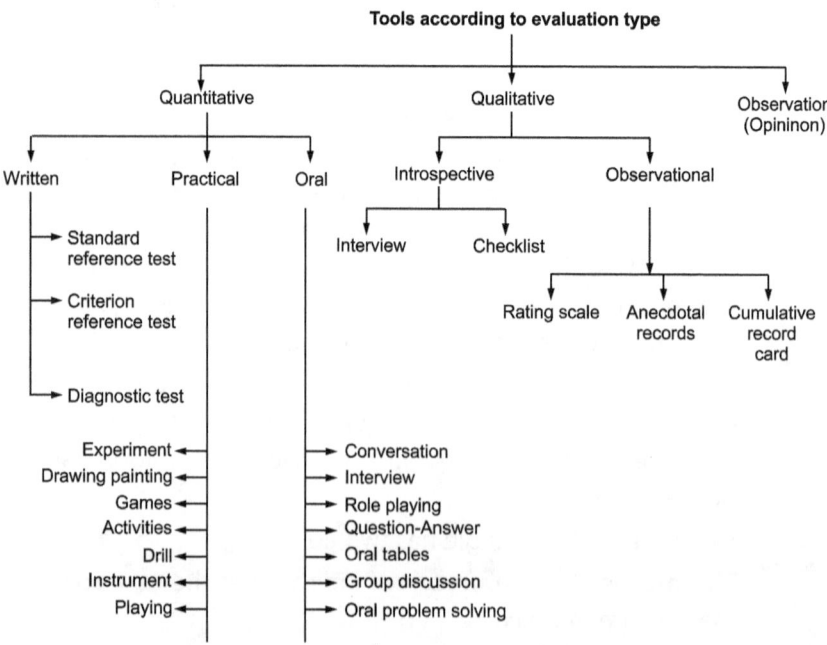

5.4.1 Tools of Evaluation Based on Mathematics Content

Primary Level (1st Lower to 5th Std.)

Contents	Objectives	Evaluation Techniques
1. Geometry	Observation of shapes, Classification, Conclusion and figure drawing	1. Daily observation 2. Orals 3. Practicals 4. Activity 5. Self study 6. Written test
2. Measurement	Observation, Practical work and use of practical work	1. Daily observation 2. Orals 3. Practicals 4. Written test 5. Project
3. Number system	Formation of concepts	1. Daily observation 2. Orals 3. Activity 4. Self study 5. Written test 6. Project
4. Operation and Numbers	Understanding of numbers, Solve examples, Use in day-to-day life	1. Daily observation 2. Orals 3. Practicals 4. Activity 5. Self study 6. Written test

... (Contd.)

Contents	Objectives	Evaluation Techniques
5. Data collection and frequency distribution	Collection of data, Classification of data	1. Daily observation 2. Orals 3. Activity 4. Practicals 5. Self study 6. Projects
6. Patterns	Observation, Find meaning, Pattern drawing	1. Daily observation 2. Orals 3. Activity 4. Practicals 5. Self Study

(I) Formative Evaluation :

Subject : Mathematics

(1) Daily Observation :

Aim:

(i) Check the understanding of concepts and use of concepts in day-to-day life by the students.

(ii) Remove the problems in teaching-learning process of mathematics subject.

For example :

1. **Number system :** Note down the given numbers/Problem with reading numbers/Wrong reading like –

   5017 - This number can be read as five hundred seventeen and the expansion form of number can be written as

   500 + 10 + 7

   And ask students whether it is correct or not.

2. **Geometrical shapes :** Shape of ball, ring is circle/round shape. If we stand in circle shape on a ground then it is called as round shape.

3. **Measurement :** While writing volume forgot to write units, or units are not considered while doing conversion of different units.

4. **Operations on numbers :**
   - From the given information students cannot form the equations in mathematical language.
   - Lack of speed to do the mathematical operations.
   - In day-to-day life they are not able to do the simple calculations.

5. **Classification of data :**
   - They can collect the information but they cannot classify the information.

6. **Patterns :**
   - They cannot match the patterns.

For above mentioned reasons the daily observation technique is very important in formative evaluation.

Also note down the bad and good statement in daily teaching-learning process.

For example :

- Ganesh has been done addition of three digit numbers accurately.
- Ganesh has been done addition of three digit numbers with speed accurately.
- He/She
  - can solve examples speedily
  - can solve examples with different method
  - is master in mathematical operations
  - is interested in mathematical puzzles/games.

(2) Oral Work :

Aim :

- To develop communication skill.
- To check reading skill.
- To check understanding of mathematical concepts.
- Are able to do the mathematical operations with speed/orally.

For example : **(i) Geometry :**
- Reading of figures.
- Characteristic/Properties of shapes, like rectangle, square.
- Difference between rectangle and square.
- Check whether the given triangles are symmetric or not.
- From the given figure, read the pair of ∠AOB and ∠BOC

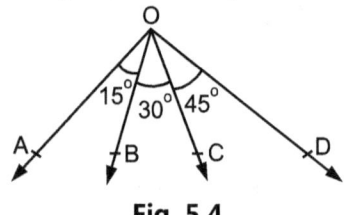

Fig. 5.4

(ii) Measurement :
- How to convert cm in metre? or 5 m = ? cm.
- How many days are in the month of February in year 2016?
- What is the difference between perimeter and area of square?
- Find the diameter of a circle if the radius is 8 cm.

In this way, we can ask the easy questions in the oral exams like –

Tables, Formulaes, Rules, Definitions, Reading of graph, Oral calculation etc.

(3) Practical/Experimental Method :

Aim :
- To check the practical skill of students.
- To check the understanding of mathematical concepts by practical method.
- To do exact or proper observation/write the correct conclusion/verification of rules/formulae/properties.

Planning :
- Decide the practical for teaching-learning process on the basis of content.
- Make apparatus available for practical. Decide whether the learning process is given to a single student or a group of students.

- First explain the aim of practical clearly and what to be observed ?

For example : Find the fractions of same value.

Apparatus/Material : Plain paper, pencil.

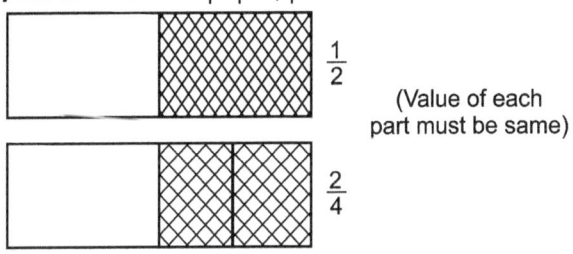

$\frac{1}{2}$

(Value of each part must be same)

$\frac{2}{4}$

Fig. 5.5

Step 1: Take a rectangular paper, fold the paper at the middle. (Ask students to draw a line on $^1/_2$ part of paper) as shown in Fig. 5.5 above.

Step 2: Again fold the paper in four equal parts.

Measure fraction on half part of the paper $= \frac{2}{4}$.

In this way, fold the paper in equal parts and observe the marked portion of paper. Check the fractions are of same value or not.

(For Practical examination give marks as per the mark distribution system.)

(4) Activity :

Aim :

- Learning with experience/Students can learn with experience.
- Develop habit of self study.
- To give a chance of learning with self study.
- To give speed to learning process on basis of experience.
- In the beginning of term fix the activities/Time management/ Required material/Field trip/Prepare list of activities.

Working :

- Fix aim of activity.
- While doing activity observe the student's communication, and co-ordination. Wherever necessary guide them and cheer them to complete the activity.

Evaluation :

At the time of evaluation, the marks can be given as
Practical work/Personal attendance performance.

Regularity.

Neat and tidyness.

For example, 3rd Std. - Measurement

- Ask students to collect different size object and take measurement of length of that objects or take two buckets and two different size or vessels to fill the bucket with water. Same amount of water measures different because different means were used to measure it.

Marks distribution :

- Collection of objects.
- Arrangement.
- Collection of information.
- Preparation of report.
- End of activity.

Give marks on the basis of above mention parts of the activity.

In the same way, give activities to the students on :

- Measure length of bench in cm.
- Measure liquids in line.
- Measure weight in kilogram.

(5) Project

Give atleast one project to each student and ask them to complete it in any one of the two terms.

For example, Subject : Mathematics 5th Std.

Unit - Pictographs.

Name of Project : Collection of information and present by pictorial method.

Aim :

- Collection of information and present the information in pictorial form.
- Learning/Study with activity/practical.

- Develop habit of careful observation.
- Use of practical knowledge in day-to-day life.

Preparation for Project :
- Make list of projects in the beginning of year.

Precaution while preparing list of projects :
- Project is of level of sixth standard students.
- Material required for project is available in school. for example, Thermometer.
- Project is such that it can be completed easily at the term end.

Project work :
Guide a student to complete the project in time. Take time-to-time information of project from students and solve their queries.

Project Report/Presentation : Students of 5th std. can
- Write detail report of collected information.
- Write the conclusion from the collected information.

(For students of 1st to 4th standard there is no need to write the project report, only oral explanation is required.)

Evaluation :
- Collection of information.
- Classification of information.
- Report writing.
- Presentation.

(6) Self-study :

Aim :
1. To develop habit of self study.
2. To use of knowledge in real life situation.
3. To develop thinking power.

Planning :
- Preparation of question bank.
- Prepare material for self-study (like card).

   (Fill in information in figures, Ask questions on figure, write information from figures,) Write examples from table, solve the given examples.)

Working :

- Give Class work/Home work on lesson. Teach in class.
- Give regular practice.
- Check class work/Home work regularly.
- Check all self study work of student's, but give marks to one of them as per the decision.

Sample of Self-study Card :

3rd Std. Subject : Mathematics

Unit : Measurement of Time : Reading of Time in min., sec. and hours.

Home work : In the table given below note down the exact time for the different required activities.

	Home work	Plying	Exercise	Sleeping
Starting time				
Ending time				
Total time				

Questions

1. Find the area of garden ?
2. Find the area of road around the garden ?

Activity :
You can make any type of self-study card with your friends.

Portfolio of Student :

Student portfolios are most effective when they are used to evaluate student learning progress and achievement.

Portfolios can help teachers to monitor and evaluate learning progress over time. Portfolios help teachers to determine whether students can apply what they have learned to new problems and different subject areas.

Portfolios can encourage students to take more ownership and responsibility over the learning process. Portfolios can improve communication between teachers and parents.

Portfolios are also useful for the future of students.

Preparation of portfolio : With the help of certificate in different competitions, Medals, Art work, Craft work, Drawing and colouring etc. with his dairy can be keep in a box, or box file or can be pasted in a notebook.

Advantages of Formative Evaluation :

1. Teaching-learning and evaluation techniques are same.
2. Evaluation can be done during the process of learning.
3. Students are more motivated to learn.
4. Evaluating students according to the same criteria.
5. Teacher can inform students about their current progress in order to help them set goals for improvement.

5.4.2 Diagnostic Test

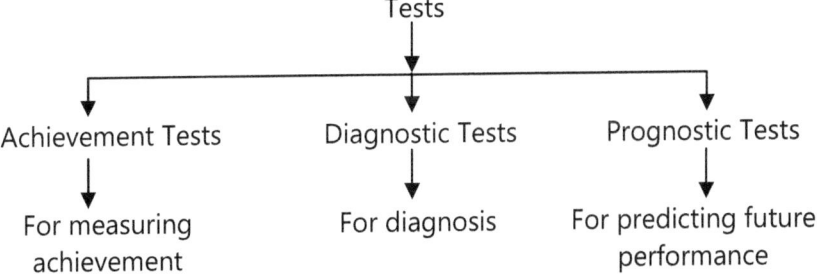

When teacher made achievement tests are organised, the progress of students can be measured. A teacher also comes to know the areas of difficulty of the students. But the cause or reason for difficulty is not made clear by achievement test. Thus, specific tests are designed to provide more information about the students difficulties. They are designed to identify particular strengths or weaknesses of the student and also reveal the cause.

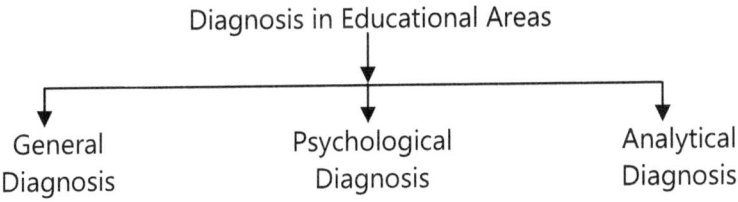

According to Ross and Stanley, the following are the levels of diagnosis :

1. Who are the students having difficulty ?
2. Where are the errors located ?
3. Why did the errors occur ?
4. What remedies are suggested ?
5. How can the errors be prevented ?

The first four levels are corrective diagnosis while the fifth level is preventive diagnosis.

Steps in construction of Diagnostic Test :

1. Identification of problem area.
2. Detailed content analysis.
3. Listing all learning points.
4. Arranging learning points in sequence.
5. Writing test items for each learning point.
6. Providing clear instructions.
7. Preparing a scoring key and making scheme.
8. Providing time limit.
9. Administration of test.

After administering the test following procedure should be used for analysing the performance and identifying the weaknesses :

1. Analysis of performance of students according to each question.
2. Identification of strengths and weaknesses.
3. Identification of causes for learning difficulty.
4. Preparing a diagnostic chart.
5. Planning of remedial teaching.
6. Implementation of remedial teaching.
7. Evaluation of effectiveness of programme.

Uses of Diagnostic Tests : Diagnostic test is useful :

1. To find out the difficulties of students.
2. To diagnose the weaknesses of students.
3. To find out inadequacies in certain skills.

4. To locate areas where individual attention is required.

5. As it serves as a basis for improving instructional methods.

Question

1. Explain the meaning of diagnostic tests and also write their importance.

5.4.3 Remedial Teaching

Only diagnosis of weaknesses and shortcomings is not enough. A good diagnosis must be followed by good treatment. This good treatment" in education means "Remedial teaching" this statement also has to be very accurate and should be done as soon as possible. Otherwise the weakness of the students will become strong.

Good diagnosis and good remedial teaching are the two sides of a coin. A teacher should be concerned with both. Most of the diagnosis done by the teacher is corrective in nature corrective diagnosis involves the following steps :

1. Finding the difficulty.

2. Finding the cause of difficulty.

3. Providing remedial teaching.

4. Preventive measures.

After identifying the difficulties and its causes, the next step is planning and applying remedial measures. The planning of remedial programme differs considerably from individual to individual. If there are two students having the same learning difficulty, this difficulty through being singular may have arise because of different causes and hence have to be tackled differently. A teacher also has to take the aspect of individual differences in consideration. If the whole class is having same difficulty, a teacher has to plan remedial teaching appropriately.

The method of remedial teaching may sometimes be a simple matter such as "Teach, Review and Reteach". In other causes it may involve hard efforts to improve motivation, correct study habits and overcome emotional difficulties.

Despite different methods and techniques used in remedial teaching, there are certain guiding principles as follows :

1. Remedial teaching should be accompanied by strong motivation programme.

2. It should take into account the psychology of learning.

3. There should be continuous evaluation.

4. Remedial programmes may not always need separate time allocation. But they will need extra work or part of teacher and students.

5. Students commit silly mistakes, so teacher should not be angry with them.

6. Teacher should see if the diagnosis is correct.

7. Teacher should try to change the wrong study habits of the students.

8. Sometimes, teaching method may also be incorrect. So teacher should teach by using another method in remedial teaching.

9. Remedial teaching without diagnosis is useless. Teacher should keep this in mind.

10. Do not publicize the weaknesses of any student. Protect the privacy and emotions of a student.

5.4.4 Criterion Tests or Criterion Reference Tests

The actual process of evaluation involves the following steps :

1. Define the objectives to be tested.

2. State objectives.

3. Selection of evaluation tools.

4. Administration of tools.

5. Interpretation of data.

6. Application of results.

Interpretability has to do with what the scores on a test mean. But unless a test provides a point of reference for interpretation it is not a useful test. There are two types of reference points that can be applied for interpretation of test. The first is to relate a student's test score to the scores of other students in that test. We call this Norm-Referencing. The second is to establish an external standard and relate the student's test score to it. We call this Criterion Referencing. In Criterion referenced tests the tools of evaluation are so constructed as to measure student learning according to a predetermined standard of achievement or performance. In other words, test based on reference to a "criterion" i.e. specific teaching learning objective fixed in advance may be referred to as a criterion referenced evaluation. Such type of test is conducted to provide results that can be directly interpreted in terms of the level of performance.

Whereas in norm-reference test, a learner's performance is compared with that of another or a group of learners.

In criterion - reference test, a criterion i.e. an accepted level of performance (mastery level) is fixed well before the beginning of the actual teaching - learning session. The results of such tests are interpreted in terms of predetermined standard of absolute performance. For example: The learner solves 15 two digit subtraction problems out of 20 in 30 minutes.

Steps in Construction of Criterion - Reference Tests :

1. Prepare content outline.
2. List the skills and knowledge that the test attempts to measure.
3. Identify performance level.
4. Write objectives and specifications.
5. Decide upon a criterion or cut-off score showing the test performance a student must obtain.

The following points should be considered while preparing criterion tests :

1. Questions should be competency based.
2. The language should be clear and understood by students.
3. Mastery level of students should be proved through the questions.
4. Questions should be appropriate according to age and standard.

Instructions should be clear.

For Example, Standard 1 :

Competency : Addition of two digit number with one digit number.

Following type of criterion - test can be prepared for the unit - Addition of two digit numbers with one digit numbers (Nos. 1 to 20).

Question : Fill in the blank squares with correct answers by doing addition as shown in the solved example :

1. $15 + 2 = \boxed{17}$ 6. $16 + 3 = \square$

2. $11 + 8 = \square$ 7. $13 + 6 = \square$

3. $12 + 3 = \square$ 8. $15 + 3 = \square$

4. $14 + 5 = \square$ 9. $17 + 4 = \square$

5. $19 + 1 = \square$ 10. $12 + 2 = \square$

Mastery level/Criterion : Students should solve at least seven problems. If student solves only 5 or less than 5, then remedial teaching is needed.

Question

1. Explain the importance of criterion tests.

5.4.5 Standards Reference Tests

In education, the term "standards referenced" refers to instructional approaches or assessments that are "referenced" to or derived from established "learning standards" i.e. concise written descriptions of what students are expected to know and be able to do at a specific stage of their education.

Standard referenced test are designed to measure student performance against a fixed set of predetermined learning standards. In elementary and secondary education, standard reference tests evaluate whether students have learned a specific body of knowledge or acquired a specific skill set described in a given set of standards.

Standard referenced test is a recent variation of criterion referenced test. "Content standards" or "Curriculum framework" are prepared for these tests which describe what students should know and be able to do in different subjects at various grade levels. They also have performance standards students should know to reach the "basic" or "proficient" level in the subject.

Tests are then based on the standards and the results are reported in terms of "levels". In some states, performance standards have been steadily increased, in that students continually have to know more to meet the same level.

Characteristics of standards of standards reference tests :

1. Standards should cover the important knowledge and skills that students should learn.

2. They should be well written and reasonable.

3. They should not include "too much" or should not be too vague.

4. This difficulty level must not be too high.

5. They should not undermine higher quality of local curriculum.

Difference between Standards referenced test and Criterion referenced test :

Standards Referenced Test	Criterion Referenced Test
1. To rank each student with respect to the achievement of others in broad areas of knowledge.	1. To determine whether each student has achieved specific skills or concepts.
2. To discriminate between high and low achievers.	2. To find out how much students know before instruction begins and after it has finished.
3. Measures broad skill areas sampled from a variety of text books, syllabi and judgements of curriculum experts.	3. Measures specific skills which make-up a designated curriculum.

... (Contd.)

Standards Referenced Test	Criterion Referenced Test
4. Each skill is tested by less than four items that vary in difficulty.	4. Each skill is tested by at least four items in order to obtain an adequate sample of student performance and to minimize the effect of guessing.
5. Items are selected that discriminate between high and low achievers.	5. The items which test any given skill are parallel in difficulty.
6. Each individual is compared with other examinees and assigned a score.	6. Each individual is compared with a present standard for acceptable achievement. The performance of other examinees is irrelevant.
7. Student achievement is reported for broad skill areas.	7. Student achievement is reported for individual skills.

5.4.6 Continuous Comprehensive Evaluation

Primary education is the base of education. With the help of primary education the child can be developed physically, mentally and also at the emotional level of the child. On the basis of these three, there is a requirement of development of ability and expertise. It is also important to check that, the development of child is going in proper way or not at the time of assessment. To take a decision about the expected behavioural changes at the time of assessment is very important. If the behavioural changes of child are compared with expected changes and both are same then the method of teaching is ok. Then the teaching work is satisfactory, otherwise the teacher has to change the method of teaching.

For primary level education, Government of Maharashtra declared a Rule on 20th August 2010 on the basis of :

(i) Kothari Ayog (1964).

(ii) Rashtriya Shaikshanik Dhoran (1986).

(iii) Dr. R. H. Dave Samiti Ahwal (1990).

(iv) NCF 2005.

(vi) SCF 2010.

(vii) 29 (2) (h) in RTE 2009.

The GR was declared on the basis of above mention references. The achievement of learning objectives can be evaluated at the time of learning is very important. The process of evaluation develops the structure of teaching-learning, and total system of education is evaluated under it. On this basis, some essential improvements in the system are to be done.

Since, examination system has concerned only with the achievements of students, evaluation is the new concept.

In teaching-learning process, the evaluation can be done as :

(i) Formative evaluation.

(ii) Summative evaluation.

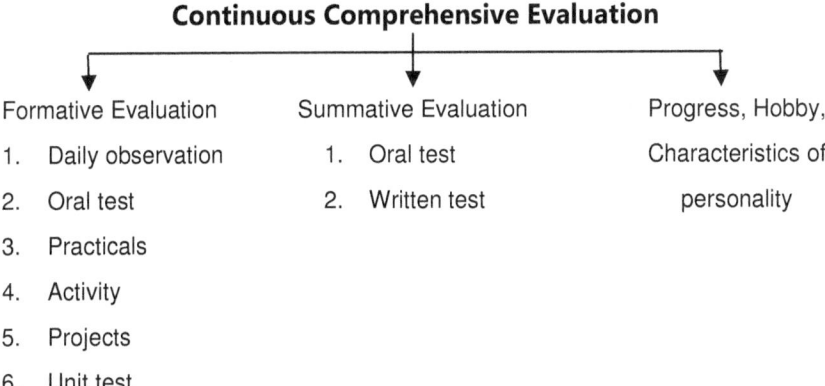

Continuous Comprehensive Evaluation

Formative Evaluation	Summative Evaluation	Progress, Hobby,
1. Daily observation	1. Oral test	Characteristics of
2. Oral test	2. Written test	personality
3. Practicals		
4. Activity		
5. Projects		
6. Unit test		
7. Class work / Home work		
8. Self study		

(At least 5 techniques are important).

(i) Formative evaluation: Formative evaluations are the evaluations FOR learning. They are often ungraded and informal. Their aim is to provide both the students and teachers with a guage of where their level of understanding is at the current moment and enable the teacher to make necessary changes in teaching methods to meet the emerging needs of the class. Formative evaluations are particularly important because they allow you to make changes that affect the current students, while the term 'end form' only affect further class.

The formative evaluation can be done on the basis of the following :

(i) Daily observation.

(ii) Oral test.

(iii) Taking practicals.

(iv) Activity work.

(v) Project work.

(vi) Unit test.

(vii) Class work/Home work.

For formative evaluation, teaching methods/aids are decided on the basis of subjects.

Subject	Methods/Technology
1. Languages, Mathematics	(i) Daily observation, (ii) Oral work, (iii) Written test and any two types of works as mentioned above.
2. Geography, Social Sciences	(i) Daily observation, (ii) Written test, (iii) Practical work and any two types of works as mentioned above.
3. History/Civics	(i) Daily observation, (ii) Written test (iii) Any three types of works as mentioned above.
4. Art, Craft and Physical Education	(i) Daily observation, (ii) Practical work, (iii) Project work.

Evaluation Techniques in Mathematics :

The techniques of evaluation for mathematics which are commonly used in schools are of two types :

(i) Quantitative Techniques,

(ii) Qualitative Techniques.

Quantitative Techniques : The quantitative techniques of evaluation are the most useful, reliable and valid for mathematics subject. The main form of this technique is :

(i) Daily observation

(ii) Oral work

(iii) Written test

These three forms are compulsory for mathematics subject evaluation. Because of these three forms.

(iv) Practical method, and

(v) Activity work is also important.

In short, the techniques of evaluation of mathematics subject on primary level i.e. (i) Daily observation, (ii) Oral work, (iii) Written test, (iv) Practical work, (v) Activity work, are important.

For some content there is need of project work also.

(A) Evaluation Techniques based on Formative Evaluation

On primary level, the content of mathematics subject can be classified as :

Low primary level (1st Std. to 5th Std.) and high primary level (6th Std. to 8th Std.). Because of this, while deciding the techniques and methods, we have to consider the content of subject, teaching - learning method, knowledge and evaluation.

Gradation method is very useful for pre-primary level. Because, the students on pre-primary level can understand the comparative words, they can differentiate the numbers; they can understand the meaning of operation and operation on number. They can draw the geometrical figures; they can collect the information and classify the information.

Percentage Distribution (G.R. : 20th August 2010) :

Percentage distribution can be done on the basis of evaluation techniques used in formative assessment.

1st Std. and 2nd Std. : 70%

3rd Std. and 4th Std. : 60%

5th Std. : 50%

For example, Total 70 marks are given for the evaluation techniques of formative assessment of Mathematics for 2nd standard.

Marks given on the basis of evaluation techniques :

Daily observation	–	0 marks
Oral work	–	15 marks
Practical work	–	25 marks
Activity	–	20 marks
Self study	–	10 marks
Total	**–**	**70 marks**

Note: For special child keep project work optional.

Points to Remember

* Meaning of formative evaluation.
* Choice of evaluation techniques for formative evaluation.
* Marks distribution of mathematics subject.
* Role of formative evaluation/assessment.

(ii) Summative Evaluation:

Summative evaluation can be done after a certain period (i.e. at the mid-term or at the end of academic year). Summative evaluation can be done with the help of the techniques such as written test, oral examinations, practical etc. at the middle or mid-term and at the end of year. The percentage can be distributed in increasing pattern from 1st standard to 8th standard and the percentage distribution in formative evaluation is in decreasing pattern.

Percentage distribution according to G.R. declared on 10th August 2010 for primary level (1st std. to 5th std.) is as follows :

Std.	Percentage distribution for formative evaluation	Percentage distribution for summative evaluation		Total percentage
		Orals/Practicals	Written exam	
1st std. & 2nd std.	70%	10%	20%	100%
3rd std. & 4th std.	60%	10%	30%	100%
5th std.	50%	10%	40%	100%

Format of Questions in Summative Evaluation :

1. In the form of written test, orals and practical tests.
2. Questions asked in examination should develop thinking level of students.
3. Avoid the questions which put burden/stress on mind of students.
4. Ask questions on the basis of syllabus only.

After the summative evaluation, check whether the expected behavioural changes are seen in students or not. If the behavioural changes are not satisfactory, then change the direction of teaching-learning process.

5.5 Unit Test

5.5.1 Preparation of Question Paper of Unit Test

A teacher has to know the learning outcomes of teaching a unit. This may be done after teaching of every unit. The teacher evaluates the students to know whether they have understood the unit or not through a test. This is called a unit test. Unit test is a type of written test which is in turn a type of teacher-made achievement test.

Any unit test or written test contains three types of questions :

(i) Objective type questions.   (ii) Short answer questions.

(iii) Long/Essay type questions.

5.5.2 Outline of Unit Test

The important steps involved in the preparation of a good unit test are :

1. Planning the test.
2. Preparation of a design or outline.
3. Reviewing and editing.
4. Providing directions.
5. Preparing scoring key and making scheme.
6. Administering the test.
7. Evaluation of test.

Preparation of outline or design or the blue print or 3-dimensional chart is most important step.

Following steps are involved in the preparation of a blue print.

1. **Summative Evaluation : Layout of Written test**
   Subject - Mathematics Std. 4th

   Sections of content and allotting weightage to the content.

   Second Term

   Std. : IV   **Subject : Mathematics**   **Total Marks : 40**

Sr. No.	Objective/Unit	Percentage	Marking Scheme		Total Marks 40
			Written 30	Oral/ Practicals 10	
1.	Geometry	20%	6	2	8
2.	Operations on Number	25%	8	3	11
3.	Mensuration	10%	3	1	4
4.	Fractions	15%	4	1	5
5.	Classification of data	20%	6	2	8
6.	Patterns / Fig.	10%	3	1	4
	Total	**100%**	**30**	**10**	**40**

2. **Identification of objectives and allotting weightage to the objectives**

Sr. No.	Objective	Percentage	Marks Distribution		Total Marks 40
			Written 30	Orals/ Practicals 10	
1.	Knowledge	05%	02	1	3
2.	Understanding	45%	13	4	17
3.	Application	30%	09	3	12
4.	Skill	20%	06	2	08
	Total	**100%**	**30**	**10**	**40**

3. **Selection of form of questions and giving weightage to the questions**

Sr. No.	Type of Questions	Percentage	Marks Distribution		Total Marks 40
			Written 30	Oral 10	
1.	Objective Type Questions	25%	08	2	10
2.	Short Answer Questions	55%	16	6	22
3.	Long (Essay) Answer Que.	20%	06	2	08
	Total	**100%**	**30**	**10**	**40**

5.5.3 Preparation of Blue Print

Std.: IV   Total Marks : 30

(According to G.R. of 20th of August, 2010)
Continuous and Comprehensive Evaluation
Second Term : Written Test
Subject : Mathematics
Blue Print

Sr. No.	Unit	Percentage	Knowledge O	Knowledge S.A.	Knowledge L.A.	Understanding O	Understanding S.A.	Understanding L.A.	Application O	Application S.A.	Application L.A.	Skill O	Skill S.A.	Skill L.A.	Total
1.	Geometrical Shapes	20%												1 (3)	(6)
2.	Operations on Numbers	25%				2 (2)	2 (4)			1 (2)					(8)
3.	Mensuration	10%							1 (1)	1 (2)					(3)
4.	Fractions : Addition / Subtraction	15%	1 (2)			2 (2)	1 (2)								(4)
5.	Classification of data	20%						1 (2)	1 (1)						(6)
6.	Figure / Pattern	10%	1 (2)		1 (1)				1 (2)						(3)
	Total	100	(2)	–	5 (5)	4 (8)	–	3 (3)	3 (6)	–	–	–	–	2 (6)	(30)

*Note : Numbers in bracket shows marks.

5.5.4 Test Paper (Written Test)

Second Term : Written Test

Std. : IV   **Subject : Mathematics**   **Total Marks : 30**

Q.1. (A) Choose the correct alternative for the give questions :

(6 Marks)

1. What is the perimeter of rectangle ABCD? Refer Fig. 1 alongside.

    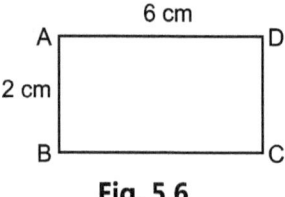

    Fig. 5.6

    (a) 16 sq. cm.   (b) 8 cm.

    (c) 16 cm.   (d) 4 cm.

2. What is the cost of 25 chairs, if cost of one chair is ₹ 700 ?

    (a) ₹ 2,500   (b) ₹ 1,750

    (c) ₹ 17,500   (d) 1,75,000

3. One bunch of flowers required 8 flowers. How many bunches will be form by 360 flowers ?

    (a) 54   (b) 45

    (c) 36   (d) 63

4. 7 km. = _____ m.

    (a) 700 m   (b) 7000 m

    (c) 70,000 m   (d) none of these

5. Find the wrong statement from the following options.

    (a) $\dfrac{1}{8} \boxed{>} \dfrac{1}{10}$ (b) $\dfrac{1}{7} \boxed{<} \dfrac{1}{6}$

    (c) $\dfrac{1}{5} \boxed{>} \dfrac{1}{4}$ (d) $\dfrac{1}{4} \boxed{\leq} \dfrac{1}{2}$

6. Observe the Fig. alongside and choose the correct option of fraction from the following.

    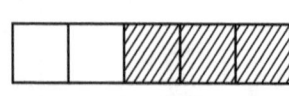

    Fig. 5.7

    (a) $\dfrac{3}{5}$ (b) $\dfrac{3}{2}$

    (c) $\dfrac{5}{3}$ (d) $\dfrac{2}{3}$

Q.1. (B) State whether the given statements are True or False.

(2 Marks)

1. We can show pattern of addition in Table of 9.
2. By reading of Pictograph, we can understand the concept of picture.
3. After reading pictograph, we can able to give information about it.
4. There is no pattern in table of any number.

Q.2. Solve the following questions :   (8 Marks)

1. The length and breadth of rectangle PQRS is 12 cm and 8 cm respectively. Find area and perimeter.   **(2M)**

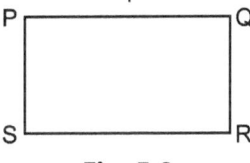

Fig. 5.8

2. Seema contributes ₹ 1,645 for a picnic. After picnic she get ₹ 269 return. How many rupees spend by Seem for picnic?

(2M)

3. The addition of two numbers is 31,426, If one number is 17,548 then find the other number.   **(2M)**

4. From the given information form an example of division. **(2M)**
   - Deepak want to purchase 35 chairs.
   - Cost of one chair is ₹ 765 in a shop.
   - Shopkeeper get ₹ 26,775.

Q.3. (A) Solve the following questions :   (6 Marks)

1. Look At The Fig. Of Nets Given Alongside.

   Which Geometrical Shape Will Be Form With This Nets.   **(1M)**

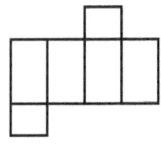

Fig. 5.9

2. Draw Fig. of Nets to prepare a shape of cylinder.   **(1M)**
3. If side of cube is 2 cm, then what is the total surface area of a cube ? (Side = 2 cm).   **(1M)**

Q.3. (B) Observe the pictograph carefully and answer the following questions : **(3M)**

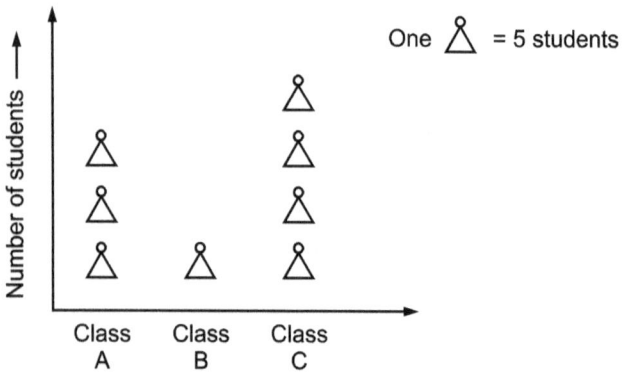

Fig. 5.10

1. How many more number of students in class C than class A?

2. What is the total number of students?

3. How many less number of students in class B than class A?

Q.4. Solve the following questions : **(8 Marks)**

1. A shopkeeper has 500 ml and 200 ml measure to measure liquid substance. If he want to give 200 *l* 700 ml oil to a customer. How he can measure it ? **(2M)**

2. Look at Fig. of tile given below, and prepare a pattern of a tile as you like. **(2M)**

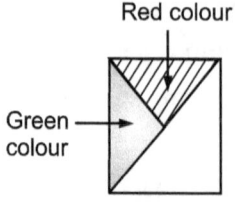

Fig. 5.11

3. Read the information in table given below. Represent this information by pictograph. (Use scale 1 picture to represent 400 animals.) **(2M)**

Types of Animals	Number of Animals	Number of Pictures
Horse	2000	
Cow	800	
Goat	400	
Dog	400	

4. Use a correct sign to show the following inequalities (>, <, =)

(2M)

(i) $\dfrac{1}{8} \square \dfrac{1}{10}$,   (ii) $\dfrac{1}{5} \square \dfrac{1}{3}$,   (iii) $\dfrac{1}{4} \square \dfrac{1}{4}$

(iv) $\dfrac{1}{12} \square \dfrac{1}{16}$,   (v) $\dfrac{3}{7} \square \dfrac{3}{7}$,   (vi) $\dfrac{1}{20} \square \dfrac{1}{15}$

Preparation of Score Key and Marking Scheme :

Preparation of scoring key is also a part of construction of a test. To make the scoring objective, scoring key is essential. It should be prepared by the test maker. In this key, the correct answer of each question is given. For objective questions, the preparation of scoring key is not a difficult task. But for long answer questions and short answer questions it is time taking and difficult task. Division of marks should also be mentioned with the each aspect of model answer sheet.

For example, Std. IV : Blue print of written test Question paper as discussed above.

Objective type Questions	8(8)
Short Answer Questions	8(16)
Long Answer Questions	2(6)
Total	**18(30)**

Knowledge	1(2)
Understanding	9(13)
Application	6(9)
Skill	2(6)
Total	**18(30)**

Note: Number in brackets shows marks.

Number of questions and marks shown in above table are same as mentioned in blue print.

5.5.5 Preparation of Model Answer Sheet

Second Term : Written Test

Std. : IV   **Subject : Mathematics**   **Total Marks : 30**

(Model Answer Sheet and Marks Distribution)

Q.1. (A) Choose the correct alternative for the given questions :

1. (c)	4. (b)		
2. (c)	5. (c)	**(1 Mark each)**	
3. (b)	6. (a)		

Q.1. (B) State whether the given statements are True or False.

1. True	2. True	**(1 Mark each)**
3. True	3. False	

Q.2. Solve the following questions :   **(8 Marks)**

1. Given :   length = 12 cm

                                 breadth = 8 cm

Find : (i) Area of ☐ PQRS

(ii) Perimeter of ☐ PQRS.

Perimeter of rectangle = $2l + 2b$

= $2 \times 12 + 2 \times 8 = 24 + 16$

= 40 cm.   **(1M)**

Area of rectangle = length × breadth

= $12 \times 8 = 96$ sq. cm.

2. Given : Contribution of Seema = ₹ 1,645

Amount paid return to Seema = 269   **(1M)**

Expenses of picnic = Total amount − Amount return

= 1,645 − 269 = 1,376

∴ Total expenses of Seema for a picnic = ₹ 1,376.

3. Given : Addition of two number = 31,426

One number = 17,548

Find :   The other number = ?

Operation : Subtraction

∴   31,426   (Addition)

              − 17,548   (One number out of two)

                13,878   Other number   **(1M)**

4. Given : Shopkeeper get amount = ₹ 26,775

Cost of one chair = ₹ 765

Chair purchase by Deepak = 35   **(1M)**

Example : Deepak purchase 35 chairs of ₹ 26,775 from a shopkeeper. What is the cost of one chair ?

Here we have to do operation of division.   **(1M)**

$$
\begin{array}{r}
765 \\
35\overline{)26775} \\
-245 \\
\overline{0227} \\
-210 \\
\overline{0175} \\
-175 \\
\overline{000}
\end{array}
$$

Q.3. (A) Solve the following questions :

2. From given Nets the shape of cylinder will form.   **(1M)**

Nets of cylinder

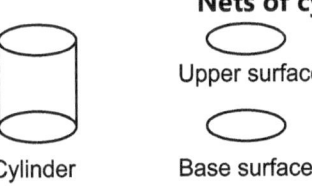

Upper surface

Base surface

Cylinder

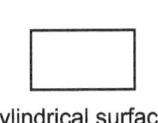

Cylindrical surface

Fig. 5.12

3. Surface area of cube = $(Side)^2$

Side = 2 cm.

∴ Surface area of cube = 4 sq. cm.

All surface of cube are equal.

∴ Total surface area of cube = 6×4 = 24 sq. cm.   **(1M)**

Q.3. (B) From given pictograph : Scale is : One picture (⚇) represents 5 students :

1.   Students in class A = 15

Students in class C = 20

∴ The number of students in class C more than class A

= 20 − 15 = 5 students   **(1M)**

2.   Total number of students $= 8 \times 5 = 40$ students   **(1M)**

3.   Students in class A $= 15$
                Students in class B $= 5$

$\therefore$ $15 - 5 = 10$

The students in class B are less than in class A by 10 numbers of students.   **(1M)**

Q.4. (A) Solve the following questions :   (8 Marks)

1.   A shopkeeper has measure of 500 ml, and 200 ml to measure oil. He wants to give 2 l 700 ml oil to a customer.

$\therefore$ $2\,l = 500\ \text{ml} \times 4 = 2000\ \text{ml} = 2\,l$ **(1M)**

$$700\ \text{ml} = 200\ \text{ml} \times 3 + \frac{1}{2}\ \text{of 200 ml measure}$$

$700\ \text{ml} = 600\ \text{ml} + 100\ \text{ml}$

OR $700\ \text{ml} = 500\ \text{ml} + 200\ \text{ml}$ **(1M)**

2.   Given pattern of tile is

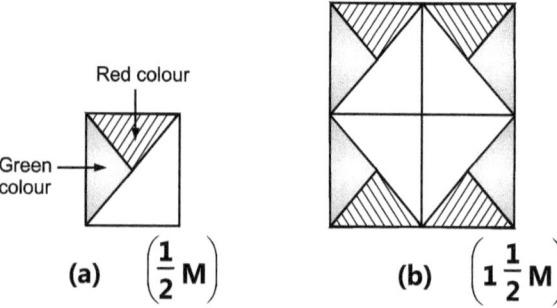

New pattern

Red colour

Green colour

(a) $\left(\dfrac{1}{2}\,\text{M}\right)$ (b) $\left(1\dfrac{1}{2}\,\text{M}\right)$

Fig. 5.13

3.   From the given information in the table (One picture represent 400 animals). Therefore, the table can be rewrite as.   **(1M)**

Types of Animals	Number of Animals	Number of Pictures
Horse	2000	5
Cow	800	2
Goat	400	1
Dog	400	1

4.   Use the correct sign (>, <, =) to show the following inequality:

(i) $\dfrac{1}{8}\boxed{>}\dfrac{1}{10}$,   (ii) $\dfrac{1}{5}\boxed{<}\dfrac{1}{3}$,   (iii) $\dfrac{1}{4}\boxed{=}\dfrac{1}{4}$ **(1M)**

(iv) $\dfrac{1}{12}\boxed{>}\dfrac{1}{16}$,   (v) $\dfrac{3}{7}\boxed{=}\dfrac{3}{7}$,   (vi) $\dfrac{1}{20}\boxed{<}\dfrac{1}{15}$

5.5.6 Preparation of Blue Print for Oral Test

Std. IV

Second Term/Practical Test/Oral Test

Subject : Mathematics

Blue Print

Total Marks : 10

Sr. No.	Unit	Objectives												Total
		Knowledge			Understanding			Application			Skill			
		O	S.A.	L.A.	O	S.A.	L.A.	O	S.A.	L.A.	O	S.A.	L.A.	
1.	Geometrical Shapes							1 (1)			1 (1)			(2)
2.	Operations on Numbers				1 (1)			1 (1)			1 (1)			(3)
3.	Mensuration											1 (2)		(2)
4.	Fractions : Addition / Subtraction										1 (1)			(1)
5.	Classification of data							1 (1)						(1)
6.	Figure/Pattern							1 (1)						(1)
	Total	–	–	–	1 (1)	–	–	4 (4)	–	–	3 (3)	1 (2)	–	(10)

* **Note :** Numbers in bracket shows marks.

Second Term : Oral Test

Std. : IV   **Subject : Mathematics**   **Total Marks : 10**

Q.1. Answer the following questions :

1. What is the formulae of perimeter of rectangle ?
2. What is the divisibility test of 5 ?
3. $31050 - 18 = $ _____ .
4. Read the table of 15 correctly ?
5. The total surface area of a cube is 54 sq. cm. What is the surface area of one face of a cube ?
6. Measure length of book.
7. Tell the bigger fraction from the given pair of fraction $\frac{2}{7}, \frac{2}{5}$.
8. To show a pictograph of 5000 people which scale is convenient.
9. Tell the pattern in table of 9.

Second Term : Oral Test

Std. : IV   **Subject : Mathematics**   **Total Marks : 10**

(Model Answer Sheet and Marks Distribution)

1. Perimeter of rectangle = 2 length + 2 breadth. **(1M)**
2. Divisibility test of 5 : The number is divisible by 5 when the digit in the units is 5 or 0. **(1M)**
3. $31050 - 18 = \underline{31032}$. **(1M)**
4. If the table is read correctly. **(1M)**
5. Surface area of cube = 9 sq. cm. **(1M)**
6. Length measure by scale correctly. **(2M)**
7. $\frac{2}{7} < \frac{2}{5}$. **(1M)**
8. Scale to draw pictograph 1 picture = 1000 peoples. **(1M)**
9. Pattern in table of 9 is = The digit of units place of each number in table of 9 are in decreasing order from 9 to 0. **(1M)**

Points to Remember

- Evaluation means finding out whether the set of objectives have been achieved or not.
- Evaluation must be comprehensive and continuous.
- Unit test is the real test of evaluation.
- Marking scheme and answer scheme gives proper direction to evaluation.
- Remedial teaching is necessary after a diagnostic test.
- Crieterion referenced tests are conducted to provide results that can be directly interpreted in terms of the level of performance.
- In norm-reference test, a learner's performance is compared with that of another or a group of learners.

Assignment

1. What is the meaning of evaluation ? Why is evaluation needed in the Mathematics ?
2. How will you prepare a unit test ?
3. Write short note on :
   (i)   Oral test
   (ii) Practical test
   (iii) Blue print.

EXERCISE

Q.1. Multiple Choice Questions :

1. _____ evaluation are the evaluation for learning.
   (a) Formative
   (b) Summative
   (c) Both (a) and (b)
   (d) None of these

2. Gradation method is very useful for _____ level.
   (a) primary
   (b) pre-primary
   (c) Both (a) and (b)
   (d) None of these

3. _____ techniques of evaluation are the most useful, reliable and valid for mathematics subject.
   (a) Qualitative
   (b) Quantitative
   (c) Both (a) and (b)
   (d) None of these

4. _____ evaluation can be done after a certain period.
   (a) Formative   (b) Quantitative
   (c) Summative   (d) Qualitative

5. _____ is a process of determining to what extent the objectives are being realized.
   (a) Evaluation   (b) Test
   (c) Oral   (d) None of these

Answers : 1 - (a), 2 - (b), 3 - (b), 4 - (c), 5 - (a).

Q.2. Answer the Following Questions :

1. What is the meaning of evaluation ? Why is evaluation needed in the mathematics ?
2. Explain the meaning of the criterion reference tests.
3. Write the importance of diagnostic test.
4. How will you prepare a unit test ?
5. Explain the concept of remedial teaching.
6. Explain the meaning of standard reference tests.
7. Write the difference between standard reference test and criterion referenced test.
8. What is mean by continuous comprehensive evaluation ?

Q.3. Write Short Note On :

1. Oral Test.
2. Blue Test.
3. Formative Evaluation.
4. Summative Evaluation.
5. Evaluation.
6. Diagnostic Test.
7. Remedial Teaching.
8. Standard Reference Test.

✍ ✍ ✍

References

- डॉ. ह. ना. जगताप, '**गणित आशययुक्त अध्यापन**', नित्यनूतन प्रकाशन, पुणे

- डॉ. कैलास बोंदार्डे, डॉ. अश्विन बोंदार्डे, शिवराज कस्तुरे '**गणित अध्यापन पद्धती**' (2010), फडके प्रकाशन, कोल्हापूर (प्रथम आवृत्ती)

- डॉ. कविता साळुंके, '**आशययुक्त अध्यापन पद्धती मूलभूत**', य. च. मुक्त विद्यापीठ, नाशिक

- मखीजा आणि पोंक्षे, '**गणिताचे अध्यापन**' (2001), नूतन प्रकाशन, पुणे

- डॉ. अ. ना. ओक, डॉ. सत्यवती राऊळ '**गणित स्वरूप अध्ययन-अध्यापन**' (1991), नूतन प्रकाशन, पुणे

- डॉ. अनंत जोशी '**आशययुक्त अध्यापन**', य. च. मु. वि. नाशिक

- डॉ. किशोर चव्हाण '**उद्याच्या शिक्षकांसाठी गणित शिक्षण**' (2008), इनसाईट पब्लिकेशन्स, नाशिक

- प्रा. सुनीता ढाके, प्रा. स्वाती चव्हाण '**अध्यापन उपागम आणि कार्यनीती**', प्रशांत पब्लिकेशन, जळगाव

- डॉ. सौ. गीतादेवी पाटील, '**शैक्षणिक संख्याशास्त्र**', मंगेश प्रकाशन, नागपूर

- मूल्यमापन विभाग, '**सातत्यपूर्ण सर्वंकष मूल्यमापन भाग 1 ते 4**', (2010) म. रा. शै. सं. व प्र. परिषद (विद्या परिषद), पुणे

- अभ्यासक्रम विकसन विभाग, '**प्राथमिक शिक्षण अभ्यासक्रम-2012**', म. रा. शै. सं. व प्र. परिषद (विद्या परिषद), पुणे

- पाठ्यपुस्तक निर्मिती मंडळ, '**इ. 1 ली ते 10 वी गणित पाठ्यपुस्तके**', बालभारती (महा. राज्य पाठ्यपुस्तक निर्मिती मंडळ), पुणे

- '**प्राथमिक शिक्षण पदविका अभ्यासक्रम 2006**'

- '**प्राथमिक शिक्षण अभ्यासक्रम 2012**' (इयत्ता 1 लि ते 5 वी)

- डॉ. वैद्य अ. का., डॉ पाटील वा. र. **'शिक्षणशास्त्र पदविका गणित'** निराली प्रकाशन, पुणे

- डॉ. अनंत जोशी, **'आशययुक्त अध्यापन पद्धती'**

- डॉ. बर्कले, डॉ. नलिनी पिचड, **'आशययुक्त अध्यापन'**

- **'अध्यापक शिक्षण पदविका अभ्यासक्रम 2004'** SCERT पुणे

- **'सातत्यपूर्ण सर्वकष मूल्मापन मार्गदर्शिका'**, SCERT पुणे

- प्राथमिक शिक्षण अभ्यासक्रम **'इ. 1 ली ते 5 वी गणित पाठ्यपुस्तके'**

- ह. ना. जगताप, **'आशययुक्त अध्यापन - गणित'**

- डॉ. वसंत देशपांडे, डॉ. सुमन करंदीकर, **'मैत्री ज्ञानसंरचनावादाशी'** निराली प्रकाशन, पुणे.

- jwi/son.coe.uga.edu/EMAT 8990/GEOMETRY

- images.rbs.org/cognitive/van-Hiele-shtml

- en.wikipedia.org/witsi/van-Hiele-moel

- www.ethicalpoltics.org/wits/vygotskydevel

- https:/en.wikipedia.org.wikipedia.org/wiki/abacus

- https:/en.wikibooks.org/wiki/vedic_Mathematics/Techniques/Addition_And_Subtraction.

- www.mastermindabacus.com/What_is_abacus.html.

- www.wikihow.com/Use_an_Abacus.

- https:/nrich.maths.org/2473.

★ ★ ★